PRAISE FOR NOVELS BY PAUL L. MAIER

A SKELETON IN GOD'S CLOSET

"Debate over the Resurrection surfaces in Maier's new novel *A Skeleton in God's Closet*. . . . The discovery not only shakes the Christian world to its foundation but has far-reaching political repercussions."

Los Angeles Times

"This plot has been crying for publication for the last nineteen centuries. . . . A colorful thriller novel!"

Houston Chronicle

"With *A Skeleton in God's Closet*, Paul Maier has crafted a new genre—the theological thriller. It reads like Robert Ludlum while expertly exploring the origins of Christianity. A superb book!"

Paul Erdman, *New York Times* bestselling author

"Maier's premise is fascinating, and his exploration of its consequences reasonable and convincing . . . an exciting story."

Milwaukee Sentinel

"This thriller keeps the reader so on edge that it is not until the last pages that the mystery is solved. Extremely well-done."

The Oregonian

"Using his historical expertise and creative license, Maier . . . sparks a new debate over whether Christ's resurrection on Easter was mythical or miraculous."

The Detroit News

"Paul Maier's explosive new novel *A Skeleton in God's Closet* . . . is extraordinary."

Newspaper Enterprise Association

"Rich with authentic detail, dialogue, and characterization, the fast-paced plot carries readers quickly to the stunning conclusion."

***Moody* magazine**

MORE THAN A SKELETON

"*More Than a Skeleton* is a wonderful rarity in that it combines a gripping, fascinating tale with sound, traditional Christian theology."

Newsday

"A fast-paced thriller . . ."

Religion News Service

"*More Than a Skeleton* is entertaining, informative, and refreshing."

Faithfulreader.com

"Historian Paul Maier has penned a fast-paced theological thriller."

The Birmingham News

The
CONSTANTINE CODEX

Hagia Sophia
1211 – 1971
31
Codex
Church of St. Paul

The CONSTANTINE CODEX

TYNDALE HOUSE PUBLISHERS, INC.
CAROL STREAM, ILLINOIS

PAUL L. MAIER

Church of the Holy Sepulchre

Visit Tyndale's exciting website at www.tyndale.com.

Visit Paul L. Maier's website at www.paulmaier.com.

The Constantine Codex

Interior architecture photographs by Barry Beitzel.

Designed by Daniel Farrell

Library of Congress Cataloging-in-Publication Data

Maier, Paul L.
The Constantine codex / Paul L. Maier.
p. cm.
ISBN 978-1-4143-3773-9 (hc) — ISBN 978-1-4143-3774-6 (sc) 1. Archaeologist—Fiction.
2. Bible. Manuscripts—Fiction. I. Title.

PS3563.A382C66 2011
813'.54—dc22 2011002146

Printed in the United States of America

17 16 15 14 13 12 11
7 6 5 4 3 2 1

BOOKS BY PAUL L. MAIER

FICTION

Pontius Pilate

The Flames of Rome

A Skeleton in God's Closet

More Than a Skeleton

The Constantine Codex

NONFICTION

A Man Spoke, a World Listened

The Best of Walter A. Maier (ed.)

Josephus: The Jewish War (ed., with G. Cornfeld)

Josephus: The Essential Works (ed., trans.)

In the Fullness of Time

Eusebius: The Church History (ed., trans.)

The First Christmas

The Da Vinci Code—Fact or Fiction?
(with Hank Hanegraaff)

FOR CHILDREN

The Very First Christmas

The Very First Easter

The Very First Christians

Martin Luther—A Man Who Changed the World

The Real Story of the Creation

The Real Story of the Flood

The Real Story of the Exodus

To Vera Thomas

and, in memoriam,

Bill Thomas

PREFACE

While this is the third in the Skeleton series, these novels may be read in any order since the plotlines are totally different. Most characters in these pages are fictitious, but in the interest of realism, some authentic personalities do appear. So that they might not be thought to endorse everything in this novel, I have not sought permission to use their names. All are famous enough to be in the public domain and will, I trust, find their portrayal in these pages both appropriate and congenial. The reader, however, should know that the dialogue I supply for them is mine and not theirs.

When *A Skeleton in God's Closet* was published in 1994 during the pontificate of John Paul II, I had designated his fictional successor as Benedict XVI, who appears also in *More Than a Skeleton* and in this novel as well. But in April 2005, Cardinal Joseph Ratzinger chose this very name for his pontificate—coincidence, rather than any prophecy on my part! The reader is therefore urged to distinguish between the two Benedicts, one fictional, the other authentic.

Special appreciation is due Marion S. Ellis, Maria Perez-Stable, Brian C. Bradford, Dr. Stan Gundry, Wayne Little, MD, Fr. Evangelos S. Pepps, and especially Dr. Timothy R. Furnish for their gracious technical assistance.

Paul L. Maier
Western Michigan University
May 2011

PROLOGUE

Shannon Jennings Weber was enjoying her lunch under the shade of a juniper tree—much as the prophet Elijah had done. She was digging at Pella on the east bank of the Jordan River, about twenty miles south of the Sea of Galilee. This was new territory for the archaeologist, who had had a string of successes with her spade in Israel. She had organized this dig in hopes of finding something—anything—to help fill one of the most crucial gaps in church history: the later first century, when Christians managed to escape the horrifying Roman conquest of Jerusalem in AD 70 by fleeing to Pella before the war started. Here, she thought, in the very capital of the earliest church, there must be clues under the soil, artifacts that would illumine the decades during which Christianity first took hold in the Mediterranean world.

Her husband, Jon, could not have been more pleased, since he too thought Pella an excavation site with huge potential. While teaching at Harvard, he regularly sent Shannon such e-mail queries as *"Have you found the personal memoirs of Jesus yet?"* or *"How about Paul's missing letter to Corinth?"* Even the messages that told of his love and loneliness usually had a playful tagline, such as *"Surely you've found one of Luke's paintings of the apostles?"* or *"If you unearth the bishop's chair of James, do excavate carefully."*

No sensational discoveries, however, had come to light, and tomorrow the team was scheduled to decamp. Before Shannon's dig, teams from the University of Sydney and the Jordanian Department of Antiquities had uncovered several Bronze- and Iron-Age Canaanite temples, and the whole site sprouted white marble columns from the Hellenistic era that merely had to be restacked. Unlike the Aussies and Jordanians, Shannon's team had focused on the fourth-century church of St. James. After clearing its base and discovering some interesting floor mosaics, curious ceramics, and a small cache of second- and third-century coins, they called it a season.

Few digs produced sensational results, and Pella was no exception. Shannon was satisfied with their results, though hardly elated. If only digs would produce treasures on demand! She grimaced, remembering a too-good-to-be-true find she'd been a part of several years previous. It had only proved the adage "If it seems too good to be true, it probably is."

As she munched on a pear, her eyes came to rest on what was likely the present-day version of the ancient church they were excavating—the Greek Orthodox Church of St. James the Just. There it sat, on a hillock just east of the dig, an aging, whitish gray structure with a blue dome that looked as if it had been plucked from an Aegean seaport. She had passed it daily en route to the dig and thought, playfully, how nice it would be if that church had kept continuous records across the centuries. It was a fanciful concept, of course, but if a church were, say, on fire, what were the two documents they would try to rescue? The altar Bible and the church records. There might be something worth seeing there before she packed up and headed home.

The next day, she paid a visit to the church and introduced herself to the priest in charge, who spoke surprisingly clear English. He was a spare little man, middle-aged, with a luxurious salt-and-pepper beard as if to compensate for his advancing male-pattern baldness. He had trouble making eye contact with Shannon, and the reason became clear when he said, "Yours is certainly the loveliest face to grace our premises in many months, Mrs. Weber. You must have Greek blood in you, no? Your dark hair, your—"

"I wish I could claim that distinction, Father Athanasius," she replied. "But no, I'm just an Irish-English hybrid who moved to America. And I love old churches like this one. How long has it been standing here?"

He pointed a pensive finger to his chin. "This building went up in the 1700s, but it was built on . . . on foundations of the church before it."

"And when was that one built?"

He smiled, shook his head, and said, "Centuries ago. Many centuries."

Shannon smiled inwardly and wanted badly to surprise the cleric with word that she was excavating what was likely the grandmother church to this one. But that would be premature; first the official dig report had to be published. "Does your church have archives? A library?" she asked.

"Oh yes, of course."

"I'm fascinated by old books. Might you be kind enough to let me see your collection?"

"But of course. Please to follow me."

They walked across a sun-drenched courtyard rimmed with trellises of grapevines and entered a library annex. The priest showed Shannon row after row of books until they came to a section whose shelves were bending under the weight of ponderous old volumes, some bound in gray-white parchment skin. Here Athanasius stopped and explained why his church was named for St. James the Just. He picked out an ancient tome. "Here we have Eusebius's *Historia Ekklesiastica*. You know Eusebius?"

"Of course! He's the very *father* of church history."

Athanasius smiled and nodded appreciatively. He laid the volume on a table and opened it to what seemed to be a bookmark of sorts, then translated the Greek that spoke of the martyrdom of James the Just of Jerusalem, Jesus' half brother—or cousin, as some would argue—and the first bishop of the Christian church.

"Eusebius writes that he got this information from Hegesippus," the priest continued. "You know Hegesippus?"

"Oh yes. My husband often raves about Hegesippus. He tells his classes that if we had the five lost books of that first-century Jewish-Christian historian, we'd know much, much more about the earliest church."

Father Athanasius beamed. "Yes, yes—it is as you say."

While he showed Shannon the text, her eyes quickly shifted to what was serving as a bookmark for the Eusebius passage: several brownish leaves of what seemed to be parchment of some sort. Their darker color showed that they had to be older than the Eusebius tome—*much* older. The writing in the text, however, was so faded as to be hardly legible.

"Have you read this material, Father Athanasius?" she asked, pointing to the dark leaves. "Have you even been *able* to read it?"

He shook his head. "I read only a few words of the ancient Greek. But it must be old. Very old."

"Yes, indeed." Obviously those pages had come from a larger collection—probably a codex, the world's first book form—and Shannon could only wonder if that codex was somewhere in the stacks surrounding them. She asked, "Do you know where these leaves came from? Do you have more of them?"

Father Athanasius merely shrugged and held out open hands. "I don't know. The former priest here showed me the old Eusebius book and how I could use it to show people why our church is named for St. James. I never thought to ask him about the pages."

"You know, we have instruments in America that could easily bring out the text, Father. Anything this old, this ancient, could be important. *Very* important." She stopped and knew she should not have been so direct, but the words escaped before she could restrain them. "Might it be possible for me to . . . to take these with me to the U.S. for a short time? I'd return them quickly—by international express—along with a clear copy of the restored Greek text."

Father Athanasius had a wounded look, staring at the bookshelves and saying nothing.

"I would guard them with my very life, good Father. The text may or may not be significant. But if it *is* important, we might gain valuable information about the early church."

He shook his head slowly and said, "Is it not for Greeks to

translate Greek, Mrs. Weber? I will take these to Athens when I visit the archbishop. Surely he and his staff will be able to . . . to read this."

Shannon's heart sank. Who could quarrel with that logic? Well, one last effort. "Perhaps they could decipher the text, Father Athanasius. And perhaps not. The script seems to have vanished at places, and the rest is hardly legible. I fear that only ultraviolet light and other equipment in my husband's office at Harvard University would be able to restore the text."

"Your husband teaches at Harvard?" Athanasius stroked his beard. "What is his name, his first name?"

"Jon. Or rather, Jonathan."

His eyes widened. "Jonathan Weber? Not *the* Jonathan Weber, who wrote *O Iisous apo tin Nazaret*?"

Shannon smiled. "Yes." Before she married Jon, he'd already become an internationally bestselling author. His book *Jesus of Nazareth* had been translated into nearly thirty languages at last count. Clearly Father Athanasius was numbered among Jon's worldwide fans.

"And you are his *wife*?"

When she nodded modestly, Athanasius broke into a great smile. "Yes, Mrs. Weber, you may certainly borrow those leaves of manuscript. Your husband's life of Christ is the best I've ever read!" He stopped, a twinkle in his eye, and seemed to reverse himself. "But no, you cannot take them . . . unless you sign my copy of *O Iisous*."

Shannon was about to object that she could hardly inscribe a book she had not written, but why quibble at the moment of success? Instead, she nodded happily.

Carefully, Athanasius removed the almost tobacco-colored leaves and hurried into his office, where the Greek edition of Jon's book was on the shelf behind his desk. "I've read it three times," the priest said proudly.

Shannon signed the book, then looked up and said, "A final favor, Father Athanasius. If you have time, *please* try to find and save any other ancient manuscript pages here, whether bound or unbound, because of their possible importance."

He nodded instantly. "Oh, indeed, Mrs. Weber."

Shannon gratefully accepted the five brown pages of manuscript, hoping they might shed a bit of new light on earliest church history. She could not know that they would, in fact, ignite a change in church history.

CHAPTER 1

JONATHAN WEBER HAD EXPERIENCED much more than the fifteen minutes of fame often allotted to mortals. The recognition brought about by his bestseller and his archaeological sleuthing in Israel that had "saved Christianity" (according to his fans) had given him entrée at the Vatican, the White House, and even Buckingham Palace. Yet despite a string of extraordinary adventures, Jon would always count the return of his wife from her dig at Pella as one of the summit events in his life. It was not only the joy of seeing Shannon again—that lithe, sapphire-eyed, pert-nosed, Irish pixie who had taken him captive—but what she had brought back with her from Jordan as a little memento of her tour.

A day after she had unpacked, Jon and Shannon took the manuscript leaves to his office at Harvard. In an adjoining room he had a small but efficient manuscript laboratory with an ultraviolet apparatus as the centerpiece. It had served him well in exploring palimpsests, vellum manuscripts on which the writing had been erased and the vellum reused. The penetrating, purplish rays of the instrument usually showed the original script quite clearly.

Shannon adjusted the window blinds to darken the room, while Jon turned on the UV apparatus. The hum of its fan covered the throb of his almost-audible pulse. "We're not looking for erasures here, Shannon," he said, "just the original script underneath those brownish accretions."

"Obviously. We could hardly make out anything at home last night, even with intense illumination."

"Okay. We're ready. Bring the first page over."

Shannon put on white gloves, opened a large portfolio, and—with care that bordered on a caress—lifted a protective muslin pad and extracted the first of the leaves. With both hands she laid it on the examining field below the instrument.

Jon peered closely at the document, studied it for some time, and then shook his head. "Here, have a look, sweetheart."

Shannon scrutinized the leaf for several moments. "Oh . . . how disappointing. I can make out a *little* more of the lettering, but . . ."

"I'll raise the intensity." Jon turned the gain knob thirty degrees clockwise, but the brighter light, while revealing more of the Greek lettering, failed to liberate enough script for them even to try to reconstruct the text without much guesswork and the insertion of long blanks.

Crestfallen, Shannon sighed. "I . . . I'm sorry, Jon. I certainly had hoped for more than this. What an utter waste of effort!"

"Not necessarily, darling." Jon kissed her cheek. Was it actually moistened with a tear? "We'll do it just like they do at Palomar Mountain."

"By which you mean . . . ?"

"Our eyes can't store up light versus dark contrast. Film can. That's why stars that couldn't possibly be seen otherwise show up on their photo plates."

"Got it!" She chuckled.

Jon opened his photo cabinet, pulled down a 35mm Nikon, and loaded it with panchromatic film. He mounted it in a camera bracket adjacent to the ultraviolet instrument and focused on the document. The shutter snapped repeatedly as he photographed at various speeds and diaphragm settings.

They achieved no results that day, since from that point on, it was trial and error—overexposure, underexposure, too much contrast, not enough contrast. Finally they hit upon a formula that worked: inside a totally opaque chamber with a very low-intensity UV illumination of the leaves, the Nikon set at f/16, time exposure, and precision film development yielded beautifully readable Greek script on almost every line of the five pages of manuscript, when printed out on photo paper.

It took Jon another week to prize out a translation of the leaves. When he had finished, he gave Shannon copies of both the Greek text and his English translation. "You know Greek, honey," he said. "Please see if I got it right."

Shannon started reading the translated version immediately.

His own pulse in something of a gallop, Jon watched as her eyes widened and the jaw of his lovely wife sagged open.

She looked up and said, "Jon, there are details here about

the martyrdom of Jesus' brother James—beyond what we have from Eusebius!"

"Exactly."

"Then do you suppose this is from . . . from Hegesippus?"

"Who else? Some old librarian at that church must have tried to keep the secondary and primary sources together. As a bookmark, no less."

"Well, this is just *fabulous*, Jon!"

"No, it isn't. You haven't come to the good part yet." The twinkle in Jon's eye had broadened into a huge expansive smile. "Read on," he said, "but it'll take a while since it's at the other end of the material."

Shannon flashed him a quizzical look and returned to Jon's typescript. Some minutes later, she looked up again. "Well, here Hegesippus seems to be talking about what he calls 'the sacred books.' Do you suppose he means the Canon?"

"Could be," he said, again assuming his mischievous grin. Soon Shannon would find the passage, he knew.

And she did, of course. She now dropped the typescript and said, very slowly, "Oh . . . my. This . . . this is just . . . beyond belief."

"It looks like you discovered more at Pella than you *ever* thought, my dear. But now, we have to keep mum on this until the authentication is complete. We'll have to go to Pella, of course, to see if there are any more leaves—loose or bound—floating around Father Athanasius's library. And we'll definitely have to include Greece on the itinerary, since I want to try to *date* this thing if possible, and I'll need help from some of their best text experts. We fly over at the end of the spring semester, right?"

Shannon nodded slowly, in wonderment. It seemed as if great discoveries were not limited to excavating the good earth. Good libraries, evidently, were also fertile ground.

✢ ✢ ✢

Must good fortune be balanced off by bad? Jon and Shannon never made the trip.

How could things go wrong so instantly, so emphatically? And why did it have to happen on one of the loveliest days in May? One moment, Jon and Shannon were looking forward to their trip to Jordan and Greece. But the next, Jon heard his own name being shouted by an angry jumble of voices from Harvard Yard below. He hurried over to the open windows of his office to see at least seventy or eighty students gathered in the shape of a crescent below Sever Hall. Many stood with raised fists waving at him in unison.

"Weber? Never! Islam is forever!"

As he listened, the chant grew louder and became a full-throated chorus: *"Weber? Never! Islam is forever!"*

"What the . . . ?" Jon asked himself; then the phone rang.

"This is Captain Rhinehart at Harvard Security, Professor Weber," the voice on the line said. "I should warn you that the Muslim Student Association on campus was granted a demonstration permit, and we just learned that you may be the subject."

"They're already here. Any idea *why* they're after me?"

"Haven't the foggiest. We're sending our men over now. I suggest you lock your office door immediately."

"Right! Thanks."

Outside the window, the mighty mantra continued, as each

leaf fluttering on the ivy-covered walls seemed to waft the message in Jon's direction. Now he saw some of the placards sprouting above the crowd:

PROF. WEBER WILL PAY
9/11 IS ON ITS WAY!

WEBER IS THE CANCER
ISLAM IS THE ANSWER!

WEBER'S A PROFESSOR?
WE NEED HIS SUCCESSOR!

Again the phone rang.

"Dr. Weber? It's George Gabriel of the *Boston Globe*."

"Hey, George. I've been meaning to call and thank you for doing that nice piece on our ICO conference. But just now we've got a big demonstration over here—"

"I'll bet! We just got an AP dispatch from Tehran that the grand ayatollah of Iran is convening a council of Shiite clergy to determine if charges of blasphemy should be lodged against you."

"What?"

"It's the new Arabic translation of your *Jesus of Nazareth* bestseller. It seems they're going to urge the faithful to buy up copies at all the bookstores and burn them. Hey, at least that should help sales!"

"But in Iran they speak Farsi, not Arabic," Jon replied, ignoring the levity. "So why would—?"

"Apparently the offending passages were translated into Farsi, and they pounced on them."

"But *what* offending passages, for goodness' sake?"

"Don't know. The only item mentioned in the dispatch was . . . let's see, here it is. 'The Iranian clergy feel that the author treated the Prophet Muhammad with great disrespect, if not outright sacrilege.'"

"Impossible!" Jon almost shouted into the phone. "Most of my book covers the *first* century, not the seventh! I mention Muhammad only in the final chapter, which does a quick summary of Christianity since Christ."

"Yeah, but you know how sensitive Muslims are. Remember the Danish cartoon business or the pope's comments in Germany?"

"But I can't think of anything in the book that would be offensive. Anyway, I gotta go; someone's at the door. I'll get back to you."

The knocking persisted as a voice resonated through the wood of the door. "Harvard Security—Captain Rhinehart here, Professor Weber. I have the president of the Muslim Student Association with me, and he'd like to speak with you."

Jon opened the door to find Captain Rhinehart standing with a tall, bronzed figure dressed in a galabia and a maroon fez. A small crowd of campus police and curious students filled the hallway behind them. The student introduced himself—in excellent English—as Abdoul Housani, an Egyptian graduate student in international studies. Jon invited him into his office, and Rhinehart followed without waiting for an invitation.

"Have a seat, gentlemen," Jon offered.

"I prefer to stand, Professor Weber," Housani said.

"As you wish. Perhaps you'd be kind enough to explain *why* this demonstration is taking place?"

"Yes, of course. You are on record as insulting the Prophet Muhammad—may his name be blessed."

"Why in the world would you ever think that?"

Housani opened the book he was carrying—*Isa al-Nazrani*, the Arabic edition of Jon's book—and turned to a bookmark he had inserted at page 490. Pointing to the last line of the text, he said, "Here, sir, you have grievously offended all of Islam by what you wrote about the Prophet—may his name be blessed. I shall read your own words back to you as I translate."

"Please do."

"On this page, you deal with the great expansion of Islam, and the last line reads, 'Undoubtedly, Muhammad introduced the greatest evil Christianity ever faced.' Now that is an outrageous—"

"I never wrote that!" Jon exclaimed as he rose, stood next to Housani, and peered at the page. His Arabic wasn't exactly conversational, but he had a reading knowledge of the language. Slowly, he read the offending line aloud: *"La yujad shakk, qaddama nabi Muhammad al-radi al-'athim allathi wajahat al-masihiyah."*

Jon stopped reading and returned to his desk, fighting the impulse to clench his fists. "Unbelievable!" he almost whispered. "That's exactly what it says!" Then he looked up and said, "You translate well, Mr. Housani."

The swarthy face of his guest warped into a grim smile of triumph. Captain Rhinehart's brow corrugated into a facial question mark as he looked on rather helplessly.

"But that's *not* what I wrote!" Jon fairly bellowed. "It should be *tahaddi*, not *radi*—*challenge*, not *evil*." He went to one of the bookcases insulating the four walls of his office and pulled off a copy of the American edition of *Jesus of Nazareth*. Quickly thumbing his way to the last chapter, he swooped down to the final line and held the book out for the student. "Now, Mr. Housani, please read what I actually wrote."

Glowering with suspicion, the student read aloud, "'Undoubtedly, Muhammad introduced the greatest . . . challenge . . . Christianity ever faced.'"

"*Challenge*, Mr. Housani. *Challenge*, not *evil*!"

The Arab student seemed perplexed and was mute for several seconds. Finally he stammered, "I . . . I don't understand. . . ."

"It's really quite simple. Either this was a wretched typographical error, or it's a translation error. Believe me, I'm going to find out which."

Slowly, Housani nodded, while Captain Rhinehart stopped wringing his hands and smiled.

Jon didn't want to overdo the injured innocence bit, but he did have a few questions he wanted answered before this student left his office. "Might I ask, Mr. Housani, why you and the Muslim Student Association didn't check the original English version of my book first before staging this demonstration? I can't imagine it would have been difficult to find a copy. I think the Harvard Coop keeps about fifteen in stock at all times."

"I . . . we . . . find Arabic easier reading than English."

Jon nodded. "Okay, understandable. But something strange seems to be going on here. How in the world did you and your demonstrators even learn about all this? The publication date for the Arabic edition isn't until a week from now."

Housani was silent for some moments. Then he answered, "We have a contact in Cairo who mailed us a copy air express in order to help us . . . stay on top of things as much as we can."

"As well you should," Jon replied, now smiling. "I trust you'll explain all this to the Muslim Student Association?"

"Yes. I'll do that, Professor Weber. But please let us know how that terrible error got into the Arabic translation."

"Of course. In fact, the moment you leave this office, I'll be phoning my publisher in Cairo to stop the presses—literally—and make that correction. Then I'll instruct him to recall as many of the faulty first editions as possible."

"Thank you, Professor Weber. And . . . I apologize if any of our people went overboard during the demonstration."

"Accepted. Thank you. By the way, how come you have such a perfect command of English—even our colloquial expressions—and hardly any accent?"

Housani smiled. "Well, as a boy growing up in Bahrain, I listened to *Voice of America* as much as I could, and I tried to imitate American English."

"VOA? Well done, sir. Your association certainly seems to have picked a worthy leader."

They shook hands. The moment Housani and Rhinehart left, Jon reached for the phone. Never mind that it was nearing midnight Cairo time. If his publisher didn't roust himself out of bed and act quickly, much of the Islamic world might erupt into rioting that could make the demonstration in Harvard Yard look like a party in the park.

✠ ✠ ✠

Jon's second call was to his translator, Osman al-Ghazali, a Christian Arab who was a professor of Islamic sudies at Harvard, but he failed to reach him either at the university or at his home in Belmont. The messages Jon left on both answering machines were quite impassioned.

His third immediacy was to compose a written statement for the media on the glaring error in translation and proofreading. His two-page statement concluded:

> The offending word in the final sentence of the last chapter of *Jesus of Nazareth* has been correctly translated as "challenge"—not "evil"—in the twenty-nine foreign languages into which the book has been printed, as will become obvious to anyone taking the time to make the search. I deeply regret that the new Arabic edition contained a typographical or translational error that is understandably offensive to Islam. The printing of the first edition has been halted, and the publisher is in the process of recalling as many of the defective copies as possible. Those who have purchased a copy of the faulty first edition may exchange it for the corrected version or receive a full refund. All future editions in Arabic will contain the appropriate correction. Thank you for your patience and understanding in this matter.

"There; that should do it, Marylou," Jon said to his secretary. "Better run off a hundred copies of this. The media will be hungry."

"Not 'will be'—they *are* hungry. Look out the window."

Below, mobile television trucks were already desecrating the sacred turf of Harvard Yard, and reporters and camera crews were milling through the still-vocal crowd of demonstrators. Jon threw his hands up in frustration. "I haven't gotten through to al-Ghazali yet, so there's nothing I can add to that statement. Please just hand it out, and they'll have to be satisfied with that for now."

"But won't you be here too? You look so nice on television," she trifled.

"No, I'm escaping, and you don't know where I am. Good luck with the media!"

Jon ducked out of his office just as the staircases and elevators disgorged the first wave of reporters. He used a remote fire escape and was on the road home to suburban Weston before the media even learned that he had left campus.

CHAPTER 2

AT THE TUDOR-GOTHIC RESIDENCE the Webers called home, Shannon was catching up on her own correspondence between loads of laundry, relishing the quiet hours she was able to devote to more domestic pursuits. But in the late afternoon, the quiet seemed doomed as the phone began ringing incessantly. Each inquiry was from a newspaper, radio, or television station—all asking to speak to Jon but giving no hint as to the cause of all the furor. Yet each time she tried to call her husband at Harvard, the line was busy. His cell phone went straight to voice mail. She finally sent an e-mail to his BlackBerry, but there was no return call.

Again the phone rang. Might it be Jon? "Weber residence," she said, trying to keep the exasperation out of her voice.

"Meeses Web-air," someone with a thick accent said, "your

husband has spoken lies about our great Prophet—may his name be blessed—and we will have our revenge. We know where you are living in Wes-tone. Dr. Web-air will be punished."

"Who is this?" she demanded.

No answer. Just a click and the line went dead.

A clutch of apprehension started building inside her. First the media inquiries about Jon, then his failure to call, and now an ugly threat. She locked all the doors in the house and spent the next hour pacing the floor, looking out the windows, and alerting several neighbor friends. Call 911? Too early for that.

Suddenly the sweet music of her garage door opening provided welcome relief. More relieved than she wanted to let on, she greeted him with a fierce hug. "What in the world is going on, Jon? The phone's been ringing all afternoon. Mostly media, but then there was a nasty call from someone with a thick accent who threatened 'Dr. Web-air.'"

Jon sighed. "Sorry you were bothered, darling. I think I've cleared it all up, and—"

"But why didn't you check your e-mail? I kept calling, but your line was busy. So I—"

"I'll give you the whole story very shortly. But until things have a chance to blow over, let's pack *immediately* for—shall we say—an 'early vacation' at the Cape. I mean now, *instantly*, Shannon. Twenty minutes and we're outta here."

"Good! You can explain on the way." And explain he certainly would. Shannon never ceased to be amazed at the way controversy and unsought fame seemed to follow her husband wherever he went. It might even be amusing if it didn't so often disrupt the quiet, scholarly life they both preferred.

Somehow, they managed their escape in a half hour. En route to Cape Cod, Jon told her all about the demonstration at Harvard Yard and that the real reason for their drive to the Cape was not the phoned threat but to escape the media. He refused to stand in front of TV cameras, a blank stare on his face, and whimper, "I have no idea how this happened." He also admitted to a tinge of conscience in *not* having personally proofread the Arabic edition before publication. Had he done so, he would have caught the error immediately. "Of course, that should have been the translator's responsibility," he told her, "and if I don't hear from Osman al-Ghazali soon, I'm going to go after him bare-handed!"

Just before reaching their hideaway at Cape Cod, Shannon asked, "So then, you think your—Mr. Housani, was it?—will explain things to the guy who threatened us on the phone?"

"Right."

Shannon hoped Jon's optimism was not misplaced. As much as she enjoyed their beach house, hiding out from the media when they had a major research trip on the horizon was not her idea of a vacation.

✠ ✠ ✠

As a strategic retreat for times of both vacation and duress, Jon and Shannon had purchased an oceanside home several miles east of the Kennedy compound on Cape Cod. Only the police at Hyannis Port, Marylou Kaiser, and several trusted friends and neighbors knew of its existence.

They loved the place. It was spacious by Cape standards with four bedrooms, three baths, and a great room with cobblestone fireplace. The exterior siding was composed of cedar shakes painted in Cape Cod gray with white window trim, and it blended in perfectly with the many thousands of other homes at the Cape, Nantucket, and Martha's Vineyard. They had named the place Thistle Do.

A broad lawn that rolled down to the Atlantic comprised their backyard, part of which fronted a small bay, where they had built a boathouse to match Thistle Do. It housed a thirty-two-foot runabout cruiser they used for excursions up and down the New England coast. Jon always apologized to his friends—piloting a tall-masted schooner with billowing sails would have been far better sport, but he just didn't have time enough for all the hassle involved in readying the ship for a sail and then stowing it all away again. Maybe after retirement, or maybe sooner if the price for gasoline rose any higher.

Because of the extraordinary success of his literary works—both scholarly and popular—Jon was by no means poverty-stricken. He tried to use his wealth wisely. He gave to charity and tithed to the church but still had little twinges of conscience each time he fired up his boat or sped off in his BMW Z4. This merely proved that the man was Lutheran, a tribe that celebrated God's grace and forgiveness all the more because of an inbred sensitivity to shortcomings and sin.

Jon and Shannon planned to stay no more than a week at the Cape and return to Cambridge once the brouhaha had blown over. Then they intended to fly to Greece and Jordan, as planned.

The day after they arrived at Thistle Do, however, Marylou Kaiser phoned, somewhat breathlessly. "You *do* have television reception out there, don't you, Dr. Weber?"

"Sure. Of course . . ."

"Then please turn on your TV. You just have no idea . . ." There was a catch in her voice. She cleared her throat and began again. "All the networks—NBC, CBS, ABC, Fox, CNN—they're all showing footage of Islamic riots across the world over your book, with—"

"*What!* Across the *world*? That's ridiculous. Don't they report that it's all an *error*, for goodness' sake?"

"No. At least, not yet, evidently."

"*Why* haven't they reported it?" he demanded. Then, realizing Marylou couldn't possibly have the answer, he quickly added, "Probably because they want to let the 'sensation' play out first, maybe to build ratings, and then sober up with the truth."

"I hope you're right. Oh, I do have a bit of good news, Dr. Weber."

"I need it about now."

"Professor al-Ghazali is trying to reach you. Shall I give him your cell phone number?"

"Yes, please! But don't tell him where I am."

"Never."

"Call me if anything else comes up. Sorry to leave you with this mess."

She chuckled, her good humor once again restored. "I think it was all part of the package when I signed on with Indiana Jones—Harvard edition."

Smiling, Jon said good-bye, then reported the conversation to Shannon. "I can't believe this thing has gotten so out of control."

Shannon gave a wry smile. "That's what you get, darling, for being so famous."

"As the Brits would say, 'Balderdash!'"

Jon turned on the wide-screen TV and watched in growing horror—high-definition horror—the Muslim riots across the world. The BBC showed footage from London of a papier-mâché Jon being hanged in effigy from a lamppost in front of the Nelson monument at Trafalgar Square. In Paris, a similar Weber dummy was ceremoniously hurled from the top of the Eiffel Tower. In Madrid, he was gored in a mock bullfight, and only Germany provided a bit of grim humor when the Weber figure was drowned in a bathtub full of beer—though Muslims there insisted others had poured the amber beverage, of course.

Jon shook his head. "This is beyond all belief!"

His cell phone chirped, and he lunged for it. It just *had* to be Osman al-Ghazali. He was not disappointed.

"We were in Poughkeepsie, Jon, at our daughter's graduation from Vassar," he opened, "and I didn't get the news until late last night, or I would have called you immediately."

"All right, Osman. I'm listening." It was not the friendliest response, Jon knew, but his translator deserved it. Unless he had some reasonable explanation for his now-notorious gaffe, Jon was ready to throttle the man.

"I . . . I can't find the words to express my concern . . . my shock," al-Ghazali said, "and you have my *profound* apologies for what happened, Jon. The typesetter in Cairo must have made the error, of course, but I should have caught it. . . . I should have caught it."

Jon said nothing, so al-Ghazali continued. "I just can't believe I didn't catch it, since *radi—evil*—sounds nothing like *tahaddi—challenge*, as you well know. Well, they rhyme, but . . ."

"That could be, Osman," Jon finally replied, softening. "Have you called our publisher in Cairo?"

"Even before calling you. I made them repeat the correct term for 'challenge' three times, and they'll e-mail me proofs before going back to press."

"Good, Osman. What in the world ever made the typesetter in Cairo do that—*if* he's responsible? He's not a Coptic Christian, is he?"

"I don't really know. But I'll find out."

"In any case, you should also have a few words with him—to say the least."

"You bet I will."

"More than that, I think you'll have to do a *careful* proofing again of the whole Arabic edition to make sure there are no other errors."

"I'd already planned to do that."

"Good. Oh, one more thing: word about the translation error seems to be a deep, dark secret as far as the media are concerned. I worry most about Al Jazeera. If they don't report that it was all a mistake, rioting will rage on in the Islamic world."

"Ah! Good that you tell me. I have a friend or two there. I'll call Al Jazeera immediately—the start of my long journey back into your good graces, Jon."

"Fine, Osman. Be sure to keep me posted."

Shannon, who had been listening intently to Jon's side of the conversation, seemed relieved and sighed. "I do hope that's the end of this bizarre business. How it can ruin a beautiful spring!" It was obvious that images of her husband being hanged in effigy had done very little to boost her spirits.

They turned off the TV, put on walking shorts, and headed down to the Atlantic shore. Perhaps a long stroll along the beach and many breaths of fresh sea breezes would clear their minds.

✢ ✢ ✢

Jon and Shannon returned from their seashore promenade eager to check the progress of Jon's story. "What was it Mark Twain said?" Shannon asked. "'A lie gets halfway around the world before the truth even puts its boots on'?"

"Yes," Jon replied. "I guess it's a corollary to Murphy's Law that wrong information—particularly of a sensational nature—gets front-page treatment in the press and opening-story status in the broadcast media, while the truth, by way of correction, shows up later with only the briefest coverage on page 6 of section D in the papers or as a small afterthought on TV."

Gingerly they turned on the television evening news, flipped through the networks, and were happily surprised. Diane Sawyer of ABC, Katie Couric of CBS, and Brian Williams of NBC all opened with a story on the error in the Arabic text of Jon's book, while CNN even showed footage of a perspiring Osman al-Ghazali heaping blame on himself, but even more on the typesetter in Cairo.

Later in the telecasts, however, Jon felt the clutch of concern return when the news programs shifted to reports from foreign correspondents. A firebomb had been lobbed into the first floor of Jon's publisher in Cairo, scorching much of the reception area until the blaze was extinguished. Footage from Lebanon showed a long column of Hezbollah marching through downtown Beirut, clad in green and white and demanding revenge against "Web-air," as they chanted the name again and again. In Tehran, where the offending sentence had been mistranslated into Farsi with an even stronger term for *evil*, enraged mullahs were preaching about possible jihad, while rioting in Pakistan had actually left five dead on the streets of Islamabad.

Jon held his head in his hands and muttered, "People getting *killed*? For nothing? *Nothing?* Good grief, it's Salman Rushdie all over again! How many died in those riots after Ayatollah Khomeini put a fatwa on his head?"

"Not just Rushdie," Shannon added. "There were dozens of deaths in the riots that followed the Danish cartoon of Muhammad with bombs in his turban. And the same after the pope's address in Germany at Regensburg."

The phone rang—inconveniently, since the evening news had not yet ended.

"Just let it ring," Jon said.

Shannon paused, then shook her head and lifted the receiver. "Weber residence." She listened for a moment before handing the phone to Jon.

"Yes?" he said into the phone, with a questioning look at his wife.

"Professor Jonathan Weber?"

"Yes . . ."

"This is Morton Dillingham, director of the Central Intelligence Agency."

"The CIA? Right! And I'm Alex in Wonderland."

"No, Professor. This *is* the CIA, and we have *very* serious matters to discuss. Are you free to speak?"

"Yes," Jon replied, meekly, in case the call was authentic after all.

"Is your phone line secure?"

"Yes, I think so."

"Is anyone else there?"

"Yes, my wife."

"No one else?"

"No. And by the way, how did you get this phone number? It's unlisted."

"We convinced your secretary that it was in the national interest and for your own personal safety."

"Okay. Sorry about my levity."

"Not a problem. Now, Professor Weber, here's the situation. Our operatives in Tehran have just informed us that the grand ayatollah in Iran, Kazim al-Mahdi—their Supreme Leader—in consultation with his Shiite clergy, has just declared a fatwa on your head because of that Arabic translation business."

"Ridiculous!" Jon nearly shouted into the phone. "Don't they know about the translation error? And it's in Arabic, not Farsi. In fact, do *you* even know about the error?"

"Of course I do—the CIA also watches the evening news! But no, evidently they don't know about that mistake in Iran. And they decided to exploit the translation error for their own purposes, even if it was in another language."

"Do you have any idea why Al Jazeera hasn't announced the error?" Jon assumed the CIA also knew about the Arab TV network's silence.

"We're working on that one even as we speak."

"Good."

"But first things first, Dr. Weber, and that's security for you and your wife. We hope, of course, that the fatwa will be lifted once they finally learn the truth in Iran, but meanwhile your lives are in some danger."

"Oh, please; this can't really be happening, can it?"

"I am *not* exaggerating, sir," the CIA director said in a credibly serious tone. "Now, we have a direct parallel in the case of Salman Rushdie and his *Satanic Verses* novel that earned him a fatwa some years ago. We've already contacted Scotland Yard to learn how the British handled security in his case with such obvious success: although his fatwa has never been lifted, the man lives on! We intend something similar in your case, although—"

Jon erupted. "Rushdie was in hiding for *months* after the fatwa was announced, and I just can't spare that kind of time!"

"A fatwa?" Shannon whispered. "Jon, what's happening?"

He covered the phone with his hand and tried to reassure her. "I'm sure it's nothing, darling. I'll explain in a minute." He spoke into the phone again. "I'm sorry, Mr. . . . ?"

"Dillingham. And that's quite all right. But we do need to take every possible precaution to protect your life and that of your wife as well. You see, all we need is for just one fanatic to take the fatwa seriously and act on it. Your death would be his passport to paradise."

Jon was stunned into silence. One stupid error was turning his life into a grotesque nightmare. Shannon's too. Finally he asked, again rather meekly, "What do you suggest?"

"Since the FBI covers the home front and we the international, we asked them to send over a security detail immediately. In fact, they'd probably have been there by now if your secretary had told us where you are."

Thank you, Marylou! Jon mused. Then he replied, "No, not here. It would disrupt the peace of the neighborhood. . . . All right, my wife and I will return to our home in Weston, and you can incarcerate us there."

"Well, we certainly don't intend to—"

"Strike that; bad humor on my part. But seriously now, we're grateful for your concern."

"We do have your home address in Weston, but we'd really prefer to have you escorted there by—"

"No, I absolutely decline that. Categorically. But thank you, Mr. Dillingham. We'll be leaving first thing in the morning and should return to Weston by, say, early afternoon."

"I'd feel better if you left this evening."

"No, morning will do just fine. The fatwa hasn't been announced over here yet, evidently."

"Well . . . all right. Thanks for your cooperation, Professor Weber."

"Yours too. Good night."

Jon hung up and turned to Shannon, who was hovering nearby with a worried look on her face.

"What is it, Jon? A fatwa? On you? You're kidding, right?"

"I'm afraid not, sweetheart. That was the CIA. They want us to head home so they can put us under official protection, at least until this thing blows over."

"Jon, fatwas don't 'blow over.' At least Rushdie's didn't. What about our trip? Our work? Oh, this is just ridiculous."

"I know; I know. But when the truth finally sinks in at Tehran, they'll lift it, I'm sure."

"And if they don't?"

Jon saw a tear or two glistening in her eyes. He tucked two fingers under her classically chiseled chin and said, "Then we'll flee Weston and fly to Tahiti."

✠ ✠ ✠

Shannon made a conscious effort to shrug off the curdling climate of fear in their lives as they drove eastward to Chatham. She appreciated Jon's attempts to cheer her up with a seafood dinner overlooking the Atlantic—one of her favorite things to do when they were staying at the beach house. It began with obligatory Lambrusco—the vintage they had shared on their wedding night—and went on to lobster for him, crab cakes for her.

Was it the edge supplied by danger? The wine at dinner? The gorgeous full moon floating over the eastern seascape? Whatever. The evening was a success as far as Shannon was concerned. By the time they returned to their hideaway, she had managed to put the fear and danger out of her mind. It was heavenly to return to their beachfront hideaway and forget, at least for the night, that anyone else existed outside the circle of their love.

CHAPTER 3

THEY HAD MISSED THE 11 P.M. NEWS, of course. But during the morning drive back to Weston, they heard it all on the car radio. In the name of Allah, the Iranian clergy had declared an official fatwa on American professor Jonathan Weber of Harvard University in Cambridge, Massachusetts. Muslim faithful were duty-bound to seek him out for apprehension, trial, judgment, and condemnation. And the penalty for insulting the Prophet, as Professor Weber had done? Death.

Jon and Shannon's new roles as moving targets? Not a felicitous feeling. Jon was quiet, but he seemed to be checking the rearview mirror more often than usual, while Shannon found herself scanning each approaching vehicle with uncharacteristic scrutiny.

Jon finally broke the silence. "Well, it's much too soon for anyone to try anything, sweetheart."

"Oh, that's *some* consolation," she replied with a bite. "But in a short time, it'll be open season on the Webers. So much for the joy you promised in our wedded life!"

"Think you made a mistake, Shannon?" His eyebrows were a pair of arches.

She put on her best imitation of a frown. "Well, it wouldn't be the first time." Then she whispered, "Oh, Jon, despite the crazy twists and turns life has taken since I met you, it's a mistake I'd make again and again and again!" She reached over and squeezed his knee.

After crossing the bridge at the Cape Cod Canal, they headed northwest on I-495 toward the Boston suburbs. It was a luminous spring morning, the air nicely scrubbed from a shower the night before. But then an intrusion. Jon noticed it first in his left outer mirror: a dark green Cadillac Escalade was following their silver Buick LaCrosse, and it seemed to *stay* behind them, even when he slowed down to encourage passing.

He tromped on the accelerator to eighty miles per hour, and the distance between the two cars lengthened. But the Escalade suddenly sped up in order to reach its apparently chosen perch just behind their car.

Shannon knew what was happening without his saying a word. She peered back anxiously and exclaimed, "Jon! They're wearing *turbans*—all four of them!"

Jon quickly looked back and saw that Shannon was right. An icy stab of terror rippled inside him. "It's just not possible that anyone would try to act on the fatwa this soon, is it?"

"Who knows? Maybe we've been followed."

"Stay cool. I have a plan." Jon started slowing down to 50 mph, then 40 and even 35. The Escalade slowed also.

"Jon, have you lost your mind?" she wondered.

"Strategy, dear. I may even stop the car. But the moment they also stop and get out, I'll floor it. Just hang on and keep your head down."

His plan came to nothing. Suddenly the Escalade sped past them, four turbaned heads so busy in conversation that they didn't even notice Jon and Shannon.

Jon broke out laughing. "We're bloody fools, Shannon. They were *Sikhs*, not Muslims! It's Sikhs who wear turbans."

"Well, cut us some slack, Jon. A death threat is enough to turn anyone a little paranoid."

+ + +

When they arrived in Weston, they expected to find a security gate across their street, police patrolling the area, and angry neighbors wanting to know why they and their families were being imprisoned. But they saw nothing of the kind. The shady little lane was the same picture of tranquility they had left.

"Obviously, security hasn't arrived yet," Shannon observed.

Jon pressed the garage door opener and drove in. Just as he was inserting the house key into the lock, a man appeared out of nowhere and said, "Sorry to startle you, Professor and Mrs. Weber. Jim Behnke, FBI." He flashed his credentials. "Do you mind if I join you inside to explain our security arrangements?"

Over coffee and rolls in the kitchen, Behnke laid it all out.

"We've set up an electronic fence around your entire property—invisible, of course—that will alert us to any attempts at intrusion. Now, do you see that aging blue Dodge van parked across the street?" He pointed. "It's really an electronic base with communications and radar. It will monitor everything in the area, including your phone calls. But just call this number first every time you need privacy, and we'll tune out." He handed them a card, then continued. "Anyone ringing your doorbell will be under the tightest surveillance. But don't worry; we won't bother the mailman or delivery people."

The briefing went on for some time. Finally Behnke gave transponders to both Jon and Shannon with panic buttons to press in case of emergency.

"But what happens when we leave the house?" Shannon wondered.

"We'll also install GPDs—global positioning devices—on both your cars so we can track your locations at all times."

"Will we be tailed . . . followed?" Jon asked.

"Perhaps. But if so, you'll never know it."

As Behnke prepared to leave, Jon had one more question. "Okay, let's imagine a worst-case scenario: what if they come here in force—more than one or two people?"

Behnke pointed out the kitchen window facing the backyard. "You have a pretty dense grove of trees behind your place. It rather conveniently hides our manpower at the western edge of your property. Not to worry!"

"Thanks, Mr. Behnke," Shannon said. "We were concerned that our neighborhood would be disrupted."

"Your neighbors won't even know we're here, Mrs. Weber."

✠ ✠ ✠

Maybe life could return to something resembling normalcy after all, they dared to hope. But one nagging concern remained: were their summer plans ruined? Both were determined to have the finest scholars in Greece examine what Shannon had discovered at Pella.

They decided to postpone their visit to Pella because Father Athanasius had written that, after an exhaustive search of their library, no other vellum sheets matching Shannon's had been discovered. In place of Pella, they decided to visit Turkey along with Greece. Both were gorgeous peninsulas thrusting themselves into the sapphire Mediterranean. Both were scattered with scenic mountains and lakes, rimmed with golden beaches, and surrounded by Aegean islands boasting homes of gleaming white with roofs of royal blue. That's what the tourist brochures promised, and yet there was so much more there.

Greece and Asia Minor were the cradles of classical civilization in the ancient world, both lands still studded with ruins of temples, colonnades, theaters, baths, aqueducts, and even latrines from antiquity. "People living in Greece and Asia Minor two and three millennia ago gave us more of our present culture than any other civilization," Professor Weber reminded his classes again and again.

Yet there was still more. The Aegean world was also the second cradle of Christianity. It was here that St. Paul did most of his missions work, where many of the earliest church fathers held forth, where the first churches were built and the first creeds formulated. And perhaps most importantly, it was here that the earliest New Testament Scriptures were written. This was what most intrigued Jonathan Weber and the ICO that he had founded.

The Institute of Christian Origins, based in Cambridge, was a think tank for discovery rather than—as was so much of recent theology—a scholarly rehashing of evidence raked over many times in the past. Their symposia dealt with cutting-edge findings from the ancient world that impinged on Jesus of Nazareth and the church that he founded. Membership in the ICO—by invitation only—was an honor roll of many of the most prestigious scholars in the world, men and women not only with expertise in their specialties but with the flexibility and courage to draw unpopular conclusions, if necessary. They regularly had to blow a shrill whistle on the increasing fakery and fraud pseudoarchaeologists were foisting on the public, such as claims that wheels from the ancient Egyptian chariots in the Exodus account had been found at the bottom of the Red Sea. Similar targets were mistranslations of the vaunted Judas Gospel or wild claims regarding the so-called Jesus Family Tomb at Talpiot in south Jerusalem. And as for Noah's ark, the ICO reminded the public that Noah must certainly have built a fleet rather than just one ship, since it had now been "discovered" twenty-one times in the last century!

At the most recent symposium of the ICO in April, Jon had told his colleagues, "So often we assume that any fresh information on Jesus and early Christianity will come from archaeological discoveries. And while that's true enough, it's not the whole truth. Perhaps we've overlooked another major source of potential evidence, and I'm sure you all know where

I'm heading: *manuscripts*! Ancient manuscripts, wherever they might be found—whether via archaeological digs, hiding in medieval and even modern libraries, or lurking in neglected monastery archives.

"But here's an important difference between these two sources: things not yet unearthed will hardly change over the millennia, but manuscripts *will* change. They'll deteriorate. Papyrus and parchment will age, rot, and crumble. Rats and worms will diet on them; water and dampness corrode them; fires consume them. Looters may steal them for sale on the black market, or they can be destroyed during war or by natural disasters, like floods and earthquakes.

"Hard artifacts will wait patiently until they're uncovered—maybe decades, centuries from now—but manuscripts are impatient. In their case, we have a time factor on our hands. We discover them, or they die."

Shouts of "Hear, hear!" and "Right on!" accompanied much nodding among the thirty-eight world-class scholars seated around the huge conference table at the ICO headquarters on Brattle Street in Cambridge. There were twenty-six men and twelve women at that particular conclave, at least a quarter of them from Europe, Africa, and the Far East.

"Tell them about biblical manuscripts alone, Dick," Jon said.

Richard Ferris was the general secretary for the Institute of Christian Origins, a lanky scholar whose crew cut seemed to remove a decade from his actual age. "Well, you all know the numbers and how our list of New Testament manuscripts has exploded across the years. For the King James translators in 1611, only six basic manuscripts were available, but by 1870, two thousand had been discovered for the Revised Version translators. Today, however, we have about 5,700 manuscripts in whole or in part. And of course, as we have to tell the public again and again, through textual research and criticism of all these manuscripts, we get more and more exact versions of what was originally written by the New Testament authors. That's the good news.

"But the bad news Dr. Weber has already expressed. There are *more* manuscripts out there, and if we don't find them in time, the world will have lost some priceless treasures. And it's not just discovery. Some of these manuscripts have already been 'discovered,' as it were, but they've not been photographed, cataloged, or even examined. For example, Dr. Daniel Wallace, executive director of the Center for the Study of New Testament Manuscripts, recently sent a team to Albania to photograph ancient manuscripts in its national archive. They found no less than forty-five New Testament manuscripts that had never been photographed before—an incredible cache of documents in one of the least-likely places in the world! In fact, he estimates that maybe a thousand Greek New Testament manuscripts are still out there, yet to be discovered." He paused to let the tidings mellow.

Heinz von Schwendener, New Testament professor at Yale, raised his pen and added, "And I'll bet there could be *more* than a thousand in the long run. Okay, my colleagues, what's our role in all this? How can the ICO contribute?"

"Glad you asked, Heinz," Jon said. "In fact, I'm a little surprised that a Yalie is still awake to hear all this."

"It's only you Harvards that put me to sleep, Jon."

Amid chuckling over the inevitable Harvard-Yale banter,

Jon smiled and continued. "Here's what I envision: an effort—hopefully an international effort—to search out every known library or archive of ancient manuscripts in the world and photograph all early *un*photographed biblical manuscripts contained therein. We'd then do further examination of the most ancient and important of those manuscripts as well."

"Sounds like a task for several lifetimes, Jon," said Sally Humiston of Berkeley's archaeology department, "and requiring resources far beyond ours."

"Exactly, Sal. I've been discussing this with the leadership at the Center for the Study of New Testament Manuscripts. They'd be delighted to cooperate with us in this endeavor, and we've sketched the following procedure."

Jon switched on his PowerPoint presentation and directed his colleagues' attention to the large screen behind him.

"First, we must reach a consensus on the most feasible modus operandi. This would determine the dos and don'ts in terms of searching out locations of libraries and archives with ancient biblical manuscripts, how to approach the respective authorities at each and secure permissions to photograph, and the like.

"Next, I recommend that we work up an overall comprehensive plan for the project, including the initial target collections. Then we would be ready to approach appropriate foundations for funding as well as recruiting scholars and photographic teams to do the job."

"But haven't many of the collections been microfilmed already?" Brendan Rutledge wanted to know. He was Princeton's prime theologian.

"Yes, but many of them ought to be redone. Microfilming is

really passé with our new technology. We'll use digital photography instead, which is much better in every way. Here, check out the difference for yourselves."

Jon passed out photocopies that showed two views of a leaf from the fourth-century *Codex Vaticanus*, one of the earliest uncial biblical manuscripts. To the left was a regular microfilmed version, and to the right a digital version. There simply was no comparison. In terms of clarity, ease of decipherment, even shadings in the lettering, the latter was far superior.

"Beyond that," Jon continued, "at critical passages, we'll also use multispectral imaging to check for text that's faded, altered, or even erased. Manuscript copyists have been known to make mistakes." A titter of laughter followed the last comment, since it seemed that nearly all ancient manuscripts had their share of errors, most of them quite minor.

A drone of discussion followed—not in challenge or objection, Jon was delighted to note, but in affirmation and enthusiasm. Suggestions and ideas rattled off the walls; scholar candidates were suggested, names of foundations offered.

At the close of the conference, Jon announced, "In order to practice what I preach, my wife Shannon and I want to participate in the project by targeting libraries and archives in Greece and Turkey—not all of them, obviously, but several that we think may be promising candidates. We plan to fly off just after the close of the spring semester."

✢ ✢ ✢

Those, of course, were the plans before the translation catastrophe struck. Now, it seemed their summer would be grotesquely transformed from the research and travel they had planned into a sickening scenario of looking behind themselves at potential danger—imagined or real—their lives hostage to the whim of some fanatic. Curse the translation error! Curse the fanaticism that could augment a tiny publishing miscue into world riots and bloodshed!

Some relief, however, came swiftly. The American and Canadian television networks had announced the error in translation earlier, and the BBC, Deutsche Welle, and the French, Italian, and Spanish networks soon followed. Jon and Shannon were greatly heartened when the ghastly riots on their TV were replaced by interviews with spokesmen for Islamic councils in the western European countries who announced that this had all been a mistake after all, that Professor Weber had apologized for it, and that the offending effigies and signs had now been removed.

"But I didn't 'apologize' for it," Jon objected. "I regretted it. There's a difference."

"Half a loaf is better than none, Jon," Shannon reminded him.

Jon nodded slowly. "At this point I should be grateful for small favors. But why hasn't Al Jazeera come clean on this? That's the most-watched TV network in Muslim countries, so for their world, I'm still a blasphemous villain."

But it was Al Jazeera that might rescue their summer after all—not intentionally, of course—and television rivalry seemed partially responsible. The Abu Dhabi television channel in the United Arab Emirates broke the news on the translation error to the Arab world, and Qatar Television immediately followed suit. Rather than be upstaged, Al Jazeera, perhaps in compensation for its late coverage, did an entire half-hour special on the typographical error in Jon's book and how it had happened. They even had footage of the typesetter at his computer inside the editorial offices of the Cairo publisher, who blamed Osman al-Ghazali for the error, followed by footage of Osman in Cambridge blaming the typesetter. The program concluded with close-ups of the corrected text in the second printing of Jon's book. Islam was now the greatest *challenge* to Christianity, not the greatest *evil.*

Sunni Muslims across the Islamic world—that broad band of latitude from Morocco to Indonesia—soon responded, almost with pride, at the corrected reading that showed their powerful counterpoise to Christianity. Still, Jon was hardly home free. The Shiites were silent. Although they represented only 16 percent of world Islam, it was the Shiite clergy in Iran who had placed the fatwa on his head. That fatwa had not been lifted.

Jon discussed the matter with Osman. They had been in continual phone contact over the past two days. Predictably, the translator took some credit for Al Jazeera's finally announcing the error, but he also took the wind out of his own sails by confiding his surmise as to their delay.

By dragging their feet in announcing the error-cum-correction, he told Jon, the Sunni Al Jazeera got the Shiites to make fools of themselves with their instant fatwa. "There's just no end to the rivalry between Sunnis and Shiites."

"You really think the grand ayatollah and his Iranian clergy are embarrassed by the fatwa?" Jon asked.

"Not embarrassed. More like mortified, I'm sure. In fact, I'll bet that they'll never even mention this again."

"What! Not even to lift the fatwa?"

"Probably not. That would look like they'd made a mistake. And of course, they did! But it's the same reason Rushdie's fatwa was never lifted."

"So I have to live the rest of my life with this hanging over my head?"

"Welcome to the club, Jon. Since I converted from Islam to Christianity, I'd also face a sentence of death in almost any Muslim country if I returned. But I think you can put away the worry beads. Salman Rushdie lives, as you may have noticed, and I understand that VOA and Al Arabiya have also been giving full coverage to the truth in their Farsi broadcasts. Truth will win, even in Iran."

Jon was neither entirely convinced nor consoled.

CHAPTER 4

A WEEK LATER, SOMETHING HAPPENED that shocked not only Jon and Shannon, but much of the Western world as well. It was a very pleasant shock. Sheikh Abbas al-Rashid—probably the most influential Muslim theologian in the world—came down on Jon's side. Al-Rashid was the grand sheikh and imam at al-Azhar Mosque and University in Cairo, the number one Islamic theological school and the oldest university in the world. Before giving the commencement address at al-Azhar, he had alerted Al Jazeera, as well as network reporters and stringers from other nations, that they might find his remarks rather more newsworthy than was usually the case for commencement addresses.

This was enough to attract a small army of media sorts, all festooned with cameras of every description, to cover the occasion. Thousands of miles away in Weston, Massachusetts, Jon and

Shannon joined the international audience in watching the televised address, which was titled "Freedom for Truth." Al-Rashid opened by telling of an observer that the Sung dynasty in China dispatched in the year 987 to survey life in the West. When he returned home, the observer reported that the Roman Empire had fallen and been replaced by two great civilizations in the West: one was Byzantine, the other Islamic. The latter, however, was *far* superior to the former. Then, as an afterthought, he also told of a third—that of the Frankish kingdoms in Europe. "But they are sunk in barbarism," he concluded.

Al-Rashid continued—in Arabic, of course, but with simultaneous translations. "The observer from the Sung dynasty was absolutely correct. Today, all scholars, both East and West, agree that Islam was *the* foremost culture in the entire world during the tenth through twelfth centuries. Our cities had the first universities, the first hospitals, the first public libraries, even the first fire departments. We were at the forefront of all branches of human knowledge: astronomy, physics—all the sciences, in fact—mathematics, medicine, literature . . . The list is endless. We preserved manuscripts of the ancient Greek and Roman philosophers that were *lost* in the West. Their scholars learned from *us*.

"Yet this is not the case today. Some even regard Islamic nations as 'backward' and in need of foreign help. What happened? The reasons are many, but perhaps two dominate the others. One, we were brutalized by the Mongol invasion when Baghdad, the center of the Islamic world, fell in 1258. But the second reason, I think, is even more significant: our academic freedoms were curtailed from that time on. In later centuries, our most creative minds were constrained by intellectual blinders, fresh ideas were suspect, and our scholars were no longer at liberty to pursue truth for its own sake. Islam and the teachings of the Prophet—may Allah's peace and blessing be upon him—were by no means responsible for this, but narrow minds that claimed to speak for Islam were."

Al-Rashid went on to cite passages from the Qur'an that stressed the importance of free inquiry and tolerance, such as Sura 2:256—"In religion, there is no compulsion"—and how later on, stringent mullahs tried to explain away such verses. He then lashed out at the current fanaticism and violence fostered by Islamic fundamentalists and jihadists that not only endangered the world but were an insult to Islam itself.

He capped his argument with a powerful illustration. "Lest you think that this is not the case today, I would call your attention to what happened very recently. The Arabic edition of a book by a well-known American professor, Jonathan P. Weber of Harvard University, contained a misprint or innocent error that has since been corrected. And yet this professor was instantly attacked by today's mullahs, and fanatic mobs inspired by them caused riots in various countries that led, tragically, to some deaths. Not only that, but straining all canons of logic, a fatwa was even issued against the professor, which should immediately be lifted. We call on our Shiite brothers in the faith to nullify that fatwa."

"Jon, did you hear *that*?" Shannon asked unnecessarily.

Jon himself was speechless. What a magnificent development—in fact, a true answer to prayer! If the fatwa were lifted, their summer plans were intact once again.

The university imam closed with an appeal that Islam resurrect its past glories and world cultural leadership by returning to the path of free inquiry, which alone could lead to truth itself in all fields of human knowledge. His final words, of course, were the formulaic "All praise be to Allah, the Lord Sovereign of the universe, and may Allah praise his Prophet Muhammad and his household."

Moments of stunned silence followed, and then deafening applause erupted, especially from the students, with shouts of *"Allahu Akhbar! Allahu Akhbar!"* "God is great! God is great!" Of the seventy-five al-Azhar faculty members sharing the platform that day, some were smiling, while others wore frowns of deep concern.

Jon shook his head. "It's the finest address by a Muslim that I've ever heard—and certainly the best since 9/11. *This* is the voice of moderate Islam that should have been *much* louder following what happened in New York and Washington. What a man! I'll bet the archconservatives in the Islamic world cordially hate him."

"Do you think it'll take some of the heat off of us?"

"It certainly should, Shannon. It looks like we may be heading for Greece and Turkey after all."

They called Washington the next morning and discussed the matter with Morton Dillingham of the CIA. He was his usual cautious—perhaps paranoid—self. Jon was sure there must be a plaque on his office wall that read, *The light at the end of the tunnel is an approaching freight train.* Yes, he admitted that the climate had improved for Jon since the now-celebrated commencement address by al-Rashid. He also reported that the CIA operatives in Tehran had reported very little public follow-up on the fatwa issue. It was no longer news there, and there were no further riots.

"Then it should certainly be safe for my wife and me *not* to alter our plans for Greece and Turkey, right?" Jon asked.

"Oh, I'm not sure *that's* the case," he demurred. "It only takes one fanatic, one unstable—"

"We're fully aware of that threat, Mr. Dillingham, but our decision is to go ahead with our plans in any case."

There was a long silence at the other end of the line. Finally Dillingham replied, "Well, you're free citizens, and we can't stop you. But please fax me your specific itinerary, along with dates, after which I'll dispatch you a complete protocol of procedures to avoid danger, CIA contacts overseas, and other security measures."

"Thank you, Mr. Dillingham. That will be very helpful."

"But while you're abroad, always look behind you. Always."

✠ ✠ ✠

A fortnight later, Jon and Shannon were on an Olympic Air jet, flying from JFK to Athens. As the plane settled into its cruising altitude, she turned to him and said, "You know, Jon, despite all the traveling we do, this trip is the first one in a long time that almost feels like a vacation."

Jon squeezed her hand. "Whoever said that business and pleasure can't be mingled?"

Shannon was almost prepared for "no dancing in the aisles" on their plane, based on Olympic's ads, but she was quite content to settle for tasty introductions to Greek cuisine. They were served calamari ("almost like chewing rubber bands," Jon commented), *angarodomata salata*, *pastitsio*, *souvlaki*, *dolmas* nicely drenched in a thick *avgolemono* sauce, with a main course of either baked lamb or chicken and potato slices bathed in lemon olive oil. To be sure, there were also olives from first to last—not the modestly flavored Spanish sort cored with pimento, anchovies, or nuts. No, these were dark and salty Greek olives—totally salty—the kind that took command of your mouth and provided a day's suggested sodium intake apiece. It took several glasses of retsina wine—Jon intentionally mispronounced it "rinsina"—to "rinse" the palate for the deliciously sweet *baklava* that followed. Cups of steaming *elliniko kafe* capped off the gustatory marathon.

Suddenly, and apropos of nothing, Shannon sat up straight and asked, "Jon, the case with the manuscripts from Pella—where is it?"

He stared at her, wide-eyed, and seemed to grope for words. "I . . . I thought I . . . I hope I . . . didn't leave it at the JFK security line."

When Shannon gaped at him in horror, Jon quickly stood, opened the overhead compartment, and extracted the case. Holding it overhead as some sort of trophy, he returned it to the compartment and sat back down.

"Are you proud of yourself, Professor Prankster?" she asked.

"Sorry, dear. Someday I'll grow up."

"Doubtful!" She gave him a playful poke in the ribs.

Over the snowy Alps, down the long peninsula of Italy, and then eastward across the Adriatic, they flew until Pelops's vast "island" came into view, hung on the Greek mainland by the slender isthmus of Corinth. Now their jet lost altitude, glided across the Saronic Gulf, and curved northeastward over Laurium Mountain to land smoothly at Venizelos International Airport, the vast new structure built just in time for the Olympic Games at Athens in 2004.

"I wonder what 'Venizelos' means in English, Shannon," Jon wondered, tongue in cheek, as they disembarked.

"It means 'Venizelos,' you dunce!" she laughed. "It's a proper name and you know it!"

"Ah yes, Elefthérios Venizélos, the prime minister of Greece in the early 1900s, a statesman with so much charisma he's often called 'the father of modern Greece.'"

"Enough lecture for now, Jon."

They breezed through passport control at Venizelos to the reception concourse, which was festooned with welcoming signs in both Greek and English. They spotted their guide even before reading the *Dr./Mrs. Jonathan Weber* sign he was holding, a bearded young man dressed from head to toe in ecclesiastical black. He doffed his cylindrical hat and bowed slightly as he said, with studied formality, "In the name of Christodoulos II, archbishop of Athens and all of Greece, I bid you a most cordial welcome, Professor and Mrs. Weber."

"Kalimera," Jon replied. "You must be Father Stephanos Alexandropoulis?"

"Nai, nai!" he said, nodding in response.

Shannon smiled, recalling her first encounter with the Greek language when she learned that something so negative-sounding in fact meant "Yes, yes."

"Please to follow me and get your luggage," Father Stephanos said.

En route to their hotel, Jon acted as self-appointed tour guide to sights along the way, since Shannon had never visited Greece. "This is where chapters 17 and 18 in the book of Acts *really* come to life," he commented as they drove through the heart of Athens and along the western side of the Acropolis on the *Odos Apostolou Pavlou*—the Street of the Apostle Paul. "There's the Parthenon atop the Acropolis." He pointed to the right. "And just northwest of it—see that rocky rise?—that's the Areopagus, where St. Paul gave his famous Mars Hill address. And we're just passing the agora, where he met the philosophers who invited him to give that speech."

Father Stephanos was nodding proudly, almost as if he had arranged all the sites for their benefit. He told them how other tourists who had money but not culture infuriated him with inane questions: "Why don't they tear down all those ruined buildings on top of that big hill?" Moments like that made the holy man want to strangle the inquirer, he admitted.

Now they drove through the Plaka to Syntagma Square and their hotel, the Grande Bretagne. Father Stephanos helped them with their luggage as they checked into Athens's most famous hotel, frequented by the crowns of Europe and greats of the past and present.

"I hope you have good rest after your flight," he said. "And I pick you up in the morning at ten o'clock. Will that be all right? Our appointment with the archbishop is at ten thirty."

"Excellent, Father Stephanos," Jon said. "You've been most kind. *Ef charisto!*"

"Parakalo."

✠ ✠ ✠

Next morning at the appointed hour, they arrived at the headquarters of *Hey Ekklesia Hellenike*—known more commonly as the Greek Orthodox Church. A smiling Christodoulos II received them, the holy archbishop of Athens and all of Greece. He was a tall, imposing figure, attired, like Stephanos, in solid black. His salt-and-pepper beard provided a modest contrast, reflecting a man of sixty-seven maturing years. In many ways, because of a very lofty forehead, Jon thought he looked like Pericles himself, though without the helmet.

"Welcome, Professor and Mrs. Weber," he opened in excellent English.

"Ine megali timi Makariotate, na'houme afton ton hrono mazi sas," Jon returned in Greek, which he hoped would pass for "It's a great honor, Your Beatitude, to have this time with you."

"Your Greek is excellent, Dr. Weber," the archbishop replied, "but please to use English. I love the English language and don't have chance enough to use it."

"I'm grateful for that, Your Beatitude," Shannon said. While his wife's New Testament Greek was as good as any scholar's, Jon knew she was not familiar with modern, conversational Greek, which was markedly different.

"I am glad," the archbishop continued, "that the fierce Muslim debate over that translation matter in your book seems to have ceased. When the news first reached Athens, I looked up that passage in the Greek edition of your book—and I saw that it was rendered correctly."

Jon expressed his thanks, then came to the point of their meeting: the biblical manuscript project, which he explained in full detail. Would the archbishop be kind enough to look over a preliminary list Jon and Shannon had compiled of libraries and archives in Greece known for their ancient manuscripts, and provide any corrections or addenda? He easily agreed.

Jon's next request, he worried, was more daunting. Might the archbishop be generous enough to provide them a letter of introduction that would be useful in establishing their credibility when they or their teams arrived at a given archive and desired permission to photograph the biblical manuscripts in their collection? Jon had prepared a list of safeguards, which he handed to the archbishop:

1. The librarian or archivist on location may always exercise his veto, with or without explanation.
2. All photography will be undertaken with utmost care so as not to inflict damage in any way on the precious materials involved. No flash photography will be employed in the process so as not to cause any fading of the texts. (Digital photography obviates any such need, provided that normal light sources are available.)
3. Full credit lines will be added to all photo collections and in all publications thereof.
4. A complete set of the resulting photographs will be deposited at all libraries and archives kind enough to permit such photography.
5. All commentary accompanying the collections involved will first be checked with the authorities at each location prior to publication.

Archbishop Christodoulos II studied the list and then excused himself to show it to the general secretary of the archdiocese in another office.

Jon smiled nervously at Shannon as they waited for what

seemed like an hour but was probably only a few minutes. What if they couldn't pass even first base on their venture? Should they have done more preliminary correspondence first? Yes, they whispered to one another, they probably should have. Would have, in fact, had the translation crisis not commandeered all of their time.

Christodoulos reappeared with another document in his hand. "Please to forgive me, honored friends, for making you wait," he explained. "Our general secretary called in several other advisers, and a debate followed. And wouldn't you expect that of Eastern Orthodox theologians?"

"Of course," Jon chuckled, relieved to learn what had caused the delay. He was well aware that even in the ancient church, it was the eastern half of it—the Greek-speaking East—that always loved to split theological hairs in debates that could rage on for decades, even centuries, compared to the more practical Latin church in the West that quickly came up with reasonable solutions.

Now the archbishop's smile faded into a frown. "Unfortunately, we cannot approve your list as it now stands."

Jon shot a glance at Shannon that said, *Well, our worst fears are nicely confirmed.*

"But there will be no problem," the archbishop added, a twinkle in his eye, "if you will add a sixth condition, which we have written out. It is similar to provision five, but stronger." He handed Jon and Shannon the second document.

6. Except in the case of heretical writings, if upon reading the ancient texts in the photographs, a word, phrase, or paragraph appears that seems in any way to

> contradict, threaten, or imperil the holy, ecumenical beliefs of Eastern Orthodoxy, the text or translation editor(s) must report this immediately to the offices of the archbishop of Athens rather than making that text public. Nor shall they in any way publicize this text but instead promise to keep this information absolutely confidential until it is released by the archbishop.

When Jon frowned a bit while reading, Christodoulos commented, "Please understand, dear friends, that this is not intended as censorship, but rather as a measure that will alert us to give a proper answer for such an item, should it arise."

Jon brightened. "In that sense, we can certainly sympathize with your concerns, Your Beatitude, since worthless reinterpretations of Jesus and the church that he founded are all the rage in the print and electronic media today. Our sensationalist novelists and theologians would just love to twist some obscure line in an ancient source to discredit Christianity. We'll gladly accept stipulation six."

"Fine, then. We shall be happy to write your letter of introduction with the stipulations listed and send it by courier to . . . Where are you staying?"

"At the Grande Bretagne."

"Excellent. It will be done."

As they were standing to leave, Jon, in a carefully rehearsed afterthought, asked, "By the way, Your Beatitude, among the many fine textual scholars in the Church of Greece, who, in your estimation, is the foremost authority on early Greek orthography?"

"Classical Greek or *koine*?"

"*Koine*. I should have specified that."

"Ah, the language of the New Testament and the early church fathers. Well, this question is very easy to answer. Our outstanding authority here is Father Miltiades Papandriou at *Oros Agiou*."

Jon concurred with a smile. "Had you replied with any other name, I would have asked you, 'Why not Papandriou at Mount Athos?'"

"So then, you were only 'testing me,' as it were?" he asked. If Christodoulos had been frowning, it would have been a sure sign that Jon had stepped over the line. But the genial archbishop had a broad smile.

"No, it was just a case of reconfirmation. Father Miltiades is famed the world over for his ability to scan Greek lettering and slot it accurately into the nearest half century."

"Probably the nearest quarter century or even decade!" the archbishop chuckled. "Do you plan to consult with Father Miltiades?"

Shannon quickly replied, "We'd be delighted to do that, Your Beatitude, if that were possible."

Christodoulos shook his head sadly. "Unfortunately, Madame Weber, that is not possible. Not possible . . . *for you*," he emphasized, then smiled. "But I can easily arrange it for your husband."

"Oh, that's right; do pardon my error!" she replied. "No female can enter the monastery enclave on Mount Athos!"

"Quite right, Madame Weber. Perhaps someday that will change, but that someday has not yet arrived. Shall I prepare a letter of introduction also for Father Miltiades, Professor Weber?"

"I would then be *doubly* grateful to you, Your Beatitude. We would also like his evaluation of a Greek text my wife found at Pella in Jordan some months ago." The words were out before Jon quite realized what he was saying. What if the archbishop wanted to know more about that text? At least, thank God, he had not used the term *manuscript.*

"Kalos," Christodoulos replied. "I shall do so and send the letter along with the other material."

Jon breathed a sigh of relief and asked, "Do you think Father Miltiades will be amenable to my visit?"

The archbishop chuckled. "*Amenable?* He will be grateful to me for sending him an internationally known scholar on the life of Christ, though he will not know he was *denied* a visit by this very lovely archaeologist who wished to accompany him."

"You are very generous, Your Beatitude," Shannon said with a shade of blush, "and we are deeply in your debt. *Ef charisto.*"

"*Parakalo*, my friends. *Parakalo.*"

CHAPTER 5

AFTER A WEEK IN ATHENS getting approval for subsequent teams to photograph biblical manuscripts at the National Library and the University of Athens, Jon and Shannon revived the tourist aspect of their journey by renting a car and driving northward on Greece's National Road 1 toward Thessalonica and Mount Athos. The "Holy Mountain" indeed, Athos had more monasteries per square mile than any place on earth.

While Shannon snoozed, Jon was ruminating to himself on the *why* of monasticism in almost every creed in the world, especially including Christianity. In the Old Testament, Elijah, Elisha, and the other great prophets each seemed to have had a desert experience—either alone or with like-minded followers. In the New, where did John the Baptist, the forerunner of Jesus, hold forth? In the wilds of Judea, of course, though near the

Jordan for his baptisms. And Jesus himself? Forty days in the wilderness at the start of his ministry, the background for his famous temptation by Satan. St. Paul? Same story. Following his celebrated conversion on the Damascus Road, he spent almost the next three years in the Arabian desert, gearing up for his ministry.

The lure of the solitary tracts, the wilderness, the wastelands. And not just in Judeo-Christianity. Five centuries before the birth of Christ, an Indian prince named Siddhartha Gautama had left his wife and nine-year-old son for meditation in the forest to explore the meaning of life. And what was a forest, in terms of solitude, but a desert with many trees? He was there for seven years until he finally found the answer while sitting under the Bodhi tree and became the first "Buddha," or "Enlightened One." Zarathustra had had his wilderness experience as well, and the list went on and on.

Clearly, you couldn't be a self-respecting religious luminary unless a desert experience was in your resume, Jon reflected. But why? Probably it was a case of clearer communication with God when one was in the wilds and far from the blandishments and seductions of life in the everyday world. Jon doubted that God spoke more loudly in the desert; it was just easier to hear him there.

Yet early Christianity was very outgoing and social, and for a time it had even seemed that it might be the first world religion without monks. Then, in the third century, a holy man by the name of Anthony fled into the Egyptian desert for a life of solitary contemplation, until the tour buses full of pilgrims, so to speak, arrived from Alexandria to see the holy hermit and the cave where he lived. Others, similarly inclined, sought out caves nearby and eventually monastic communities were born.

Except for anchorites like St. Simeon Stylites, who climbed atop a pole in Syria and sat there for the next thirty-plus years, monasteries were the rule thereafter. It remained only for St. Benedict, in the sixth century, to provide his famous threefold vow of poverty, chastity, and obedience to guide monasticism thenceforth.

But the monastic to whom Jon and his colleagues owed an incalculable debt was Cassiodorus, the sixth-century monk who had suggested that monasteries not only worship the Lord seven times a day and grow their own groceries, but also recopy ancient manuscripts so that priceless information from antiquity would not be lost. And so it was that monks in the medieval world preserved so much of the past tense of Western civilization.

Now they neared Kalambaka on the plains of Thessaly, beyond the halfway point to Thessalonica, where Jon left the main roads for an inevitable visit to Meteora. They *had* to take in Meteora, of course, and its series of monasteries that were perched precariously atop huge towers of rock. Quite aside from their role as tourist magnets, the monasteries were second in importance only to Mount Athos itself.

"Wake up, Sleeping Beauty!" Jon said as he parked the car at a vista observation point. "You're about to see something that's unlike *anything* you've ever seen before!"

✠ ✠ ✠

Shannon opened her eyes and gasped. Before them was a sight that came directly out of a fairy tale or fantasy novel. Or was it the most outlandish panorama that Disney artists or Steven Spielberg or George Lucas could ever have contrived? It was as if some colossal device in the earth's crust had extruded broad, thousand-foot columns of sheer rock that loomed so dizzily over the plains below that the Greeks had named the place Meteora, meaning "things hanging in midair." And, impossible to believe, atop each of these gargantuan sandstone pinnacles was perched a monastery complex.

"When the Ottoman Turks invaded the Balkans," Jon explained, "hermit monks sought refuge atop these gigantic rock piles, which were quite inaccessible to the Muslim occupiers."

"How could they ever have built those structures way up there? Wasn't that in the Middle Ages?"

"Yes, thirteenth, fourteenth century. The story goes that St. Athanasios, founder of the first monastery, was carried to the top by an eagle."

They both chuckled.

"Well, truth to tell," Jon went on, "they scaled some of the cliffs by cutting steps into the rock, though often they used long, rickety ladders lashed together."

"Horrifying!" observed Shannon, who admitted to a touch of acrophobia.

"There used to be more than twenty monasteries here. Now there are six, and only four are still active. As in all branches of Christianity, monasticism is not exactly overrun with applicants."

"It's an incredible view," Shannon said appreciatively. "Which one are we headed for?"

"Our appointment is with Father Simonides, the abbot of the second-largest monastery up there to the right: Varlaam." Jon pointed up to structures that seemed to belong to the heavens rather than terra firma. Varlaam was perched atop a cliff towering nearly twelve hundred feet above the valley below. "With any luck, he'll give us permission to inventory and photograph their most ancient manuscripts, and maybe he will even persuade his fellow abbots to do the same."

As they walked to the base of the enormous butte below Varlaam monastery, Jon pulled out his cell phone to announce their arrival. After many nods of the head and choruses of *"Nai . . . nai . . . nai,"* Jon pocketed the phone and said, "Bad news and good news, Shannon. Which do you want first?"

"The bad, of course."

Jon was grinning, so even the "bad" news couldn't be all that devastating. "Well, we were going to drive up to the mesa opposite Varlaam and take the bridge to the monastery, but cracks were discovered at one of the bases of the bridge and it's closed for inspection."

"And the good?"

"I couldn't be happier. They're going to winch us up in a large netted basket or raft, just as they used to do for people and goods in past centuries." Jon gestured to the contraption as they walked toward it.

Shannon laughed. "I don't think so."

"What do you mean?"

"I'm not going. If *you* are suicidally minded, you can go, Jon. I'm staying here."

"Aw, c'mon, Shannon. It's perfectly safe. Where's your spirit of adventure?"

"Where it should be: next to my feet, which are planted firmly in the realm of sanity."

"Look how sturdy these lines are—one-and-a-half-inch hemp. Now they're calling to us from the top. *Please* hop on board?"

Shannon looked very skeptically at the contrivance. It had a small wooden floor, something like a raft that was covered with netting underneath and along the sides. The netting was bunched together at the top, where it was secured to the main hoisting rope cable. Two smaller ropes were attached to each side to stabilize the rig. It was interesting to look at, to be sure, but hardly worth risking one's life, she concluded.

Just then, a monk came along to join them for the trip to the top. Smiling genially, he climbed onto the conveyance as if it were an Otis elevator. His confidence seemed to melt Shannon's qualms, and she finally boarded also.

"Hoist away!" the monk called up in Greek.

Slowly the ascent began. Shannon actually enjoyed the first part of their voyage upward because of the spectacular view. But when they were two hundred feet off the ground, she made the mistake of looking down. She gasped and clutched at Jon's arm.

"No, darling," Jon soothed. "Don't look straight down. Just keep looking out over this once-in-a-lifetime panorama."

"But what's that *clickety-click* sound up there?"

"Just the ratchet wheel on the windlass that's hoisting us up. You *always* want to hear those clicks."

"Why?"

"They prevent the winch from turning the other way."

"In which case we'd hurtle back down?"

"Well . . . exactly."

"Oh, how *delightful*! I wonder if that's ever happened."

"I understand that the windlass works perfectly. *Most* of the time, anyway."

"Jon! Not a time to be joking."

By now they were over halfway up to the monastery. While the view outward was breathtaking, any glance downward was terrifying. They were higher now than most radio towers, suspended between heaven and earth, and held only by hemp cables that looked quite worn. Now they themselves were also *meteora*.

Shannon was sorry that she had ever let Jon talk her into this exquisite bit of torture. She cast another glance at the hawsers that spelled life or death for them. "How often do they replace those ropes, Jon?"

He turned to the monk and asked the same question in Greek. When he had the answer, he turned to Shannon and smiled. "He thought the last time was when Lord Byron visited Greece in the 1830s."

Both men hardly concealed their mirth. Shannon pondered which of them to hoist overboard first, but she decided their weight in the basket was beneficial to her own safety.

The monk then added another comment, which Jon translated. "The brother here was only spoofing," he said. "As good stewards of property, they replace the ropes only 'when the Lord lets them break!'"

"Not helpful, Jon!" she cried, *Jon . . . Jon . . . Jon* echoing across the entire valley. The men, however, were doing a miserable job of trying to stifle their laughter.

Suddenly the *clickety-click* stopped and the ascent upward

was halted. A wind from the west had arisen, causing their rude gondola to start swinging from side to side. "What's going on?" she demanded, her hands clammy.

Jon asked the monk, then replied, "He says that you should not be concerned. The machine breaks down sometimes, but they're usually able to repair it in less than twenty-four hours."

Her heart momentarily stopped. But then her mood changed to one of steel as she said, "Now listen closely, Jon. If I could let go of the edge of this witch's basket you've arranged for me, instead of my holding on for dear life, these two hands would gladly wrap themselves around your throat until you begged for mercy. And the same goes for your new Greek friend there, monk or not! Now get me out of this mess, *and I mean now.*"

Realizing that once again he had stepped over the line, Jon admitted, sheepishly, "It was only a little joke, honey."

The *clickety-click* resumed, and soon they were at the summit. Though Shannon's knees were wobbly as she emerged from their netted elevator, she refused to give Jon the satisfaction of accepting his help in ascending the final steps to the courtyard of Varlaam monastery.

"Shannon, honey," he called. "I'm sorry. Really."

"Later, Jon," she said through clenched teeth. Honestly, sometimes she wondered if her husband would ever grow up. As much as she loved the man, there were times she could hardly stand to be within ten feet of him.

A violet-robed warden of diminutive stature extended them a warm greeting, and Shannon tried to arrange her features into a more neutral state. The warden showed them to their quarters for the night, and Shannon was pleased to see that the room was nicely appointed—not the monastic cell she had expected—with twin beds and a window looking out over the valley below. Shannon quickly chose the bed away from that window.

By now it was late afternoon, a golden yolk of sun starting to drop onto the western horizon. The vesper had rung, and the brother monks gathered in the monastery chapel to chant their evening prayers. Jon and Shannon, however, were escorted to the refectory, where they were treated to a simple, though tasty, dinner of seafood broth, green beans, white fish, dark bread, and—of course—black olives. A pungent retsina wine, served in wooden goblets, assured them that they were in the very heart of Greece.

Early to bed, Jon finally admitted to her why their "ascension to heaven" was momentarily delayed. On the cell phone, he had asked the brother in charge of the windlass to halt the hoisting for a minute or two when they were near the top "so that they could gather in a final view."

"I'm sorry, honey." His voice was contrite. "I shouldn't have taken your acrophobia so lightly. I really thought . . ." He paused.

"I'm listening."

"I really thought the magnificent view would take your mind off the circumstances. I didn't mean to scare you out of your wits. Truly I didn't."

Shannon took a deep breath. It wasn't the first time Jon's enthusiasm had overridden his better judgment, and she knew it wouldn't be the last. Despite his sometimes-childish pranks, she did love him. And she somehow always found it in her heart to forgive him.

"Okay, Jon. I . . . I'll try to forgive you. But if you want a good-night kiss, you'll have to come over here. I'm not getting any closer to that window than I have to."

Almost before she'd finished speaking, Jon appeared at her side. She squeezed over against the wall to make room for him on the narrow bed. He snuggled in and wrapped his arms around her. "Thank you, darling. I love you."

Surrendering to his embrace, she once again thanked God for bringing this wonderful, unpredictable, albeit exasperating, man into her life.

✠ ✠ ✠

The meeting with Abbot Simonides the next morning went well enough, although it was complicated by the fact that the rotund, white-bearded archimandrite insisted on using his broken English instead of Greek—this in deference to Shannon. In responding to Jon's manuscript project, Simonides promised to secure the cooperation of the other monasteries at Meteora, but admitted that they were better known for their museums, icons, and relics than their libraries. "Here at Varlaam," he said proudly, "please to believe it: our museum has a finger of St. John the apostle, and also a shoulder blade of the apostle Andrew, brother of St. Peter!"

Shannon exchanged a glance with her husband that told it all: privately they would share a chuckle over the dear brother's sincerity, but a simple smile and a nod were far more appropriate here.

"For your purposes, I would go to Holy Mountain," the patriarch continued.

"That is indeed our plan, Your Grace," Jon replied. "Mount Athos, in fact, is our next destination. But for the very reasons you mention, the collections at Meteora have been overlooked, I think. If you and your colleagues at the other monasteries here took a complete inventory of your manuscript collections, something priceless might yet be discovered and the world would be in your debt."

The abbot's eyebrows arched. Slowly he nodded and said, "Yes, we will do this. We will do this. And yes, let the photo people come too and make pictures of our treasures."

"We could not ask for more, Your Grace," Jon said.

Shannon knew that he was probably restraining himself from doing cartwheels in his delight. "We also deeply appreciate your hospitality at Varlaam," Shannon added. *"Ef charisto!"*

"Parakalo!" Abbot Simonides replied. "It is nothing. It is nothing."

"*Ouxi!* In fact, it is everything," Jon commented.

Shannon's favorite memory of their visit to Varlaam was when the abbot announced, in parting, that the crack at the base of the pedestrian bridge from the monastery to the adjoining plateau had been repaired, and that Varlaam's service vehicle would drive them down to their car. She would not have to risk her life again on that netted raft, since the trip down the cliffside would have been even more terrifying, she assumed, a virtual descent into hell.

God was good! Her husband, on the other hand? Well, the jury was still out in his case.

CHAPTER 6

ON THE DRIVE NORTHWARD TO SALONIKI—as Greeks referred to their second-largest city, Thessalonica—Jon gave Shannon the gist of the phone call he had put in to Marylou Kaiser. To his surprise, sales of the Arabic translation of his Jesus book were booming in moderate Muslim nations like Morocco, Egypt, and Jordan, with brisk success even in Syria, Iraq, Pakistan, and Indonesia—and not just as fuel for book burning.

"Then again, chalk it up to controversy, Marylou," he had said. "Controversy is always the mother's milk of sales."

"But it may be more than that, Dr. Weber," his secretary had replied. "Because of your other comments on Islam in that chapter, all sorts of debates are springing up between Muslims and Christians in various cities here, including Boston."

"Nothing wrong with that—so long as it remains dialogue and no one gets steamed. By the way, anything from the Iranians?"

"Do you mean, has your fatwa been lifted?"

"Yeah, I guess that's what I mean."

"No. Which reminds me, Mr. Dillingham—the CIA, you'll recall—has phoned several times to complain that you aren't checking in with their operatives in Greece, as you should have."

"Darn. I plumb forgot. But hey, I haven't been assassinated yet, have I?"

"That's so comforting, Dr. Weber. Now please do the right thing?"

"I promise. Oh, and please ask Osman al-Ghazali to try and monitor some of those Christian-Muslim debates and get back to me, okay?"

Shannon had not worried about the fatwa for several days, but Jon's mention of it restored a furrow or two to her brow. He saw it and immediately switched the subject to their favorite topic of late: the five leaves of brown parchment that had such explosive implications—provided they were authentic and could be dated.

"Those just have to be pages from Hegesippus's lost memoirs, honey. And no, you don't have to ask if I packed them. The attaché case went into the trunk first."

"Let me play devil's advocate, Jon, and ask why you seem to be so sure that this is material from Hegesippus. After all, those pages are anonymous—no author's name anywhere."

"True enough. But they provide new detail on the death of James the Just that doesn't appear anywhere else. So when Eusebius states that he got his information from Hegesippus, and the expanded version of this material shows up inside Eusebius just at that passage where Eusebius tells of the death of James, I think any scholar would support our conclusion that yes, this obviously older text must come from Hegesippus."

She nodded. "I only hope the experts agree, especially because of what Hegesippus wrote about the Canon."

"Yessss!" Jon dragged out the sibilants in his enthusiasm. He would never forget the tidal wave of excitement that had splashed over them both in Cambridge when they read the passage:

> *After blessed Luke wrote his first treatise to Theophilus, which we call Luke's Gospel, and his second treatise to Theophilus, which we call the Acts of the Apostles, he wrote yet a third treatise to the same person, which we call the Second Acts of the Apostles.*

"Second Acts, Shannon, Second Acts!"

She beamed as if it were fresh news. "No less than a missing book of the New Testament!"

"What do you think Luke wrote in the second book of Acts?"

"I think it's obvious, Jon. He must have finished off St. Paul's story, since he really leaves us hanging in the last verse of Acts, where Paul is in Rome for two years, waiting for his trial before Nero."

"True. Luke loved reporting about trials—think how many times Paul shows up before Greek and Roman authorities in the book of Acts. Wild horses couldn't have prevented him from telling about Paul's biggest trial of all—before the emperor himself. And yet, no report of it in Acts."

"So that's why he must have told of it in Second Acts."

"Exactly. I'd give my left arm—no, maybe both—if I could find that third treatise, O Theophilus."

"Think it will ever be found?"

"Unlikely. Nobody ever mentioned it in other sources from that era."

"Except for Hegesippus," she corrected him.

"Except for Hegesippus—if dating those pages can authenticate their antiquity. Which, of course, is why we're heading for Mount Athos. You and I have dealt with frauds before, but this particular find is different. Concocting those pages would be virtually impossible, and their random discovery all but shouts authenticity. Frankly, the main reason I want Father Miltiades to look at our treasure is less to see if they're genuine and more to gauge their age—no rhyme intended."

"Assuming they're authentic, Jon, how do you think the public will react once we break the news?"

"The reference to Second Acts alone is going to shake the whole world of biblical scholarship."

✠ ✠ ✠

By now they were approaching Thessalonica on the national road, the inky blue Aegean Sea to the east and the towering hulk of Mount Olympus to the west, its top lost in the clouds. Jon opened the window and yelled up to the mythological home of the gods, "Hey, Zeus! How's your dysfunctional family?"

"Jon, have you lost it?" Shannon wondered.

"Shhhh! I'm waiting for his answer."

"You *have* lost it!"

"Probably. But we don't skirt Mount Olympus every day, now, do we?"

They reached Thessalonica in time for dinner at their hotel, the Macedonia Palace, which stood proudly over the eastern waterfront of the city. Jon noticed that Shannon's ire over his performance at Meteora had moderated, a mood change fostered by the delicious Greek cuisine they were sampling at a table on the hotel terrace overlooking the harbor. Below them was a band shell, where a small orchestra was filling the warm evening air with syrtaki music in general, Mikis Theodorakis in particular. Jon looked at Shannon and found her especially lovely when gilded by the setting sun. He took her hand in his and gave it a gentle squeeze. When she squeezed back, he assumed all was well again and that they could look forward to a beautiful evening.

✠ ✠ ✠

At breakfast, they discussed Jon's overnight trip to Mount Athos. While Shannon stayed at their hotel with plans to visit the museums and excavations in Thessalonica, Jon would embark on a ferry for the voyage to the port of Dafni midway down the western shore of the Athos peninsula.

Shannon would much rather have accompanied Jon to discuss the age of her documents with Miltiades Papandriou. She asked, "What about that strange rule excluding women from Mount Athos, Jon? Isn't it the only place on earth with that restriction?"

"Probably."

"Well, I think it's antiquated at best, and sexist, medieval, discriminatory, demeaning, and an insult to women everywhere at worst."

"I really wish you'd have an opinion on the subject," he trifled. "But I don't think women ought to feel singled out by that policy since it applies also to all female members of the animal kingdom."

Fortunately she caught the slight smile at the corner of his mouth or she would have given it an affectionate slap.

"Wait . . . I think I made a mistake," Jon confessed. "They do allow hens on Mount Athos. They need the fresh egg yolks to supply the tempera for painting their icons."

"How very generous of them!"

"Oh, and feline femmes too. If it weren't for cats, rodents would overrun all twenty monasteries on the Holy Mountain."

"And that's it for females on Mount Athos?"

"So far as I know."

"But why, Jon?"

"The monks don't want any of you sexy creatures around. These are holy men, my darling, and they don't want to be tempted or seduced by womankind. At least, that's the standard impression across the world."

"Well, what's the real reason, then?"

"I still think that what I told you is the real reason. Officially, though, they claim that women would distract them from their prayers and meditations—the higher purposes for which they chose the monastic life."

She was pensive for some moments, her fingers turning an orange juice glass around several times.

Somewhat warily, Jon asked, "So what exactly are you thinking, my darling? I can see the wheels turning inside that lovely head of yours."

"Oh, nothing really." She gave him a teasing smile. "Just toying with the idea of somehow disguising myself as a man and accompanying you."

"Shannon, it wouldn't—"

"I could wear jeans, carry equipment, and don a cap to hide my hair. I'd speak very little—using the lowest voice I could manage when I had to—and simply go along as your aide?"

"I don't think so, Shannon."

"Why not?"

"Okay, it'd be possible, I suppose, but if you were discovered, it would doom our mission in Greece. By the way, it did happen before, I recall—earlier twentieth century, I think. Some beauty queen who won the Miss Greece title did disguise herself as a man and snuck into Mount Athos. She was discovered, of course, and it wasn't pretty."

"What happened?"

"The monks were so outraged they stoned her to death."

"What?"

"All right, I jest. Her little escapade doomed Greek beauty contests for decades after that."

Shannon shook her head, laughing. "Well, I wasn't really serious. It's just that it's going to be hard sitting here waiting while you have all the fun."

"I promise to give you hourly updates by cell phone."

Shannon supposed that she would have to be content with that. After Jon drove off for the embarkation port east of Thessalonica, she returned to their hotel room to wash her hands. There, next to the wall socket, lay Jon's cell phone, resting comfortably in its charger. So much for the hourly updates.

✢ ✢ ✢

Jon was convinced that if ever some precious ancient biblical manuscripts were waiting to be discovered, they would likely be lurking in a monastery archive at Mount Athos. For centuries, the holy men living in these monasteries had devoted themselves to worship, meditation, and prayer, as well as to preserving the relics and manuscripts in their possession. Who knew what ancient treasures lay buried there in plain sight, for those who knew where to look? The authorities at the Holy Mountain were well aware of this potential as well and had begun a lengthy project of cataloging every manuscript on Mount Athos. That was the good news. The bad was this: the process might take thirty years. Jon's other mission, then, would be to ask Abbot Miltiades if his ICO might send scholars and photographers to Mount Athos to assist in accelerating the process.

Miltiades Papandriou was the *hegoumenos*—abbot, archimandrite—of Megiste Lavra, the Great Lavra monastery at the tip of Mount Athos, which had the primacy on the peninsula. He was a rare combination of gifted administrator and world-class manuscript scholar. Both Jon and Shannon knew of his reputation long before their trip to Greece.

Attaché case in hand, Jon boarded a wooden Greek ferry painted royal blue and blinding white, the national Hellenic colors. He quickly donned sunglasses in order to save his eyesight. Aboard were a curious collection of robed clergy and monks in black, along with supplies for the monasteries. Nothing female was in sight, of course, except for several crates of cackling hens. Jon could only hope that the weather would stay favorable, recalling that a fierce storm had destroyed an entire Persian fleet off the coast of Mount Athos in 492 BC, two years before the great Battle of Marathon. The Aegean, however, was on its best behavior that morning, a placid, quiet sea interrupted only by the chug-chug-chugging of the ancient diesel engine propelling their craft.

An hour into the voyage, Jon reached for his cell phone to give Shannon the first of his promised updates. It was then that he remembered where it was: plugged into his charger at the hotel in Thessalonica. Mentally kicking himself, he quickly glanced down to see his attaché case safely nestled at his feet. Evidently, absentminded professors must be selective in what they forget, Jon assumed.

In late afternoon, they sailed into the port of Dafni. Disembarking, the passengers went through a customs check at the port and were waved through turnstiles by a white-helmeted official—all, that is, except for Jon. Because Archbishop Christodoulos in Athens had generously cleared the way for Jon, he had not stopped at the Pilgrim's Bureau in Thessalonica to get a diamoneterion—a special three-day pass to visit Mount Athos. Each of the other passengers had one; Jon did not. The customs agent, who knew no English and seemed not to understand Jon's more classical Greek, let fly with torrents of angry shouts at Jon, almost as if he were a female interloper. Next the agent turned his anger on the boat's captain, evidently for his daring to bring along a passenger without a diamoneterion. As calmly as he could, Jon opened his attaché case and handed the official the authorizing letter from the archbishop of Athens and all Greece.

Scowling, the officer had just started reading the letter when a jeep pulled up, driven by a purple-robed monk. The brother stepped out of the vehicle, saw Jon being detained, and then unloaded an even louder torrent of furious Greek at the customs official. The agent took umbrage at that and unleashed a response in stentorian tones, complete with gestures to suit the occasion. Jon had always thought that two Italians arguing after a traffic accident usually set the record for altercation volume. He was wrong. The decibels of this disagreement topped them all.

Suddenly all became quiet. The monk looked at Jon and said in a thick accent, "Welcome to you, Dr. Weber! And please to forgive this unpleasantness. This man's father was a donkey! I give you ride to the monastery."

Rather sheepishly, and avoiding eye contact, the customs agent handed Jon the archbishop's letter and retreated into his guard shack. Jon thanked the monk and climbed into his jeep. They drove southward along the coastal road for a brief time and then headed up into the mountains, where the drive became an adventure. Roads were not paved on Mount Athos but consisted of stabilized gravel. The driver himself seemed to have studied not at a seminary but at Daytona. Whether or not he was trying to impress his passenger, some of his speeding around hairpin curves was just plain dangerous, and Jon expressed his concern as best he could. The driver merely offered Jon a toothy smile, almost as if to say, "Yes, I know; you want me to go faster." Was this man from al-Qaeda, a terrorist in training?

After twenty harrowing minutes, they skidded to a halt at the Great Lavra monastery, perched at the very tip of the Athos peninsula. Jon stepped out and tried to take it all in: the great gray walls, the fosse, the turrets, the crenellated terraces.

What surprised him most, however, was the unexpected presence of Miltiades Papandriou himself, who walked across the courtyard to greet him, wearing a warm smile that seemed to soften his otherwise-formidable bearded countenance. His spare frame stood erect at more than six feet, his shoulders not hunched over nor his eyes bleary from a lifelong perusal of manuscripts. This man was clearly in charge on the Holy Mountain.

"Greetings in the name of our Lord and Savior, Jesus Christ, Professor Weber," he said in flawless English. "We are honored by your visit."

"Quite the contrary, Your Grace. I am the one honored."

"Ever since we received word from Archbishop Christodoulos that you would come to Mount Athos, many of our brothers have read or reread your remarkable book on Jesus. I think it is a model of excellent scholarship."

"Thank you, but the chapter on sources rests heavily on your own brilliant manuscript research, Your Grace."

Miltiades held up the palms of his hands as if to ward off the compliment, then showed Jon to his guest quarters.

At dinner that evening, Jon was invited to give a brief talk to the resident monks in the refectory, which was enthusiastically received. *Only because these poor fellows have such limited exposure to diversion of any kind.*

The next morning, he was given a guided tour of the monastery, during which he paid special attention to the archives.

Archimandrite Miltiades joined Jon in the refectory after the tour, and they both climbed the stairs to his office in a turret overlooking the entrance to the monastery. The office was well insulated from the heat of summer or the cold of winter by books of every description, including the sort that caught Jon's eye: ancient tomes covered in tattered leather, some with spines missing. Atop the broad desk of polished maple lay a beautifully illuminated medieval codex.

"My—how you say it?—my *hobby* is to bring out a modern edition of the sermons of St. John Chrysostom," the genial abbot said, pointing to the codex, "as annotated by medieval monks."

Jon registered appropriate awe but thought, *Why their annotations? Today's scholars have far more resources for commentary than medieval monks!* But he held his tongue; he had more important fish to fry.

"And now, my esteemed professor," Miltiades continued, "please sit down and let us discuss that manuscript of yours about which the archbishop wrote. First of all, where did you find it?"

"I didn't find it, Your Grace. My wife Shannon did. At Pella in Jordan."

"Pella, you say?" The face of the archimandrite brightened. "I've always thought that if any important early manuscripts were to be discovered, it would be at Pella. Or perhaps at St. Catherine's on Mount Sinai."

"Or Mount Athos," Jon quickly added.

The abbot smiled and agreed. "Or Mount Athos."

Jon proceeded to give the whole history of the find before

opening his attaché case. First he took out only four of the five ancient leaves, then renderings of the writings on them enhanced by ultraviolet, providing a much clearer text. Miltiades put on a pair of gold-rimmed glasses and began reading the Greek immediately, occasionally glancing at the originals.

Minutes passed. Jon said nothing. Nor did his host, who reached for a magnifying glass from time to time and held it over the texts. Silence filled the office more audibly than Jon had ever experienced.

Finally Miltiades looked at Jon and said slowly, "This is quite remarkable. I have read some of these words before. I think it was when Eusebius quotes Hegesippus on the death of James the Just of Jerusalem."

"Exactly, Your Grace. I wanted you to discover that for yourself, rather than with any prompting from me. I congratulate you on your marvelous recall."

"It is nothing," he objected. "But here we have more from Hegesippus than what Eusebius quotes. It tells how Jesus' cousin Symeon became the next bishop of the church in Jerusalem."

"Precisely. And this is why my wife and I believe these pages come from the lost writings of Hegesippus."

The abbot shook his head in astonishment. "This is . . . this is remarkable, Professor Weber, remarkable! But I had not heard of this discov—"

"Only three people on earth know about these pages, Your Grace: yourself, my wife, and I. The priest at Pella knows about the leaves, of course, but not what they contain. Obviously, we wanted to determine their provenance—and even their authenticity—before going public with them. Hence my visit."

"Yes. Yes of course." The abbot exhaled heavily. "To me, it looks as if the writing comes from . . . well . . . from as early as . . . the third century. But wait. . . ."

He reached for a reference book on orthography, which compared Greek lettering styles across the centuries. Now his head shifted from one side to the other repeatedly in comparing the shapes of letters, almost as if he were watching some ancient tennis match. Finally he looked up. "Yes. Yes, it is third century indeed. Here, look for yourself."

Jon compared the evidence and nodded—affecting surprise only because he had also done this comparison with a similar text on Greek orthography back in Cambridge. But yes, it was important to have his conclusions tested by the world authority on ancient Greek texts.

Their conversation now turned to the origin of the ancient leaves. If they came from the third century, then they could well be a first-generation copy of Hegesippus's original, which had to have been written before his death in AD 180, the abbot told Jon, confirming what he and Shannon had already surmised. "If that is the case, more such leaves from Hegesippus would be priceless. Did your wife inquire about this at Pella?"

"Most certainly. Unfortunately the priest who was using them to hold his place in an aged copy of Eusebius's *Church History* had no idea where they came from or when." Jon went on to disclose his plans for the ICO to do an exhaustive inventory of all written materials at the church in Pella, pending the local priest's permission.

Next they focused on the question of authenticity. The archimandrite examined the brownish leaves under additional lamps, using his magnifying glass almost constantly. His scrutiny, however, was fairly brief. He lifted his head and said, "Really, Professor Weber, there is no question but that these leaves are genuine and ancient. I think it would be totally impossible to . . . to . . . What is the word?"

"To forge, to falsify something like this?"

"Yes, that is what I want to say."

Jon smiled appreciatively, almost as if his host had made it all possible. Then he reached into his attaché case and extracted the fifth brownish leaf and its enhanced copy and laid them on the abbot's desk, his own heart increasing its tempo as he said, "This final page, Your Grace, is of such great importance that I didn't want it to color your conclusions."

Miltiades resumed his reading, showing no response whatever. Halfway through, however, he looked quizzically at Jon before returning to the text. Slowly, his head turned across each line, which he seemed to read and reread. This time he also had much recourse to the original on the left side of his desk, poring over it again and again.

He finally sat up, shook his head, and muttered, *"Thaumadzo!"*

Jon recognized the verb from the opening lines of St. Paul's letter to the Galatians: "I am amazed." Then a torrent of words poured out of Miltiades's mouth. "Now Hegesippus is talking about the Gospels and how they were written. After Mark and Matthew, he comes to Luke, and . . . and he writes . . ." He grabbed the magnifying glass and immediately translated into English. "He writes, 'After blessed Luke wrote his . . . first treatise to Theophilus, which we call Luke's Gospel, and his second treatise to Theophilus, which we call the Acts of the Apostles, he wrote . . . also a third treatise to the same person, which we call the Acts of the Apostles, Beta,' that is, the Second Acts of the Apostles."

The abbot laid down the magnifying glass on his desk between the original leaves and the enhanced version and was silent for some moments. Finally he said, "Now I know why you think these pages are . . . are so important!"

"Indeed, Your Grace. They could even mean that there is biblical material out there that never got included in the Bible."

The abbot made a triangle of his fingers and thumbs and nodded pensively.

Jon continued. "Have you ever found any reference to a third treatise to Theophilus?"

Slowly the abbot shook his head. "No. No, I have not. This . . . this is astonishing."

"And it may help explain why Luke seems to break off so abruptly at the end of his narrative in Acts, chapter 28. Here he brings St. Paul to Rome, and the reader can't wait to read about the greatest crisis in the apostle's life: his trial before Nero. But Luke seems to do a . . . a fade-out on us, as Americans put it. No trial, just a few words about Paul preaching openly in his rented dwelling for two years."

"Ah yes. I've often thought that this was the most . . . the most . . ."

"Frustrating?"

"Yes, the most frustrating passage in all of Scripture."

Both were silent for a while. Then a wan smile crossed the abbot's face. "What a treasure it would be for the church—for the world—if that 'third treatise' could ever be found."

"How very true! But do you think that's even possible?"

A slight frown furrowed the cleric's brow and he shook his head sadly. "No, I don't think so. It would have been discovered long ago and be part of our Bible today." He paused, drummed his fingers on the desk, and resumed speaking. "But your discovery, I think, will be very helpful to explain why the book of Acts ends as it does. Luke had more to say."

"Yes. Luke had more to say indeed. This is exactly what my wife and I concluded."

"Just so. But what are your plans for this discovery? When will you publish?"

"Not until a total inventory of the St. James Orthodox Church at Pella is completed—for obvious reasons."

"Oh yes, yes. That is very, very important. And I promise you that I will tell no one about this until you give me permission."

"Thank you, esteemed Archimandrite. I was about to ask you for that favor. If the news ever got out, hordes of amateur scholars and sensationalist sleuths would converge on Pella and crowd out the true specialists."

"Yes, and probably destroy further parts of this manuscript, if they were discovered."

✠ ✠ ✠

After a brief but nourishing lunch, Jon broached to Father Miltiades the ICO's offer to help accelerate the inventory project at Mount Athos and its many monastery archives. He feared a negative response since the monks there were known to be a fiercely independent lot. One of the monasteries, in fact, had so opposed any ecumenical outreach to Roman Catholicism that it had to be excommunicated from Eastern Orthodoxy.

The genial archimandrite, however, surprised him and said, "This is an answer to prayer, dear Professor. Scholars across the world have been begging us to hurry up, to . . ."

"Expedite?"

"Yes, to expedite our inventory search. But we have not had enough resources or specialists to do that. But now you come here and promise us both. In the name of the Great Lavra and of all the other monasteries on the Holy Mountain, we offer you our thanks."

Jon proffered enthusiastic thanks of his own, promising to stay in close touch with Abbot Miltiades. It was a very pleasant way to end his visit. Perhaps it was the mellow mood that actually enabled him to avoid panic on another breakneck jeep ride back to the port of Dafni. On the ferry back to the mainland, he found himself clutching the attaché case closer than ever.

After a quick drive back to Thessalonica, Jon stopped at the hotel's convenience venue to pick up a newspaper. Glancing at the news rack, he was shocked to see his own picture on the front pages of the international newspapers. He snatched up a copy of the *International Herald Tribune*.

But before he could even read the article, Shannon rushed over to him. "Jon, you won't believe what's happened!"

CHAPTER 7

AS THEY HURRIED TO THEIR ROOM, Jon was treated to a string of wifely admonitions about a forgotten cell phone, as well as an inventory of the torrent of messages that had arrived for Jon in the last twenty-four hours, including Reuters from London, the Associated Press in New York, the U.S. Embassy in Athens, and the CIA. Marylou Kaiser and Richard Ferris had been calling every hour. Fortunately no one had revealed their whereabouts in Greece, except for phone numbers Marylou had been all but forced to give the government. Otherwise, the press would have besieged the Macedonia Palace.

"It's been *crazy*, Jon," Shannon said, "absolutely crazy."

Jon shook his head in disbelief. "So what in the world is this all about?"

Shannon shrugged expressively and threw her hands up.

"I don't know what to say. Just read the papers. I picked up all the English newspapers I could find. They're spread out on the bed."

Inside the bedroom, Jon opened the blinds and turned on the light. For all her exasperation, Shannon did have them neatly arranged and crying to be read. On a top row lay the London *Times*, the Manchester *Guardian*, and the *Financial Times*. On the second row was another copy of the *Herald Tribune* from Paris, as well as overseas editions of the *Wall Street Journal* and the *New York Times*. All featured his photo on the front page (except for *WSJ*'s traditional line-sketch version), but the anomaly hit Jon from the start: next to his photo in many of the papers was that of a Muslim in traditional headdress.

He picked up the *Herald Tribune*'s version of the story. It was on the lower half of the front page.

WORLD ISLAMIC LEADER CHALLENGES HARVARD PROFESSOR TO DEBATE

Cairo (AP)—Dr. Abbas al-Rashid, regarded by most Muslims as the leading theologian in Islam, has challenged Jonathan P. Weber, well-known professor of Near Eastern studies at Harvard University, to a public debate on the topic "Christianity or Islam—Which Is More Credible?"

Al-Rashid is the grand sheikh or imam at al-Azhar University in Cairo, a much-published author of books on Islam, especially his widely read *Muhammad—A Life Blessed by Allah*. "He is preeminent in Sunni Islam," commented Haroun Nasir, president of the Islamic Council of New York. "I have no doubts whatever that he will win this debate."

Weber is the Reginald R. Dillon Professor of Near Eastern Studies at Harvard University, the founder of the Institute of Christian Origins in Cambridge, and a bestselling author of books on early Christianity. His *Jesus of Nazareth*, published several years ago, is in its thirty-second printing in the American edition, with twenty-nine foreign translations. One of these, the Arabic edition published several weeks ago in Cairo, contained an error in translation that brought him to the attention of the Islamic world, although the error has since been corrected.

No summitlike debate between Christianity and Islam has taken place for twelve centuries. The last such was in the year 781, when Timothy I, Patriarch of the Assyrian Christian Church, held a celebrated debate with the third caliph of the Abbasid dynasty, Muhammad ibn Mansur al-Mahdi.

In an interview today in Cairo, Dr. al-Rashid stated, "I must apologize to Professor Weber that I was unable to reach him first with a personal invitation to such a debate. This news is therefore premature, the mistake of a press secretary at our university, who has since been disciplined. I do, however, welcome the possibility of debating Professor Weber, for whom I have great admiration."

Dr. Weber could not be reached for comment. At

present his whereabouts are unknown, although reliable sources place him in Greece. The Associated Press promises full coverage of such a debate should it occur, especially in view of its controversial topic.

Jon put the paper down and stared vacantly across the room. He finally said, "This is hard to believe, Shannon. Here we thought al-Rashid was our *friend.* He gave that wonderful commencement address in Cairo. It helped take the fatwa off my head. Oh, oh, I forgot; the fatwa's still there but harmless."

"You hope," she replied. "Maybe he still is our friend. Notice that he admires you."

Jon nodded. Then he quickly scanned the other newspaper reports. Essentially they had the same story, though with different local commentary on the merits of the potential opponents.

The phone rang. Marylou Kaiser and Richard Ferris were calling from adjoining phones in Jon's office at Harvard. Their relief in finally getting through to "the boss" was palpable. They gave a lengthy rundown on the U.S. reaction to the debate challenge, which consumed at least twenty minutes' worth of transatlantic phone charges. At the close, Jon said, "Yes, we'll have to fly back. I can't tell you how much I hate to interrupt what we're doing since we're really on to something here." He swept the papers aside in frustration and sat on the edge of the bed. Raking his fingers through his hair, he forced himself to calm down and focus on the matter at hand. "But let's convene a meeting of the ICO executive committee for this coming Monday. Of course Osman al-Ghazali needs to be there too. Can you set everything up?" The two easily agreed. "Great! See you soon, then."

When he had hung up, Shannon commented, "I guess that means you *will* accept the debate, then?"

"Is the pope Catholic, Shannon?"

"And that our great little tour of Greece is over?"

"We'll be back, my darling. And that's a promise."

The manager at Hertz Rent-a-Car in Thessalonica grew apoplectic when Jon informed him that they would be unable to drive the car back to Athens, as they had agreed, since they had to fly home directly from Thessalonica. Why were Mediterranean types so excitable? he wondered. He could have fibbed that his mother was dying, so they *had* to get back, but his Lutheran conscience wouldn't permit it. A couple of American fifties laid on the counter took care of everything instead.

✠ ✠ ✠

Olympic Air flights from Thessalonica to Athens, then Athens to New York, and finally the Delta shuttle to Logan in Boston, and they were back in Cambridge. Large, dark sunglasses seemed to protect them from the press at the three airports, where they carefully avoided anyone carrying a camera or a nosy cell phone–cum–camera. Lately, though, that seemed to be every other person on earth.

Sunday back in Weston was devoted to unpacking and jet lag recovery. Incredibly the FBI was still keeping their house under surveillance. The government was nothing if not persistent. The phone kept ringing, but caller ID enabled them to answer only the most important calls, mostly from relatives and close friends.

Early Monday morning, Jon stopped at his Harvard office to check the mail, ignoring the almost-continuous ringing of his office phone. Among his letters was an elegant envelope from Cairo that turned out to contain al-Rashid's invitation to debate. It was in English, not Arabic, very proper, nicely worded, and almost friendly. To Jon, this only compounded the mystery of his challenge.

Then he hurried over to Brattle Street off of Harvard Square, where his think tank was assembling in the board room of the Institute of Christian Origins. Unfortunately the media had put two and two together over the past several days and had the ICO under surveillance. When Jon appeared, they thronged around him until Cambridge police cleared his way. He was bombarded with questions, mostly variations on the same theme: would he accept the challenge to debate or not? Finally he held up his hands for quiet and announced simply, "We'll have a press release for you this afternoon." Then he ducked inside.

Osman al-Ghazali was already sitting at the board table, Jon was relieved to see, since his advice regarding the debate would be crucial. Osman was half a head shorter than Jon but likely weighed more. The man had a bald pate that somehow failed to detract from his appearance. He made no attempt to cover it by combing long remaining strands of thinning hair across his bare dome, as happened so often, but kept his remaining dark thatch well trimmed along the sides. His velvet brown eyes always seemed to have a playful quality, and his classes at Harvard were packed, thanks to his excellent communication skills.

Since al-Rashid had supplied his e-mail address in the letter of invitation and had even suggested that they use the electronic medium to facilitate arrangements, Jon opened the meeting by reading the e-mail he proposed to send to Cairo:

"Dear Dr. al-Rashid:

Thank you for the honor of your invitation to debate the topic 'Christianity or Islam—Which Is More Credible?' I am pleased to accept. Perhaps we might first decide issues of time and place for the debate, then draw up mutually agreeable guidelines for our discussion.

I would also like to thank you for the remarkable address you delivered at the commencement of al-Azhar University this past June, not only because you were kind enough to give me favorable mention, but also in view of your splendid championing of academic freedom in the cause of truth. Yours is a most welcome voice in the Muslim world."

"Well, my colleagues, what do you think?" Jon asked.

Heads nodded in approval, until al-Ghazali commented, "What do you want to send there, Jon, a love letter? This man wants to trounce you in a debate!"

Jon was taken aback. "Are you serious, Osman?"

"No, I guess not," he said, smiling. "I'm just a little ticked that he went public before reaching you."

"He claims it was someone else's error. That sort of thing can happen, Osman, right—the 'error' bit?"

Al-Ghazali threw his arms up and chuckled. "*Touché!* I plead guilty!"

"Okay, then. Marylou, please send this to Cairo. The e-mail address is on al-Rashid's letterhead."

"Done."

Jon turned to al-Ghazali again. "Now, please tell us, Osman, why in the world would al-Rashid issue this debate challenge? We all thought he was progressive, a Muslim moderate who was anything but doctrinaire."

"Simply because that's exactly what al-Rashid is."

"What do you mean?"

"I heard from my contacts in Cairo that he got a tremendous amount of flak after that address you raved about—and it *was* worth raving about, believe me! But some archconservative mullahs started scheming to have him replaced. He learned of it, and in a steamy faculty meeting, he announced, 'It is easily possible to be faithful both to Islam *and* the cause of academic freedom!'

"That led to more hot debate, until one of their reactionaries, who inclines a bit to the right of Genghis Khan, yelled out, 'Prove it, then! Prove that you are indeed faithful to Islam by taking on that Christian professor from Harvard in debate!'"

"But why *me*, for goodness' sake?"

"Glad you asked," Osman said with a twinkle. "Whether or not you know it, Jon, you are big in the Arab world, *big*—thanks to that innocent mistake in the Arabic edition that seems to have catapulted you into stardom!"

"Can't be."

"Remember those Christian versus Muslim discussions you had Marylou ask me to monitor after you spoke to her from Meteora?"

"Yes."

"Well, they're starting also in the Muslim world. Not Christian-Muslim debates so much as Muslim-Muslim discussions on some of the issues you raised in your book. Al-Rashid simply had to put his money where his mouth was."

Marylou was staring at her laptop when she suddenly raised her hand. "Sorry to interrupt you all, but a return e-mail has just arrived from Cairo."

"Please plug your laptop into the projector so we can all read it at the same time, Marylou."

When the screen at the far end of the conference table lowered from the ceiling, they read the following message:

Dear Professor Weber:

Again I apologize for the premature announcement of our possible debate, and I thank you for accepting. I am certain that you and I can discuss the topic without the high emotion that often characterizes such exchanges, and the result might even benefit Muslim-Christian relations.

I would suggest that we consider the event for sometime within the next two or three months. As to place, we would be happy to invite you here to al-Azhar University. I am sure that the Coptic Christian population in Cairo would be glad to welcome you here as well. We are, of course, open to other locations.

Yours truly,
Abbas al-Rashid

"How come his English is so good, Osman?"

"Who knows? He could have used someone from the American University in Cairo."

"Well, team, what's your opinion? Is Cairo a good location?"

"I'd prefer New York," Richard Ferris said, half-joking. Then he added, "No, I think it's a very *bad* location, Jon—bad for your health. Not the climate, but the security situation. Cairo's the home of the Muslim Brotherhood—many of them jihadists—and of al-Gama'a al-Islamiyyah, the people who assassinated Anwar Sadat. And when you win the debate, they could even take it out on the Copts. Not a season goes by in Egypt without some Christian church getting burned. Plus, it would be al-Rashid's home ballpark."

"You seem a little optimistic about the outcome of the debate, Dick."

He laughed. "Is there any question?"

"You bet there is!" Jon glanced out the windows and saw an even larger media crowd outside. "Uh-oh, time to throw them a fish. Marylou, let's work up a press release that says I not only accept but look forward to the debate, since al-Rashid will be an excellent opponent, and that it will take place within the next three months at a location still to be determined. Okay?"

"Got it."

"Then bring it back here and we'll check it out."

✠ ✠ ✠

This set the pattern for other such meetings to come. An international debate like this might come off with apparent technical brilliance—or not!—which only masked the immense amount of preparation involved. Jon's "cabinet" met twice a week and exchanged hundreds of e-mails with Cairo until everything was nailed down. A long checklist was involved.

The hardest nut to crack was the location. Al-Rashid wanted a venue with a large Muslim population, in order to demonstrate his theology of loyalty yet flexibility within Islam. For obvious reasons, Jon preferred a large Christian presence. They exchanged suggestions for neutral sites or those with something of a religious balance between Muslims and Christians, like Beirut. But Beirut was finally rejected by both in view of the violence that so often and so tragically disrupted that beautiful city.

They finally agreed on a place that brought gasps to Christians but smiles to Muslims: Istanbul, Turkey. Had Jon lost his senses, agreeing to a location that was overwhelmingly Muslim? Not really, he claimed. Turkey was the most Westernized of the Muslim countries and a secular—not religious—state, thanks to Mustafa Kemal Atatürk, the father of modern Turkey. Geographically, too, it lay almost at the interface between Muslim and Christian lands.

But it was a third reason that had finally convinced Jon. He received a letter from no less than "the eastern pope," His All Holiness, Bartholomew II, Archbishop of Constantinople, New Rome and Ecumenical Patriarch, pleading with Jon to have the debate in Istanbul. The Eastern Orthodox Christians there were a small minority and needed all the recognition they could get in that quarter of the world. Although Jon's advisers were against the idea, he was adamant. The debate would take place in Istanbul. Once that was settled, the other details quickly fell into place and were outlined in a forty-page document.

Specific Location: *Hagia Sophia, the Church of Holy Wisdom, constructed by the Byzantine emperor Justinian in the sixth century, now a public museum.*

Date: *September 3, two months away.*

Time: *9:30 a.m. local time, with as much of the afternoon as necessary.*

Audience: *Exactly half Muslim and half Christian; ticket distribution to be administered by each side, independent of the other.*

Seating: *Christians will occupy the western half of the nave, Muslims the eastern half.*

Moderator: *Two will serve concurrently: the Ecumenical Patriarch of Constantinople and Mustafa Selim, the Muslim mufti of Turkey.*

Translation: *Simultaneous translations of the debate will be provided in Turkish, Arabic, English, Greek, Farsi, French, German, Spanish, Italian, Russian, and Chinese.*

Media Coverage: *Live radio and television coverage will be permitted. All cameras and all representatives of the press will be limited to the second-story galleries of the basilica.*

Publications: *All official printed materials resulting from the debate, whether in pamphlet or book form, will be carefully checked for accuracy by both sides against master audiotapes of the debate.*

Video: *Similarly, all DVD reproduction will be mutually approved, and all proceeds from sales of any media* *products subsequent to the debate will be shared equally by the Muslim and Christian parties involved.*

Security: *Metal and nitrate detectors will be in place at all entrances to the basilica, and no packages will be permitted inside. The government of the Republic of Turkey will have final responsibility for security and will provide same at both the civil and military level.*

A sheaf of many more pages covered everything from prohibition of camera flash to how many porta-potties should augment the regular toilet facilities at Hagia Sophia.

In the weeks following, the international media wanted details on every aspect of the debate plans. Apparently they could not leave the story alone. Some of the press reports overdid it, of course. London's *News of the World* brought out a headline—it must have been a slow news day, Jon opined—bellowing, *MOST IMPORTANT CHRISTIAN-MUSLIM CONTACT SINCE THE CRUSADES!* But even the more responsible media often used phrases like "could be historic," "rather unprecedented," "huge potential consequences," and the like.

"All in all, it promises to be *quite* the event," Shannon commented after reading through one day's particularly intense news coverage.

"Mm-hmm," Jon agreed, "although *quite* the detour for our research plans."

CHAPTER 8

SHANNON ATTENDED MOST of the ICO cabinet meetings at Jon's side, and both were aching to report her find at Pella and its significance. But they had to be absolutely sure about the physical properties of the five brownish leaves to ward off any potential claims of forgery. In fact, fraud had reared its ugly head with some frequency in the world of antiquities of late. Unfortunately this could taint genuine finds as well, prompting a "guilty until proven innocent" attitude among both professionals and laity. Inevitably, the more important the discovery, the greater the temptation to call it a forgery.

Shannon flew to Washington, D.C., to deliver one of the leaves to Sanford McHugh at the Smithsonian. "Sandy" had helped them with determinations of authenticity before, and he promised Shannon to have the results of his tests in about two weeks.

For his part, Jon, with Shannon's permission—it was her find, after all—cut off a small corner of one of the leaves, put it in a lead pouch, and air-expressed it to Professor Duncan Fraser at the radiocarbon labs of the University of Arizona in Tucson. Fraser and his TAMS apparatus—tandem accelerator mass spectrometer—had provided crucial assistance to Jon and Shannon several years earlier through his meticulous dating of a crucial manuscript by carbon-14 analysis.

And yes, Jon did have an ethical problem here. He should first have asked permission of the priest at Pella. But *cui bono*? To what good? If the priest had said yes, all was in order. If not, one of the best testing methods for an ancient manuscript would be denied. The chances that the priest would even notice a small cut from one corner—no writing whatsoever involved—were about one in a thousand. And even if he had an eagle eye and did notice it, he would quickly see that no damage had been done. It seemed a justified cut.

Jon and Shannon had a larger problem with his agreeing to Istanbul as the site for the debate. With Turkey 98 percent Muslim, she thought it was almost suicidal, especially in view of the fatwa still lingering over his head. Nor was the CIA, which quickly caught wind of it, especially pleased. If Jon would not change his mind, they wanted to review all security procedures in Istanbul and could not promise his safe return.

For his part, Jon defended his decision by pointing out that Turkey was Sunni, not Shiite, territory; he was debating the very person who had called for the lifting of his fatwa; and strict security measures would be employed. "It's a done deal, Shannon," he said, "a dead issue."

Her voice quivered as she warned, "I hope your words aren't prophetic!"

Jon just stood there, wondering if he might not have made a better choice of words. It was a bad moment.

Maybe things could be salvaged with a little levity. "Well, honey," he said, "don't forget that third reason I agreed to Istanbul: the Eastern Orthodox Patriarch begged me to come to Turkey, which wins me some points with him."

"And why do you need those points?"

"I'm really desperate to get into his archives. Otherwise, he might have said no."

Shannon merely flashed a wry smile and shook her head.

That, at least, was better than tears.

✠ ✠ ✠

Jon was not too concerned about preparation for the debate. Although he had not debated often, he could draw on a professional lifetime acquaintance with the sources and histories of both Christianity and Islam, and he was well aware of the unprecedented importance of an encounter like this. No debate of this kind between Christianity and Islam had taken place for centuries. And of course, due to the modern media revolution, the audience for this encounter would dwarf anything previous.

Jon had not read the Qur'an in some years, so it was high time for a reread as cornerstone for whatever preparation he did. Doubtless, his opponent was doing the same with the Bible. Some years earlier, a devout Muslim, hoping to convert Jon, had sent him a beautifully illuminated copy of the Qur'an, along with instructions on how to use it. *Read it*, for goodness' sake? Not so fast. First, the reader should always wash his hands before touching it. He should never hold it below his waist. He should never put anything on top of it.

For some reason, Jon had not exactly followed these rules. On the other hand, he had no reason to desecrate it but treated it like the Bible or any other book. A book was a book was a book. Claim more than that, and you're on to fetishism. He recalled that, in fact, some Christians were also guilty of "bibliolatry," worshiping the book itself or using it for other than reading as a good-luck charm or talisman against evil.

Or even for fortune-telling, like the fellow who used his Bible for divine guidance on career choices. Praying for revelation, he shut his eyes, opened the Bible, and pointed randomly to a passage. *"And he went away and hanged himself."*

Couldn't be, he thought. *I'll try again.*

After repeating the procedure, he opened his eyes and read, *"Go, and do thou likewise."*

Impossible! Third time's a charm. This time he prayed harder, spun himself around three times, flipped through the pages, and pointed. Opening his eyes, he read: *"What thou doest, do quickly!"*

Jon found the Qur'an about the same size as the New Testament, with a curious arrangement for its chapters: the longer ones first, the shorter last—rather than being placed in chronological order. Much of the historical material covered the same ground as the Bible, but by no means in the same way. There seemed to be dozens of differences, some minor, some major. As he read, Jon wrote down a list of the most important of these, along with locations in the Qur'an through its suras, followed by his own written comments:

Noah's flood did not take place until Moses' day.
(Sura 7:136; 7:59ff)
Impossibly late.

One of Noah's sons was drowned because he wouldn't come along with the rest of the family in the ark. (S 11:43)
Nice lesson in obedience!

Abraham's father was not Terah but Azar. (S 6:74)
Making him an Arab?

Abraham tried to sacrifice not Isaac but Ishmael.
(S 37:100ff)
To be sure: Ishmael as patriarch of the Arabs.

Baby Moses was adopted not by the daughter but by the wife of Pharaoh. (S 28:8ff)
Augmenting Moses? Strange for Islam.

God struck the Egyptians with not ten plagues but nine.
(S 27:12)

Zechariah, father of John the Baptist, was not struck dumb for nine months until the birth of John, but only for three days. (S 3:40-41)
Interesting sympathy for the voiceless one.

Mary gave birth to Jesus not in a cavern-stable but under a palm tree. (S 19:23)

Christians believe in three gods: the Father, Jesus, and the Virgin Mary. (S 5:116)

Misunderstanding of the Trinity.

Jesus did not die on the cross. Someone took his place. (S 4:157)

Probably the *most decisive difference between the Qur'an and the Bible.*

Beyond these differences from Scripture, Jon found the Qur'an even contradicting itself. In Sura 7:54, for example, it took God six days to create the world, but in Sura 41:9, it took him *two*. And the most notorious, of course, were the so-called satanic verses, in which Muslims were to seek the divine intercession of two goddesses and one god in the Arab pantheon, though later Muhammad was told that this had been Satan interjecting a revelation and that it was thereby abrogated. Salman Rushdie had suffered enough on that one.

At times, Jon was ready to throw down his pen and mutter, "Why even bother debating when the Qur'an has many such problems and is so obviously derivative from prior, biblical sources?"

"Be careful!" Osman cautioned him when he vented such thoughts. "You have to treat the Qur'an *very* carefully in debate—unlike the Bible—since in Islam, it's not only authoritative but unimpeachable as God's *only* totally reliable and uncorrupted revelation. In that sense, you should compare it not to the Bible, but to Christ himself. Muslims even believe there's a word-for-word copy of it in heaven—in the original Arabic, of course."

Jon also noted that many of the prophetic passages in the Bible that predicted a future messiah were transferred from their fulfillment in Jesus and made to refer instead to Muhammad, especially Deuteronomy 18:18: "I will raise up for them a prophet like you from among their brethren; and I will put my words in his mouth, and he shall speak to them all that I command him."

Nay, more: Muslims even made Jesus himself prophesy the advent of Muhammad each time he referred to the coming Comforter, as in John 14:16: "I will pray the Father, and he shall give you another Comforter that he may be with you for ever." And here Christians had always thought the Comforter was the Holy Spirit!

✢ ✢ ✢

Some personal correspondence also took place between Jon and al-Rashid regarding ground rules for the debate. They both agreed not to politicize the exchange or try to make points in the West–versus–Middle East debate as was done so often in Christian-Muslim discussions across the years, since this was to be a purely religious exchange. In view of al-Qaeda and militant Islamic extremism, however, this would be very difficult to accomplish, but at least they could move beyond the "Is Islam a Religion of Peace or War?" question.

The answer to that one, of course, was simply yes, since you could find both peace and war in the Qur'an. But the answer was yes also in Judeo-Christianity, Jon knew, since you could find both also in the Bible. For example, God's orders through Samuel for Israel to annihilate the Amalekites—"Kill both man and woman, infant and suckling"—were hardly any waving of the olive branch. Still, there was this critically important difference: Jesus never preached violence; Muhammad did.

They also agreed not to use any cheap shots in trying to denigrate each other's faith, since there were skeletons in both Christian and Muslim closets, primarily due to believers' not living up to the ideals of their religions. Both traditions had their horror stories. If thoughtful Christians were embarrassed by the Spanish Inquisition, the medieval burning of heretics, or Galileo's house arrest, thoughtful Muslims were similarly haunted by the Egyptian sultan Hakim's destruction of Christian holy places in the eleventh century, the mass execution of Christian monks in Tunisia by the al-Muwahhids in the twelfth century, the betrayal and execution of the surrendered Christian garrison on Cyprus by the Ottoman Turks in the sixteenth century despite promises of safe conduct, and the Turkish annihilation of Armenian Christians in the early twentieth century—not to mention all the suicide bombings across the world since.

On the other hand, when al-Rashid wanted even more safeguards, such as no criticisms or negative references whatsoever to either Muhammad or Jesus, Jon drew the line and, as diplomatically as he could, explained that they ought not let their exchange become too bland. He knew, of course, that he had no reason to worry about the personal record of Jesus Christ.

In the case of Muhammad, Jon felt it was high time to reexamine his life story in detail. Unfortunately this was more difficult than in the case of Jesus, since the first definitive biographies of Muhammad were not written until 150 years after his death. The Gospel accounts of the life of Jesus were written within a generation.

Another matter galled Jon. Some years previous, a self-appointed pundit had published a list of the greatest or most influential people who ever lived, at least in his opinion. Jon was chagrined to find that Muhammad, not Jesus, was number one. Why? Because Christianity was cofounded by Jesus and St. Paul, it was claimed. Jesus had to share the honors, whereas Muhammad was the single founder of Islam. Never mind that Christianity had—and has—twice the following.

Unquestionably, though, Muhammad was an extraordinary personality, and his life story was fully unique. Born in Mecca circa 570—though that date was disputed—Muhammad claimed to trace his lineage back to Abraham's firstborn, Ishmael. Muhammad's father died before he was born, and his mother when he was only six years old. The orphan shepherd boy was raised by an uncle and early developed attractive moral traits such as never telling a lie, caring for those in need, and managing fiscal accounts with total honesty and reliability. In directing caravan operations for a wealthy widow named Khadijah, he did so well that she ultimately married him, despite being fifteen years his senior.

Jon especially noted that Muhammad was also a meditative and mystic sort who left his family for days at a time for meditation in favorite caves near Mecca, where he experienced dreams and visions. Around 610, when Muhammad was about forty—so his final wife, Aisha, reported—Muhammad was sitting at the mouth of a cave named Hira when a luminous being—he later claimed it was the angel Gabriel—seized him by the throat and commanded him to read.

"I cannot read!" Muhammad replied, for indeed, he was illiterate.

"O Muhammad, read!" Gabriel said a second time.

Again Muhammad responded, "I cannot read!"

When this happened a third time, the angel embraced him so tightly that he could not breathe. Finally he released him and said, "O Muhammad, give utterance: Allah is God, and you are his Prophet!" Additional revelations followed.

Muhammad was understandably shocked, and he wondered if the revelations were genuine. He had his doubts and expressed them to Khadijah. What if an evil spirit or *jinn* had seized him and these were *not* the words of the Lord communicated through Gabriel? Worse yet, what if they were satanic? That the revelations ceased for a time only compounded the problem.

At that moment, Jon realized, the future of Islam—and much subsequent world history—hung in the balance. Had Khadijah sided with his doubts, Islam would never have existed. Instead, however, she firmed him up with the assurance that the revelations came from God himself, and that he should be obedient to them.

Muhammad was persuaded, and Islam was born. He preached this revelation on the streets of Mecca. Against the rampant polytheism of the many desert tribes in Arabia, the new Prophet announced that God was *one*—not many—and that Muhammad himself was the one he appointed to proclaim this message.

At first, few paid him any heed, not even relatives or members of his own Quraish tribe. He was called crazy, a liar, and a sorcerer, and once, while he was at prayer, dung and bloody camel intestines were dropped onto his back—until removed by his daughter Fatima. His small following was scorned by the wealthy merchants who controlled the city government at Mecca. They were particularly worried that Muhammad's new teaching would undermine all the pilgrimages that took place to visit the great Kaaba situated at the center of Mecca. That black rock was home to the many desert spirits of Arab polytheism, and its sacredness would be doomed were people to believe Muhammad's message.

Still, more and more people in Mecca were accepting Muhammad's message, and so the merchants now decided on a violent solution. Warned in time, Muhammad and his companions, or disciples, fled from Mecca to Medina, some two hundred miles due north of Mecca. The flight, called the *Hijirah*, took place in 622, which became year one in the Muslim calendar.

The people of Medina, not controlled by a merchant aristocracy, eagerly accepted Muhammad's message, and the first mosque was built there. Now he could deal from a position of growing political strength. The pagan Quraish in Mecca tried to halt the spread of Islam by military action, and Islam's first battle took place at Badr, an oasis halfway between Mecca and Medina. Although outnumbered 1,000 to 314, the Muslim forces were victorious. Further battles took place over the next eight years, until Muhammad was able to command an army of ten thousand, which advanced on Mecca. When the dust settled, the Meccans, tired of war, accepted Muhammad, especially in view of his promise to give the Kaaba a major future role in Islam.

He entered Mecca triumphantly in 630 and formally cleansed the Kaaba of its evil spirits. Then he made it an obligation for every Muslim at least once in a lifetime to make a pilgrimage to Mecca to visit the Kaaba, if physically and financially able. Jon knew that if he himself were a Muslim and made the hajj—the pilgrimage—he could thenceforth be known as Jonathan Hajji-Weber.

Muhammad issued a general amnesty to his opponents in Mecca, which only added to his reputation, and a firestorm of conversion to Islam swept across Arabia. The polytheistic desert tribes had been looking for something to unite them, and Muhammad now provided that.

But his own lifestyle seemed to go beyond his teachings, Jon noted. His male followers were limited to no more than four wives—actually making something of a women's liberator of Muhammad, strange as that may seem, since previously there had been no limit to the number of wives a man might have. But did Muhammad limit himself to four? He was faithful to Khadijah for as long as she lived, but when she died, the Prophet married no fewer than eleven other wives. One of them, Zainab, had been the wife of an adopted son, who willingly stepped aside when he learned of the Prophet's interest in her. Muhammad's last wife—little Aisha—was just six years old when he married her, but nine when the marriage was consummated. And it was in her arms that the sixty-three-year-old Prophet died at Medina in 632, where he was also buried.

Jon now pondered a dilemma. How many of the questionable details in Muhammad's life would be off-limits for discussion in the debate because, were they discussed, they could cause riots worldwide? In contrast, he thought wryly of all the current attacks on Jesus and the church that he founded. In the world's new double standard, evidently it was politically correct to attack only Christianity but no other religion on earth. Not fair. Not fair at all.

Imagine if a distorting book like *The Da Vinci Code* had targeted Muhammad instead of Jesus. The fatwa imposed on the author would have been far more lethal than was his, Jon knew—at least to date. In Christianity, at least, multiple targets—like Jesus, Paul, Peter, John, or Luke—helped cushion the attack. In Islam, there was only one person and one book: Muhammad and the Qur'an. Both were regarded by pious Muslims with sacrosanct awe and were barred to criticism of any kind. He was preparing for a debate with the cards stacked against him, Jon finally realized.

While Muhammad's wives should have been fair game in the forthcoming debate, Jon wondered whether to play that card. He knew the Muslim response. The marriages were conducted for political and social reasons, such as to give protection for women in need of such; most of the women were nonvirgins—if that could be considered justification—and Henry VIII's reason: Muhammad wished to have a son. And of course, al-Rashid would raise an even more obvious precedent: the polygamy among Old Testament leaders. Solomon, after all, made Muhammad look like a master of restraint when it came to wives.

Perhaps the Prophet's wives, then, would have to be off-limits. Again, though, how superior was the analogous situation in Jesus' case, who had no multiple-wife problem whatever—in fact, no wife at all, despite recurring attempts among sensationalist authors to get Jesus married off to Mary Magdalene.

And finally there was the question of whether or not to bring up Muhammad's fabled night journey from Mecca to Jerusalem. He claimed to have mounted a winged horselike creature and flown to Jerusalem, and thence to the seven heavens—all in one night. While in Jerusalem, he also claimed to have seen the Jewish Temple—a historical impossibility, since the temple had been destroyed by the Romans 550 years earlier. Even his beloved Aisha said that Muhammad was at home that night, and the whole thing was a vision. Since it was not mentioned in the Qur'an—only in the hadith, the traditions—Jon decided not to use it. After all, medieval Christianity also had its own collection of legends.

✠ ✠ ✠

Other aspects of Jon's preparation involved direct research, such as wandering into a local mosque and checking out its tract rack. Here there was plenty of free literature, including short biographies of Muhammad, guides to understanding Islam, excerpts from the Qur'an, as well as CDs and DVDs on Islam. Jon stocked up on this material and even left appropriate cash in a contribution box nearby.

What intrigued him the most, however, was a broad display sign across the whole width of the tract area with the words:

ISLAM IS THE WORLD'S FASTEST GROWING RELIGION
FIND OUT WHY!

He had heard this claim so often in the secular press and even among Christians that he was intrigued enough to test it out. It took a bit of doing—more than simply checking Wikipedia.

The careful research of David Barrett, who had been tracking religious numbers for years, proved very helpful. Statistics in the *World Christian Encyclopedia* easily demonstrated that the banner over the tract rack in the mosque was quite mistaken and that the world's fastest growing religion was, in fact, Christianity. With the southern hemisphere—Africa in particular—exploding for the faith, the conversion rate to Christianity was double that of conversion to Islam, and in some places, triple.

Even more compelling was evidence from Islam itself. Nearly by accident, Jon stumbled across comments by Ahmad al-Qataani, who was interviewed by Al Jazeera on December 12, 2006. Al-Qataani, leader of an organization advancing the science of Islamic law in Libya, stated, according to the translated Web transcript from Al Jazeera, "In every hour, 667 Muslims convert to Christianity. Every day, 16,000 Muslims convert, and every year, 6 million Muslims convert to Christianity. These numbers are very large indeed."

Jon doubted, though, that there would be any value in using statistical claims in the debate, since numbers alone did not prove all that much. When the Christian church was founded on the Day of Pentecost, it numbered only some three thousand members.

Osman al-Ghazali proved very helpful in marshalling the most important arguments that Muslims use in defending their faith, and Jon found books by other Muslim converts to Christianity, such as by the Caner brothers, to be very helpful as well. The literature on Islam and Christianity was becoming a major genre in the publishing industry.

So, once again, it would be the Crescent versus the Cross,

and the Cross versus the Crescent, Jon reflected. Would their forthcoming debate bring anything fresh to the table or become nothing more than a footnote in a fourteen-century face-off?

CHAPTER 9

TWO WEEKS BEFORE "THE GREAT DEBATE," Jon, Shannon, Richard Ferris, and Osman al-Ghazali were on a Turk Hava Yollari jet—Turkish Airlines flight 25 from JFK to Istanbul, a ten-hour odyssey. With a nod to American presidential election debates, they had already had a practice session at Harvard, in which al-Ghazali had presented Islam with such passion that Jon nearly thought he had returned to the teachings of the Prophet.

Jon had planned to use frequent flier miles to upgrade them all to business class, but Richard Ferris told him it was unnecessary. Although the ICO had made no fund appeal in any medium, financial gifts had poured into their Cambridge headquarters anyway. The American public was clearly sensitive to the world importance of this particular Muslim-Christian engagement.

Two members of Jon's party did not have their expenses

underwritten by the ICO. Instead, American taxpayers footed their bill, and no one was even supposed to know they had anything to do with Jon's group. They were, of course, two agents from the CIA, one sitting by himself at the rearmost seat in business class on the left side of the plane, the other taking the same position on the right. Jon grinned as he noted their navy blue serge suits and ties. If they were supposed to look like tourists, wouldn't khaki Dockers and sport shirts have been more appropriate?

The plane landed with an emphatic bump at Ataturk Havalimani, the international airport west of Istanbul. The Turkish morning was bright and hot as Jon's party descended the lofty aluminum port-a-stairway from the front of the plane, a strong semisirocco blowing up from Africa to the south and sending swirls of dust into the air.

At passport control, a welcoming committee from the Turkish Ministry of Culture greeted them amiably, led by the dapper and amply mustachioed director himself, Adnan Yilmaz. He would be their liaison with the Turkish government throughout their visit. Once their baggage was in hand, he whisked them through the various gateways set up to screen out troublemakers. Curbside, he reminded them of the final planning meeting for the debate, to be held in three days at the U.S. consulate in Istanbul, then ushered them inside two black Mercedes limousines emblazoned with insignia from the Turkish government.

✠ ✠ ✠

So far, so good, thought Shannon, who was torn between the thrill of finally visiting one of the most exotic cities on earth and the fear that somewhere in that vast metropolis of thirteen million, there had to be at least a dozen or so fanatics who felt that they would please Allah by assassinating her husband—or both of them.

Her dread, however, was soon drenched by the improbable vista unfolding before them. To the south were the sparkling sapphire waters of the Sea of Marmara, alive with ships of every variety sailing eastward or westward. Ahead and to the left, the central skyline of Istanbul grew ever larger, not with skyscrapers, as in other cities, but with huge, domed mosques, each surrounded by several stately minarets that looked for all the world like two- or three-stage guided missiles in stone, as if to guard the sanctity of the mosque.

Further eastward, and occupying the most commanding view of the waterfront, were the vast grounds of the Topkapi Palace—for centuries, the home of the great sultans of the Ottoman Empire that had at one time controlled the Mediterranean world and all of Balkan Europe as well. This was not one palace, but a virtual palatial city of its own, full of structures housing the sultans' treasures in art and women too. From 1453 to the late nineteenth century, much of the world was ruled from here.

Jon was exuberant as he directed Shannon to the sights left and right. Their limos turned northward and were mounting the hill overlooking the Bosporus when he suddenly asked the driver to slow down.

"There, Shannon!" Jon exuded. "See those two great structures? The one to the left, with the six minarets, is the Blue Mosque. And the one to the right, with only four—" he suddenly shifted to a tone of near reverence—"is probably the greatest Christian monument in the entire world: Hagia Sophia." He said the last in a choked whisper.

Shannon, too, was deeply moved. Hagia Sophia—Greek for "Holy Wisdom"—had been constructed 1,500 years ago by the great Byzantine emperor Justinian, who, on dedication day in AD 537, declared proudly, "Solomon, I have outdone thee!" He had indeed, with this first and largest domed structure in the world, the Christian exemplar from which every domed Muslim mosque since that time was patterned. And Hagia Sophia would be the place where the Muslim-Christian debate would take place that could change all of their lives.

"It's such a shame that the Muslim conquerors added those minarets," Shannon said. When Constantinople was taken over in 1453, the cathedral had been converted into a mosque. *A mosque? Wait a minute. . . .*

"Jon, you can't be planning to debate a Muslim opponent inside a mosque?"

He looked surprised. "Why not? I'm a generous sort and don't mind giving him some home-field advantage."

As he chuckled, the rest of her history knowledge fell into place. "Wait, I recall now. Atatürk, the founder of modern Turkey, converted Hagia Sophia from a mosque into a secular public museum."

"Precisely." Jon grinned. "But you were worried there for a minute, weren't you?"

She swatted him playfully and sat back to enjoy the sights. Through crowded streets scented with dozens of different spices and jammed with humanity buying or selling at hundreds of open-air markets, the limos threaded their way down to the waterfront of the fabled Golden Horn. This was the inlet from the Bosporus—gilded each sunrise and sunset—that split the city and set off the triangular peninsula tip that was the heart of Istanbul. They crossed the Galata Bridge and drove up another hill in the eastern sector of the city, atop which stood the Istanbul Hilton, their headquarters while in Turkey.

Jon and Shannon's suite was on the top floor of the Hilton, and they walked out onto their balcony to take in the commanding view to the south and west. Below them sprawled the great Turkish metropolis, with millions of citizens packed into its boulevards, parkways, streets, and alleys. To the south flowed the majestic Bosporus, that great waterway channeling water from the Black Sea into the Sea of Marmara and eventually into the Aegean and Mediterranean. The ominous drone of ships' horns filled the air as ferries scuttled between Europe and Asia—a distance no more than the width of the waterway at that point. On a north-south axis, the ferries had to interweave themselves between the huge cargo ships sailing an easterly-westerly vector, their staccato horn blasts advertising a near miss from time to time.

A knock on the door of their suite interrupted Shannon's reverie. They walked back from the veranda, and Jon opened the door. It was their two "guardian angels" from the CIA who wanted to sweep the room for any listening devices. Their code names were merely Click and Clack—perhaps in honor of the Tappet brothers on National Public Radio?—and they brushed off all requests for further identification, genially but firmly. Despite their best efforts, no bugs were found.

"Still," Clack advised, "I wouldn't mention anything super-sensitive inside here."

"Do we go out onto the balcony, then?" Jon asked.

"Never! Anyone down below could home in on you with telescopic audio."

Shannon sighed. It seemed that from now on, the panoramic view would have to be enjoyed from within the safe confines of their suite.

✠ ✠ ✠

Early the next afternoon, Jon and Shannon had an audience with the personage who had innocently lured them almost halfway across the world, the man with the official title, His All Holiness, Bartholomew II, Archbishop of Constantinople, New Rome and Ecumenical Patriarch, who was the 271st successor to the Apostle Andrew. Jon had already met and enjoyed instant rapport with the eastern pope at the Vatican III Council in Rome, the ecumenical conclave where a potential disaster to Christianity had been avoided.

The Eastern Orthodox Patriarchate was located on the eastern edge of the old city just north of the Sultan Selim mosque and overlooking the Golden Horn. The patriarchate was heavily walled—as was so much in that area of the world—but here with more reason. It had been subject to repeated bomb attacks by Muslim terrorists in recent years—a fact deplored by the secularist government of Turkey and the reason there was an official guard station near the entrance.

Inside the gate, Jon and Shannon received a warm welcome from an aide to the patriarch and were given a brief tour of the premises, including St. George's Chapel with its great chandeliers of shimmering crystal. In the reception hall stood a lofty dais on two levels. On the upper dais was a throne to seat not a human being but a beautifully illuminated Bible, attesting to the supremacy of Scripture. Immediately in front of it but on the lower dais stood the patriarch's throne of gold with red silk cushions that Bartholomew would have occupied were this a state reception.

Jon and Shannon were received instead at the patriarch's residence across the courtyard, where the great man himself greeted them with surprising warmth and excellent English. "I bid you welcome in the name of our sovereign Lord, Professor Weber, and also to you, madam."

"This is my wife, Shannon, Your All Holiness," Jon explained. "Thank you for this gracious audience."

He bowed slightly. "No, it is our Christian community in Turkey and I who must extend gratitude to *you* for coming to defend our faith here in the heart of Islam."

Bartholomew closely matched Jon in height, though with a stockier frame. He was a figure of authority in his late sixties, attired in a robe of basic black and clutching what was either a bishop's staff or something of a tall cane—perhaps both. His face, animated with a pair of blazing blue eyes and a broad smile, was edged by a great beard of almost gleaming white that began at his temples and plunged downward halfway to his cincture. A large golden medallion with the heraldry of his office dangled from a chain, apparently having escaped the frosty forest that covered half his chest. By any standards, this was one striking man.

The patriarch ordered refreshments and led them to his office, which had an expansive view of the Golden Horn. Predictably, they first discussed the forthcoming debate and their respective roles in that exchange. When Shannon joined the conversation, her queries were usually about security matters, particularly when Bartholomew told of the series of bombings at the patriarchate. Inevitably, this begged her question, "How safe *are* Christians in Turkey, Your All Holiness?"

"As you must know, Madame Weber," he replied, "even though Istanbul is at the dividing line between the Christian West and the Muslim East, Christians number less than one percent of the Turkish population, and we do have a militant Muslim minority that does not mean us well. However, the founder of modern Turkey, Mustafa Kemal Atatürk, decreed that this nation would be a *secular*—not a religious—state, and the army has always enforced that mandate, even to the point of overthrowing several Turkish governments in the past that tried to favor Islam. At present, even though the religious parties seem to be growing in power, I truly believe the Turkish government will remain secular and provide us the protection that we need."

Jon could hardly wait to bend the conversation in a new direction. Truth to tell, his ultimate goal was less to pit Christianity against Islam—he had not sought the debate, after all—and more to search the archives of the Eastern Orthodox Patriarchate for precious manuscripts. He used history as his segue.

"Your All Holiness," he began deliberately after a slight lull in their dialogue, "here in Constantinople—and I prefer to use its time-honored name—we have probably the most extraordinary city in the world. I find it remarkable that after Rome fell, New Rome—Constantinople—survived for another thousand years. It was this city, this cork in the bottle of Muslim expansionism, that virtually saved Christianity in eastern Europe. In the West, Islam rolled across North Africa, crossed at Gibraltar, conquered Spain, and then invaded France until the Muslim forces were *finally* stopped just south of Paris. But for Constantinople, the same could have happened in the East."

"Well, for a while, it seemed as though it might," Shannon joined in. "When this great city fell in 1453, Islamic hordes poured into the Balkans, conquering everything up to Vienna, where they were turned back by a Christian Europe that could now finally defend itself. What if there had been no Constantinople?"

Bartholomew had been nodding his concurrence. "Eastern Islamic forces would have joined with their Western forces and European Christianity would probably have been vanquished—as it has been wherever Muslims have conquered."

Shannon added, "I have little patience with some of our bleeding hearts who point to the church's great 'sin' in the case of the Crusades. That's a myopia that sees only halfway into the past. If we ever ask 'Who took more from whom—Islam or Christianity?' there's no contest. Christianity has taken not one square foot of territory from Islam that it did not originally possess, whereas Islam has taken Asia Minor, Syria, Lebanon, Egypt, all of North Africa, and part of the Balkans from Christianity."

"How very, very true, Madame Weber. I wish all Christians were as well informed. So often they can see back only to the Crusades."

Jon saw his opening and plunged in. "And the losses to Christianity have been staggering, particularly here in Constantinople. Think of the precious church documents that were destroyed here—some probably from the time of Constantine or even earlier. By the way, wasn't Constantine buried here?"

"Oh yes, indeed," Bartholomew replied. "He was buried in the *Hagioi Apostoloi*, the Church of the Holy Apostles. He built the church and wanted to gather relics of all twelve apostles for the sanctuary, but he got only St. Andrew. Well, also the bones of St. Luke and St. Timothy. So yes, Constantine and his sons were buried here, and so were Justinian and Theodora and their family, as well as many of the Byzantine emperors and my patriarch predecessors—St. John Chrysostom, too. That wonderful basilica was second in importance only to Hagia Sophia itself."

"Is it still standing?" Shannon asked.

Bartholomew shook his head sadly. "The Holy Apostles was rebuilt by Justinian in the year 550, just after Hagia Sophia, and it stood nine hundred more years until the Ottomans conquered Constantinople. That's when the conqueror, Sultan Mehmed II, turned Hagia Sophia into a mosque and moved our patriarchate into the Holy Apostles. But when that church got surrounded by Turkish settlers who were hostile to Christians, Mehmed demolished the church and built the *Fatih Camii* on the site, the Mosque of the Conqueror. In fact, he's buried there. And that mosque still stands, almost in the center of the Old City."

"Where did the patriarchate relocate?" Jon inquired.

"To the Church of St. Mary Pammakaristos in the Christian district—and eventually, of course, to this place."

"What happened to the treasures of the Church of the Holy Apostles—its icons, sculptures, sacred books, manuscripts, and—"

"The Venetians," the patriarch muttered darkly, then, more distinctly. "What history calls the Fourth Crusade—although it was conceived and born in hell—invaded Constantinople instead of the Holy Land in 1204 and plundered the city. The Venetians even looted the Church of the Twelve Apostles, opening the tombs of the emperors—even the sepulchre of Justinian—and carting off their silver, gold, and jewels!"

Bartholomew had visibly changed. Gone was the genial patriarch. In his place was a scowling prophet with flushed countenance who had again wrapped his hand, or rather fist, around the knob of his staff as if to cudgel Venetians off the pages of history. "You know of the Emperor Heraclius?" he asked.

"Byzantine emperor soon after Justinian?" Shannon suggested. "Lived in Muhammad's time?"

"Yes, exactly, Madame Weber. The Venetians broke open his tomb and stole the golden crown right off his head—with some of his hairs still attached to it! You can see it yet today at St. Mark's basilica in Venice."

The disaster at the beginning of the thirteenth century seemed to impinge even into Jon's twenty-first. His hopes of finding any written materials from the time of Constantine seemed to vanish with the Venetians. Almost timidly, he asked, "What about the other treasures at the Church of the Apostles—the library, the codices, the manuscripts? The Venetians carted those off also?"

Bartholomew thought for several moments, each of which

seemed an endless span of time to Jon. Finally the patriarch shook his head. "No, those barbarians, those putrid pirates, couldn't even read. They wanted gold, not books."

Jon tried not to look too elated. Swimming in relief—at least preliminary relief—he asked, "What . . . whatever happened to the written materials? Did the Turks destroy them?"

"Some were lost in the fires that burned at various parts of Constantinople after the conquest, but the church saved a goodly number of important documents."

"And . . . where are they now?"

"Some are at church and seminary libraries of the Orthodox churches across the world—St. Vladimir's in New York, St. Catherine's at Mount Sinai, Mount Athos—but many are here in the patriarchate."

Glorious news! Now was the time for Jon to bare his heart. How abrupt should he be? A bald, frontal assault with an unvarnished confession of what he and Shannon ultimately desired? A series of gradual insinuations and hints? No, plain honesty would be best, he decided.

"Your All Holiness," Jon began, "I wonder if you'd be generous enough to let us see some of the written materials—the documents, the older manuscripts?"

The patriarch seemed somewhat puzzled, hesitant.

"Well, certainly not today," Jon quickly added, almost in panic. "But perhaps before we leave Istanbul?"

Bartholomew finally nodded. "I only wonder why we have not talked more about the matter that concerns me most, concerns the church most, which is—"

"The debate, of course?" Jon broke in.

"Yes, the debate, Professor Weber. I am to be joint moderator with Mustafa Selim. Don't you think we should talk more about the debate?"

"Yes, certainly. This must indeed be our central concern. How well do you know Mustafa Selim?"

"Well, we are not the closest of friends, obviously, but we do respect one another. Each time Christians are attacked somewhere in Turkey, he publicly deplores it and tries to build tolerance among the more fanatic elements in Islam. Several times when our patriarchate was bombed, he even sent workers over to help in the repair. A good man. But now, Professor and Mrs. Weber, please to join me for lunch so that we can plan together at table."

✠ ✠ ✠

Both the patriarch and Jon had checklists for items related to the debate. Jon was most concerned for the safety of the Christians inside Hagia Sophia and whether there were really enough in Istanbul to constitute half the audience. To his surprise, the patriarch said they could have filled the entire structure with Christians, since many were coming to Istanbul for the event from Asiatic Turkey. He also reported that he and Mustafa Selim were in charge of ticket distribution, and the latter passed them out only to known, moderate Muslims. And yes, the police would be able to assure the safety of those inside.

For his part, Bartholomew wanted to know the main thrust of Jon's opening remarks and the strategy that he planned to pursue. In response, Jon unpacked his arsenal of Christian arguments as well as the principal points in Islam that he felt were open to challenge. The patriarch's repeated noddings in affirmation were a welcome sight for Jon, but his concluding caution was quite sobering. "You must walk a very careful line, Professor Weber. If you triumph in the debate—or, I should say, *when* you triumph—please do so gently. Were you to mortify your opponent, there could be 'blood in the streets,' as you Americans put it. On the other hand, our faith must be defended with vigor, for it is God's own truth. The way will be narrow—and difficult."

"That's very sage advice, Your All Holiness, and I thank you for it."

As they stood up from the table, their host said something in Greek to an aide. This translated itself when an aged, scholarly monk appeared and greeted them in the courtyard below the patriarch's quarters.

"This is Brother Gregorios," Bartholomew said. "He is our archivist and librarian. I have instructed him to let you examine our entire collection of ancient records and documents anytime you wish."

Jon felt like wrapping his arms around the patriarch for a big hug, but he checked himself. Offering most genuine gratitude, they left the patriarchate.

On the drive back to the Hilton, Jon was pensive, even crestfallen. Shannon asked what the problem might be.

"What a study in contrasts," he commented, shaking his head. "We've just conversed with the spiritual head of the second-largest church in Christendom—the eastern pope, so to speak. But the patriarchate is so much smaller than the Vatican, so very modest by comparison. It just . . . doesn't seem fair."

Shannon sighed. "Well, you can thank the Ottomans for that. Just imagine what might have happened had the Turks *not* conquered the Byzantine Empire."

"Or what if they had converted to Christianity rather than Islam? We'd have a very different world today."

"We'd have a *better* world!"

"I couldn't agree more." He leaned over and gave her a kiss, thankful that their driver was so engrossed in fighting his way through Istanbul traffic that he took no notice.

CHAPTER 10

THE DEBATE WAS ONE WEEK AWAY. All eight thousand portable seats on the main floor inside Hagia Sophia had been spoken for. Additional folding chairs would surround the basilica on all sides, with closed-circuit television screens and loudspeakers conveying the program inside. Representatives of Christian church bodies would have VIP seating—meaning they could sit inside the basilica—as would an equal number of Islamic leaders, 84 percent of whom would be Sunni and 16 percent Shia, in accord with their relative numbers in the Islamic world.

Already the lofty galleries of Hagia Sophia were getting cluttered with television cameras, cables, and broadcast paraphernalia, next to which a special section was reserved for the world press corps. The rest of the surrounding galleries were given over to additional seating. Adjacent to the three main entrances to the basilica were security checkpoints with turnstiles, first-aid facilities, and of course, additional porta-potties.

Nothing was left to chance. Click and Clack, who suddenly had additional security help from the CIA, were putting in twelve-hour days. Each evening, they briefed Jon, Shannon, Dick, and Osman. Ferris seemed to be in constant phone or e-mail contact with Marylou Kaiser and the ICO in Cambridge. Jon himself was keeping his wits sharp through verbal duels with Osman.

Yet Jon was acutely aware that there was such a thing as too much preparation. Two days before the debate, he and Shannon decided to take a break. Perhaps an excursion on the Bosporus? A museum tour of the Topkapi Palace? Never! Like iron filings drawn to a powerful magnet, they were back again at the Eastern Orthodox Patriarchate to explore the archives. This time their host was not the patriarch himself but Brother Gregorios, the librarian-archivist.

A diminutive older figure with a pointed gray beard and sallow skin, Gregorios seemed to have spent his entire life in row after row of book stacks. At first he was somewhat cool toward Jon and Shannon, as if his assigned task of showing them around his domain would cut into his beloved affair with words—printed, written, painted, pictured. But their obvious interest and apt queries seemed to melt the old man's heart as he recognized them as genuine bibliophiles.

They had seen much larger libraries, of course—here there were only six hundred thousand books—but they had not come for the printed word. Instead, manuscripts were their target, early codices and documents from times of yore, the older the better. They had to be looking at the right place. It was in Istanbul that the Greek scholar-churchman Philotheos Bryennios had discovered the famous Didache, lost to the world since the third century, when Eusebius, the father of church history, almost included it in the New Testament canon. *The Teaching of the Lord to the Gentiles through the Twelve Apostles* was the real name of the work, lost for fifteen centuries until 1873 and Bryennios's discovery.

In the reading room there were ten computers, at three of which young, black-suited students were peering into screens. Jon looked at one of the keyboards and winced, not because the lettering was Greek but because several letters were interchanged from the regular QWERTY keyboard. Then again, he hadn't really planned to use those computers for overseas e-mail but in place of a card catalog.

Gregorios showed them row after row of book stacks and explained what sorts of titles were shelved on each. This was important, since they were hardly using the Library of Congress cataloging system. Yet all these were printed materials and thus of only secondary importance to Jon and Shannon. Still they registered appropriate interest until Jon finally asked, "And the archives, Brother Gregorios? Where are the archives?"

"Oh yes. Please to follow me."

He led them to the far northern end of the library's ground floor and down a metal stairway into a broad hall. All four walls were completely lined with bookshelves laden with ledgers organized by year. Jon looked around and asked, "I wonder if my wife and I could examine some of these volumes for . . . perhaps the next hour? When we've finished, we'll come to your office."

"As you wish." He bowed slightly and left the archives.

"All right, my darling; let's peruse all this with a passion!" Jon said, exulting in their solitude.

"Oh, of course, Jon; I'm sure we can read all of this in an hour." She grinned.

Jon chuckled and pulled a book off the shelf. It began with events at the patriarchate in January 1848. Much of it was in a flowing Greek script that was at first difficult to read, but soon Jon had made out several pages. He put the book back where he had found it and said, "Now let's find the earliest year here."

Chasing down row after row, he found a really tattered tome with fading leather covers. "It's from 1503, Shannon, just fifty years after the Muslim conquest." Then he found another section of the hall devoted to the oldest printed books as well as manuscripts that predated them. He was overjoyed. "We have incunabula here," he called out. "Incunabula!"

"Great!" She hurried over and looked at the title page. "Fabulous, Jon. Look at the date. It's 1483!"

"The year Martin Luther was born. He could have read this book." It was Hartmann Schedel's *Nürnberger Chronica*, the great picture book of the Middle Ages. Jon carefully paged through it. Then he laughed. "Never mind that this elaborate woodcut of Padua is exactly the same as that for Verona—here fifty pages earlier."

"They must have counted on medieval readers having short memories," Shannon said, smiling.

The manuscripts, however, were Jon's Holy Grail, the potential treasure that had lured them from Cambridge to Istanbul. They were indexed on a large placard posted over the wider stacks where they were stored. The dates ran back from the 1400s and 1300s to the 600s and 500s. A rippling thrill tingled through Jon, although he realized it would take a much longer visit to know what they contained. Today's was only a quick survey.

They retraced their steps to Gregorios's office to extend their thanks and take their leave. "I think we have a general impression of the layout here, good brother," Jon said. "We have seen it all, haven't we?"

He nodded. "All but the *geniza,* of course."

Jon chuckled at the man's use of a Hebrew term. "The *geniza*? I didn't know you were Jewish! A sacred dump for old Scriptures?"

Brother Gregorios joined in the laughter. "Well, that's what we call our room for . . . bad manuscripts—I want to say—for leaves missing from books or . . . or codices with bindings cracked and pages that are not readable or are too torn to save. We do try to save some of them when we can. And maybe even try to rebuild them—no, what is the word?"

"Rebind them?" Shannon offered.

"Yes, rebind them."

"And where is your *geniza*?" Jon asked.

"In the basement."

"The basement? I hope you have humidity control."

"Oh yes, the whole library and archives—and basement—are at 48 percent humidity and twenty degrees temperature."

"Twenty degrees, you say?"

"That's centigrade, Jon," Shannon said. "In Fahrenheit it would be about . . . sixty-eight degrees."

Jon made a mental note: *Think first; speak later.*

As they were walking out of the library, Jon did an about-face. The opportunity was simply too good to pass up. He walked back to Gregorios's office and asked, somewhat sheepishly, "I wonder, good brother—just to complete our tour—if we might briefly visit also the *geniza*?"

"Well, there's not much to see there, but . . . as you wish."

He led them into the basement. The room was poorly lit. Next to the light switch was a clear plastic cube with temperature and humidity barrel graphs, showing that at least the proper environment was being maintained. As Gregorios had assured them, the temperature was a slightly cool but comfortable twenty degrees Celsius and the humidity was carefully controlled. Otherwise, mold would have blanketed everything in this literary catchall and ruined it.

It was hardly a picture of disciplined order. On the east side of the room were torn books, orphaned printed pages, and empty bindings. In the center was an apparently uncataloged miscellany of dusty manuscripts in partial state of preservation, and at the extreme western edge of the room were stacks of ponderous old tomes bowing the wooden shelves with their weight.

"Ugly as all this appears, Jon," Shannon said, "I suppose our teams will have to photograph every bit of it?"

"Most of it, I think. There may be some golden nuggets in this junk heap."

Jon tried to discern the arrangement of materials in the room, but there seemed to be little or none. Shannon walked over to the fat tomes, pulled one off the shelf, and blew dust off it. She opened to the title page, and her eyes widened. "Listen to this,

Jon: *Omile Hrisostomou*, 491–496. That would be Sermons of Chrysostom, AD 491–496, written in Constantinople in 847."

"Interesting," Jon said. "Even though we have those sermons elsewhere, a ninth-century codex is nothing to sneeze at."

"Ye—yes it is!" Shannon snorted in nasal tone, as she inhaled suddenly and let loose with a colossal sneeze. "Sorry. It's the dust."

The other ancient tomes offered more sermons by Greek church fathers. Shannon turned to another codex that was almost on the floor, since its weight had bulged the too-thin wooden shelf supporting it. Holding her nose, she blew the dust off the faded calfskin stretched across a thin wooden board cover. "This one looks like it's fairly complete, although the back cover is missing." Opening to the title page, she read aloud: *"Biblia Beta. Kaine Diatheke tou Kuriou Iesou Christou. . . ."*

She read on silently, then asked, "What do you think? This one could be interesting."

Jon made no response. He was busy in the miscellaneous manuscript section.

"Jon, did you hear me?"

"What's that, Shannon?"

"We have an interesting title page here, in very elegant lettering." She repeated the Greek for what, in English, would be "Book Two: The New Testament of our Lord and Savior Jesus Christ, one of fifty copies."

Jon hurried over to Shannon's side and examined the page. His eyes narrowed. He glanced further down the title page and read aloud the rest of the Greek, followed by his translation, as he would write it out later that day in the same relative positioning as the Greek:

One of fifty copies commissioned by
Caesar Victor Constantinus Maximus Augustus
and servant of God
who authorized Eusebius Pamphili to have these
prepared by his scribes in the church at Caesarea
Palaestina and distributed throughout
Constantinople in the year 1088 AUC

Jon realized he was breathing heavily. His face grew flushed. His pulse accelerated, and his hand actually trembled as he paged quickly through random sections of the codex. Finally he halted his frenetic paging and stared at her. "My darling," he began, in what sounded more like gargle than elocution. He cleared his throat and tried again. "Do you have any idea what you've found here?"

"Well, Constantine's name is on it, so it must be significant. But what about that date? Constantine died in 337, but this is from 1088, and we have many materials from the eleventh century."

"That's 1088 AUC, Shannon. *Ab urbe condita*—from the founding of the city."

"Rome, of course—founded 753 BC!" Shannon recalled. "Okay, so our date is 1088 minus 753 or . . . AD 335?"

"Right. And that's exactly when Eusebius says Constantine commissioned him to do this."

"So this could be the real thing, Jon?"

He slowly shook his head. "I'd hate to be premature, but yes, it could well be." He broke into a great smile. "It's well known that Constantine had commissioned Eusebius to prepare fifty elegant copies of Scripture, but none of them has ever been found. And just look at the layout: four handsome columns of beautiful Greek lettering on each page of vellum, just like the *Codex Sinaiticus*, which dates only a bit later."

Jon paged further in growing excitement. "Aside from the *Sinaiticus*, we have only two other codices from that time: the *Vaticanus* and the *Alexandrinus*. This is . . . this could be . . . well, I'm not given to superlatives. Let's just say that this might be a . . . a simply stupendous find. Depending on what the text says, this could . . . well, it could be a discovery far more important than even the Dead Sea Scrolls! How in the world, Shannon, do you have such off-the-wall great luck, such over-the-top serendipity, that—?"

"Oh, Professor Weber," said Brother Gregorios, who had just appeared in the doorway, "have you seen enough of our tattered collection?"

"Yes, thank you, good brother." Then he whispered to Shannon, "Just put this back exactly where you found it."

✠ ✠ ✠

On the way back to the hotel, Jon unpacked his strategy. "We had no time to get into the text, Shannon, so telling anyone there what we found would have been totally premature. And foolish! If the thing *is* authentic—and how in the world could it *not* be?—it will stun the entire scholarly world. Report it too early, and it would become a cause célèbre and complicate any evaluation. We could even be denied further access to it." If Jon had one questionable habit, it was his proclivity to overexplain things to people, born of many years' teaching university undergrads, who, in fact, needed his careful reiteration of what might have seemed obvious.

The moment they returned to the Hilton, Jon headed for his laptop, found the folder on the early church fathers, and opened a work by Eusebius called *Vita Constantini—The Life of Constantine*. He paged through the document until he came to chapters 36 and 37, where he read aloud, for Shannon's benefit, the dated though colorful translation from *The Nicene and Post-Nicene Fathers of the Christian Church*. It began with Eusebius's transcription of Constantine's own letter, written from Constantinople to Eusebius in Caesarea.

VICTOR CONSTANTINUS, MAXIMUS AUGUSTUS
to Eusebius,

It happens, through the favoring providence of God, our Savior, that great numbers have united themselves to the most holy church in the city which is called by my name. It seems, therefore, highly requisite, since that city is rapidly advancing in prosperity in all other respects, that the number of churches should also be increased. Do you, therefore, receive with all readiness my determination on this behalf. I have thought it expedient to instruct your Prudence to order fifty copies of the sacred Scriptures, the provision and use of which you know to be most needful for the instruction of the Church, to be written on prepared parchment in a legible manner, and in a convenient, portable form, by professional transcribers thoroughly practiced in their art.

The procurator of the diocese has also received

instructions by letter from our Clemency to be careful to furnish all things necessary for the preparation of such copies; and it will be for you to take special care that they be completed with as little delay as possible. You have authority also, in virtue of this letter, to use two of the public carriages for their conveyance, by which arrangement the copies when fairly written will most easily be forwarded for my personal inspection; and one of the deacons of your church may be entrusted with this service, who, on his arrival here, shall experience my liberality. God preserve you, beloved brother.

Jon looked up from the screen in jubilation. "What you found was written on parchment, Shannon. You found one of the fifty. Scholars have been looking for that edition since the early centuries of the church!"

"Yes, but don't the 'Scriptures' ordered by Constantine include the Old Testament? I just found the New."

"Well, they were supposed to be portable, so they were most likely in two volumes, exactly as the title 'Book Two' implies. Anyhow, in the next lines, Eusebius tells how he responded to the emperor's letter."

Such were the emperor's commands, which were followed by the immediate execution of the work itself, which we sent him in magnificent and elaborately bound volumes of a threefold and fourfold form. This fact is attested by another letter, which the emperor wrote in acknowledgment. . . .

"'Threefold and fourfold form'? Whatever can that mean?" Jon wondered.

"Maybe three or four columns of writing per page?" Shannon suggested.

"Why not? Excellent, Shannon! What we saw were four columns per page, and remember how carefully the calfskin cover had originally been tooled? That's it! That's one of them!"

Shannon smiled, but her reserve showed that she wasn't quite ready to celebrate. She shook her head and asked, "But why would they put something so incredibly valuable as that in their junk room?"

"Well, who knows when it landed there? We'll try to find out. But probably they did it for some stupidly simple reason, such as a missing back cover. That room was full of mangled books."

"Okay, Jon, let your mind roam. What, finally, is the 'world-shaking' importance here? Might it not be simply an early edition of the New Testament that we all know? And if so, what's the big deal?"

"You know the rule, Shannon: the earlier, the more authoritative. The Bible has come down to us with thousands of tiny variations. None of them amount to a hill of beans, despite sensationalizing claims to the contrary. But now textual scholars will have a tremendous new source to work with in getting us the best possible reading of what the biblical writers actually wrote. And who knows what else we might find in the text? For openers, even issues regarding the Canon come into play here: what books are included in that early New Testament, and which are left out?"

Shannon quickly found Jon's enthusiasm contagious and said, in a beaming smile, "I bet you'll have trouble sleeping tonight!"

"You bet, and for the next two nights, my darling, since the debate is tomorrow. But after that, I'm loading up our cameras with freshly charged batteries to photograph every last inch of that incredible document."

In a great bound, Jon now leaped to the mini fridge in their suite, hauled out a bottle of Dom Pérignon, popped the cork, and filled two glasses with bubbly. "I know this is too traditional, sweetheart, but . . . a toast to Shannon Jennings Weber, amazing archaeologist, scintillating scholar, dauntless discoverer of precious codices, and magnificent mate! By the way, we'll both have trouble sleeping tonight!"

CHAPTER 11

THE NIGHT BEFORE THE DEBATE was indeed rather sleepless for Jon, and not only because he and Shannon were celebrating God's magnificent gift of marital love—itself a proof of his existence. He was also chagrined to realize that instead of fighting nervous concern over the forthcoming debate, his mind was focused on the ancient codex Shannon had discovered. It was almost as if he had told himself, "Let's get this debate thing out of the way so I can finally *read* what's in that document!"

Now, on the sun-drenched morning of September 3, while their motorcade wound its way to Hagia Sophia, he came to his senses. How selfish, how very solipsistic could he get? Millions across the world would be watching the debate—either live or later on DVD, and over the next hours he had to defend the faith as best he could rather than fixate on a dilapidated manuscript. The Crusaders were unable to succeed militarily against Islam eight centuries in the past; was he, perhaps, supposed to try making up for that intellectually? Then again, he was glad he had not ventilated such wild thoughts to Shannon, for she would have replied, "The faith will survive nicely without your success or failure, dear!" Shannon was God's gift to Jon for many reasons, not least of which was to keep her husband humble. As the magnitude of the event finally registered with Jon, he wondered why it had taken him so long to invoke divine help. Although he was not in a private oratory but in the midst of urban bedlam, he offered up the most earnest silent prayer of his life.

It was difficult for them to get inside the basilica, since it was surrounded by a host of humanity even an hour before the debate was to begin at 9:30 a.m. The lovely park that extended between Hagia Sophia and the Blue Mosque several blocks to the west had turned into a temporary parking lot for television and communications vans, each sprouting relay dishes aimed toward their counterparts outside the western upper gallery of the basilica.

Surrounded by Turkish gendarmes, Jon's party made its way through the small west portal into Hagia Sophia. Overhead inside the passageway they saw a magnificent, semicircular mosaic of Constantine offering the city of Constantinople to the Virgin Mother and Jesus. To the right was Justinian, offering Hagia Sophia to the same pair—all against a gleaming background of golden mosaic. Jon offered up another quick prayer to the Christ who received these gifts to bless the debate.

Inside, they walked down a side aisle, under the vast dome overhead, and toward a dais erected at the southern end of the sanctuary. Several times Jon stopped at a given row, exchanging a glad hello with a friend from the States who had made the long trip to Istanbul. Shannon, in fact, had to shoo him on several times.

On the eastern side of the sanctuary, Abbas al-Rashid and his party were approaching the dais. It was the first time Jon had seen his debate partner in the flesh, but he answered well to the many photographs he had seen of the sheikh in the press and on television. He was a fair Islamic counterpart to Jon—the same solid, broad-shouldered frame, medium-tall height, and square-cut visage, but perhaps five years older and with dark hair and deep brown eyes. He was wearing a Western-style suit but with Islamic headdress, perhaps a compromise to please both extremes among his faithful seated in the eastern sector.

As they took their seats in the front row on the opposite side, Jon—almost instinctively and without forethought—got up and walked across the aisle to shake the sheikh's hand. Abbas unleashed a broad smile and shook Jon's hand with evident enthusiasm. Both sides of the audience erupted into applause. It was an unanticipated and pleasant touch.

At 9:33 a.m., three men emerged from somewhere in the apse and stepped up to the dais. One of them Jon had already seen emblazoned on the Turkish lira, no less than the president himself—all six feet of him and his trademark mustachioed face that resembled a latter-day Süleyman the Magnificent. He moved to a central microphone and opened in Turkish, then English: "In the name of the Republic of Turkey, it is my privilege to welcome you to Haya Sofya and this important debate between Imam Abbas al-Rashid, the grand sheikh of al-Azhar University in Cairo, Egypt, and Dr. Jonathan P. Weber, professor of Near Eastern studies at Harvard University in Cambridge, USA. To my right is the Muslim mufti of Istanbul, His Excellency Mustafa Selim, who will be one of the moderators, and to my left is His All Holiness Bartholomew II, the Eastern Orthodox Christian Patriarch, who is the other moderator. May Allah-God guide all our proceedings here today."

He then stepped down from the dais.

The Muslim moderator stood and approached the microphone, directing the audience, again in three languages, to don their headgear. From now on, there would be simultaneous translations of all speakers in the agreed-upon languages of Turkish, Arabic, English, Greek, Farsi, French, German, Spanish, Italian, Russian, and Chinese. The appropriate language would be transmitted via Bluetooth wireless technology to all earphones mounted on the thousands of heads in the audience. The expense for this arrangement—well into six figures—was the gift of a Saudi oil magnate.

Mustafa Selim announced the rules of the debate, which both sides had agreed upon weeks earlier. It would be a much freer exchange than U.S. presidential debates, in which the contest was merely "Who can answer the same question better?" rather than the rough-and-tumble of give-and-take. Next, Patriarch Bartholomew presented a brief commentary on the rules, promising that both moderators would intervene as little as possible and cautioning the audience against raucous responses of any kind, which would result in ejection by government police. Both parties in the debate were then invited to offer brief opening statements.

Abbas won the coin toss but elected to go first. He began with an air of confidence. "I am honored to have this discussion with one of the foremost Christian authorities in the world today, a man whose scholarship is admired by all, including Islamic scholars. But I will try to show him—and the world—that Islam has superseded both Judaism and Christianity as Allah's, as God's, greatest, fullest, and final revelation and that the prophet Muhammad—may Allah's peace and blessing be upon him!—is greater than the other prophets that we both respect, namely Abraham, Moses, and Jesus of Nazareth.

"I will liken Judaism to the elementary school in our knowledge of Allah, Christianity to the secondary or high school, but Islam as the university. I will point out the impossibility that God could be three rather than one or marry a human woman and have a son by her. I will honor Jesus of Nazareth as a great prophet, to be sure, but not as God or the Son of God. Nor was he crucified, as claimed by the Christian Scriptures, which suffered errors early on in their transcription from the original authors.

"I will also demonstrate that Islam has higher moral standards than Christianity, and for that reason Allah has blessed his believers with greater territorial success and conversion rates than Christianity. And at the close of our debate, I hope that Professor Weber will recognize the truth of Allah's revelations through his holy Prophet—may Allah's peace and blessing be upon him!—and perhaps even accept the one true religion as proclaimed in the Holy Qur'an."

At that, Abbas sat down and received thunderous applause from the eastern side of Hagia Sophia.

Jon had taken in every syllable of al-Rashid's opening statement, parts of which were predictable, others not, such as his opponent's ingenuous hope for his conversion. Jon squeezed Shannon's hand and walked to the dais.

Noting the contrast between the two halves of his attentive audience, he began. "I find it a privilege to dialogue with one of the great theologians of Islam. Grand Sheikh Abbas al-Rashid is known not only for his vast knowledge but also for his generosity and wisdom. If you'll permit a personal reference, his was the major voice in averting great danger from me some months ago due to a mistranslation in one of my books. I remain in your debt, my friend."

Spirited applause broke out from both sides of the sanctuary, which al-Rashid acknowledged with a gracious nod of appreciation to both Jon and the audience.

Jon resumed. "As a Christian, of course, I will have to maintain that all knowledge about Jesus Christ is *far* more reliable from contemporary and eyewitness sources rather than from a differing version that first arose six centuries later. I will have to correct some misinterpretations that Islam has about Christianity and its doctrine of the Trinity and affirm that Jesus did indeed die on a cross, and that he rose again as he and the prophets had predicted. I will have to challenge the claim that the Qur'an is God's greatest revelation—" he heard murmuring from the eastern half of the sanctuary—"and that the Christian Scriptures suffered errors as they were recopied across the centuries.

"While I have great respect for the second largest religion on earth, I shall have to point out problems in the claims of

Islam, while finding those of Christianity provable by a massive amount of outside evidence. In any case, I look forward to a fascinating interchange with the grand sheikh."

As Jon left the podium, parallel applause broke out on the Christian side.

The debate then moved into the format they had agreed to, which was now announced by both moderators:

Islam's problems with Christianity
Christianity's defense
Christianity's problems with Islam
Islam's defense
(Both parties are limited to fifteen minutes each in the above segments)
A general exchange
Final summation: Christianity
Final summation: Islam

The moderators also announced the schedule: two morning sessions, separated by a break, and two similar afternoon sessions following an interim for lunch. "And lest anyone complain that this is too long," Patriarch Bartholomew added in a genial touch, "debates in the past lasted for *days*, not hours. Martin Luther's famous debate at Leipzig in 1519, for example, lasted *eighteen days*. We don't intend to inflict that on you!" Laughter followed intermittently, depending on the varying speed of the translators.

Jon and Abbas now took their seats, each at the end of a table on the dais so that they could face one other, while the two moderators sat in the middle. Both sides had agreed that only the person speaking at a given time would stand and use a lectern.

Abbas al-Rashid stood and opened with warm enthusiasm. "Thank you, people of all faiths, for joining us today for what we believe will be a very important discussion, which is long overdue. And yet this is not the first time Christians and Muslims have debated their respective beliefs. In fact, major discussions have taken place for the past fourteen *centuries*, and we are pleased to add our own efforts to that proud tradition.

"As for problems I find in Christianity, let me begin with simple logic and mathematics. The program began today at a specific time—not three different times. And so, if Christianity confesses one God—as do Jews and Muslims—they cannot also confess that God is three. This is not monotheism, but polytheism, specifically, tritheism: the worship of three different gods. To be sure, Christians try to speak of one divine essence and three personalities in what they call the Godhead, but this doctrine of the Trinity, so-called, fails all tests of logic. By no calculation does one equal three, or three equal one. This point alone, I believe, refutes Christianity as a viable religion for any who believe that God is one."

Loud partisan applause again broke out, until silenced by the moderators. Jon was less than comfortable in realizing that Abbas had immediately attacked the one logical weak point of Christianity. Only the problem of evil was greater, but that was common to all three monotheistic religions. Jon looked at Osman Al-Ghazali to see if the Arabic translator was doing an accurate job. Much of Abbas's Arabic Jon could understand, but he wanted to be sure. He had had a bitter enough experience with mistranslations! Each time that he heard "Allah" in Arabic, the translator rendered this as "God," which was perfectly acceptable, since that was the generic term for God in Arabic.

Abbas seemed to press his lips together, perhaps to keep from smiling. He glanced quickly at his notes and then resumed. "We who follow the Prophet—may Allah's peace and blessing be upon him!—also find it nearly blasphemous that Christians should think that almighty God had a marital affair with a human woman in conceiving Jesus. The sovereign Lord is certainly beyond that sort of thing, unless you equate him with mythologies invented by the Greeks and Romans: Zeus and his many affairs with anyone in skirts in heaven or earth." He paused briefly for the laughter greeting his remark. "We esteem Mary highly, of course, but we refuse to make her part of the Godhead. We also regard Jesus as a great prophet. Indeed, we believe that he was virgin-born and that he shall return, as he has promised. But to include him in what you call your Trinity? Never!

"And speaking of Jesus, whom we call Isa, we agree that he performed miracles and wonders, but he did so as God's prophet—no more, no less—a holy man who was so favored by God that he never would have permitted him to suffer such a horrible death as crucifixion, as Christians claim. Never! Allah could not have done that to his faithful prophet. And this very point proves the greater reliability of the Holy Qur'an over the Bible. Your New Testament—all four Gospels—claim that Jesus died at Jerusalem, and he most certainly did not. Sad to say, errors intruded into the Gospels when the manuscripts were recopied across the decades and centuries since, which is why God had to correct the record by revealing to his holy Prophet what truly happened—may Allah's peace and blessing be upon him."

✝ ✝ ✝

Shannon looked carefully at her husband. She noticed a slight tightening of his jaw muscles, although his face registered total neutrality. She knew that hers did not, since she was angry at what she thought a mistaken attack on her faith, and the murmuring behind her from the Christian audience showed that she was not alone in that respect. Osman, sitting to Shannon's right, merely seemed fascinated by Abbas, while Richard Ferris, on her left, wore an eloquent frown.

Abbas swallowed a sip of water and continued. "And of course, there are many other teachings in Christianity that we cannot accept, such as the supposed resurrection of Jesus. That prophet died a normal, natural death, as did the blessed Muhammad—may Allah's peace and blessing be upon him!—so no resurrection was needed for either of them. The story that Isa—Jesus—rose from the dead was merely what psychologists call 'wish fulfillment' by his partisans, perhaps grieving that he had somehow forsaken them. Furthermore, his supposed suffering and death had no redemptive quality, as the Christians claim, nor are they saved by faith in what never happened. What they call their 'sacraments' are fine—*if* they find comfort in them—but intrinsically they are useless. The water of their 'baptism' is just plain water, and if they feel cleaner afterwards, fine. The bread and wine in what they call their 'Eucharist' cannot have been ordained by God or Isa, since all strong drink is forbidden in the Holy Qur'an—just another example of how their Scriptures have been corrupted.

"And finally, while many of Jesus' teachings are noble and we Muslims can support many of them, they do not seem to have had the power of those taught by Muhammad—may Allah's peace and blessing be upon him—because look at how, generation after generation, century after century, Christians have failed to follow the high moral teachings of their master. If Jesus taught peace, then why did they go to war? If he taught giving to the poor, why did they steal and seek after riches? If he taught the commandments, why did they break them? If he taught purity, why did they indulge in impurity? If he taught humility, why did they prefer pride and adorn their highest officers with embellishments that would have embarrassed their founder?

"It is for these reasons that the teachings of Muhammad—may Allah's peace and blessings be upon him—clearly have had greater divine sanction than those of Jesus, which is why we regard him not only as greater than Jesus, but as Allah-God's final revelation for all mankind. Thank you, Professor Weber and everyone here, for your kind attention."

Thunderous applause erupted from the eastern half of Hagia Sophia, punctuated by cries of *"Allahu Akbar!"* "God is great!" While Christians sat on their hands, the ovation across the aisle was not only loud but apparently interminable. The clapping and shouting cascaded everywhere, reverberating up to the golden dome, then down across the galleries and reechoing over the entire audience.

Shannon looked pointedly at the moderators. Wasn't this the sort of emotional display they were supposed to contain?

Patriarch Bartholomew finally lifted his gavel and started pounding. His Muslim counterpart seemed hesitant but eventually did the same. The double pounding, augmented electronically, had its effect, and the vast sanctuary stilled to a hush.

She was relieved when Jon stood up to his lectern. Thank goodness they'd hear the truth now. He began, "Thank you, honored Sheikh, for your candor, which is clearly the product of honest conviction. You've presented the principal objections Islam finds in Christianity with eloquence, and I'm sure there are more."

Following the ripple of laughter, he continued. "At this point in our debate, I am to respond to those objections, and the first is certainly of paramount importance, namely what you claim as 'the mathematical impossibility of the Trinity.' In fact, in many of the historic encounters between Muslims and Christians across the ages, this doctrine has prompted the most debate.

"I'm reminded of the celebrated discussion between Caliph Muhammad ibn Mansur al-Mahdi of the great Abbasid dynasty and Timothy I, patriarch of the Assyrian Church. This took place in 781, when the caliph opened the debate by asking, 'If God is one, he is not three; and if he is three, he is not one. What is this contradiction?' The Christian patriarch replied that the sun also has three dimensions—spherical shape, light, and heat—and yet it remains one sun. Similarly three golden denarii are three in number but one in essence: gold. The one does not contradict the other. But I would add to the patriarch's explanation the fact that we cannot hope to know and understand the ultimate essence of God, who is so dimensionally different from his creation that the mystery of the Holy Trinity stands at the ultimate threshold of our attempt to understand God with this message: 'Unless three equals one, thus far, and no further.' For this very reason Augustine could say, *'Credo* ut *absurdum est!'*—'I believe *because* it is absurd,' in the sense that human logic alone could not have 'invented God,' as it were."

Shannon tried to gauge the general reaction. Abbas was merely looking down at the table in front of him, apparently lost in thought. The reaction of the audience was similar. *Time to move on, honey.*

Jon continued. "As to whether God engaged in any marital act with the Virgin Mary, Christians absolutely agree with you that this would be demeaning to our Lord and certainly did *not* happen in human fashion. No, not at all. This was clearly spiritual, not physical, as you yourself would agree, since Islam believes that Jesus was *born of a virgin.* If the begetting of Jesus were physical, carnal, Mary would not have been a virgin.

"As to Jesus' crucifixion and death in Jerusalem, probably no fact in all of history is better attested to than this one. Not only are the Gospels, the entire New Testament, and all the earliest Christian writers in unanimous agreement on this point, but so is the witness of non-Christian writers, such as the Roman Tacitus, the Jewish historian Josephus, the rabbinical traditions of Judaism, and such pagan philosophers who opposed Christianity as the Neoplatonist Celsus. The plain fact is that no one in the world denied that Jesus was crucified until a Gnostic heretic in Egypt named Basilides did. Whether or not the Prophet Muhammad knew of him is not the point here, but this is: Muhammad's claim arrived *six centuries* after Jesus' crucifixion. Accordingly, the burden of proof on this point must shift to Islam."

Shannon glanced at the eastern half of the nave and heard a murmuring grumble.

"To the claim that errors intruded into the Christian Scriptures through recopying across the centuries," Jon continued, "tiny variations in spelling and syntax *did* indeed occur in the surviving Greek manuscripts of the New Testament. Yet none of these dealt with any doctrines of Christianity or facts regarding the person and statements of Jesus, and not one of these denied that Jesus died on the cross—*not one* of the 5,700 Greek manuscripts of the New Testament that have come down to us in whole or in part.

"Furthermore, any claim that the biblical documents were subject to error compounding error in recopying was disproven by the discovery of the Dead Sea Scrolls in 1947, in which two surviving Isaiah scrolls from circa 200 BC were compared with the oldest known manuscript of Isaiah at that time, from AD 1006. The text is 99 percent the same, showing that there was remarkable care and accuracy in recopying biblical manuscripts.

"My worthy opponent also concludes that the resurrection of Jesus never happened, nor was his work redemptive for believers. *If*, in fact, Jesus never died at Golgotha but lived on, as claimed by Islam, then indeed there was no necessity of any resurrection. But, again, Jesus' death on the cross is as solid a fact of history as is, say, the *hijirah*, the flight of the Prophet from Mecca to Medina."

Angry whispering erupted in the Muslim audience, which seemed to get louder, as if by contagion. Shannon shot a worried glance at her husband. He might have been wiser not to have used the sacred *hijirah* as a parallel. Speech was not as free in the Muslim world. Looking over to Abbas, she saw Jon's scholarly opponent apparently unaffected by his statement, merely jotting down notes. When the moderators' gavels brought silence, Jon resumed.

"As for questioning the resurrection, it is clear that Jesus either did or did not rise from the dead. If he did not, why was his body not found in Jerusalem still occupying the tomb in which he was buried? The authorities there who crucified him would certainly have pointed to his dead body in order to refute claims of his resurrection, *if* it were available. All the traditional claims of a 'stolen body' are worthless in terms both of motive and execution. That Jesus' tomb was indeed empty is now a sober fact of history.

"My worthy opponent also questioned the efficacy of the church's sacraments. Christians themselves have differing opinions on whether they are merely symbolic or very powerful means by which God penetrates the lives of believers, the clear majority of Christians favoring the latter interpretation. But I wonder why the grand sheikh claims that God in Christ could not have authorized the Holy Eucharist because wine was involved. The Qur'an claims that in paradise, there will be 'rivers of wine'—Sura 47:15—and yet sharia law prescribes eighty lashes for one imbibing wine.

"Finally, the argument that Christians do not fully follow the high moral standards of their Founder is very true indeed, and I certainly agree! Unfortunately, however, *every* religious faith on earth has followers that fail to uphold the high teachings of their respective prophets or founders, and Islam is no exception. I find it strange that my worthy opponent should have accused Christians of making war when, in the present climate, it is the extremist followers of Islam who seem to be the world's terrorists, inflicting death and destruction in New York City, Washington, D.C., London, Paris, Madrid, Somalia, Afghanistan, India, Indonesia, and elsewhere.

"Add to that the obvious cruelties Muslim jihadists have inflicted on their own kind, such as the Taliban in Afghanistan throwing acid onto the faces of schoolgirls trying to get an education, or mangling a young boy's arm in Indonesia for stealing a loaf of bread, or the so-called honor killings in which families put to death their own innocent daughters who have been raped. And what about the Iranian who wanted to divorce his innocent wife, so he framed her for adultery and she was stoned to death?

"I hasten to add, however, that Dr. al-Rashid is as bitterly opposed to radical Islam as is the rest of the world, for which I am extremely grateful and will always call him my friend. But I note from the moderators that my time has expired. Thank you, ladies and gentlemen, for your kind attention."

Jon sat down to waves of powerful applause from the Christian side, along with cries of "Hear! Hear!" Shannon breathed a sigh of relief. It seemed the first volleys had been exchanged with minimal bloodshed. Mercifully, it was also time for the first morning break. Black Turkish coffee only exacerbated the limitations of the human bladder.

✠ ✠ ✠

Inevitably, the break lasted longer than the appointed twenty minutes, but by 11 a.m., all had returned to their seats. It was now time for Jon to air what Christians found amiss in Islam, an area in which he knew he would have to thread his way very carefully across a field strewn with traps and mines. It wasn't fair, of course. In the free West, anyone could say outrageous things about Christianity and not only be tolerated, but even be applauded for it, while in the Middle East—as Jon had learned from personal experience—one wrong phrase regarding Islam could set off riots, destruction, and even death. Still, the truth must come out, Jon decided, as he began.

"Some of the problems that Christians see in Islam have already been cited in my response to those that Islam finds in Christianity, so they need not be repeated here. Basically, we must question the revelations that Muhammad claims to have received from the angel Gabriel." As he'd anticipated, this statement met with murmuring from the eastern contingent. "But in this we are only following the Prophet himself, who also questioned his early revelations until firmed up in his beliefs by his wife Khadijah.

"We also find difficulties in the life of Muhammad that we do not find in the life of Jesus. One of them involves wives, that is, those after the death of Khadijah, to whom Muhammad was always faithful. Jesus had no wives, but the Prophet had twelve. My distinguished opponent will point out that the patriarchs in the Old Testament also practiced polygamy, but the real point here is one of consistency. While the Prophet limited the number of wives a man might have to four, he himself chose twelve. Someone has well said, 'No true prophet must ever exempt himself from his own mandates.'"

Again, murmuring—this time a bit louder than before.

"As for claims that the Holy Qur'an is God's final and

greatest revelation, Christians find that problematical because the book contains inconsistencies that seem incompatible with the perfection of God. In Sura 7:54, for example, we are told that the world was created in six days. Fine. Yet in Sura 41:9-12, we are told that it took God *two* days. Again, in Sura 2:256 we have the noble statement: 'There is no compulsion in religion.' Excellent! Yet Sura 9:29 advises, 'Fight those who do not believe in Allah.' And of course, when one of the most documented facts of history—the crucifixion and death of Jesus—is denied, then one must naturally question the source of such denial."

At this point, the murmuring took on a distinctly angry tone.

"Your great *Shahada*—'There is no God but God, and Muhammad is his Prophet'—is excellent in terms of leading people to one God, but it has also led to the belief that Muhammad is God's only prophet or at least his greatest prophet. But please contrast Jesus and Muhammad. Christians believe that Jesus performed miracles and rose from the dead. Muhammad did neither. His immediate successor, Abu Bakr, said at the Prophet's funeral in Mecca: 'If you are worshipers of Muhammad, know that he is dead. If you are worshipers of God, know that God is alive and does not die.'

"Finally, Christians find the sharia law set forth in the Qur'an to be demeaning to women—placing them helplessly under male control with only half the rights of men. Punishments mandated in sharia also seem excessively brutal: cutting off a hand for stealing, stoning a woman to death for adultery, 'honor killings' to which I referred earlier, and, worst of all, the penalty for conversion *from* Islam is death."

"AND YOU ALSO DESERVE TO DIE!" a voice shouted in plain English from nearby, *Die . . . die . . . die* echoing and reverberating across the marble walls of Hagia Sophia.

Now a young Muslim stood up in a row very near the dais. He clenched a fist held high and shouted, "You are a satanic infidel whom Allah will surely strike down, Weber, and then condemn you to hell where you belong! Your days are numbered, Web—"

The voice was instantly silenced when Turkish police rushed in, grabbed the man, and gagged him, then hustled him out of the basilica. But a great commotion had arisen as a result, which ended with the banging of two gavels.

"You may continue, Professor Weber," Patriarch Bartholomew said.

"No, I've finished my response, honored moderators." Jon sat down and looked to Shannon, but her lovely face was warped with concern. Osman and Richard on either side of her, however, were smiling and flashing Jon thumbs-up signals.

Abbas al-Rashid stood with an enormous frown and opened, "As for the terrible interruption just now, ladies and gentlemen, you have just heard Islam at its *worst*! And yet this was not Islam at all, which is a religion of submission to Allah and respect for humanity, but a misguided fanatic who *thought* he was a Muslim. I apologize to you, Professor Weber!"

A humble bow accompanied his words, but Jon shook his head, held up his hands, and said, "It is nothing!"

Abbas's features relaxed into a warm smile as he took up the defense of Islam against points that Jon had raised. "My worthy opponent questions the revelations given to the Prophet—may his name be blessed—because Muhammad himself questioned them at first. But *of course* he did, which is exactly what one would expect of a very rational person not given to delusions. The very questioning proves his rationality, and I am grateful for it. Clearly, Allah provided his wife Khadijah to reassure the Prophet—may his name be blessed—perhaps much as he sent Aaron along with Moses to confront the pharaoh of Egypt.

"Now, regarding wives, the Hebrew Bible—which Christians call the Old Testament—does indeed provide us precedents. With David having ten wives and Solomon supposedly a thousand, one need not quarrel over just twelve for the final prophet in their line."

Jon squirmed as the audience laughed, regretting that he had ever raised the wives issue against his earlier intentions. Never mind that Abbas had deftly dodged his main argument—the issue of Muhammad's inconsistency—he had evoked laughter, which would endear the audience and win points while making Jon look foolish. Abbas was shrewd, no doubt about it!

He continued. "My worthy colleague questions the Holy Qur'an because of 'inconsistencies' he claims to find in its pages. Well, so be it. There are contradictions also in the Bible, as in every literary work, whether written by man or God. But this is no problem whatever, since Islam alone provides the solution."

Abbas reached for a copy of the Qur'an lying on the table, picked it up, and said, "I read from Sura—that is, chapter 2, verse 106: 'Whatever communications we abrogate or cause to be forgotten, we bring one better than it or like it. Do you not know that Allah has power over all things?' Clearly, then, the later statements of Allah in the Qur'an replace the earlier statements in every point of perceived disagreement."

Applause broke out in the eastern half of the sanctuary, which was promptly silenced by the moderators.

"However, there is no disagreement in the Holy Qur'an that Jesus escaped death on the cross. No, not at all. Again I read, this time from Sura 4:57: 'They killed him not, nor crucified him, but so it was made to appear to them, and those who differ therein are full of doubts with no certain knowledge . . . for of a surety they killed him not.' Do you see, Professor Weber, the historical references that you cite *thought* Jesus had been crucified—'so it was made to *appear* to them.' Allah would never have permitted his faithful servant Isa to endure this. God would not allow any of his prophets to be killed.

"And now to Jesus and Muhammad—two great prophets. You seemed to deny that Muhammad could perform miracles. But our hadith—our traditions—tell us that once when the Prophet was asked, 'Why don't you do miracles as did Jesus?' he responded by holding his thumb and index finger around the full moon, then passing his other index finger through the middle of the orb, and half the moon fell east of Mecca, and the other half fell to the west. No, I don't believe that this *physically* happened, but the miracle is that bystanders saw exactly that—which is a miracle. And what of the Prophet's miraculous midnight ride from Mecca to Jerusalem and up to heaven and back?"

Good heavens! Jon thought to himself. *Can Abbas really believe all that—this rare voice of Muslim moderation? And yet if I poke fun at such credulity, the place will go up in flames. He must just be trying to please his own right wing.* That, in fact, seemed to be the case, since Abbas hurried on to the next point. "How shall I respond to my colleague's concerns as to how sharia law is being applied today and how women have been treated in Islam? I would ask you all to prepare for a shock. . . . I agree with him! Yes, *I agree with him*!"

Amid rumblings of surprise, he declared, "The words of the Prophet—may his name be blessed—have been followed too literally by some in the world of Islam, who forget that he was often speaking to followers in very difficult military situations, rather than laying down rules to be observed at all times and places. This is no more and no less than the same problems Christians have with how they interpret some of the words of Jesus, who also often spoke harshly. He said, for example, 'If your eye offend you, pluck it out!' I sincerely hope that no Christian would be insane enough to take that advice literally.

"And so, I would like to close this phase of our discussion on an irenic note: Professor Weber and I have much in common, since we both oppose any hateful fanaticism in religion that would lead believers to think that violence is obedience to Allah's, to God's, commands. It is not!

"Thank you, ladies and gentlemen."

Both sides of the sanctuary now joined in spirited applause, which grew even louder after Jon and Abbas shook hands.

It was now noon, and time for lunch.

CHAPTER 12

IN ORDER TO AVOID THE PRESS and the crowds, Click, Clack, and a detail from the CIA and the Turkish special police escorted Jon, Shannon, Richard, and Osman through a small exit in the southern apse of Hagia Sophia and into several black Mercedes sedans. They were whisked eastward around the basilica and into the gates of the Topkapi Palace grounds, where walking tourists parted ranks to let them drive by. Stopping at the eastern end of the enclave, they descended a steep flight of stairs to the Konyali Topkapi restaurant and its beautiful view overlooking the Bosporus. Here they all sat down at outdoor tables in an area separated from the rest of the restaurant terrace.

Osman and Dick were ebullient over the first half of the debate. Ferris, in fact, gave Jon a big hug and ordered champagne. Shannon was finally smiling again too, though she voiced her apprehension over the fanatic who had yelled his hatred inside the basilica. Kemet Bankasi, one of their Turkish liaisons, overheard her and said, "Again, we're *very* sorry about that. He turned out to be a young student from Bodrum who is studying under a radical cleric there."

"But how did he ever get a seat so near the front?" Dick Ferris asked.

"That's still a mystery. He wouldn't tell police, but it could be as simple as using a chair that was unoccupied for some reason. We thought we had screened everyone properly, but—well, one in eight thousand isn't a bad average, is it?"

They all chuckled.

In discussing strategy for the afternoon, the talk was so spirited that they barely noticed the delicious seafood luncheon the chef had specially prepared. Jon passed on the champagne, since he wanted to keep all his wits in gear for rounds three and four.

Ferris's cell phone rang, and he excused himself from the table. Minutes later, he returned, wearing a big grin. "The debate won't air in the States until 3 p.m. our time, which is 8 a.m. Eastern time in the U.S. But Europe's just an hour behind, and the BBC is reporting a *huge* audience. They even set up big projection screens at various points in London—Waterloo Station, Trafalgar Square, St. Paul's—you name it. The same with Télévision Française. And at the Reichstag in Berlin, they even suspended a morning meeting of the Bundesrat so all could watch."

"No riots so far?" Jon asked almost timidly.

"Not that I've heard." Then he added, impishly, "And that's all due, of course, to the high plane on which the debate is taking place."

"Well, we'll change all that this afternoon. That's when we take our gloves off, so prepare for fireworks!"

"Jon . . ." Shannon's plaintive tone was corrective enough.

"Just hyperbole, dear," he soothed. *Though maybe not,* he mused.

✢ ✢ ✢

By 2 p.m., all had reseated themselves inside the immense basilica, having lunched at hundreds of different eateries in the heart of Istanbul. Although Jon half expected the audience to diminish—who watched all-day debates anymore?—this time it was the opposite. Even the crowds outside had swelled. All seemed to know that the fun was about to begin. This would be the open, free, unstructured segment of the debate, in which the moderators promised to intervene as little as possible. Abbas, Jon, Bartholomew, and Selim had reminded one another of that agreement moments before the debate resumed, and the moderators opened the afternoon half of the debate by reminding the audience of that arrangement as well.

Again, Abbas al-Rashid seemed interested in starting off. "Dr. Weber, your explanation of the Christian Trinity is interesting in terms of how you illustrated it with the sun, or gold, or whatever, but I find it less than convincing. Please, once again, kindly explain how one can equal three. The word *Trinity* is not even in your Bible."

The Trinity again, Jon reflected, then replied, "You are absolutely correct, Dr. al-Rashid. The term was first used by our church father Tertullian, but it faithfully reflects both the unity of God as well as his 'plurality' as Creator, Savior, and

Sanctifier, qualities that we find all over the Old and New Testaments."

Jon went on to cite the appropriate passages, then marshaled the traditional and philosophical evidence Christians have always used. The bottom line, in any case, was that mathematics alone stands as a warning sign that—unless one equals three—humanity, this side of eternity, cannot hope to probe the essence of God who is dimensionally different from his creation. "But permit me, honored Imam, to deal with the most significant problem that Christians have with Islam. It is so basic that all the other difficulties we find become secondary to this one."

"Indeed? I look forward to hearing it!"

"And that, of course, is the role of Jesus and what happened to him in Jerusalem on the day we call Good Friday. To deny his crucifixion flies in the face of all historical evidence. You explained that as best you could, by claiming that 'it was made to appear' that he was on the cross. This, however, will simply not do. It would have required something of a mass hallucination on the part of all bystanders at Golgotha—which was not possible. And what about the Roman executioners? The Romans were grimly efficient when it came to executions: no one escaped."

"With Allah, everything is possible. But you, worthy Professor, claimed that there are no records stating that Jesus did *not* die by crucifixion, other than that Basilides person. I fear you are mistaken on that point. *The Gospel of Barnabas* reports that someone else took Jesus' place on the day of crucifixion and that Jesus escaped death. Now, the—"

"Honored Sheikh, *The Gospel of Barnabas* is a medieval *forgery*! It has no historical value whatever."

"Well, perhaps a forgery based on facts, on a true secret tradition of what actually happened."

Jon simply shook his head. "As I recall, one reason you deny Jesus' crucifixion was because God would not allow such a punishment for one of his faithful prophets. Well, there we have a problem. Quite a few of God's prophets have indeed suffered and died for his sake despite their faithfulness. Elijah had to run for his life, Jeremiah was cast into a pit, Zechariah was stoned to death, and John the Baptist was beheaded."

"Well, Jesus was perhaps a favorite son among the prophets. In any case, you Christians have been fearfully wrong in turning him into a god, when there is no God but God."

"What about Jesus' own claims to deity?"

"He never made them. This is only another example of how your Scriptures have been corrupted, or, to phrase it better, an example of how errors have intruded into their texts when manuscripts were recopied. In fact, here is what Jesus did say on this subject." Abbas picked up his Qur'an, paged through it, and said: "Here it is. I quote from Sura 5:116:

> *"Then God will say, 'Jesus, son of Mary, did you ever say to mankind, "Worship me and my mother as gods besides God"?' Jesus will answer, 'Glory be to You. I could never have claimed what I have no right to. If I had ever said so, You would surely have known it. . . . I told them only what You bade me. I said, "Serve God, my Lord and your Lord."'"*

Al-Rashid closed the book and looked directly at Jon.

Jon again shook his head and said, "Jesus would never, *ever* have said, 'Worship my mother and me as gods.' This drastically violates *everything* we know regarding his relationship with his mother, Mary, and so—"

"So you agree with me, then?"

"No, I do not. In his ministry, Jesus took great care to distance himself somewhat from his mother, most probably so that any worship of his mother would never take place. Accordingly, God could never have asked a question like that."

"But the Holy Qur'an says that God *will* ask Jesus this question."

"And our Holy Bible shows that it would be utterly *impossible* for God to ask Jesus a question like that, especially in view of everything we know about God, Jesus, and Mary from the pages of the New Testament."

"So, then, you also deny that Jesus ever said or ever would say what the Holy Qur'an plainly states are his very words?"

"Yes, I simply must deny that Jesus ever said, or ever would say, the words that you quoted."

"Then are you calling the Prophet—may his name be blessed—a *liar*?"

"No—" Jon started to reply but was forced to pause as loud, agitated murmuring arose from the crowd. He raised his voice a bit. "No, I would never call him a liar. Muhammad did not write down those words himself, since he could neither read nor write. They were first written down—as the Qur'an—under his successor Caliph Uthman twenty years after his death. How can we be sure that those were the actual words of the Prophet?"

This prompted an even louder drone of disapproval until silence returned when the crowd seemed eager to hear Abbas's response.

"It is an article of faith in Islam that they actually were the Prophet's words—may his name be blessed. And certainly the same could be said about the words of Jesus in the Gospels. He never wrote them down."

"This is true enough, Dr. al-Rashid. But the overwhelming evidence of the different followers of Jesus who wrote down his words is consistent in reporting what he said. Many were eyewitnesses. The same cannot be said for a source six centuries *after* Jesus."

Silence followed. It was a very powerful argument, not because Jon had come up with it, but because it was simple, logical, historical fact.

Finally Abbas responded, "I must prefer the true and final revelation of God himself in the Holy Qur'an against that of human beings, whether they wrote as eyewitnesses or were removed even thousands of years from what they reported."

Jon waited out the inevitable applause from the Muslim half of the audience, then replied, "I respect you for your faith, worthy Imam." He suppressed what he wanted to add: *even though no historian in the world would agree with you.* What he did add was: "And I trust that you will respect mine."

The moderators rang a bell, indicating that it was time for the midafternoon break. Both sides of the sanctuary offered applause, clearly enthusiastic enough to exceed what was merely routine or polite.

✠ ✠ ✠

Jon's luncheon group, along with their detail from the Turkish police and the CIA, retired to what would have been the green room in any other public venue, but at Hagia Sophia it had to be a robing room in the apse of the basilica. More than anything else, Jon wanted to hear Osman al-Ghazali's reaction to the afternoon debate, thus far. As a convert from Islam, his opinions were of utmost importance.

"Brilliant defense of the faith, Jon," he opened. "And you really scored some potent points against Islam. By the way, it seems that most of the national television networks in the Muslim countries are making use of Al Jazeera's feed from their big camera crew in the east balcony."

"Great. But why are you frowning?"

"Oh, was it that noticeable? Well, I'm . . . just a little concerned . . ." His voice trailed off.

"Concerned about . . . ?"

"Well, during the debate, I've been watching the other side very carefully, particularly several of their well-known mullahs whom I recognized, sitting near the front. Some Shiites were there too. One, in fact, was Ayatollah al-Kazim from Tehran, not the one who laid a fatwa on your head, but his lieutenant. And then there was Imam Chasbullah, who evidently came all the way from Indonesia, Amir Ahmad Riza Khan from Pakistan too. Among the Sunnis there were several princes from the royal family in Saudi Arabia, as well as a big Egyptian delegation—mainly faculty colleagues of al-Rashid. But I digress. My concern is this: every time you scored a debating point against Islam, I watched their reaction. We're talking narrowing of the eyes, clenching fists, and corrugated foreheads. Lots of frowning, too."

"You mean they weren't exactly applauding me?" Jon quipped with a wink to Shannon that was intended to forestall any worry on her part.

"Well, put it this way: I wouldn't want to break bread with any of them afterward."

"Hadn't really planned to, Osman." Jon looked up. "Uh-oh, here comes Ferris with that cell phone molded to his left ear."

"Hi, team," he said. "Our debate's been on for an hour now in the States. It's replacing the morning shows on NBC and CBS, with ABC cutting in from time to time on *Good Morning America*. CNN is covering everything from gavel to gavel, but with a commentary team that's half-Christian and half-Muslim."

"Excellent!" Jon said. "I'll bet watching that would be more fun than the actual debate!"

"Yeah, but—" Ferris's face fell a bit—"the NBC studios at Rockefeller Center received a bomb threat from someone who called in with a Middle Eastern accent."

Shannon bit her lip and glanced at Jon with a look that all but shouted, *I* knew *something like this would happen!*

"What are they doing about it?" Osman wondered.

"Well, they have to take it seriously, of course," Ferris replied, "but that sort of thing is quite routine nowadays, unfortunately."

"We have to go back shortly," Jon said. "Any further advice, Osman?"

"Just beware of any traps that al-Rashid may try to set for you. If you're caught in one, he could win the debate. I'd only suggest that you continue walking that tightrope, Jon. You have to defend the faith, of course, but try to do it as diplomatically as you can—"

"Without enraging the other side. Got it, Osman." *Blasted restraint,* he almost muttered. *How I'd love to cut loose!*

✠ ✠ ✠

On the way back to the dais, Jon weighed the obvious. They were now on the last lap. What if he got tired—or impatient—and let his guard down? One ill-chosen phrase, evidently, could ignite the Islamic world. Again that dreadful double standard: Curse Christ as much as you wish in the West, or draw caricatures of his church, or place a crucifix in a pan of urine and call it art (duly funded by the government), and you easily get away with it. Try the same with Islam or Muhammad and you're dead!

Just before stepping onto the dais, Jon looked at row ten on the Christian side of the sanctuary, because it seemed to be filled with Roman collars. And on the aisle, whom should he see but the wonderfully familiar face of Kevin F. X. Sullivan, "my personal ambassador to the Vatican," Jon often told friends. He immediately walked over, and they exchanged several slaps on the back.

"And what brings *you* to Istanbul, Kev?" Jon asked. "Converting to Eastern Orthodoxy, are you?"

"Right! But only when you return to Mother Church, Jon. The Holy Father sends you his blessings."

"And mine to him, Kev. Gotta run. What're you doing for dinner?"

"No special plans."

"Great! We're at the Hilton. Say 7 p.m.?"

Before Kevin could answer, Jon had to return to the dais. But he looked back and saw his friend flashing a thumbs-up sign.

The moderators now announced that the same, freewheeling dialogue would govern the final session of the debate, with a minimum of their interference. Applause actually broke out at that point, which both the patriarch and the primate took graciously.

"I have a question for you, Professor Weber," Abbas al-Rashid began. "What in Islam do you find the most difficult doctrine to accept?"

Clever, Jon thought. *Makes Abbas look like he's ready for anything, while luring me out on a dangerous limb. Why didn't* I *think of that one first?* Jon finally opened his mouth and said, "The doctrine of abrogation."

Abbas looked puzzled. "The doctrine of abrogation?"

"Yes, the idea that God could lay down one precept and then—in what is claimed as a subsequent revelation—change his mind and say something entirely different. I find that demeaning to God's perfection."

"But the later command is an *improvement* on the previous one, as Allah tells us. Isn't that gracious of the Divine Majesty?"

At that point, Jon had to bite his tongue, for he wanted to say, *Well, why didn't the deity get it right the first time? Didn't he have a second cup of coffee that day?* What he actually said was "One only wonders why anything that God did or said would need improvement." This was met with applause from the Christian contingent. Then he added, in tit for tat, "And what in Christianity do *you* find the most difficult doctrine to accept, esteemed Imam?"

"Two claims, really," he replied. "The Trinity, of course, is still incomprehensible to any Muslim. But the other is what you Christians call the doctrine of the Incarnation, that the God of the universe could have taken on human flesh in Jesus. That is impossible by any standards and is far more demeaning to God than the idea of God improving on his commands."

"Well said! And I certainly agree that the Trinity and the Incarnation are the two greatest mysteries, the two greatest miracles of the Christian faith. Again, though, I side with Augustine who said, 'I believe *because* it is absurd'—absurd to human logic, to be sure, but our minds are so dimensionally different from that of God that what seems absurd to us may be entirely logical in the divine dimension. And what greater revelation could God give us than to cross the cosmic divide into humanity, forming the divine bridge by which we can truly know God and experience the blessings of having our sins forgiven by faith in the suffering, death, and resurrection of Jesus Christ?"

"Very well, then, let me ask you the most important question any Muslim can ask of anyone else. May I?"

"Of course." *Here it comes,* Jon thought, with no idea how *it* might be defined.

Al-Rashid asked, "What is your true opinion, your *honest* opinion of the Prophet Muhammad—may his name be blessed?"

A sudden, tense silence filled the vast reaches of Hagia Sophia. *Well,* it *was dynamite,* Jon realized. Or better, his tightrope was now stretched across the caldera of a volcano bubbling with hot lava and threatening to explode whether or not he fell off the tightrope first. What he wanted to say was not what he *could* say at that place and time. Yet he had to be honest.

Jon smiled. "I have many good things to say about the Prophet Muhammad." A loud stirring on both sides of the aisle showed that he had startled the entire audience. He paused to let the strange tidings digest, then continued. "First of all, he led his people away from the terrible error of paganism, polytheism, and their worship of many different desert deities to monotheism, since there can be only one God. Belief in the one God sets Judaism, Christianity, and Islam apart from all other world religions then or since. We surely have that in common."

"Well said!" al-Rashid replied. "I heartily agree."

"Muhammad also taught people to abandon idolatry and other sad practices of paganism. He taught them spiritual disciplines, such as prayer, fasting, and concern for the poor, and he set higher ethical standards than had previously been the case among the desert tribes of Arabia. His reforms aimed in the right direction, for example, reducing the number of wives a man might have to only four. Previously, there had been no limit."

"Again I must agree. Well spoken. Why, then, can you not also become my brother in the true faith? All you must do is define Jesus correctly as one of the greatest of the prophets, yet less than God—and thus restore unity in place of trinity. But are there any other reasons you cannot join us?"

"Yes, there are. But first I must thank you for your fraternal spirit. We need much more of that in Muslim-Christian dialogue. There are indeed many other reasons that I cannot follow Islam, but a single day's debate is not long enough to air them. Since our time is expiring, let me mention only one. I find it extremely unwise to hazard my entire spiritual future by believing in *one* person's *claimed* revelation, whether that person be man or woman, boy or girl. What if that one person should be wrong? And I do believe that *every* religion founded by just one person has indeed been mistaken."

At the loud Muslim murmuring, al-Rashid held up his hands for silence, then replied, "Well, I would agree with you in the case of Zoroaster, or Gautama Buddha, or Mithra, or Joseph Smith, or Mary Baker Eddy—all single founders—but you have just admitted, then, that Christianity is false, since it was founded by one man: Jesus of Nazareth."

"No, my honored opponent! Christianity had *many* founders who lived and taught God's revelation across many centuries. We believe the testimony of God's patriarchs and prophets in the Old Testament, who predicted matters that were fulfilled with incredible accuracy many centuries later. We believe the further testimony of God's evangelists and apostles and missionaries in the New Testament, as well as in the ultimate embodiment of God's revelation in Jesus Christ. Now *that* is what we call a whole 'cloud of witnesses' who can be trusted since their testimony is unanimous."

Spirited Christian applause filled the basilica.

The moderators now tinkled their bells, indicating that it was time for a final summation by each side. Al-Rashid was given the favored position of having the last word, due to the essentially Muslim environment.

Jon started his summation with a surprising twist. "I am most grateful to everyone in this basilica for your attendance and for your patience, as well as to all who had a hand in preparing this event. I don't think a final summary of the Christian position is necessary at this point, since that should be quite obvious by now. Instead, I would like to close with an urgent appeal for further dialogue and tolerance between Muslims and Christians. Both sides have been guilty of failures in this respect. In the West, we've been traumatized by radical Islam—especially since 9/11—and so there the debate rages as to whether Islam is a religion of peace or violence.

"The answer, of course, is *yes*, meaning that one can find both in the Qur'an. Yet so often when Muhammad advocated violence it was more in the form of a general inspiring his troops prior to actual warfare, since the Prophet had been attacked militarily. Does anyone think that—were Muhammad alive today—he would have condoned the attacks in New York or Washington, the subway bombings in London and Madrid, the assassinations in Beirut, the bombings of mosques in Pakistan, the murderous rampage in Mumbai, and dozens of other acts of Islamic terrorism across the world?"

"Never! He would *not* have!" al-Rashid interposed.

Jon smiled and continued. "And so I would plead that the great moderate majority in Islam across the world become *far* more vocal, *far* more active in curbing the incendiary rhetoric of radical mullahs and other militants who preach violence. I would plead that their governments become *far* more active in eradicating terrorist cells in their own nations and elsewhere. These fanatics have killed *far* more *of their own Muslim brothers and sisters* than the Western Christians they have targeted!

"To be sure, Christians in history have also failed to follow the teachings of the Prince of Peace. But in general, our period of religious violence ended centuries ago. Today, we do not see Christian or Jewish terrorists blowing up Islamic mosques, do we? Sadly, the reverse is often the case, which is why I would rejoice to see a true Islamic reformation take place in terms of the same mature moderation now achieved in both Judaism and Christianity. If you forget everything else in our discussion today, please remember this vision, this plea.

"Thank you, ladies and gentlemen." Amid applause that bordered on ovation, Jon sat down.

Abbas al-Rashid stood with slow deliberation and said, "I, too, thought of using this summation to 'win for Islam,' as it were, but I agree so thoroughly with my opponent's plea for peace, dialogue, and moderation that I am pleased to say that I agree with his statements in almost every respect. Even in the Christian West, however, we also hear radical voices denouncing Muslims as 'camels' or 'towel heads.' This is not to say that our radicalisms are the same. Ours, I must confess, are far more violent, far more dangerous, and far more in need of correction.

"For that reason and others, I join with Professor Weber in appealing to all Muslim authorities in both state and religion to *denounce* radical Islam, to curb terrorism, and finally to end it. They must admit this truth to their people: that terrorism has *never—anywhere in history or anywhere on earth*—succeeded in establishing a successful government or society. Its history instead has been one of bloodshed, civil upheaval, anarchy, and general chaos. For that reason, reason itself must prevail. If it does, I have great hopes for another golden age for Islam—as was the case in the Abbasid era, for which I was named—but only if it escapes the clutches of those who would restrict it. These are the same false leaders who have prevented Muslim progress in so many fields in the centuries since. I hope people of goodwill everywhere may support this effort.

"Thank you, ladies and gentlemen, Christians and Muslims alike, for your presence at our discussion today."

Al-Rashid received applause similar to what Jon had evoked, though actually more from the Christian than the Muslim audience. In the eastern half, some had refused to applaud, especially Shiite representatives. Abbas and Jon walked toward each other, met near the center of the table on the dais, shook hands, and then actually embraced. Instantly, the applause became a vast, genuine ovation.

CHAPTER 13

PUNCTUAL AS ALWAYS, Monsignor Kevin Sullivan was in the chandeliered lobby of the Hilton at 7:05 p.m., when Jon and Shannon stepped off the elevator. This time nattily attired in clerical grays, the dark-haired, ruddy-faced son of Ireland gracefully kissed Shannon's hand and then squeezed Jon's.

"We really wanted to take you over to the Sultan's Table on the Golden Horn, Kev," Jon said, "but the CIA vetoed it—especially tonight—so we'll have to make do with the hotel restaurant."

"The Bosphorus Terrace? Not a bad alternate! Hey, kabobs and beer would do. This time it's the company, not the food."

The maître d' seated them next to a sliding-glass door overlooking the city, and the conversation lagged not a moment from that time on. In fact, they hurried their drink order for one bottle of local merlot so they could get on with it. The three had been through several extraordinary adventures together recently that could massively have affected the Christian faith, and they wondered if this would be another.

"You turned in a virtuoso performance today, Jon," Kevin observed. "The Holy Father was particularly pleased—I was on the phone with him an hour ago—and if only you were a good Catholic, I really think he'd give you a red hat!"

"Hmm . . . Jonathan Cardinal Weber," Shannon said. "It does have a nice ring to it, doesn't it?"

"Ah, but then I'd have to give you up, Shannon," Jon said, "and become a solitary celibate like Kevin!"

"And you'd *never* want *that*, Jon!" Kevin played along. "The beautiful Shannon alone is worth your staying Lutheran." After smiles and chuckles, Kevin grew serious. "I'll say again, this was an important day in the fourteen-century interface between Christianity and Islam, and you did our faith proud."

Jon shook his head. "Both you and I know that I could have hauled out some really *heavy* artillery against Islam, but I had to limit myself to a handgun. And you know why."

Kevin nodded, pensively.

Shannon said, "I think when the debate comes out on DVD and especially in printed form, it may pack even more power. Any word on how it was received in Rome, Kevin, apart from Benedict XVI, that is?"

"Well, I also spoke with Cardinal Buchbinder, the Vatican Secretary of State, and he told me business nearly ground to a halt today, with everyone hooked to a TV screen. Same for the general public in Italy, I understand, since Radiotelevisione Italiana covered everything. But, thank God, no riots anywhere so far."

"And you can thank Jon's pulled punches for that," Shannon commented.

When they had ordered the main course, Jon shifted the conversation. "Okay, team, enough about the debate. Frankly, I'm debated out. But now," he said grandly, "let us tell you, Kevin, about the *fabulous* thing that happened this week, and it's not the debate. . . ."

Kevin looked at him quizzically. Shannon had a slight smile on her lips.

"But before we tell you, we'll need your pledge to keep this *absolutely confidential* for now, okay?"

At Sullivan's emphatic nod, Jon said, "Do you see that lovely proof for God's existence sitting at our table?" All eyes focused on Shannon, a slight flush tinting her cheeks. "That woman with the face of an angel also has the mind of a Solomon and the luck of the Irish. Please start off, Shannon. Begin with Pella."

Hardly needing any persuasion, Shannon eagerly unpacked her discovery in Jordan, capping it off with her find in the basement of the Eastern Orthodox Patriarchate. In the telling, Kevin's eyes grew wide, and when she told of the title page identifying the codex as one of the fifty copies of Scripture ordered by Constantine, his jaw dropped open.

"My . . . my goodness," he stammered. "That could revolutionize New Testament scholarship! Up to now, among the great uncials, our earliest are the *Vaticanus*, the *Sinaiticus*, and the *Alexandrinus*. But this version—authorized by Constantine and prepared by Eusebius, no less—would easily trump them all. This is a . . . a scholar's *dream*!"

Kevin pushed what was left of his juicy filet to one side of the plate and seemed to grow incandescent with excitement. "Okay, we have the title page, but what about the rest of the text? What's the format? How many columns per page? How many lines per column? What books are inclu—" "We don't know, Kevin," Shannon said. "Or rather, we don't know *yet*—except for four columns per page."

"What in *very blazes* do you mean?"

Jon explained. "Just as we were ready to get into the text, the curator of the archives returned, and we instinctively 'covered our tracks,' as it were. Maybe we should have been open about it from the start, but then, I think, the patriarch would have invited his Greek scholars by the dozens to pore over the codex, and we could have been last in line."

Kevin nodded. "I think you did the right thing."

"But now you'll start to understand that, ever since Shannon found that codex a couple days ago, my mind has been *there* and not on the debate."

"Well, your mind on autopilot doesn't do a bad job. But when are you going back to examine that codex and photograph its pages?"

"Tomorrow morning, of course."

"Great! I have to fly back to Rome tomorrow, but *do* keep me informed, Jon, and let me know when I can tell the Holy Father."

"Right, but only if you keep a buttoned lip in the meantime."

As Jon leaned over to refill Shannon's wine glass, they heard a sharp crack from outside. The bottle of merlot shattered in his hands, gushing crimson all over the tablecloth and onto their laps.

"Get under the table!" someone yelled.

As the three dove for cover, another shot demolished Jon's plate into shards of crockery that spattered off the walls. Shrieking and panic filled the restaurant.

Several men from adjacent tables ran to the sliding-glass door that had been ten inches ajar, permitting a breeze—and two bullets—easy admission. Guns drawn, they stormed through the door while Turkish police rushed into the room and surrounded Jon, Shannon, and Kevin. For some moments, a surrealistic scene of bedlam transformed the Bosphorus Terrace into a chamber of horror. Commands were barked, only adding to the cacophony of shouting and screaming that filled the place.

Shannon, Jon, and Kevin were hustled out of the restaurant and onto the first available elevator. As its brass door was closing, Jon saw that the other diners were being similarly herded out. *But who will pick up all their tabs?* he wondered, then worried about his own sanity for posing such an inane question in such an emergency.

Safely inside their suite, Shannon sat on the edge of their bed trembling, trying with only limited success to put on a brave front. The men took turns pacing the floor and glancing at the door. Jon tried to redeem the situation, without really knowing how, except to say that a small army of police now controlled the hall leading to their suite.

Presently, Richard Ferris and Osman al-Ghazali appeared with Click and Clack, who explained that the men at nearby tables in the restaurant were from the CIA and the Turkish government police. They had just recovered the weapon at the edge of the broad lawn in back of the hotel, an old U.S. Army Garand rifle with telescopic sight. The perpetrator, evidently, didn't believe in suicide bombing, although simple murder was fine. Had it been the other way around, or if he had simply shown up with a firearm at point-blank range just outside the open glass door, Jon would be no more.

The phone rang. It was Adnan Yilmaz, the Turkish minister of culture who had met them at the airport. He explained—with official regrets on the part of the Republic of Turkey—that they were doing ballistic tests on the bullets and checking the rifle for fingerprints. Meanwhile, however, Jon and his party were not to leave the Hilton—advice they found quite unnecessary.

Minutes passed, yet time dragged. Although he was not supposed to, Jon briefly parted the opaque sleep curtains in their suite to look below. He saw a long column of police cars with flashing red and blue lights and heard the alternating dual wail of European emergency vehicles. And of course, right behind them were the news trucks and television vans.

Reaching into the suite's mini refrigerator that was stocked full of overpriced goodies, Jon pulled out several mini bottles of cabernet and poured glasses for all who wished. "You'll recall that there was an unfortunate accident with our original bottle," he added, trying hard to add a bit of levity to the general mood that had all the gaiety of a séance in Transylvania.

Again the phone rang. It was Morton Dillingham of the CIA. After several remarks in the I-told-you-so category, his comments quickly focused on a predictable theme. "Now, how are we going to get you out of there?"

"But we're not ready to go back yet," Jon advised.

"So here's what we've arranged," Dillingham continued, brushing off Jon's comments as those of a madman. "We're text messaging your homeward itinerary, flights, and times over our high-security line, since we don't trust the phones—"

Jon chose his words carefully. "With all due respect, Mr. Dillingham—and with gratitude for all your efforts on our behalf—Shannon and I have no intention of leaving Istanbul for at least a week."

A long silence ensued. "Are you out of your mind?" Dillingham finally responded.

"Ordinarily, we'd be glad to go, but something of *phenomenal* importance has just come up here that we simply have to deal with. It'll require about a week—well, maybe only five days—after which we'll be delighted to have you arrange our transportation."

"Nothing could be *that* important, sir!"

"Oh, but it is."

"More important than your life? And that of your wife?"

Jon pondered for a moment, then replied, "Yes . . . that's exactly the case."

Dillingham lost all control of his tongue, blurting out, "*Listen*, Weber, whatever your ding-dong, dad-blasted reason may be, we're sick and tired of tryin' to keep you outta trouble when all you do is go out of your dag-blamed way to *find* trouble! You don't stay in touch; you don't follow the rules—what are you, some kind of suicidal jerk? Hey, maybe we should just wash our hands of you and let the terrorists use your blessed body for target practice! Yeah, that'd be a lot less expensive for us, and never mind that you'd be toast!"

Jon cringed but made no reply. Better to let Dillingham's steam get vented.

Finally Dillingham cleared his throat. "Well . . . sorry, Dr. Weber. That was . . . that was rather unprofessional of me."

"No apologies necessary, Mr. Dillingham. I realize I've been an exasperating case for all of you. I'm very sorry about that."

Dillingham sighed. "Don't mention it. I still feel bad about how I blew off. Let me try to show you that I'm not some pompous federal idiot. And please call me Mort rather than Mr. Dillingham, all right?"

"Fine—if you call me Jon."

"All right, then. But what detains you, Jon? What's so blasted important?"

"It involves a manuscript . . ."

"A *manuscript*, you say? What sort of manuscript?"

"Awfully sorry, but that's all I can say at this point."

Dillingham released another sigh of frustration. Then he said softly, "One last time, Jon; if they don't catch the gunman, he'll try again. And there may well be more than one out there. After that debate today, you're not exactly a hero in the Muslim world."

As Jon pondered the point, Dillingham asked again, "So—this manuscript of yours—is it *really* worth your life?"

"It really is, Mr. Dill—er, Mort. You'll understand when I can finally explain it all."

After a few moments of silence, Dillingham finally said, "Well . . . have it your way, then. We'll postpone your return arrangements for exactly one week. But *only* if you follow the added security measures I'm going to text message to our people."

"We'll do exactly that . . . Mort."

When he hung up, Shannon observed, "Sounds like you were speaking for both of us, Jon."

"Uh-oh, you're right." Jon looked at her. For a time, the room was silent. Then he asked, "Do you really want us to go back immediately?"

"Yes, I'd really *want* to—*if* we hadn't come across that manuscript!"

Relief washing over him, Jon gave her a big hug. Ferris and al-Ghazali wanted to know all about "that manuscript," whatever it was.

Swearing them all to total secrecy, Jon and Shannon launched into the story for the second time that evening, Kevin Sullivan adding further comment with the sort of enthusiasm only the Irish can generate. The Vatican ace didn't even have to change his plans for the flight back to Rome the next morning. He rather served as guinea pig for the escape route from the hotel that Jon and Shannon would use on a daily basis that week.

Several hours after Sullivan's jet had left Turkish airspace, Jon, Shannon, and their security took the service elevator down to the Hilton's basement parking garage. They climbed into a special Citroën that looked like a surviving specimen from the 1970s, but in fact had armor-plated sides and bulletproof glass. Anyone peering inside would have seen not the Webers but a Turkish couple, the husband with tanned skin and Muslim headdress and the woman veiled. The cars preceding and following them were equally nondescript, but they all had a common destination: the Eastern Orthodox Patriarchate.

CHAPTER 14

INEVITABLY, PATRIARCH BARTHOLOMEW INVITED JON and Shannon to a celebratory breakfast. The churchman was overflowing with appreciation for Jon's defense of the faith, which he thought an inspiration for all Christians living in Muslim lands, particularly for those in Turkey. Jon, in turn, thanked him in advance for editing the Greek translation of the debate for both the DVD and print versions. After a final coffee, Jon explained that—with the patriarch's kind permission and that of Brother Gregorios—they wished to finish their research in the archives, which might take several days.

"Certainly, dear professor," the patriarch agreed. "And do let me know if you find anything of . . . of particular interest."

Of particular interest? Jon mused. *How about a manuscript codex that will become one of the great landmarks of biblical research?* But for now, he simply agreed.

Brother Gregorios readmitted them to the patriarchate's *geniza*, though Shannon preferred to call it the "Manuscript Retirement Home." He stood in the doorway for a minute or two but then generously returned to his own duties. Jon's pulse was at a swift gallop as they made their way to the southwestern corner of the room. There it was—the ancient bookcase . . . and its bottom row of dilapidated materials . . . *and* the Constantine Codex.

Wordlessly, and almost worshipfully, Jon put down his attaché case that was crammed with photographic equipment and, with exquisite care, lifted the volume off the shelf. Then he opened it with a gentleness he usually reserved for Shannon.

For her part, Shannon opened her own case, which contained several photo lights—including ultraviolet and infrared—spare batteries, 6.0 gigabyte flash drives, filters, and dozens of 35mm film canisters—yes, film, since they would photograph each page both digitally and via film emulsion. A random static electric charge could destroy the memory cards if they went only the digital route or if they were, say, hit by lightning. "We would die, of course, but the film would most probably survive," Jon had explained, helpfully.

Both put on white cotton gloves to prevent any of their skin oils from touching the vellum of the codex. Gently they opened the tome and, for the first time, were able to examine material beyond the title page in some detail.

"Incredible, Shannon!" Jon exclaimed. "Just *look* at that magnificent writing—it's biblical uncial—just like the *Sinaiticus* and *Vaticanus*. And four columns per page versus three in the *Vaticanus*."

Shannon shook her head in awe. "It's stunning, absolutely *stunning*. And ancient, all right; look at all those words run together. I still wonder why they didn't have enough sense to separate words in the early documents."

"It's called *scriptio continua*. And it's the same with the Greek and Latin you find on most of the monuments in the ancient Mediterranean world. Actually, it was the Hebrews who had the great idea of separating words."

Jon turned on his mini tape recorder and dictated. "September 4: In what we term the *geniza*—the decaying manuscript repository of the Eastern Orthodox Patriarchate in Istanbul—we are examining an extraordinary document, a codex with pages of vellum sewn together inside a front cover of thin wooden board layered over with thick dark tan vellum. The back cover is missing. This codex is most probably one of the fifty commissioned by Constantine late in his career and prepared by Eusebius. It is written with a very fine hand on leaves of vellum parchment—probably antelope or donkey skin, I think. Each page is about—" he pulled out a pocket tape measure—"about thirty-eight centimeters wide by . . . thirty-five high—similar to the *Sinaiticus*. There are four carefully justified columns per page, with slight variations in the lengths at the end of each line. There are about . . . twelve to . . . fourteen Greek letters in beautiful biblical uncials in each line, without serifs or any adornments. The lettering seems very similar to that of the *Sinaiticus* in the British Library in London—hence early fourth century. This accords very well with statements on the title page."

They now carried the precious codex over to a table nearby, where they would carefully photograph each page. First, they had to see how many pages there were and which biblical books were included—or excluded. Again Jon pressed the Talk button on his recorder.

"The title page was found almost separated from the rest of the material but still joined at the highest sewn stitching. I suspect that the missing back cover is the reason this codex landed in the *geniza*. The page of material following the title page begins:

"TO KATA MATHAION AGION EYAGGELION."

"The Holy Gospel According to Matthew," Shannon whispered. Jon heard the emotion in her voice, which echoed his own.

Shifting the heavy pages of the large codex from right to left with extreme care—almost as if they were a volatile mix of nitroglycerin threatening to explode—Jon came to the last page, which had only two columns and ended with a postscript:

APOCALLYPSIS IOANNOU TOU THEOLOGOU

"The Apocalypse of John the Theologian," Shannon again translated. "That's the book of Revelation! We probably have the whole New Testament here, Jon!"

Jon nodded, eyes momentarily closed, breathing a prayer of thanks to God for having permitted such a discovery as this. Wiping his eyes, Jon had a catch in his voice as he said,

"First we should survey the whole document. Only then the photography."

Now began the painstaking process of paging through the codex. The plan was easy, the accomplishment difficult. Time and less-than-ideal storage conditions over its probable seventeen-hundred-year history had apparently glued some of the pages together, likely due to excess humidity. These they would have to deal with on the morrow, but as they paged through the accessible text, their excitement was only compounded, because *Kata Mathaion* was followed by *Kata Markon*, next *Kata Loukan*, and then *Kata Ioannen*—Matthew, Mark, Luke, and John—the same order of the Gospels as in all later versions of the New Testament.

Nay, more. In turn followed Acts, Romans, 1 and 2 Corinthians, and the rest of the Pauline corpus, the general epistles of James and Peter—virtually the same order of canonical books that appeared in contemporary Bibles. This was beyond all expectation, since the great *Sinaiticus*, while it also had all of these books, included the apocryphal Epistle of Barnabas and the Shepherd of Hermas too.

"I counted 151 pages, Jon. And you?"

"The same. Exactly."

"You say this is vellum. So how many animal hides do you think were necessary to create this codex? A dozen or two?"

Jon thought for a moment, then replied, "No, more like eighty or ninety animals had to die for this codex—and that's just for our New Testament segment here."

"Incredible! Don't tell the SPCA about this!"

"Sad, but true. It's been estimated that the cost of one of

these codices was a laborer's lifetime earnings. That's why they used papyrus instead of parchment as much as possible for biblical manuscripts. But even a papyrus scroll was expensive—not because of the material cost—reeds *are* cheaper than animals—but the huge effort in *copying*."

Shannon nodded. "And that's one reason, I suppose, that each of the Gospels is comparatively short."

"Exactly. The early church had very limited resources."

To test their equipment and the lighting, they took a small number of photographs in both digital and film. Then they carefully lifted the tome off the table and replaced it on the basement shelf.

They called it a day—but what a day! On the drive back to the Hilton, they said very little—both caught in the wonderment of their discovery.

✠ ✠ ✠

When Ferris and al-Ghazali invaded their suite that evening, they brought a huge sheaf of media reports on world reaction to the debate. Predictably, most Western reviews in the print and broadcast media were "categorically certain" that Jon had won the debate, while reports from the Islamic world claimed victory for Abbas al-Rashid. Pleasant, though, were the reactions from neutral and Third World countries, which clearly gave the nod to Jon.

All remaining meals in Istanbul would be catered to their suite, according to the new arrangements, and Morton Dillingham phoned them periodically with further security plans. At ten o'clock that night, however, came a most welcome telephonic interruption. It was Adnan Yilmaz with news that the would-be assassin had been arrested. He turned out to be the *brother* of the student hothead from Bodrum who had cursed Jon rather vocally inside Hagia Sophia. Both militants had driven to Istanbul in a VW microbus well stocked with hate-America pamphlets, as well as assorted fireworks that included eight pipe bombs, four pistols, five rifles, and enough ammunition to supply this arsenal. Under separate interrogation, the brothers implicated no one else and proudly claimed to be "the only men in Turkey who served Allah properly."

For some time, the conversation in their suite centered on how the shooter could have known Jon was staying at the Hilton or where they would have dinner that night.

"That's really no mystery," Ferris opined. "With all the press hanging around the entrance to the Hilton, it was pretty obvious. I think *Hürriyet* even wrote that you were staying here."

"Yes, but that kid was just a little too bright, figuring that we'd also be dining at the hotel restaurant. I wonder if he was tipped off . . ."

While they pondered that possibility, Jon suddenly slammed his fist on the table. "No, he wasn't. It just came to me. I noticed that during his tirade, the hothead was standing at the aisle of the ninth or tenth row at Hagia Sophia on the Islamic side. And who was sitting directly opposite him on the Christian side? Kevin Sullivan! When the debate resumed, I had asked Kevin to come to the Hilton for dinner. The shooter, the brother of the loudmouth, must have been sitting next to him and overheard."

That was plausible, even probable, and a welcome blanket of relief seemed to descend on everyone, especially when Yilmaz called again to say that both brothers would be in prison for weeks before they were even arraigned in Turkish courts.

Dick Ferris, however, wondered why Jon and Shannon were not more enthusiastic about the debate triumph or more relieved that the would-be assassin and his brother had been caught and that theirs seemed to be a solo operation. "Do you have something else on your minds?" he asked.

Jon just smiled at him. Of course, the men knew what Jon and Shannon had been up to, but he was not going to divulge any more information than was absolutely necessary at this point.

When everyone had left that night, Jon and Shannon transferred the photos they had taken of the codex onto Jon's laptop. When they appeared on screen, he had no trouble enhancing the images using only the contrast control of his favorite photo program.

"Great!" he commented. "These will print out with razor-sharp clarity."

"But what about the pages that are stuck together?"

"Yeah, I've been worried about that. Tomorrow let's use something as simple as steam. If that doesn't work, then we simply *have* to declare our find to the patriarch, and he'll have to bring in a team of his own museum restoration people. But I'd *hate* to have to do that before we know what's actually in the text of the codex. Still, we dare not destroy a single line—a single word—so if steam doesn't work, we'll photograph the rest of the codex and then let Bartholomew in on *the* greatest manuscript find of the twenty-first century." He grinned at her. "Or am I exaggerating?"

"Probably not, provided it's authentic."

"I know, Shannon. We've been duped before. But not this time. No one on earth could *ever* have managed to forge all that."

She nodded. "That, and its totally accidental discovery. No wonder you had your mind on this rather than the debate, my darling."

Her use of such a tender term in the context of cold scholarly research added sudden, renewed warmth to their relationship. That, combined with their natural elation over the codex was all they needed to call it a night. There simply was nothing like love to banish all concern and restore the soul.

CHAPTER 15

EN ROUTE TO THE PATRIARCHATE THE NEXT MORNING, Jon and Shannon's security escorts maintained the same dispassionate silence they had observed from the start, never bothering to ask *why* they were making this daily trip as Jon surely thought they would. *Real professionalism,* he thought. They raised no questions even when Jon asked the driver to stop at a hardware store, where he purchased a hot plate, a teakettle, some flexible tubing, a hose clamp, a screwdriver, a roll of paper towels, and a long extension cord. Somehow, he managed to pack it all into Shannon's tote bag so that when they arrived at the patriarchate, no curiosity was aroused. Again, Brother Gregorios admitted them into the *geniza* without asking any questions. But how long would *that* last?

When he had left them, Jon searched for an electrical outlet.

It was maddening; he could find none. And why would you need one in a manuscript morgue in the first place? He felt the same ugly frustration he had encountered at so many airports when the battery in his laptop was draining, but could he find an outlet at any of the gates? Evidently, the miserly masters of the aerodrome were afraid of losing three cents' worth of electricity.

Alternate options boiled up in his brain. Go to the kitchen or refectory of the patriarchate and beg a steaming teakettle? But then their secret would be out, quite apart from the fact that the teakettle would lose its steam before reaching the *geniza*. Well, there *had* to be an outlet in the room somewhere. Surely the place had served some other purpose before being converted into a manuscript dump.

"Jon, look overhead at the light fixture," Shannon advised.

And there it was: salvation hanging just above the lightbulb. It was a compound socket that included not only a screw-in cavity for the lightbulb but two regular outlets as well.

Jon smiled broadly. "Shannon, you're a dream—also in the daytime!"

But where to get the water? Not a problem, since Gregorios had helpfully pointed out a little WC near the *geniza*.

The extension cord proved just long enough to reach from the light fixture to the table beneath it, so he plugged in the hot plate, set the teakettle upon it, and waited for the water to boil.

The light had dimmed visibly when he plugged the hot plate in. "Please, Lord, don't let the fuse blow." While the water was warming, Jon put a hose clamp over the flex tubing and screwed it tight over the circular nose of the teakettle.

Soon came the wondrous simmer of heating water and finally the welcome gurgle of boiling. When a clear jet of steam emerged, Jon and Shannon lugged the codex over to the table.

"There aren't all that many stuck pages, honey, and here's the first." Jon paged through to the end of Mark's Gospel that adhered to the first page of Luke's Gospel. Now he directed the jet of steam around the three available edges of the two stuck pages. Moment after moment passed. Jon tried to distribute the steam as gently and evenly as possible, but it seemed to have no effect whatever, raising the level of his frustration. "Rats!" he said. "I guess we'll not be able to do it ourselves after all."

"Look at the upper right corner, Jon."

"Hey, it's starting to part!" He aimed the steam jet to this vulnerable spot, opening it further. "Yessss . . . ," he crooned.

Slowly, and with admirable cooperation, the two pages started parting from one another, providing additional avenues for the steam to penetrate.

"Fabulous! It's working."

Soon the pages separated entirely. Jon quickly scanned the material for any damage, but while the uncial lettering was damp and even wet at places, the ink had not run. Evidently, a deposit of ink that had clung to its parchment for seventeen centuries was not going to be deterred by a little steam.

"Thank God!" Jon whispered. Triumphantly he put a paper towel under both parted pages and then small weights at the edges of the pages to keep them open. "Let's go get some coffee, sweetheart," he said. "We can't do a thing until these pages dry."

And they did remember to unplug the hot plate.

When they returned, the pages had dried, but just to make

certain, they inserted paper towels between the now-parted pages to absorb any remaining moisture. Matthew and Mark were now ready for photographing. Starting at the beginning, they photographed each page digitally, then with film, and finally with ultraviolet and infrared light to detect whether any of the vellum had been used previously and erased—a palimpsest. While this was unlikely in view of Constantine's commission, they would overlook nothing.

This consumed the rest of the day and might even have been deemed tedious were it not for the critical importance of the codex for future New Testament manuscript research. When they had finished, around 4 p.m., Matthew and Mark had surrendered their texts. Tomorrow, Luke, John, and perhaps Acts would hopefully do the same.

✢ ✢ ✢

Under any other circumstances, Jon and Shannon would have spent the evening at one of the more prominent night spots in Istanbul—or perhaps on a dinner cruise along the Bosporus. In view of their enthralling project, however, they hardly felt deprived at the lack of time for such comparatively frivolous pursuits. They excused Ferris and al-Ghazali for that purpose. Instead, it was time to "view the rushes" of the day's shooting—to borrow a phrase from Hollywood. Jon had brought along his Eberhard Nestle Greek New Testament—the latest edition of which contained the optimal readings of the ancient Greek manuscripts in attempting to provide the most exact version of what Matthew and the others had originally written down.

Jon found remarkable correlations between the readings in the codex and the latest Nestle edition. Again and again, as he plowed through Matthew's text, he would comment, "Right on! . . . Yes. . . . Three cheers for textual scholarship!" Still, there were a few interesting variations in the Constantinian text. "Future editions of Nestle will have to take these into account," he told Shannon.

"Provided that all this is authentic," she cautioned.

"Right. But I'll bet my very life that it is."

After their catered dinner, Jon said he was particularly concerned as to how well the adhering pages would show up in the photography after their steam treatment. Filling his laptop screen with the now-liberated last page of Mark's Gospel, Jon said, "Look, Shannon, no difference from the others. They all reproduced *very* nicely."

Then she noticed a growing frown on the face of her husband. He was staring so intently at the screen of his laptop that she wondered if some electronic genie might be hypnotizing him.

"What's wrong, Jon?"

"Something's . . . very strange here. We're at Mark's last chapter, but it should end with . . . with about a half of one column, not three." Jon hauled out his Nestle and compared it with the codex. Then he seized a pen and began translating the three extra columns of the codex.

Shannon realized he'd be busy for a while, so she rinsed out the coffeemaker and put on a fresh pot to brew. She suspected it would be another late night. But who was complaining?

She glanced at Jon to see how he was progressing. He must

be getting tired, poor guy. His hand seemed to be trembling as he wrote feverishly on the notepad beside his computer.

"Honey, would you like some coffee?"

Jon seemed to be in a trance as he responded oddly, "What time is it, Shannon?"

"Nine thirty. Why do you ask?"

"Remember that time well." He put down his pen and turned in his chair to look at her. With an obvious tremor in his voice, he said slowly, "Seventeen centuries of New Testament scholarship will change from this point on, darling. You *will not believe* what we have here!"

"What? What is it?"

He shook his head as if trying to clear his thoughts. "This seems to be . . . seems to be nothing less than . . . the lost ending of Mark, the incredible, mind-boggling *lost ending of Mark*!"

"No way. What are you talking about?" Shannon knew that Mark could not possibly have ended his Gospel account with the downer clause "And they [the women] said nothing to any one, for they were afraid," while describing the glorious resurrection of Jesus. And yet that was how the *Sinaiticus*, the *Vaticanus*, the *Alexandrinus*, and many other early manuscripts ended. It had been the greatest problem in New Testament scholarship for many centuries. To be sure, later hands added their versions after Mark 16:8. The King James Bible, for example, and many later versions included verses 9 through 20, but these were not in the earliest Greek manuscripts. The problem was even more acute in that Mark was probably the earliest evangelist to report the Resurrection.

Jon sat down and clasped his head in both hands. "Eusebius

must have found a very early manuscript of Mark that had the complete text!"

Shannon stared in wonderment at her husband. "This is simply beyond belief, Jon! What in the world does the text say?"

Jon seemed to be in another world, from which he was returned by Shannon's question. "The text? Oh yes, the text . . ."

For the next three hours, Jon pored over the new material and wrote out sentence after sentence in translation, occasionally consulting the Arndt-Gingrich-Danker *Lexicon of the New Testament*, which he had brought along on disk. Finally he banged his fist on the desk, and with a great "YES!" he stood and said, with contrived pomposity, "Please take your seat, madam. You are about to hear words that the Christian world has not seen or heard since a generation or two after Jesus himself.

"This, of course, is a rough translation, which we'll improve later on. It picks up after Mark 16:8, where the women flee from the Resurrection tomb and quote, 'said nothing to any one, for they were afraid'—that puzzling and totally unsatisfactory ending. Now, however, read how Mark *really* continued his Gospel immediately after that verse." He handed her his translation:

> But immediately Jesus met them on the way and said, "Greetings!" In great joy, they rushed to him and fell down on their knees and worshiped him. And Jesus said, "Don't be afraid. I told you that I would rise from the dead, just as the prophets had predicted. And now you must take heart and tell the brethren to go to Galilee, where I will meet them at the mountain where I was

transfigured before their eyes." And then they saw him no more.

In glad exultation, they immediately rushed to tell the eleven disciples what they had seen. At first they did not believe the women but thought that their words were idle tales. But then Jesus himself appeared to them in the room where they were hiding in Jerusalem for fear of the Jews. He criticized them for their unbelief and showed from Scripture that he would indeed rise from the grave. He even ate something before their eyes to show that he was not a spirit, as they had feared. Then he left them again.

In great joy, the eleven immediately went to the mountain in Galilee where Jesus had directed them. Again Jesus appeared to them and said, "Go and make disciples of all people in all nations, baptizing them in the name of the Father and of the Son and of the Holy Spirit. You must also teach them to obey all my commandments, for I will be with you always."

Again he left them but reappeared to them and the other believers for forty days after he rose from the dead. At last, in Jerusalem, where they had returned, Jesus again reminded them that they, as his witnesses, were to proclaim repentance and forgiveness of sins in his name to all nations. Then he led them out of the city to the Mount of Olives near Bethany, where he ascended into the heaven from which he had come. And the disciples returned to Jerusalem with great joy, telling the good news to all, and awaiting the blessing of the Holy Spirit.

Shannon put down the script and looked at Jon. He said nothing, clearly overcome with a profound sense of the sacred. Shannon found herself blinking back tears. It was some moments before their silence was broken.

She finally looked out the windows skyward and said, "Thank you, St. Mark! Your version of what happened at that first Easter will silence all the catcalls of the critics who bellyache about all the 'discrepancies in the Resurrection accounts' and whether the ascension took place in Galilee or Jerusalem."

Jon nodded. "Mark does wind it up very nicely. Too bad that ending was ever lost."

"But now it's *found*, my darling!" Shannon jumped up and gave Jon a great hug. Then she asked him if she could read it again. Flipping open her own Bible, she compared the new Markan material with the Resurrection accounts in Matthew and Luke. Meanwhile, Jon poured himself another cup of coffee and slowly savored it.

"Well, Jon—" she finally looked up—"the new material certainly seems authentic enough."

"It does, but how did you come to that conclusion?"

"It's the old Synoptic question, isn't it? Most scholars assume that Matthew and Luke drew from the earliest Gospel—Mark—then added separate material on their own, especially more sayings of Jesus. This passage, interestingly enough, has the basic resurrection material common to *both* Matthew and Luke, plus Mark's usual signature touches, especially that adverb *immediately*."

Jon thought for a moment, then threw his arms around Shannon. "You're right. I should have thought about the Synoptic issue immediately."

"See, that's why you need me, Jon," she said with a sly little smirk.

"Was there *ever any* question about that?"

He gathered her in his arms and kissed her deeply, passionately.

✢ ✢ ✢

The next morning, they finished all necessary steam treatments by noon, since there were only seven other conjoined pages in the codex, and all yielded their secrets this time, however, with the loss of a few words that had probably faded long before the adhesion. Jon was confident that he could reconstruct them. In the afternoon they photographed their way through the Gospels of Luke and John, as well as the book of Acts—the earliest history of the church. At the Hilton in the evening, they checked out the rushes—all of which were fine—so they decided to discontinue the infrared and ultraviolet photography, since all the parchment skins used for the emperor were apparently fresh and new, not palimpsests full of erasures. Using secondhand materials, of course, could have damaged the close relationship between the historian Eusebius and his close friend, the emperor Constantine.

Jon and Shannon calculated that they could finish the project in the next two or three days. The following morning, curiosity finally got the better of Brother Gregorios. He put it into quaint English as he opened the door of the *geniza* for them yet another time. "It is very bold to ask, Professor Weber, but what do you and Madame Weber find so . . . so interesting in our 'manuscript cemetery'—we call it? We have much better volumes in the rest of our library."

Jon smiled in what he hoped was a charming and innocent manner. "We're just sampling the sort of debris that you store inside that room, Brother Gregorios. That information will help us in America if we decide to do the same with our old materials." While that, of course, was only a half-truth, it would have to serve for now. The librarian nodded and left the *geniza*.

After lugging the big tome onto the table they'd been using, Jon and Shannon prepared their equipment.

"Well, since we finished Acts yesterday, Paul's letter to the Romans is next, Shannon. Ready?" Jon opened the codex to the bookmark they had left. An unusual superscript that he hadn't noticed earlier caught his eye. He stared at the page for a moment, saying nothing.

"What is it, Jon?"

"Strange. Look at that superscript. Shouldn't it read '*Pros Romaios*'? 'To the Romans'?"

"Yes . . ." Shannon peered over his shoulder at the page that held him transfixed. "Hmm. It looks like it says '*Praxeis Apostolon B*'—'Acts of the Apostles, Beta,' Book 2. What could that mean?"

What could that mean indeed? Jon's pulse pounded as the possibilities started to sink in. He pulled out his handkerchief and held it to his brow. Truth be known, he was suddenly feeling a little faint.

After giving Shannon's hand a quick squeeze to ground himself in reality, he put a trembling finger onto the document's opening words, words he knew he would never forget. Indeed this moment, which seemed to be unfolding in slow motion, would forever be burned on his memory. "*Touton men triton logon, O Theophile . . . ,*" he read.

Shannon looked at him, eyes wide. In a hushed tone, she translated, "This *third* treatise, O Theophilus . . ."

They stared at each other for what seemed an eternity but must have been only seconds. "Third treatise, Shannon," he repeated. "*Third.* Luke's first treatise to his friend Theophilus, of course, is his Gospel. The second is the book of Acts, so this third treatise must be a continuation of Acts, hence *Acts 2* or Second Acts!"

"And it most probably picks up where Acts leaves off, just as Acts started where Luke's Gospel ended." Shannon sat down slowly, clearly overwhelmed by the implications. Propping her chin on two fists, she slowly shook her head from side to side. "Beyond . . . all . . . belief! Hegesippus and Eusebius—those leaves of manuscript from Pella—were right after all. There has always been a Second Acts, but we never knew it for certain until now."

Jon met her eyes and voiced what both of them were thinking. "This . . . this and the end of Mark could make every Bible in the world obsolete."

CHAPTER 16

WITH A FEELING OF AWE, almost bordering on worship, they started to photograph Second Acts. Jon felt something of a sacred tingling in his arms and fingers as he understood, for the first time, what the Jewish high priest must have sensed when he went into the Holy of Holies at the Jerusalem Temple just once each year. He and Shannon were penetrating something of a verbal inner sanctum in this process, treading onto freshly uncovered holy ground.

The new document seemed to be only about a quarter as long as the original Acts.

"This seems to be a sort of codicil appended to Luke's main document in Acts," Jon noted, "probably to cover what happened to Paul in Rome, because he really leaves us hanging where Acts stops in chapter 28."

"I really hope that's it," Shannon added. "I've always found the last verse of Acts the most frustrating passage in the entire Bible."

"Well, darling, we may now be able to find out what happened next." He flashed her an incandescent smile.

The quest for answers, however, would have to be delayed until the evening rushes. For now, they had to finish the photography with only three days left, and the final day was reserved for the report to the patriarch.

Immediately after the sacred pearl of their discovery—Second Acts—followed the expected epistles: *Pros Romaios*—Romans, then *Pros Korinthious A*—First Corinthians, and *Pros Korinthious B*—Second Corinthians.

After a break for lunch, they returned to photograph the rest of St. Paul's writings, also appearing right where they should be: *Pros Galatas*—Galatians, *Pros Ephesious*—Ephesians, *Pros Philippasious*—Philippians, *Pros Kolossaeis*—Colossians, *Pros Thessalonikeis A*—First Thessalonians, and finally, *Pros Thessalonikeis B*—Second Thessalonians.

Having finished for the day, they took their leave of Brother Gregorios and were at the gate of the patriarchate at the agreed-upon time of 4:30 p.m. Again, their security convoy was faithfully waiting on the street just outside. Jon only hoped that they had found something to do with their time during the day.

✠ ✠ ✠

They could barely wait to finish supper that evening so that they could delve into Second Acts. But they were detained by the nightly visit of Dick Ferris and Osman al-Ghazali. Both complained that it was getting harder every day to hold off the media, who were pressing them for information about Jon and Shannon—what their plans were, their schedules, and when Jon would be available for interviews, photography, press conferences—whatever. Ferris, per usual, delivered his sheaf of continuing response to the debate. This time he supplied an overseas edition of *Time*. The cover was a wide-angle photo of Hagia Sophia, with vignettes of Jon and Abbas al-Rashid burned in. The cover story was titled "The 1,400-Year Challenge to Christianity," with sidebars that included brief biographies of both debaters, the main tenets of Islam and Christianity, and even a précis of the debate itself.

Next, Ferris placed a copy of *Newsweek* on the table, the cover depicting a huge crescent on one side of a diagonal and a cross on the other. "Jesus and Muhammad" bannered the story, with treatment similar to *Time*'s.

Osman did the same for media in the Muslim world, where the coverage was also copious. "Actually, the Turkish and Arab press treated you rather well, Jon," he said. "One would have thought they'd be down on your case. They particularly liked the relationship you seemed to develop with al-Rashid. Well, that is, except the Shiites. *Kayhan* claimed that al-Rashid sold out the Islamic side, just as he's been doing for months with his plea for moderation, et cetera, et cetera—predictable stuff. Victory for them would have been a Shiite mullah making you look like an imbecile in debate, Jon, and then grinding your infidel face into the cold marble floor of Hagia Sophia."

"So they still haven't lifted Jon's fatwa yet?" Shannon wondered.

Osman shook his head. "Probably it would take a miracle, like the return of Muhammad from the dead, announcing, 'Weber is innocent!'"

Again, Ferris and al-Ghazali commented on how Jon seemed less than enthusiastic about all the world media attention, his mind apparently elsewhere. Which it was. He was only waiting for an opening, which came when Ferris asked, "By the way, how goes your exploration of that codex?"

Instantly Jon came to life with an explosive smile. "Now that you ask," he replied with a wink at Shannon, "you'll understand why we must ask—no, demand—an even stronger pledge of *absolute* confidentiality. Agreed?"

Both men nodded.

"No, more than that. Arms up as if you were taking an oath, which this actually is . . ."

Both raised their palms, as if in court, curiosity dominating their features.

"Well, to discover one of the fifty actual copies Constantine commissioned Eusebius to prepare was sensation enough, you'll recall. But in photographing it, we found two other items that merely escalate this 'sensation' into—shall we say—the *cosmic* category."

"What in the *world* do you mean, Jon?" Ferris asked.

"How about both the lost ending of Mark *and* Second Acts?"

"Huh-*what*?" Ferris bellowed. "There's another Acts? Maybe to finish Paul's story?"

Jon nodded happily. "I haven't translated it yet, but here's the missing ending of Mark." He handed printouts to both men, then gave a detailed account of how it all happened.

Slowly they recovered. Osman shook his head. "No wonder you didn't seem all that impressed with what we brought you. All we had were merely your international headlines and stories!"

Jon chuckled. "But isn't this more important?"

They agreed. Ferris then added, "Unless there's some bombshell that hasn't been discovered yet in your Second Acts, *yes*, Jon, this *is* more important—important enough to make *every* Bible . . . *ever* printed . . . in *any* language . . . *anywhere* in the world . . . outright outdated!"

It was a powerful and very sobering statement. Jon caught the danger immediately and said, "That's most probably true, Dick, but if you put it that way, millions of Christians across the world may panic or go loony if they think their Bible has been supplanted. What we've found doesn't subvert the Scriptures at all but instead *supports* them."

Shannon, who had been silent for most of this, now spoke up. "Here's another way to put it: the Bible is an immense and colorful mosaic of God's revelation, but two important tesserae of that mosaic were missing. Now they're back in place."

The three men nodded slowly, then enthusiastically. "By george, she's got it," Ferris said.

Osman shook his head in wonder. "One ancient document changing history. How large did you say it is?"

"I didn't say, but the pages measured about thirty-eight by thirty-five centimeters."

"And the codex itself. It's about, what, say, five inches thick?"

"About that—a shade more. Why do you ask?"

"I simply can't wait to see it. When can we?"

"Only photos for now, my friends."

They discussed future plans regarding the discovery, in which Richard Ferris and the Institute of Christian Origins would have to play a major role, and then their immediate plans for the return flight to the U.S. three days hence.

"Thanks for all your help, gentlemen," Jon said. "Couldn't have done it without you. I trust you'll tie up all the loose ends with our Turkish hosts over the next two days? You will? Great. Now please get out of here so I can translate Second Acts."

✠ ✠ ✠

Second Acts proved much more reluctant to offer up its secrets than had the lost ending of Mark's Gospel. Since none of this material had ever before appeared, none of the passages had the familiarity of the standard New Testament verses Jon had known since childhood and which had always eased the translation process. That awful running together of words in the codex was hardly a help either. Often, when he had just about parsed a sentence into separate words, the result made no sense and drove him back to try again with different word divisions. Here he was veritably *lusting* to learn what the document said, yet found it difficult to pry open the text. The new section from Mark had been so much easier because of common themes in the resurrection accounts.

Finally he threw down his pen. "I'll never get this translated tonight, Shannon. I'm sure even modern Greeks would find some of these uncials hard to crack. But now that I'm getting a bit used to them, I *will* scan the whole text for key words so that we can get a general feeling of where it's going and what it says."

"That sounds like a good plan, dear. Would it help if I took notes?"

"That would be ever so kind of you."

Jon went back to his computer screen and scanned the four columns of each page of Second Acts from the codex.

"Okay, here we go: 'Paul . . . when Paul was released . . . Caesar—yes, Nero Caesar—*great,* Shannon! . . . Paul again . . . and Luke! . . . judged . . . Seneca? . . . Rome . . . Spain? Yes, Spain!"

Occasionally he used a magnifying glass to zoom in on faint lettering. "Crete . . . Titus . . . Ephesus . . . Alexander . . . Helios? . . . Praetorian Guard . . . Timothy . . . Via Ostiensis—the Ostian Way . . . fight . . . race . . . victory . . ."

After an hour of this, Jon felt a little defensive about failing to supply a quick, running translation. "It's a little maddening with the words all run together."

"Come, come now, Jon," she teased. "The ancients could do it."

"Okay, dear. Just see how it goes—even in English." He quickly typed out the first two lines of his translation without spaces between the words and handed her a printout. "There you go, Shannon. Have at it. It's all in perfect English."

She read:

ThisthirdtreatiseOTheophilusdealswithallthatbefellPaul afterAristarchusandIarrivedwithhiminRomeandwestayed inhisownrentedhousenearthePraetorian . . .

"And now imagine all that in a *foreign* language too," Jon continued, "and in lettering so different from the norm that you nearly have to relearn the alphabet."

"Point taken, Jon. I *am* impressed. You manuscript sleuths must be geniuses."

"Hmmm . . . you wouldn't be patronizing me now, would you?" A slight grin was warping his mouth.

"Of course I am. I want to patronize you for the rest of your life!" Then she gave him a lingering, passionate kiss.

After the embrace, Jon returned to the desk and turned off his laptop. "I'll certainly have enough reading material on our flight back to the States! In fact, I'll be lucky if I get all this translated in a month."

✠ ✠ ✠

On arrival at the patriarchate the next morning, Jon assured Brother Gregorios that this would be the last time he would have to descend to the *geniza* on their behalf since they were nearly finished. The archivist actually seemed disappointed. Perhaps, like colleagues in his profession, he cherished every part of his collection—even cast-off manuscripts—and he had enjoyed a fresh bond with two people strangely interested in the same.

Jon and Shannon settled in for their usual routine, opening the codex to where they had placed a simple bookmark. And sure enough, the pastoral epistles followed as part of the Pauline collection: *Pros Timotheon A* and *B*—1 and 2 Timothy—after which they photographed *Pros Titon*—Titus.

Jon smiled as he found this to be fresh ammunition against critics who claimed that Paul didn't write the pastorals.

Then came the shortest book in the Bible, *Pros Philamona*—Philemon—and the anonymous *Pros Ebraious*—Hebrews. They even managed *Iakobou Epistolay*—Epistle of James—before lunch.

In the refectory, they were in an expansive mood with the end in sight for their epic project. While they dared not discuss it with the other churchmen and monks with whom they had become increasingly conversant, there was much else by way of luncheon topics—primarily, Jon modestly trying to deflect the praise heaped on him by black-robed fellow diners, all of whom had been present at Hagia Sophia. Before they finished their lunch, the secretary to the Ecumenical Patriarch assured them that His All Holiness would indeed welcome a parting visit from them at 10 a.m. the next day.

Returning to the *geniza*, they could now coast. *Petrou A* and *B*—1 and 2 Peter—quickly succumbed to their photo scrutiny, as did *Ioanou A, B,* and *G*—1, 2, and 3 John. The pages of *Iouda*—Jude—and *Apokalypsis Ioanou*—Revelation of John—presented some problems, since they were becoming detached from the end of the codex. But with the tenderest care they could offer, Jon and Shannon managed to secure perfect images of these also. Their photography of the codex was finally complete.

✠ ✠ ✠

A quick look at the rushes that night confirmed successful photography of every page, as did a final scan of the entire codex. The film would have to await development in the States.

Jon now inserted CD-ROMs into his laptop to make three copies of the Constantine Codex: one for Shannon, another for Ferris, the third for himself—in case anything went wrong with his hard drive. He would leave nothing to chance—absolutely nothing.

And yet, a final, nagging problem remained. Simply put, it was how to handle their discovery and, indeed, the codex itself. Eventually, of course, there would be a public announcement, but who should know about it before that announcement? Calling a press conference to break the news was totally out of the question, they knew, and ridiculously premature. Jon had not even translated Second Acts, as yet.

"You know what I'd love to do, Shannon?" he asked.

"Keep the lid on all this as tightly as possible."

"Just that."

"And not tell the patriarch?"

Jon thought for some moments, then replied, "We have a moral obligation to tell him, of course. But what if he tells any of his staff? The news would soon be out."

"Probably so. By the way, what about the codex?"

"Well, we could just put it back where it was and let it sleep until the public announcement, couldn't we?"

"Not a good plan, Jon. What if they finally do a housecleaning of the *geniza*? They could easily throw it out. Or how about a fire at the patriarchate burning it to ash? Or a terrorist bomb lobbed in through a basement window?"

"I know; I know." Then he sighed and said, "How I'd love to just smuggle the codex out of Turkey and bring it safely to the U.S. . . ."

"But—"

"We could put it in your tote bag, cover it with leather goods from the Grand Bazaar, and—"

"But that would be—"

"Just kidding, dear. I could also be caught and imprisoned for trying to steal a priceless antiquity, and wouldn't that do wonders for our reputation in the scholarly world? Frankly, I don't look good with numbers under my head." Then he grew serious and added, "We now have the complete text and can take *that* home, in any case. But somehow, the codex has to be given VIP treatment at the patriarchate from now on—but in total secrecy, obviously."

Shannon pondered the problem. "Well, Jon, our one and only option is this: Bartholomew and Gregorios have to be sworn to secrecy, and I'm sure they'll know how to keep the codex in fine condition in a better environment."

Jon mulled it over, drumming his fingers. "It's really the only way, isn't it?" He returned to his laptop and inserted a fourth disk to make another copy of the Constantine Codex—this one for the patriarch.

Shannon preceded him to bed. After finishing replies to several urgent e-mails, he crawled in as well. Sleep did not come. Too many thoughts were whirling in his brain to allow him to fall asleep easily. He had a strange feeling—hoping against hope that it was not a premonition. Things had developed so very well, no, so *magnificently* well that they just could not continue. He and Shannon could not be *that* fortunate, could they?

In any case, their conversation with the Ecumenical Patriarch on the morrow could easily become one of the most intriguing of their lives, he reflected, before dozing off.

CHAPTER 17

"AH, MY GOOD FRIENDS," Bartholomew II said as he extended an openhanded welcome to Jon and Shannon inside his office. "Brother Gregorios tells me you've been spending many hours in research here at the patriarchate over the past week. That is good! We are pleased!"

"Thank you for your kindness in permitting it, Your All Holiness," Jon replied.

"And did you find anything worthwhile? Any lost or previously unknown manuscripts?"

Jon smiled broadly. "Yes, we certainly did."

"Well, no matter if—*what* did you say?"

"Yes, Holiness—a *very extraordinary* manuscript came to light. Are we in private? Can we be overheard?"

Bartholomew quickly moved to close the door and offer seats

to his guests. His velvet brown eyes, now arched over with Gothic eyebrows, peered at them with blazing interest. "Now you may speak freely. What is it that you have found?"

"When I tell you, you will understand at once that this information is *for yourself only*—at least for now—and must *not* be shared with anyone. I . . . very respectfully ask your agreement on that."

"*Nai, nai*—yes, yes, of course!"

Only Shannon smiled again at the Greek-English oxymoron.

Jon now unloaded the full account of their week of research. During the telling, Bartholomew's eyes constricted with intensity as his head began a very slow oscillation from side to side. Scholar that he was, the patriarch instantly caught the significance of the ancient codex and interjected, "One of Constantine's fifty, you say? Well, then . . . then it's greater than the *Sinaiticus*! Or the *Vaticanus*!"

Jon could only agree, but when he went on to report that they had found the lost ending of Mark in the codex, Bartholomew's jaw simply sagged open while he stared at Jon.

"Perhaps a little slower, dear," Shannon cautioned. "You and I had a week to digest all this, so you really shouldn't burden the patriarch with so much all at once."

"Do you mean . . . do you mean that there may be *more*?" Bartholomew asked.

Jon nodded. "There is, but I think my wife is right in suggesting that we take a little breather—a break, an interim." *Thank you, Shannon,* Jon thought. *It wouldn't be kind to inflict a heart attack on the aging Ecumenical Patriarch.*

Bartholomew seemed to descend back to reality. "Some tea? Yes?" he offered, then picked up his cell phone to order it.

Before the second cup of tea, the patriarch had to know more, so Jon resumed his narrative. But when he came to the discovery of Second Acts, Bartholomew's cup went flying as both his hands seemed to attack his forehead while he bent over his desk in a prayerful posture. Jon was amazed that great news could have the same shock value as very bad news.

When Jon had finished, Bartholomew crossed himself and finally looked up. "Please forgive my bad manners, dear friends, but I am . . . I am quite overcome with what you report. This is of . . . staggering importance to the whole Christian church on earth. How . . . how do you plan to let the world know? And when?"

"Any premature announcement could be disastrous to the cause of serious scholarship, Your Holiness. I think the announcement should come only after we've concluded the authenticity tests and are ready with a prepared edition of the codex, an official translation, and a commentary—at least on the new material. The rest can come later."

He nodded. "Yes, that should come first. And where should the announcement be made when all is ready?"

"Why not from your own patriarchate, here in Istanbul?"

"That is very kind of you, although there may be other options. And what about the codex itself?"

Jon handed Bartholomew a CD copy of the photographs they had taken. "Again, for now, this copy is for your eyes only. Please guard it carefully. The codex itself, of course, is your property, but I would urge that you retrieve it immediately from the 'manuscript cemetery' in the basement of the patriarchate and keep it under extreme security in a humidity-controlled vault of some kind. Before any public announcement, we *may* need the codex in America for a time for evaluation and authenticity tests—not that there is the least chance of forgery, but the world will demand it."

Bartholomew nodded readily, to Jon's relief. But then his face darkened as he pursued a different line of thought. "And so this . . . this incredibly important manuscript has been in our possession—who knows how many centuries?—and we *didn't even know it*? This is terrible! This uncovers a great failure in how we manage our archives! Brother Gregorios must answer for this! There is absolutely no excuse for such utter—"

"With all due respect, Your Holiness, this sort of thing happens again and again in many libraries across the world that have manuscript collections. With many thousands of documents and books, things *do* get misplaced, so please do not let our good fortune become Brother Gregorios's misfortune!"

Shannon joined the dialogue with an important suggestion. "We would, however, recommend that a *very complete* inventory be taken of *every* document and manuscript inside your basement 'cemetery,' Your All Holiness. Who knows what additional treasures might be found there! Our Institute of Christian Origins in Cambridge will be glad to assist you in this respect."

"*Nai, nai, nai!* A very good suggestion, Madame Weber. I thank you for it. We certainly *will* do that very thing. But now we must all go and see the codex, yes?"

The three descended the ornate staircases of the patriarchate and walked to the archives, where Gregorios, without even being asked, hastened over with his keys, knowing full well that their target had to be the basement document charnel house. Without a word, he admitted them. Jon pointed out the various sectors to the patriarch, and presently they stood before the ancient bookcase in the southwest corner. There rested the codex on the bottom shelf, where it had lain for countless, unknown centuries, looking the same as when Shannon first spotted it, except that the gnarled old leather-clad board cover was no longer gray with dust. Very gently, Jon again lifted it off its shelf and carried it to the table where they had photographed it.

The torrent of Greek spouting out of Bartholomew's mouth as he spoke to Gregorios came too rapidly for Jon to decipher, but it sent the monk running out of the room. Then the Ecumenical Patriarch approached the codex, touched it gently, lovingly, and fell on his knees in prayer before it, doubtless thanking God for its discovery.

When he arose, Jon opened the codex to show him the four magnificently written uncial columns on each page of vellum. He had, of course, opened the tome to the newly found ending of Mark's Gospel. Bartholomew read several lines, then broke out in tears. In silent, sympathetic reverence, Jon closed the codex and said nothing.

Gregorios returned with a large gilded blanket—probably from their liturgical supply room—but before he could wrap it around the codex, Jon asked him to wait a moment so that he could take final photographs of the cast of characters in this improbable drama: the Ecumenical Patriarch and Brother Gregorios, as well as Jon and Shannon with them. Only then did Gregorios reverently enshrine the codex in the blanket and carry it to the office of the patriarch.

Just as he returned to them in the main reception hall, the Turkish sentry called from outside to say that the government's car convoy had arrived to transport Jon and Shannon to the airport. The farewells were genuine and even passionate. When Jon stooped to try to kiss the patriarch's hand—as was customary among the eastern faithful—Bartholomew would not permit it. In most unliturgical fashion, he put his arms around Jon, and with tears in his eyes, he said, "All of Eastern Orthodoxy is grateful to you, dear Professor Weber, not only for defending our faith so brilliantly before a watching world, but also to you both for discovering a most priceless treasure of the church. God has been good to us through you!"

"We, in turn, are grateful for both your original invitation to Constantinople, Your All Holiness, and also for your extraordinary hospitality during our visit here. I know we shall be in frequent touch from now on. And so we say to you and Brother Gregorios, with all the sacred solemnity of our Lord's use of the term on the night before he was betrayed, *ef charisto*!"

✠ ✠ ✠

En route to Ataturk International Airport, Jon and Shannon regaled Dick and Osman with details of their delightful morning at the patriarchate. "Let me tell you, fellas," Jon said, smiling broadly, "it was quite an honor to be hugged by no less than the eastern pope himself—and even be kissed on both cheeks."

"I'm sure he won't wash his face for weeks," Shannon chirped.

Everyone in the car seemed to be in an expansive mood, and

why not? They were finally returning home, knowing secrets that would make for a fabulous future.

When their motorcade arrived at the airport, the doors of the lead car opened, and out stepped Adnan Yilmaz, the Turkish minister of culture, with several aides. In a formal, nicely crafted little speech, he apologized to Jon and Shannon, in the name of the Republic of Turkey, for the terrorist attack at their hotel and hoped that they might return to Turkey with no bitter memories.

For his part, Jon was very genuine in his appreciation of how well the Turks had cooperated in terms of security before, during, and after the debate, and he apologized to all whose schedules had been brutally wrenched because of their visit—including especially their drivers. He would later say the same, of course, to all the CIA operatives—especially Click and Clack, who had kept them alive during their visit to a chancy part of the world.

Just before they checked in at the departure hall, Yilmaz said, "It should all go well from here on." Then he handed Jon his card. "But call my cell if you have any problems."

"Thanks much, Mr. Yilmaz!"

Bags checked and with boarding passes and passports in hand, Osman, Dick, and Shannon were ahead of Jon in the security line, which moved along better than they had expected. After shedding shoes, laptops, change, and sundry metallic items, they reached the metal-detecting doorframe. Jon asked that his camera bag full of film canisters and photo memory cards be passed *around* rather than *through* the frame. In earlier years, he had had too many high-speed films ruined by X-ray exposure in more primitive scanners. This looked to be one of them, and he didn't trust it. If those photos were ruined, only one set on earth remained.

When Jon tried to hand the photo bag around the frame, the security guard said, "No. Must go through X-ray machine."

"But I'll be glad to let you examine everything inside this bag," Jon replied.

"*No! Must* go through X-ray!" the guard fairly shouted and tried to take the bag out of Jon's hands to pass it onto the belt going through the scanner. Jon held on for dear life.

The guard blew a shrill whistle. A squad of guards quickly surrounded the security line and was closing in on Jon. He snatched his cell phone before the gray plastic box with his metallic effects went through the scanner and madly reached in his pocket for Adnan's card. That move prompted the guards to take out their revolvers and aim them at Jon. He held up both arms while trying also to dial Adnan, his photo bag between his legs. The other three looked on in horror. It was a very *bad* moment.

Yilmaz, thank goodness, answered his cell.

"This is an emergency, Adnan!" Jon yelled into his cell phone. "I'm being held at gunpoint in security because I wanted my films passed around the scanner, not through it!"

Adnan yelled some curse in Turkish, then said, "Dr. Weber, give your cell to whomever is in charge of security there. I'll explain!"

Jon handed his cell phone to the officer who seemed to have the most metal on his shoulders. Frowning and skeptical, he put it to his ear and said, *"Merhaba . . ."* Since he knew no Turkish, all Jon heard was a long recitation of *"Evet. . . . Evet. . . . Evet . . ."* then a shocked *"Hayir!"*

Finally the officer, now sheepish, handed the phone back to Jon. Said Adnan in the receiver, "I told him that if they didn't release you *at once*—with apologies—my next call would be to the prime minister of this republic! I'm coming back now to make sure all is in order."

"Thank you, Adnan—if I may. But I don't think that will be necessary."

While he had been talking, the officer stepped over to the rude security scanner, slapped him on both cheeks, and relieved him from duty. Then he returned to Jon and said, "In the name of Allah the All Compassionate, I ask your forgiveness, Professor Weber. This should never have happened."

"It is nothing. Thank you for your help."

Jon's expansive mood returned when he saw his photo case being passed *around* the scanner and into his hands.

CHAPTER 18

THE NEXT MEETING of the Institute of Christian Origins took place a week after the four had returned to Cambridge. Now fully recovered from jet lag, Jon was eager to learn the American reaction to the debate, and the forty-some members attending that morning were only too happy to oblige.

It seemed that more Americans had watched the debate than the seventh game of the World Series the previous October, and far more than the Academy Awards in March—yes, despite the extraordinary length of the debate, which exceeded even that of the awards, Hollywood's annual attempt to model eternity. With so huge an audience, every shade and stripe of response was being collated by several secretaries at the ICO, but Jon and Shannon got a general picture from the comments of institute members, prompting a long discussion over the next several hours.

A large secular sector of the viewing audience thought it "engrossing . . . good theater," but no one expected such to join church or mosque once they had switched off their TVs. The general Christian response was overwhelmingly positive, although fundamentalists complained that Jon had not sufficiently "proclaimed Christ in that citadel of Satan," while radical liberals like Harry Nelson Hunt objected, "Too bad Weber couldn't have gotten beyond that Trinity thing. It's been a millstone around the neck of Christianity for twenty centuries now. And Weber even seems to believe in the Resurrection—a Harvard professor, no less!"

"I plead guilty!" Jon laughed, holding his hands up in surrender.

Heinz von Schwendener commented, a twinkle in his indigo eyes, "I think the most careful, in fact, *the* finest response to your debate that I've heard, Jon, came from the mouth of . . . Melvin Morris Merton."

"You've *got* to be kidding, Heinz!" Richard Ferris thundered. Everyone knew that Merton was a prophecy freak who had always been Jon's nemesis.

Barely able to keep a straight face, von Schwendener continued, "Merton announced that the debate was a meeting of the 'Two Antichrists.' I don't know where he got that idea, maybe somewhere in Revelation. But there you were, both of you sitting in the temple of God—guess he meant Hagia Sophia—so the second coming of Christ and the end of the world are just around the corner!" Then his shoulders shook with released laughter.

Jon and the rest joined in. If an institute could have a court jester, Heinz von Schwendener filled the bill for the ICO.

Next, Osman al-Ghazali, who had spent the week assembling reactions from the Muslim world, gave his report, which was a shade more sobering. Jon and Shannon had received daily updates after the debate, but these were the first details many institute members had heard about the Muslim reaction.

"The Islamic response—to put it mildly—is less nuanced than what we've just heard from the West. They seem to love you or hate you, Jon. The moderates, the leading intellectuals, and the secular leaders thought it a very fair debate, and they particularly appreciated the near-friendly atmosphere you developed with al-Rashid. Some thought it a model for future Christian-Muslim dialogue." Sounds of approval rose from those gathered.

Osman went on. "Then, of course, there's the broad middle of Islam. The faithful there seemed to range from neutral to bewildered. We've heard reports of believers rising from their prayer mats to ask some penetrating questions of their mullahs regarding the Prophet and the Qur'an."

"But I find it interesting," Shannon interposed, "that the reaction from the Islamic conservatives was not as vocal as we anticipated. Right, Osman?"

He nodded. "Most of the noise is coming from the radical clerics—those we call our 'usual suspects'—the firebrand mullahs in London, radical cells elsewhere in Europe, the Muslim Brotherhood in Egypt, jihadists in the Middle East, the Taliban in Afghanistan, and, of course, al-Qaeda wherever. Actually, they're attacking Abbas al-Rashid nearly as much as you, Jon. It's almost as if we're back to where we started. Well, things *are* a bit better; we don't have another fatwa on Jon's head, for example."

"At least, not yet," Jon offered, helpfully. "Fanaticism, in any form, replaces reason with madness. It's the greatest enemy of truth ever devised."

Lunch and a backlog of business consumed the rest of the day. At the close, Jon made an announcement that he knew his conferees would find startling. "Two items, my colleagues. One, thank you all once again for your deliberations and advice during the weeks before the debate in Istanbul. Two, which you may find more interesting, Shannon and I came across something of *extraordinary* importance during our time in Turkey that I want to share with you once we've arranged everything. I know that our next meeting isn't scheduled until two months from now, but might we make an exception and hold a special conclave—I hate to say it—about three weeks from today? I well realize this is terribly short notice and your schedules may not permit it at all, but that's how *very* significant this matter is."

For some time, silence ruled the room. But then Katrina Vandersteen coaxed, "Come on, Jon, give us a little hint . . . ?"

"You'll understand when you hear what it is, Trina." Jon grinned at her. Then he reconsidered. "Well . . . on second thought, I guess I'll have to give you a bit of a hint anyway since I'll need your permission to invite a few guests. Might you members of the ICO be kind enough to allow members of the Center for the Study of New Testament Manuscripts to join us for that meeting?"

Much oohing, aahing, and nodding at the clue signaled an affirmative.

"Another semi-hint: the Eastern Orthodox Church is already involved in this matter, so I think it only fair that Roman Catholicism be represented also. I have a close friend at the Vatican—Monsignor Kevin Sullivan—whom I've also asked to fly over and attend—*if* you agree. Would that be acceptable?"

Agreement seemed unanimous, punctuated by comments like "I don't have a problem with that." "Of course, Jon." "Why not?"

Pleased with the response, Jon said, "Fine. Dick will be in touch as to the specific date and time."

The conference adjourned. Had an artist rendered the scene in a cartoon, he would have drawn thought clouds over each head with just two characters: a question mark and an exclamation point.

✠ ✠ ✠

Shannon was uncharacteristically glad for the ICO meeting to adjourn. Ever since their return from Turkey, Jon had been busy at work translating Second Acts. After a day or two battling jet lag—it was always worse on the homebound trip—he had taken a happy plunge back into the AD 300s, to see what a scribe in Caesarea, writing for an emperor in Rome, would have to say to them in Massachusetts—and of course, to future Bible readers everywhere.

As they drove to the ICO meeting, he told her he had translated the first third of Luke's final treatise, and he planned to let her read it when they got home. The text had proven so challenging that they both agreed it would be best to wait until he had a good chunk of it completed for her to read, rather than his trying to share it word for word, as he'd tried to do at first.

While driving back to their still-guarded home in Weston,

Jon resisted all of Shannon's efforts to pry any nuggets of information out of him.

"No, darling, I really think it's best if you read it for yourself. Although, I admit I got so caught up in the account that I couldn't resist adding paragraph divisions in the text, as well as some of my own comments—in brackets, of course, or at the margins. Obviously, they'll be removed when the text goes public. I really can't wait to hear your reaction."

Shannon could hardly wait and had earlier been tempted to tease out a translation for herself. But Jon's printout, presented on their return home, was much more convenient.

"Here's what I have so far, sweetheart," Jon said. "Our final, authoritative version will look much more biblical in format, and I left out a few 'he said,' 'she replied'—that sort of thing. Chapter and verse divisions can come later too."

She took a deep breath, walked over to the sofa, and started to read.

> This third treatise, O Theophilus, deals with all that befell Paul after Aristarchus and I arrived with him in Rome, where we lived in his own rented house near the Praetorian camp for two years, awaiting his trial before Caesar. No one from the priests and the Sanhedrin in Jerusalem had come to Rome to speak against Paul in his appeal to Caesar, for they preferred that he simply languish in house arrest.
>
> But our Lord intervened. On the Ides of May, in the eighth year of Nero Caesar [May 15, AD 62] we learned that Titus Flavius Sabinus, the prefect of Rome

[mayor of the city!] whose wife was a believer, asked the emperor to hear Paul's appeal. He agreed, provided that his friend Ofonius Tigellinus could serve as substitute accuser [prosecutor] and Sabinus himself as defender. It was agreed.

At Paul's hearing, a board of assessors served as advisers to the emperor, including the philosopher Lucius Annaeus Seneca. Paul took great heart at this, because Seneca was the brother of Gallio, the very proconsul of Achaia who had heard Paul's case in Corinth ten years previous and had set him free, as noted in my second treatise [Acts 18].

Tigellinus, who had read the documents of indictment against Paul that the centurion Julius had saved from our shipwreck on the way to Rome, now stood up and said, "Hail, beloved Caesar, you who guide our empire and our lives with the same wisdom that Jupiter employs for the world itself; you who have spread the marvelous blanket of peace and prosperity over all provinces surrounding Our Sea [the Mediterranean]. We thank you for all you have done to make Rome glorious. But now, so as not to detain you, this defendant—one Paul of Tarsus, a Jew—had the insolence to appeal to you from the courts of our procurators in Judea, Felix and then Festus, because of accusations made against him by the Jewish high priests in Jerusalem."

Nero Caesar asked, "Is he really a Roman citizen?" Flavius Sabinus produced a record from the city clerk in Tarsus, attesting that this was so.

"What are the charges, then?" Caesar asked.

Tigellinus read them word for word from Julius's documents: namely, that Paul was a pestilent agitator among Jews throughout the world and a ringleader of the sect of the Nazarenes.

Caesar asked, "And who are the Nazarenes?"

"Most now call them 'Christians,' noble Caesar," Tigellinus replied.

"Oh yes—the Christians. I've heard of them. Continue."

Tigellinus returned to his document and said, "He even tried to profane the Jewish Temple in Jerusalem by bringing a Gentile inside the sacred Temple boundaries."

Nero Caesar then said to Paul, "Oh yes, you Jews can get very exclusive. I've heard that even if I myself stepped over that barrier in Jerusalem, you Jews could kill me since—alas, I am a Gentile. I must keep reminding my dear Poppaea of that, since the empress is very interested in Jewish ways. But do continue, good Tigellinus. What penalty are you seeking for this . . . this Paul of Tarsus?"

Tigellinus replied, "The death penalty of course, noble Caesar."

"Very well, then. The defense may speak," said the emperor.

Flavius Sabinus arose and said, "My governing the city of Rome is so much more pleasant due to your wise administration of the entire Empire, great Caesar. The people of Rome and all the urban officers are most grateful to you. I, too, have examined the documents against Paul of Tarsus and would ask that you immediately dismiss the second and the third charges.

"The second charge, O Caesar, that Paul of Tarsus is a 'ringleader of the Christians' means little or nothing, since Christians are just a Jewish sect that has never been rendered illegal by any law of the senate and the Roman people. As for the third charge, the defendant did not violate Jewish law by introducing a Gentile into the sacred courts of the Jerusalem Temple because it was a fellow Jew with Paul who was mistaken for a Gentile by Paul's accusers. Here is the deposition on that matter from our tribune in Jerusalem, one Claudius Lysias [Acts 23:26]."

Sabinus handed Nero the document, and he said, "I respectfully ask that you dismiss these two charges, great Caesar."

Nero consulted with his assessors, particularly Seneca, for some time. Finally he announced, "We do indeed dismiss them. Now what is this first charge, that this Paul causes riots wherever he goes? Tigellinus, give us more information on that."

"As suffering and death follow the plague, noble Caesar, so rioting and disorder erupt wherever this agitator travels. In Asia Minor, he was driven out of Antioch in Pisidia. Then he was attacked in Iconium and stoned in Lystra. Next he carried the disease to Greece. They had to imprison him in Philippi and expel him from Thessalonica. He caused a riot among

Jews in Corinth and silversmiths in Ephesus. He created his last uproar—thank the Fates—in Jerusalem, where he was arrested."

The emperor was amazed and said, "This one man did all these things—a man that small could cause such big trouble?"

"Yes, and much more, wise Caesar. Rome has not had such a treasonable troublemaker since Spartacus himself!"

Caesar then asked Flavius Sabinus for the defense. He stood up and said, "Paul of Tarsus has never caused a riot anywhere, great Caesar. He only proclaimed the Christian message of peace everywhere he went, but those who disagreed with him and were unwilling to open their minds to accept what he calls the Good News often tried to stop him by resorting to violence. They caused the disturbances, not this innocent Roman citizen."

"So," said the emperor, "what is this 'Good News' that you teach, Paul of Tarsus?"

Paul rose and said, "Long have I waited for this opportunity to tell you, O Caesar, but I knew that one day I would stand before you since the God who made heaven and earth promised that I would do so. And here I am. He is the God of the Jews, yet also of the Gentiles—the supreme Father of the universe—who made us all and preserves us all. But because we, his children, fell into wickedness and disobedience, he might have destroyed us all in his anger. Yet in his great mercy, he decided to save humankind by sending us a

Savior—the emanation of God himself in the form of Jesus of Nazareth. Although Jesus lived a perfect life, he was unjustly condemned and crucified by one of your governors, Pontius Pilate. But God raised him from the dead, as he will do for all who believe in him, and this is the Good News that he has commanded us all to proclaim to all men everywhere."

Caesar looked at him strangely and said, "Do you really believe all this, Paul of Tarsus? What proof do you have that this is not some daydream? Or nightmare?"

Paul now told of his conversion on the road to Damascus in words similar to those I recorded several times in my second treatise to you, O Theophilus [Acts 9, 22, and 26]. When he had finished, Tigellinus said, "This man must have mental afflictions, illustrious Caesar, and we must not let this Christian delusion of his take root in Rome."

Said Caesar, "This does seem to be true, Tigellinus. What do you have to say for yourself, Paul of Tarsus?"

"This is not delusion but divine truth, O Caesar. And I have done nothing worthy of death or further imprisonment, as one of your own assessors here should be able to confirm."

"And who might that be?"

"I call on your wise tutor and adviser, Annaeus Seneca, who honors me with his presence today. Your own brother Gallio, dear Seneca, judged my case ten years ago in Corinth and found me totally innocent. Surely he must have mentioned this to you?"

Seneca replied, "Yes, I seem to remember that. My brother is back in Rome, and I will get further details from him."

"Finally, honored Caesar, I will ask my traveling companion—his name is Luke—to provide a copy of the statement made by King Agrippa II, who heard my case in Caesarea about three years ago. The king is Jewish and should therefore best be able to judge my guilt or innocence."

I then presented a copy of what I had previously written in my second treatise [Acts 26:31-32]: "'This man is doing nothing to deserve death or imprisonment.' And Agrippa said to Festus, 'This man could have been set free if he had not appealed to Caesar.'"

Now we waited for Nero to give his judgment. The evidence showed that Paul was clearly innocent, but Tigellinus, the accuser [prosecutor], was Nero's closest friend, and Caesar wanted to reward him. He made a show of consulting with his assessors, but then he announced his decision as to condemnation or absolution.

"Paul of Tarsus," he said, "I herewith condem . . . I con . . . I ca . . ." He stopped speaking. His face grew red, and he started coughing. Then he said softly, "I absolve you."

God, the Father of our Lord Jesus Christ, again stood by Paul to control Caesar's speech, and he was set free. All the brethren in Rome rejoiced that he had been restored to them, offering prayers of thanksgiving to God, who had again delivered his servant.

We remained in Rome for several months, confirming fellow believers in the faith, and then we left the city in great joy for Puteoli [on the Bay of Naples], where we spent another week with the brethren there. Then we found a ship bound for Spain and set sail aboard it.

Shannon put down the translation and realized she'd been quietly weeping. She wiped her eyes, shaking her head back and forth in awe over what she had just read. Finally she said, "So *that's* what happened after the record in Acts breaks off! Jon, this is just . . . fabulous new information—absolutely *fabulous*! But help me a bit with these new characters. Seneca I know, but who is that Tigellinus character?"

"Seneca and Tigellinus were the good and bad influences, respectively, in Nero's life. Seneca tutored young Nero and really did a great job of running the Roman government for the first five years of Nero's administration while that teenager was still growing up. But shortly after the events you just read, Seneca retired because Tigellinus, the nasty new prefect of the Praetorian guard, was gaining more and more influence over Nero. From then on, that walking glob of garbage pandered to Nero's every whim and seduced him into the debauchery for which he would later become notorious."

"Well, maybe that explains why Nero doesn't seem to be the brutal monster here that we usually expect, even though his bias for Tigellinus was pretty disgusting. But in your translation, he seems almost 'normal,' shall we say?"

"Yes, he was. Exactly. Seneca ran Rome for Nero's first five years—wrote his speeches, handled his appearances—and he did such a great job of it that the later emperor Trajan would claim that the *quinquennium Neronis*—the first five years of Nero—were the finest government Rome ever had. And Trajan was right: Seneca was also the great Stoic philosopher, you'll recall."

"And was he really Gallio's brother?"

"Yep!"

"Why didn't they have a common name, then?"

"Gallio's original name was Annaeus Novatus, brother of Annaeus Seneca, but he was adopted by a wealthy, childless senator named Lucius Junius Gallio the Elder. The one who judged Paul was Gallio the Younger."

"And Paul knew all that?"

"He must have, which probably is why he appealed to the tribunal of Nero in the first place. Paul had *some* kind of friend at court—the very brother of the man who had set him free in Corinth!"

Shannon grinned and nodded. "That Paul was a survivor. But one of the arguments raised on his behalf was that Christianity was not illegal. If so, then why did Nero persecute believers? He's notorious for that."

"This is AD 62, Shannon. The Great Fire of Rome didn't ignite until July of 64, two years later. When Nero got blamed for that, he switched the blame to the Christians in order to save himself. Christianity was illegal only from that point on."

"And that Flavius Sabinus person? Was he really mayor of Rome at that time? And a Christian?"

"'Yes' to the first, and 'we're not sure' for the second. His mother-in-law was Christian, and his sons definitely were since one of them died as a martyr. But I haven't told you yet who his brother was, have I?"

"No, but I didn't ask."

"Ask."

"Okay, who was Sabinus's brother?"

"Merely a fellow named Flavius Vespasian, the future emperor of Rome."

She laughed. "Oh, Jon, this is unbelievable. That part of Second Acts pulls it all together, doesn't it, like some kind of crossroads of the past."

"Now you see why I'm just a wee bit excited over all this?" Then he stopped smiling and added, "It's just . . . so sad that the church couldn't have had this document over most of the past centuries."

CHAPTER 19

THREE WEEKS LATER, Jon called to order the special session of the Institute of Christian Origins and welcomed twelve guest scholars from the Center for the Study of New Testament Manuscripts. He also introduced Monsignor Kevin Sullivan, who had flown in from Rome. Under one roof, then, were many of the world's finest experts on textual scholarship. Some had been on translation committees of such modern New Testament versions as the RSV, NRSV, TEB, NIV, Jerusalem Bible, ESV, NLT, and an alphabet soup of others. Almost all had managed to massage their schedules, simply canceling any impediments in view of the important announcement they suspected was awaiting them in Cambridge.

"Ladies and gentlemen—fellow scholars," Jon opened, "I thank you all for disrupting previous plans in order to be present today. I hope you'll find that effort more than rewarded. What I'll announce shortly is something so unparalleled, so very extraordinary, that your critical faculties *must* immediately question these discoveries, and I actually look forward to any decent skepticism in that regard."

Smiles broke out around the two long boardroom tables that had been set up.

"When you do digest the tidings I bring—*and* if you're able to put your skepticism on a short tether—your first impulse will be to call home, call friends and colleagues, call your university, or call the media. Doing so, however, will only complicate the very exciting task ahead of us. And so I'm pleading for a latter-day miracle, namely, that even though there are fifty-eight people in this room, we maintain strict secrecy until we've made all appropriate preparations prior to a general announcement to the world. Might we agree on that?"

The last phrase raised a buzz around both tables, along with the expected affirmations. The irrepressible von Schwendener, sitting to the chair's left, whispered, "What is this, Jon—another Dead Sea Scrolls discovery?"

"No, Heinz, it's much more important than that."

"What?" he erupted in hardly a whisper.

Jon resumed. "Since context is of utmost importance, let's begin by giving you the background of what we found. First, archaeologist Shannon Jennings Weber—who also happens to be my wife—will discuss her dig at Pella last summer."

Shannon summarized her experiences in the Trans-Jordan, focusing on her serendipitous trip to the little Greek Orthodox church, her dialogue with the priest in charge, and her discovery of the Hegesippus copy that mentioned Luke's third treatise to Theophilus, presumably "Second Acts." This raised a fusillade of questions from the group, many of them answered when she flashed a slide of the manuscript page involved on a screen at the end of the conference room.

"This gave us the first hint that our New Testament canon *might* not be entirely complete," Shannon concluded. "Yet later, when Jon and I were on our manuscript hunt this past summer and inquired of archivists and authorities at Athens, Meteora, and Mount Athos, no one had ever heard of a second Acts, and so it dropped from our 'desktop,' so to speak."

"Did you find any other references to it since then?" asked Henry Innes MacAdam of Princeton.

"Stay tuned, Mac," Shannon said with a little smile.

Next, Jon reported briefly on their experiences at the other Greek archives but devoted the lion's share of his time to their dialogues with Bartholomew II and their experiences at his Ecumenical Patriarchate in Istanbul. His graphic report was only enhanced as he flashed image after image on the screen of the patriarchate. When he reached the *geniza*, however, the room stilled to a hush. These scholars knew that this was where many great discoveries had been made in the past.

They were not disappointed. First Jon showed a series of photographs of the ancient bookstand in the southwest corner of the room, then a close-up shot of the codex itself. Several photographs of the codex followed after it had been placed on the worktable.

Jon would have signaled a drum roll, if such had been available, for he announced, "The next photograph, my colleagues, you will never forget." On a full screen, he projected the title page of the codex and waited silently for it to sink in.

One by one, little whimpers of recognition broke out along both tables as they translated the Greek, then louder and louder comments until Jon finally said, "Yes, my friends. As you have no doubt discerned for yourselves, this is one of the fifty copies of the New Testament that the Emperor Constantine authorized Eusebius of Caesarea to prepare on the finest vellum available!"

After a moment of sepulchral silence, boisterous applause broke out at the conference tables. Edwin Yamauchi of Oxford exclaimed, "Good heavens! Scholars have been searching for one of those ever since textual scholarship began with Erasmus in the sixteenth century! *Please* tell us you have the entire Bible here."

"Wish I could, Ed. But here's a consolation prize: how about the entire . . . New . . . Testament?"

Bedlam took over the chamber. There was cheering and roaring and raucous celebration. Jon finally had to remonstrate, tongue in cheek, "Tsk, tsk, my colleagues. As critical scholars, aren't we supposed to be cool and dispassionate about this?"

When the chuckling ceased, Jon continued. "Well, my friends, all future editions of the Greek New Testament will have to take this manuscript into account." He flashed page after page of the beautiful four columns of Greek on vellum. "Obviously, we now have one of the great uncial codices of the New Testament, which is clearly the equal—if not the superior—of the *Sinaiticus*, the *Vaticanus*, and the *Alexandrinus*."

"Oh, *that's* for sure," Brendan Rutledge said. "I think this, not the *Sinaiticus*, could well be the new *aleph*!" He referred to the "א" symbol designating the first and greatest uncial text.

"Now jest a cotton-pickin' minute," called out Jesse Trumbull of New Orleans Baptist Seminary. "We've all heard the expression, 'This is too good to be true,' and then that lit'rally *is* the case: *not* true! Professor Weber has shown us some mighty intriguin' material here, but it's only slides and images—not the actual document itself. Now I'm sure he doesn't mean to trick us, but aren't we all critical scholars here? Why do we fall all over ourselves to assume that this is authentic and then go hollerin' and cheerin' and carryin' on? Remember Bernard Madoff? He was the best in the business when it came to Wall Street—until they found out that he was only the biggest Ponzi around. Hey, I'm not sayin' that Jon's any Madoff, and all this may be right as rain, but don't we have to ask the good professor about the codex itself and its whereabouts?"

"Yes, I think we do," Jon responded, smiling. "And I'm so glad you brought this up, Jesse. Shannon and I were also somewhat skeptical at first, but when we photographed page after page after page, we realized that this could not possibly be forged. Still, we plan to do appropriate authenticity testing of the codex itself as soon as we can. And in answer to your question about its location, we left it with the Ecumenical Patriarch in Istanbul, since it *is* the property of the Eastern Orthodox Church. To be sure, we gave him some firm suggestions as to optimal security arrangements and preservation of that extraordinary document."

"Well, I'm happy to hear that," Trumbull replied.

"Have you read it all yet, Jon?" Sally Humiston wondered.

"'Checked it all out' might be the best answer, though I have read some parts in much greater detail than others. The material reflects the same general manuscript tradition as the *Sinaiticus*, but with several *very* important differences: our codex, for example, does *not* include the Epistle of Barnabas or Shepherd of Hermas as does the *Sinaiticus*."

"What does it include?" Mac MacAdam asked.

"Simply and happily, all twenty-seven books of our canonical New Testament—no more, no less." Then he caught himself and added, "No, sorry. I misspoke."

"You did?" Mac persisted. "Would you care to unpack that?"

Jon paused for several moments, then said, "Well, I guess it's time to unload another little surprise for you." He pressed a button on his laptop and flashed more columns of beautiful, uncial Greek onto the screen. It was the last chapter of Mark. "Here we have the last chapter of Mark from the codex," he added.

For some time, the room was silent, since the Greek lettering, while clear, was very difficult to decipher in its run-together form.

"Anyone notice anything amiss?" Jon finally asked.

The eagle eye of Trina Vandersteen suddenly picked it up. "Hold it!" she said. "There's too much material there—it should be only eight verses' worth, no? You've got—what?—looks like almost three times that much text."

Jon nodded, letting the implications slowly sink in.

Von Schwendener suddenly exploded. "Omigosh! Give us a break, Jon. You're not going to tell us that . . . that this is the lost ending of Mark, are you?"

Quietly he replied, "You've got it, Heinz."

A wild potpourri of surprise and awe filled the room, supposedly staid scholars ripping off their glasses or putting them on—depending on their ocular needs—as they tried to scan the text more closely.

Several minutes later, Jon announced, "I'm passing out my rough translation of the lost ending, although I'm sure one of the committees to come out of this group will do a better job."

Silence reigned as each read the words Mark had actually written at the close of his Gospel. Scholars joined other scholars sitting nearby in a sudden buzz of discussion that picked up tempo and intensity.

Brendan Rutledge spoke up first. "Tends to support the Synoptic hypothesis, doesn't it?"

Jon smiled at this and winked at Shannon.

Daniel Wallace, from the Center for the Study of New Testament Manuscripts, raised his hand. "Thanks, Jon, for inviting our group to this *historic* occasion. And I don't use that adjective lightly, since there's no question but that this codex, if authentic, is the greatest find in centuries of textual scholarship. Our group has dreamed of coming across a text like this, yet we dismissed it as wishful thinking. We were wrong! Now, what do you propose as a modus operandi for this discovery?"

"Thanks, Dan! I was coming to that." Jon distributed another handout. "I propose that we establish a 'Mark 16 Blue Ribbon Task Force' and charge it with items listed on what I've just distributed."

The conferees read:

- Compare the uncial lettering of the new material in this manuscript with the Markan text immediately preceding it. This will determine if another ancient hand tried to supply the ending, as happened subsequently in later texts.

- Do a complete linguistic analysis of these verses, again comparing them with the grammar and syntax in the rest of the Markan text.
- Provide an authoritative translation of these final verses into English. (Other translations can follow later.)
- Write an official commentary on these verses, explaining how Mark's ending had originally been lost—if true—and the significance of these verses for Synoptic scholarship and especially in the reportage of the resurrection of Jesus.

The silence was quickly broken. "Hear, hear!" "Good plan!" "Let's do it" and other affirmatives welled up from both tables. Just before lunch, the ICO and CSNTM had even appointed twenty of their finest New Testament scholars to the task force. To these, Jon handed out enhanced digital images of all pages of Mark's Gospel in the codex.

"Just remember, good colleagues," Jon cautioned, "every last page of the codex is now copyrighted—my Harvard colleague Alan Dershowitz prepared an airtight instrument for us—so don't run off to publishers and try to get rich on Mark!"

Jon was smiling and the rest chuckled, but amid the mirth the message was quite loud and quite clear.

✣ ✣ ✣

Not one person in the group recalled, a year later, what they had eaten for their catered lunch. They were less diners and more a buzzing beehive of excitement over the codex.

Sitting adjacent from Jon and Shannon, von Schwendener

asked, "Anything important for this afternoon, Jon? Or can we wrap it up early? I'd like to catch the four o'clock train for New Haven."

Sure, take off, Yalie yahoo, Jon thought, *and miss more of the biggest story of your life!* But all he said, charitably, was "Try to stick around, Heinz."

Jon began the afternoon session by flashing two pages from the codex on the screen side by side: the last page of Acts and the first of Second Acts, though with the title hidden. The two pages simply hung on the screen for endless moments, but this time no one got the message. Kevin Sullivan knew, of course, but he held his tongue.

"All right," Jon said. "I suppose I'd best drop a hint. The left-hand page is the close of *Praxeis Apostolon*. . . ."

"Okay," Rutledge offered. "Acts of the Apostles . . ."

"Right, Brandon." Jon flipped a switch. "And what's the title of the next book on the opposite side—Romans?"

Rutledge stared. "It's . . . *Praxeis Apostolon Beta* . . . *Beta*? What in the world?"

Sally Humiston screamed something unintelligible, followed by a more coherent "Not Acts 2? I mean, Second Acts? That reference in Hegesippus that Shannon found?"

Jon caught Shannon's eyes and grinned and nodded.

"It's *really* in that codex?" Sally asked, almost shouting.

"Yes it is, Sal."

Silence in the room was deafening. The conclave of world-class scholars sat around the conference tables collectively stunned, many with open mouths and wide eyes.

Finally Edwin Yamauchi collected himself enough to ask, "Well, what does it say? Have you been able to read it?"

"Yes, we have, Ed," Jon replied. "It's shorter than our lengthy book of Acts. Luke beautifully ties down all the threads he left hanging in Acts. It turns out that he faithfully stayed with Paul for the rest of his days, so it has all the eyewitness appeal of his previous writings. It begins with a précis of Paul's trial before Nero—and the *fascinating* reason he had appealed to Nero in the first place—and then goes on to his acquittal—yes, his acquittal! Their voyage to Spain followed. They landed there at Valencia—Valentia in those days—where they spent fourteen months establishing a mission that not only survived but flourished."

Heads shook in bewilderment. Looks were exchanged around the tables, until finally everyone turned toward Jon to hear if there was any more.

Jon resumed. "From there we have something of a fourth missionary journey, when Paul and Luke sailed first to Sicily and then on to Crete, where Paul ordained Titus to carry on the work there. Then it was back to Miletus and Ephesus, where Timothy rejoined them, Paul all the while confirming early Christians in the faith.

"Again he faced opposition in Ephesus—why in the world couldn't he have stayed out of that trouble spot?—but this time a human glob of scum named Alexander the Coppersmith got all the metalworkers in Ephesus to riot against Paul once again, as they had in Acts 19. But this turned out to be a dangerous embarrassment to the Roman governor of Asia because Nero was just across the Aegean at the time, giving his infamous concert tour of Greece in the year 65. So Paul was quickly arrested and shipped off to Rome again, where he was imprisoned for the second time.

"This time, though, Paul was in mortal danger because the Great Fire of Rome had broken out the year before, for which Nero blamed the Christians to save his own hide. Now they were outlawed. And now Paul stood trial again, not before Nero—who was still singing his recitals in Greece, if you can believe it—but before Nero's man Helius, who condemned Paul to death. And yes, he was indeed taken out on the Ostian Way and executed about a mile outside the Ostian Gate—where the Basilica of St. Paul Outside the Walls stands today. Constantine was right on target when he built the original basilica where he did.

"Well, that was a long speech, but I wanted to hit the high points of what's in Second Acts."

Dead silence continued until Katrina Vandersteen put her head down on the conference table and broke out sobbing. Others also had tears either in their eyes or coursing down their cheeks, so strong were the emotional currents swirling through the room on that memorable day. Jon, however, knew there were *two* reasons for Vandersteen's tears; she had just completed a commentary on the Book of Acts and sent it off to her publisher, but now it had become virtually obsolete.

A pall of shock continued to shroud the conference. It was like breaking the news to Bartholomew II all over again, this time multiplied by the fifty-eight people present in that crowded room. Jon knew he was seeing church history made that day, as, very slowly, each one present came to terms with the implications not only of the rediscovered ending to Mark, but of Second Acts as well. Both of them could conceivably be added to the canon of Holy Scripture, provided the texts warranted it.

Predictably von Schwendener broke the silence. "I think I'll take the four o'clock back to New Haven, Jon—next Tuesday."

Jon chuckled. "No, Heinz, we just can't have you on our hands that long! Now, patient colleagues, I'm passing out my preliminary translation of Second Acts. I finally completed that task—and it *was* a task!—yesterday. Please know that it's *not* an authoritative translation, just a possible first draft. Now, if you'll permit, I think we should take a break so you can all read it. I think you'll . . . well, I think you'll be entranced."

✢ ✢ ✢

When they had finished the reading and refilled their coffee cups, all wanted to know: "Where's the final scene? Or did Luke break off just before Paul's execution—and leave us hanging *again*?"

"No, he provided it all," Jon replied. "I merely wanted the opportunity to read it aloud to you first. It's very, very . . . moving." He picked up his script and read:

> When word came that Paul was to be executed, Timothy, Mark, and I, as well as elders of the church at Rome, accompanied Paul on his final journey from the Castra Praetoria, where he had been imprisoned, to the Ostian Gate at the south of Rome. He wore a purple cloak that Lydia had made for him. We passed through the gate and

walked a Sabbath day's journey down the Ostian Way to avoid the curious. Finally we came to a green, open spot called the Waters of Sage, which the centurion approved.

Paul now took leave of us all and commended the church to God. He said, "This is only the beginning of a cause that will one day become far greater than the Roman Empire. The Caesars will perish, but Christ will triumph, my beloved, and you will all be his ambassadors in building the greatest structure this world has ever seen: the holy Christian church. And we will all see each other again in the paradise that he has prepared for us. So do not weep for me, but comfort one another with these words."

When the centurion said that all was ready, Paul said, "The time of my departure has come, my beloved friends. As I once wrote you, Timothy, I have fought the good fight. I have finished the race. I have kept the faith. And now the prize is waiting for me—the crown of righteousness that the Lord, the perfect Judge, will award to me on that great day. And not to me only, but to you as well—and all who await his coming. May the grace of our Lord Jesus Christ, the love of God the Father, and the fellowship of the Holy Spirit be with you all."

Then he fell to his knees, bared his neck, and bowed his head in prayer, saying, "Into your hands, O Lord, I commend my spirit."

The centurion raised his sword with both hands and brought it down in one strong sweep. In our anguish, we buried this greatest apostle in a sepulchre nearby that was provided by one of the elders of the church. On his breast we placed a small cross of wood, the emblem of what has become the center of everything he preached and taught.

Then we returned to Rome, grieving and yet thanking and praising God for having given us so great a representative of our Lord and Savior Jesus Christ. Amen. Thanks be to God.

Jon's voice broke toward the end, and he found it difficult to regain his composure. Finally he cleared his throat and said, "That's it, my colleagues. Now I'll pass out these final two pages of my translation. Please add it to the others."

A sacred silence hovered over the conference tables, not one voice daring to break the mood of profound awe. All had returned to Cambridge at Jon's request, expecting that they would, no doubt, be privy to some fascinating discovery, but Jon knew that the codex and its surprises were vastly more than they could ever have anticipated. It was almost as if their minds were now out of breath, so to speak, and needed some downtime.

It was the chair's responsibility to bring the conclave back to life. Again Jon cleared his throat. "Now, perhaps, it's time to . . . to get a few reactions from the group? Comments of any kind?"

That opened the floodgates. Torrents of response poured out across the room like a deluge-swollen waterfall, and Jon was hard-pressed to keep those with hands raised in numerical order for recognition. Many of the comments were variations on the theme of how much the new material sounded like the rest of what Luke wrote in his Gospel and the book of Acts, citing example after example.

"Not to pat ourselves on the back," Mac MacAdam said, "but the way many of us had theoretically reconstructed what happened to Paul after Acts breaks off turned out to be pretty close to the mark. It's exciting to see hypothesis turn into fact—well, once again, with that nagging proviso: authenticity."

"And on that subject," Jon responded, "I have not the slightest doubt *whatever* that our codex is authentic. Who, in the name of God-given common sense, could have faked page after page after page of this codex in fourth-century Greek uncials? The answer, of course, is no one, no one at all. *Still*, because the masses out there would be howling otherwise, we plan to test the codex as much as if we suspected that it was a crude fraud."

"What sort of tests?" Ed Yamauchi wondered.

"Two kinds: linguistic and material tests. Clearly, the Mark 16 Blue-Ribbon Task Force is our exemplar here, and the same procedures will apply also to Second Acts, which, obviously, will take much longer to implement in view of the larger amount of material."

Brendan Rutledge raised his pen. "Why, then, don't we change the name of the Mark 16 group to . . . say . . . the Constantine Codex Task Force, in view of its added responsibilities?"

Much affirmative nodding followed. "I like it, Brendan," Jon said. "What about the 'Blue Ribbon' part of it?"

"*Forget* the Blue Ribbon!" von Schwendener bellowed. "Who ever attached that stupid phrase to task forces in the first place? It was good only for Pabst beer!"

General laughter erupted, a welcome release.

Dan Wallace raised a sober warning. "You realize, of course, that it'll be next to impossible to keep a secret of this colossal size under wraps for very long, don't you, Jon? It would take God's own miracle to keep the news from spilling out over the months it'll take to do a full commentary."

"Right! I guess that's part of the package: the greater the discovery, the less the chances of keeping it secret. And yet, somehow we *must*. We've *got* to hold the news or our work will be constantly interrupted by the media. Any bright ideas?"

Shannon volunteered. "Why don't we suspend the commentary part of it? Commentaries on the Mark material and Second Acts will be written for years to come in any case. If we wait until we also produce any sort of 'official commentary,' it could take years and years—like the notorious delay in getting all the Dead Sea Scrolls edited and translated. Over that long a period, confidentiality would be outright *impossible*. So I propose that on the day we go public with this, we provide only the Greek text, as well as an official English translation that will have just a few commentary footnotes on each page, very much like our present-day study Bibles."

The conference mulled it over. Finally Sally Humiston said, "That's good, Shannon, *really* good! I'm all for it. I really think that's the way we ought to go."

Shouts of "Hear, hear!" rattled across the room, and it was so decided.

"Now you see why I married this wonder woman," Jon said gallantly—and honestly. He bent over and gave her a big hug.

"Not here, Jon," she whispered in embarrassment.

"On another matter," he resumed, "I wonder if those whom

we haven't shanghaied for the Constantine Codex Task Force might be willing to serve on another committee with an almost equally crucial function. Its charge will be to ponder two very simple questions, but their recommendations might really shake this planet. Here, I think, are the two questions: One, should the ICO suggest that the New Testament canon be opened to include not only the true ending of Mark's Gospel, but also the second book of Acts? And two, if so, how can this best be achieved?"

There were many indrawn breaths, yet no one volunteered a word.

"Good," Jon said. "Any attempt at an answer would be utter folly at this point. After I pass out copies of the Greek text of Second Acts, will those not on the Constantine Codex Task Force be kind enough to serve on the second committee?" He looked around the room and saw more than enough hands raised to form that committee as well.

"Excellent!" he said. "As we close, let me remind all of you how much I hate slogans, cutesy acrostics, and above all, convention themes, all of them ruined by speaker after speaker inflicting deadly boredom on their hearers through mindless repetition of the theme. And yet it seems that I myself have succumbed. Please let the initials of the USA inform our procedures from this point on: Urgency, Secrecy, Action!"

CHAPTER 20

JON INVITED KEVIN SULLIVAN to spend the night with them in Weston, and he was delighted to accept. After dinner, they had a predictably lively chat—a fireside version since it was a cool night in late October.

"I should have kept you in better touch, Kev," Jon said, "but all this broke rather quickly for us, as you now know."

"Wouldn't have missed today's meeting for the world, Jon. I think it was the start of a great chapter in church history—heck, in general history—and I was here to witness it. But when can I tell the Holy Father?"

"Thought you'd never ask! And the answer is obvious: just as soon as you return to Rome. For the moment, please reproduce the handouts only once and for his eyes only. Benedict will understand, I'm sure."

"Of course he will, and he'll also be elated beyond measure."

"He *will*? I worry that you conservative Catholics might find a potential *new* New Testament upsetting."

"Only if any of the new material contradicted the old, but that doesn't seem to be the case at all. Instead, it corroborates and expands on our present New Testament. Nothing wrong with that . . . in fact, everything *right* with that."

"You think he might even consider . . . opening the Canon, then?"

"Well, I didn't say that. Besides, I think it would take nothing less than an ecumenical council to decide that."

"Yes, I think so too. Hard to imagine what that would even look like, isn't it? But that's getting *way* ahead of ourselves. Right now, somehow, I've got to pry the codex out of the hands of the Ecumenical Patriarch in Istanbul so we can test it here in the States. And getting it here could be quite complicated. Any inspired ideas on how to pull that off?"

"Oh, just have him send it surface mail. Ships are quite reliable when it comes to delivery. That should do."

Jon did a double take, at which Kevin broke out laughing. "I really know how to pull your chain, don't I, Jon?"

"Ever the Jesuit jester! Okay, let's get serious. I think I overdid it in claiming I'd have to 'pry' the codex out of the patriarch's hands. I'm sure he'd cooperate, but that doesn't solve the political problem or the logistics. Even though the codex would merely be on loan to us, the Turkish government might not let it out of the country, especially if they had any inkling how incredibly important it is."

"I'm afraid that's true. All the Mediterranean countries are now supersensitive about antiquities being 'plundered' from them, as they put it."

They pondered the problem for some minutes. Suddenly Kevin said, "Wait a minute; I do have an idea. When's the last time Bartholomew visited the U.S.?"

"I'm not sure he ever has."

"Better yet! Why not have, say, St. Vladimir's seminary in New York invite the eastern pope to America? That way he could bring the codex along as part of his official sacred baggage, so to speak. Pope Benedict has visited the U.S. several times; why not the eastern pontiff?"

"Why not indeed! Good thinking, Kev."

"And if a Turkish customs official dared to check out Bartholomew's carry-on items, he could say that the codex, although old, was to be used in liturgical worship while he was in America. He wouldn't have to tell them *how* old it is. Or the testing that's planned. Or why."

Jon frowned. "But it's not the whole truth, Kev. See, that's what I dislike about you Jesuits. You never got beyond 'the end justifies the means' mentality with your Jesuitical lies . . ."

Kevin stared in shock at his friend.

"Ha! Gotcha." Jon burst out with a huge guffaw. "Tit for tat! I really know how to pull *your* chain, don't I, Kev? No, it's a *great* plan! Wish I'd have thought of it in the first place!"

✠ ✠ ✠

Over the next weeks, the plan was implemented. First, Jon Express Mailed the patriarch all the materials he had passed out to the scholars in Cambridge. Next, St. Vladimir's Orthodox

Theological Seminary at Crestwood in Greater New York City was more than cooperative. Not only would they be honored by such a visit, but so would the Eastern Orthodox Church bodies in the United States and their members, nearly two million strong. The seminary would also be glad to arrange cross-country appearances for Bartholomew, if he wished, and they sent the Ecumenical Patriarch a warm and enthusiastic invitation.

When he received the glad word that Bartholomew had accepted, Jon arranged a phone conversation with the patriarch over a secure line through the U.S. consulate in Istanbul. Bartholomew understood immediately the other purpose for his visit and even assured Jon that the whole transaction would be absolutely ethical, since the codex was clearly the property of the Eastern Orthodox Patriarchate, not the Republic of Turkey.

Jon was elated and had already set up a testing schedule for the codex both at the Smithsonian in Washington and the radiocarbon labs at the University of Arizona in Tucson. Both institutions had reported that the five brownish leaves Shannon had discovered were datable to the third century and fully authentic.

The patriarch's visit was scheduled to begin just after Epiphany. Jon and Shannon could barely wait to see the codex again. The document had become part of their very lives. Never had Advent seemed more anticipatory—or longer. For once, their central focus at the close of the year was not Christmas but Epiphany.

By some divine intervention, apparently, the great scholarly secret seemed to be holding, and the two codex task forces were making dedicated progress. Perhaps, with testing complete, the public announcement could come later that spring.

✢ ✢ ✢

On January 8, Jon and Shannon were in New York to be part of the welcoming party at JFK, along with a delegation from St. Vladimir's. In the process of receiving the Ecumenical Patriarch, of course, Jon was virtually lusting after his literary special delivery. The arriving coterie of Eastern Orthodox clergy stood in marked contrast to the other travelers as they emerged through customs—uniformly black gowns, suits, and hats against a cavalcade of color among the other passengers. Jon and Shannon spied Bartholomew before he saw them, that tall figure of patriarchal dignity who seemed almost haloed from the rest. They hurried to greet him.

"A most cordial welcome, Your All Holiness!" Jon said. "How very delightful to see you again!"

"Ah, my most worthy professor and his lovely wife! It is most kind of you to receive us! May God bless our time together!"

Now, the usual rituals had to take place. After introductions by the welcoming delegation from St. Vladimir's and the metropolitans of the various Orthodox jurisdictions, there was the usual posing for photographs by the media, prying microphones, network reporters pleading for sound bites, and a nice but mercifully brief welcome from the mayor of New York. He presented the Ecumenical Patriarch the ceremonial key to the city that would, Jon knew, open nothing.

Per advance agreement, Bartholomew and his delegation stopped at the international VIP sky lounge at JFK for some brief R & R before the ride into Manhattan. While members of the patriarch's party took their afternoon coffee—or ouzo—

Bartholomew and Gregorios met with Jon and Shannon in a small private conference room. With an air of relief, the patriarch handed Jon a large, padded, black leather attaché case containing the codex and offered a brief prayer for its safety during the testing process.

With gratitude and an equal sense of relief, Jon accepted the case and tried the latches, just to make sure everything functioned properly. When the bronze latches popped open, he lifted the lid and there it was, lying in a red velvet-covered cushion of foam rubber on all sides: the document that had become the center of their lives, the document that would change history. The patriarch had taken good care of it indeed, even having that special case fashioned to the contours of the Constantine Codex.

Jon pushed one of the latches shut and was ready to do the same for the other when Shannon said, "Please, let's sneak another peek at it before you close it, Jon."

"We just saw it."

"I mean, I only want a quick glimpse of a page of text again. I've actually . . . missed it, strange as that may seem."

"I don't think it strange at all," Jon said. "I feel the same way."

Bartholomew and Gregorios looked on and smiled, sharing an almost-sacred sympathy for the text.

The clasps popped open again, and Jon carefully lifted the codex out of the cavity prepared for it.

"Strange," Jon said. "I don't recall that the cover was this well preserved." He opened the codex . . . and gasped. He turned several pages frantically and gasped even more loudly. There was no vellum, no uncials written in four neat columns, *nothing*—other than several hundred pages of cheap, bare white foolscap.

Jon stood, pulse coursing wildly, and asked the patriarch to step over to his side of the table. Bartholomew did so, a quizzical look in his eyes.

"O The Mou!" the Ecumenical Patriarch cried. "This cannot be! Gregorios, come! Look!"

When he did so, his face contorted into that of a gargoyle. He turned several pages, teetered, and then collapsed into a chair. "This . . . this is not possible!"

The scene had become surreal. *Yes, this is not a bad dream,* Jon had to remind himself. *Yes, we are in New York. Yes, the people are real.* Yet they were all staring at an impossibility.

Jon came alive with a fusillade of queries. "Did you check this through with your luggage or as a carry-on, Your All Holiness?"

"As a carry-on, certainly."

"And was it in your possession the whole time?"

"Yes, yes, it was."

"Ever since you left the patriarchate?"

"Yes."

"Did you open the case and the codex just before leaving the patriarchate?"

"Oh yes, it was the last thing I did."

"You opened it up and saw the vellum pages, the uncials . . . ?"

"Yes. I even read the opening words of Matthew's Gospel: 'The book of the genealogy of Jesus Christ, the Son of David, the Son of Abraham.' Then I closed it and blessed it."

"How did you get to the airport?"

"We drove in a BMW owned by the patriarchate. When I

entered our car, Brother Gregorios put the case into the trunk, along with our other luggage."

"When you arrived at the airport, did this case stay with you?"

"I carried it myself for the patriarch," Gregorios said.

"Did you open the case at the airport?"

"Yes . . ."

"And the codex was inside?"

"Yes."

"Did you open the codex?"

He paused and frowned. "No, I . . . I did not."

"Was there, perhaps, some reason why you did not?" Jon felt he had to tread gingerly here to avoid giving the impression that he was some sort of grilling prosecutor.

"We were at the customs line, and everyone seemed to be rushed. Besides, the codex was there."

"What happened when you went through customs?"

"They waved us through," the monk replied.

"But the case had to go through security just before the gates, right?"

"Yes."

"And it went through?"

"Yes."

"And this was the only time it was not in your hands? Or those of the Ecumenical Patriarch?"

"Yes, the only time."

"And you had it with you at all times in the departure lounge?"

"Yes. I hardly ever took my eyes off it."

"But you didn't open the codex again?"

Gregorios hesitated—was it embarrassment?—and said, "No."

"And on the flight to New York—where did you stow it?"

"In the overhead storage bin, where there was plenty of room."

"And when you went through customs here in New York?"

"They just told us to go through. Nothing was searched."

Jon worked on the options, one by one. At last he said, "Now, this is important. When is the last time you saw the actual pages of vellum and the uncials written on them?"

Gregorios looked at Bartholomew and both had to agree. "When we left the patriarchate."

"And that was the last time you opened the codex? Not after you went through security?"

"No, that was the last time. Now I see that this . . . this was a terrible failure on our part . . ."

While Jon was tempted to agree, he guarded his tongue. "Well, with the case intact—this *is* the original case, isn't it?"

"Oh yes. . . ."

"With the original case in your hands, you'd really have no reason to open it. Please don't be too hard on yourselves."

It seemed only a modest comfort for the patriarch and his archivist. Both were terribly distraught. Shannon looked quite pale. Jon fought off the feelings of despair welling up inside him with a boiling anger that the prize should have been snatched from them just before the moment of victory. He paced around the conference room, one hand wringing the other for an explanation.

Clearly, the codex had been stolen sometime between

Bartholomew's leaving the patriarchate and his arrival in America—a bewilderingly broad span of time and place. One obvious, unguarded period of time would have been while the case was in the overhead bin on the transatlantic flight. They had flown business class, so the perpetrator most likely also had a business-class ticket, although he might have penetrated the business-class cabin if the flight attendants were chatting among themselves, as was often the case.

Jon explained his thinking to the others. Then he asked, "During the flight, did either of you notice anyone opening or trying to open your particular overhead bin?"

The two Greeks looked at each other; both shook their heads.

"Then, if it did happen on the flight, it would have to have taken place while you were both sleeping."

"But even if they were, Jon," Shannon interposed, "what about the others in their delegation? Wouldn't they have noticed someone disturbing their overhead bins? *Were* the others near you on the flight, Brother Gregorios?"

"Yes, Madame Weber. We were all on the left side of the cabin."

"And you had daylight throughout your flight?"

"Yes, we 'chased the sun,' as we say it in Greek, all the way across the Atlantic."

"Good point, Shannon," Jon said. "So the only other times the case was out of your hands had to be when you left the patriarchate and it was put into the trunk of your limo and when it went through security at the departure in Istanbul. Please recall again everything that happened there—I mean, every last detail."

The patriarch took a deep breath. "We arrive at the airport.

We check in at the counter. All the time I am watching the black case, and so is Brother Gregorios. We take our boarding passes and carry-ons to the security line. We start to go through the line. But then they direct us to a special security line—probably to make it easier for us. We put our things in those gray plastic boxes and push them along the moving track. Here I watch the black case very carefully. The belt starts to move. It stops; it reverses. It starts again, then stops again and reverses several times. It often happens this way at airports."

"It happens *all* the time," Shannon commented.

"Yes. Then, as our case again goes through the machine, the scanner person looks at his screen and calls over a supervisor. They study the screen for a while. I worry that they may want to open the black case and give us problems with the codex. But this does not happen. Finally the belt moves on; we collect our things and walk to the gate."

Jon desperately wanted to get to the bottom of this, but he realized that it was time for the two to rejoin the rest of their delegation and get on with their American tour. "Clearly, this is a terrible setback for New Testament scholarship," he said. "I would ask your permission to let me have the Federal Bureau of Investigation check this fake document for fingerprints—which is always the first step. Then, with the cooperation of the Central Intelligence Agency, they'll want to analyze that worthless paper and the board cover for any clues as to their origin. It's just possible that the perpetrator was too clever by half in providing a substitute like this."

"Shouldn't we call the police in on this?" the patriarch wondered.

"Ordinarily I'd say, 'Yes, certainly,' Your All Holiness, but then our entire effort would no longer be confidential. It may, of course, come to that eventually."

"Well, thank God we have photographic copies of the entire text, Professor Weber," Bartholomew said. "You and your wife were wise to preserve those precious words."

✠ ✠ ✠

The following days were a hurricane of intelligence sleuthing for Jon. While the Eastern Orthodox faithful were giving the Ecumenical Patriarch an enthusiastic welcome, Jon convinced the CIA's Morton Dillingham to put the resources of the federal government, including the FBI, behind the case of the missing codex. In view of their past relationship, this had not been an easy task, but when Jon revealed the secret of the document's extraordinary importance to Christianity—and the world—Dillingham gave in. He was also impressed with Jon's savvy in trying to keep the find confidential as long as possible. Not a religious man himself, Dillingham nevertheless worshiped at the shrine of secrecy.

Over the next days, the FBI and CIA examined the fake codex in every way possible. They requisitioned the passenger manifest of everyone on the patriarch's flight, including the flight crew, and did background checks on every name on the list. CIA agents in Istanbul asked the Turkish equivalent of Dillingham to do the same with all security personnel on duty that morning at Ataturk International Airport.

To Jon's happy surprise, they pledged full cooperation. At first he wondered why Muslim authorities there would be willing to assist Christians in finding a stolen church document. He assumed it was because Turkey was a secular—not religious—state, a fact that the Turkish army had to remind the government of from time to time. So there was no Muslim fanaticism impeding their investigation. To be sure, the colossal significance of the codex was not mentioned to the Turks.

One overriding item, however, could not be overlooked. The possibility—indeed, the probability—had to be weighed that this was an inside job. How else could the perpetrator know the approximate size of the codex in order to plant the substitute? Or even know that the patriarch and his party would have the codex with them en route to the U.S.?

And why was a fake codex necessary in the first place? Why not outright theft with nothing left behind as a potential clue? Jon found a quick answer to that one: the perpetrator didn't want the theft discovered until the patriarch's party had left Turkey—perhaps banking on the attaché case not being opened until their arrival in the U.S.—in order to provide lead time to escape detection and apprehension.

In this scenario, someone at the patriarchate—perhaps their airport chauffeur?—could have been the perpetrator, either a Judas sort of Christian, or a crypto-Muslim member of the staff who somehow learned about the codex and its significance to the church. His motive? Eliminate a powerful prop for Christianity and do it in such a way as to leave the theft undetected as long as possible so all tracks could be covered. The perpetrator probably would have engaged several others to bring it off, either while unloading the limo's trunk at the airport or at airport security in Istanbul, or—less likely—on the flight itself. Jon would discuss these suspicions with the patriarch by phone while he was on his American tour.

The week that followed presented no meaningful clues. Background checks on all business-class passengers showed nothing unusual, nor for the other main cabin passengers and flight crew. Quite a few of the passengers had Turkish, Middle Eastern, or Arab names and were therefore most likely Islamic, but this proved nothing. CIA labs showed only that the paper used in the fake codex was common throughout the Middle East, with most of it manufactured in Egypt. But the page size was foolscap, or sixteen by thirteen inches, a now-rare dimension that nicely approximated the size of the pages in the codex.

✢ ✢ ✢

At dinner a week after Jon had returned from Washington, Shannon asked him, "Do you think we might be making too much of this?"

"What do you mean?"

"Well, we already have *every last word* of the text of the Constantine Codex, including the true ending of Mark and Second Acts. We have all anybody needs for the authoritative edition of the codex. In fact, scholars will be using our enhanced copies, not the codex itself, so why are we falling all over ourselves at the loss of the codex? It would have been a disaster if the material hadn't been copied, but it has. Sure, it would have been nice to have the codex on display, but at the end of the day, we really don't need it all that much, do we? Certainly not because of the testing."

"On that last point, sweetheart, sure, *we* don't need it for testing, but the rest of the world does. I can just hear critics of our discovery complain: 'Hey, these may be nice pictures of what's *supposed to be* in that old book, but *where's the real thing?*' Scholars wouldn't have a problem working from our copies, but we're talking *acceptance* here. Is the Constantine Codex just going to be a scholarly footnote in history, or will it be universally welcomed as the magnificent addendum to Scripture that it is?"

Shannon smiled wistfully at him. "You'd really like it if the last of Mark and Second Acts were added to the Canon, wouldn't you?"

Jon thought for a moment, was preparing something evasive, but then blurted it out. "Yes. With every fiber of my being, in view of how it fills two major gaps in the biblical record. I have no idea if the new material will land inside the Canon even *if* the codex were returned, but I do know this: it will *never* happen without the codex."

Shannon thought for a moment, then replied, "I hate to bring this up—and you may think I'm some sort of traitor—but isn't our discovery of the Constantine Codex enough in its own right? Why is it so important that the new material be added to the Canon? As a Christian, I don't really need it."

"I don't either. Not at all. But the non-Christian *world* does, Shannon. You know how heavily the Bible is being attacked today, and not just by atheists and agnostics. It seems to be a target for any half-baked pseudo-scholar with a new pet theory with which he hopes to pry Scripture apart and raise a sensation. Christ shows up as caricature in their put-downs, and the Resurrection is denied—for one reason, by the way Mark's

Gospel ends. The new material is *strong* support for the reliability of the New Testament."

Shannon had started nodding halfway through his statement. "I'm hoisting a white flag on that one, Jon. Most anything is better if its two missing parts are found."

✢ ✢ ✢

Jon's near mania to recover the codex led him down an extraordinary parallel track. Early the next morning, he put in a call to Kevin Sullivan at the Vatican. When he heard Sullivan's *"Pronto"* on the line, he said, "Sorry to interrupt your siesta, Kevin, but we have to talk."

"I don't do siestas, Jon. Wastes time. But what's so urgent?"

"For openers, how has Benedict XVI responded to the Constantine Codex?"

"Didn't you get my letter yet? I put it into hard copy since I also wanted a permanent record. The Holy Father greeted the news as if it were some sort of beatific revelation. And after he had read the new material, he seemed to be on cloud ten."

"Isn't that supposed to be cloud nine?"

"No, papal privilege. I've never seen him so enthused, never seen him happier. Don't forget, he's also a biblical scholar, and he saw at once how magnificently it all fit. He sends you his warmest greetings and, above all, his profound gratitude."

"Wow! Coming from the pope himself, that's . . . quite humbling."

"But he does have an urgent question for you, and here it is: '*When* may I share this glad news?'"

"In response to that, I have some . . . some very bad news."

Jon went on to report the theft of the codex and the status of its attempted recovery. Sullivan asked questions parallel to the queue of queries Jon had raised with Patriarch Bartholomew. Summing up the unhappy situation, Jon said, "So we've lost our main material link to one of the greatest manuscript discoveries ever. But I do have an idea for another route, Kevin. Before I suggest it, what's the security arrangement on your phone lines at the Vatican?"

"No problem there at all. They're fully secure."

"Still . . . can you get back to me this evening, using the private line at your apartment?"

"All right, Jon. If you insist."

"Have to. Thanks, Kev. Ciao!"

✠ ✠ ✠

That evening, were an earwitness present in Sullivan's Rome apartment, he would have heard one side of a dialogue that included comments like:

"You really *must* be kidding, Jon."

"Are you really playing with a full deck?"

"You know, of course, that what you're asking is impossible."

"*Obviously* the Holy Father can't be involved in this. . . ."

"Do you really want to commit professional suicide?"

"Well, I'll help you as much as I can, even though I think it's absolute lunacy."

CHAPTER 21

A WEEK LATER, KEVIN PICKED JON UP at Leonardo da Vinci Airport, and they drove into Rome over the same route as the ancient Ostian Way, the final road that the much-traveled apostle Paul had used on his way to execution. About a mile before they reached the Ostian Gate, Kevin pulled his car off to the right side of the road and parked in front of the Basilica of St. Paul Outside the Walls.

"Well, there it is, Jon, the Basilica di San Paolo fuori le Mura," Kevin said with a grin. "The scene of the crime."

"Oh, thanks for that vote of confidence, Kevin."

"I assumed you'd want to get the lay of the land—even before getting settled in."

"You've got it."

They walked into the colonnaded forecourt of the basilica.

There, in the midst of a well-clipped lawn guarded by two sentinel palm trees, stood a great stone statue of the apostle Paul, the sword of the Spirit in his right hand.

"Much too old and much too bearded," Jon commented. "Why do so many artists and sculptors get Paul wrong? He couldn't have been more than around fifty-five or sixty at the time of his death—not this aged geezer. And he had only a pointed, trimmed gray beard, not those cascades of hair hanging down from his chin."

"You're sure of all that? You knew him well?"

"I did. We studied together in Jerusalem." Jon smiled, then added, "*All* the earliest images of Paul in Eastern and Western art—even the catacombs here—show the fellow I described, not this one."

"And of course, you Lutherans know more about Paul than us Catholics, who are fixated on Peter, right?"

"Guilty as charged!" Jon was glad that they could continue their banter despite Sullivan's obvious concerns about Jon's mission.

When they'd met at Johns Hopkins years ago, Kevin Sullivan had been a brilliant but bigoted student who was quite sure all Protestants were destined for hell and that salvation was impossible outside of the Roman Catholic church. For his part, Jon, the son of a Lutheran pastor in Hannibal, Missouri, was equally sure that Martin Luther had saved Christianity from the clutches of an apostate papacy. They'd spent many an evening in Baltimore hauling out theological ammunition and firing at each other, Jon ticking off all the points where he thought Catholicism had veered away from biblical doctrine while Kevin countered that Protestants wouldn't have the Bible in the first place were it not for Catholics.

As they matured, however, each had moved from a right-wing conservatism to a centrist, more ecumenical stance. They quickly buried the religious hatchet, knowing that the *true* struggle was not Catholicism versus Protestantism, but Christianity versus a non-Christian world. In fact, for many years now, Jon and Kevin had been the closest of friends.

As they walked the perimeter of the forecourt and sauntered into the great sanctuary, Kevin gave a running commentary. "Okay, Jon, you know the background here. The site goes back all the way to Constantine and even earlier. But why, do you suppose, the emperor built the original basilica specifically *here*?"

"Eusebius might have told him. His *Church History* tells of an elder in the early Roman church in the 200s, a fellow named Gaius, who could point out the very spot on the Ostian Way where Paul was beheaded and buried—here!"

Sullivan nodded. "It still gives me a thrill. We're standing at the very place where Second Acts ends. But now, fast-forward twenty centuries to the year 2000—Rome's Jubilee year. Pilgrims came here from all over the world, but when they visited this basilica, they raised a howl of protests because they couldn't get any access to Paul's tomb under the high altar. And so Vatican archaeologists started digging here from 2002 to 2006, exposing what we'll see in a moment under glass at the eastern end of this long sanctuary."

"Right. I remember the international sensation when that Vatican archaeologist—what was his name?"

"Giorgio Filippi."

"Right. I remember when Filippi announced that they had probably discovered the very tomb of St. Paul in a crypt under the high altar. Many of my Protestant colleagues were skeptical, of course, but Filippi's claim had a lot going for it, including that marble slab over the crypt with the Latin inscription—**PAULO APOSTOLO MARTYRO**."

"To Paul, apostle and martyr indeed. And while the earlier basilicas erected here were oriented to the west, this latest version looks to the east, yet all of them pivoted about this central shrine."

"How come we haven't heard a word about Paul's tomb since then, Kev, not a word? *Why* haven't they opened the sarcophagus to see if Paul's remains are actually inside? I thought they would for sure in 2008–09—the so-called Year of St. Paul . . ."

"Well, the archpriest here is Cardinal Andrea Cordero Lanza di Montezemolo, and he'd have to give his permission first. But he hasn't done so, at least not yet. I don't know why. Maybe because many Italians would be horrified at any plan to examine the possible skeleton of St. Paul—*if* it's inside. And yet this same wonderful breed of people can happily view the mummy of St. Francis encased in the glass altar at Assisi. Go figure!"

Now they had reached the end of the long colonnaded sanctuary, where the high altar dominated the basilica. Just below it were steps leading down to the crypt area. Along with a column of visitors, Jon and Kevin descended the stone staircase. There, behind a metal latticework screen, they saw the Vatican excavations under a slab of glass and one side of the actual sarcophagus exposed. Since photographs were permitted, Jon pulled out his small, slim Nikon and took a long series of shots—especially of the partially cleared lid above the exposed side of the sarcophagus. He had to wait his turn at times, since pilgrims were kneeling in front of the tomb and offering prayers.

Gathering in as much as possible, Jon spied a threshold at the opposite end of the excavation pit with a small access door. Made of simple crossed bars, the door seemed to have only a simple latch, not a lock. The passageway behind it was too dark to discern, but flash photography would take care of that. In fact, Jon's camera was on a photography marathon, focusing on details large and small. All the while, Sullivan easily guessed what Jon might be up to but simply stood back and let him compound his own folly.

Jon thought that the passageway from the crypt must have led to a similar access door near the high altar, and his hunch was confirmed when he emerged from the crypt and found such a door directly in line with the access door inside the crypt. It also had just a latch, not a lock. More photographs.

Finally he said, "I have everything I need, Kevin. Let's go check the visitor's center."

They walked over to the mini emporium at the south transept, where the faithful could purchase candles, rosaries, crucifixes and crosses of all kinds, imitation icons, plaster saints, and a multitude of guidebooks to Rome's holy places. Like the tourist pilgrims around them, Jon purchased several color postcards as well as a booklet on the history of the basilica. On the wall over the cash register, there was a large plaster replica of the lid of Paul's putative sarcophagus, complete with the holes through which pilgrims used to drop their written petitions and treasures centuries earlier—holes now mortared in.

The lid held a special fascination for Jon, and he photographed it from various angles. Later, he would compare the photos with his earlier shots of the real thing to determine if it were a faithful replica. Certainly the Latin phrase **PAULO APOSTOLO MARTYRO** seemed to shout that this was indeed St. Paul's sarcophagus.

Just before they left the basilica, Jon remembered to pluck one of its flyers out of the tract rack. He wanted to know the basilica's hours of admission.

✠ ✠ ✠

The "hotel" where Jon was to stay for his three days in Rome was Kevin's apartment on the Janiculum Hill with its great view of the Eternal City. That evening they indulged a bit at Kevin's favorite restaurant on the Via Veneto in view of the dangers implied in the famed adage, "All work and no play . . ." But *la dolce vita* it was not, just a modest Italian dinner that began with pasta and minestrone and then proceeded through the next four courses, all nicely lubricated with Chianti.

After returning to Kevin's apartment, their discussion turned to options other than the one Jon seemed to be pursuing.

"Why don't you involve the Holy Father in this project?" Kevin wondered. "You know how much he admires you, Jon, and just a word of approval from Benedict would end Cardinal Andrea's indecision in the matter. Your plan would then be lawful—even blessed by the church—and anything you found inside Paul's tomb would be regarded as valid and aboveboard.

But you know well enough how ugly things could turn out if you do it your way."

Jon said nothing for some moments. He sat there, staring at the thousand pinpoints of light below that were Rome. Then he nodded. "You're quite right, Kevin. If I were going to an alternate plan, that one would be the best option—far and away the best option. So why don't I go that route? Several reasons. Benedict could, of course, say no—we really have no assurance that he'd say yes. And then our project—sorry, *my* project—fails. I'd never go against the pope's decision on this. And is it really fair to Benedict to ask him to make such a decision? I think not. Furthermore, I could well come up with no results whatever—meaning that St. Paul is *not* inside that sarcophagus—and that could be embarrassing to the Vatican and disillusioning to pilgrims. Do I have the right to take away the object of their spiritual quest?"

"Nicely thought out, Jon. But what if you *do* discover St. Paul inside that sarcophagus? The clandestine nature of your discovery would certainly reduce its credibility, don't you think?"

"Yes, it certainly could. And that's why I would *never have done this*. You and I would visit Benedict, privately inform him of the great news, and then Vatican archaeologists could continue their work and make 'the discovery.' And think how nicely that would support the close of Second Acts."

"Fair enough. But what if *you*—not St. Paul—were discovered 'in the act of tomb desecration,' as the tabloids might banner it? Then what?"

"I don't really have a good answer there, Kevin. Possibly I'd have something of a ruined career after that. Or possibly not—once my motive was explained, namely, my desperation to find some material link to the close of Second Acts since the codex had been stolen. Besides, there'll be no desecration or damage to the tomb whatever."

Neither said anything for some time. Finally Jon spoke. "If all else fails, maybe I can get Benedict XVI to write me a letter of recommendation so I can get a new job somewhere."

On that inanity, they laughed and called it a day.

✠ ✠ ✠

The next morning, Kevin drove Jon to a builder's supply store in western Rome so that he could, inexplicably, purchase overalls and—even more inexplicably—a dark green plastic tarpaulin. Then they returned for another visit to St. Paul Outside the Walls, where Jon spent several hours watching the tourists between 11 a.m. and 3 p.m., noting when they were crowding into the basilica or leaving it comparatively empty. He also looked for any surveillance cameras inside the sanctuary and, in particular, where and when guards who patrolled the premises passed by the crypt on their appointed rounds.

At Kevin's place that evening, Jon unpacked the special objects he had shipped inside his checked luggage on the flight to Rome. He had thought of taking the items as carry-ons, but their very exotic nature might have provoked too many questions at the security lines. Mercifully, his baggage had arrived with him, which seemed to be quite unusual lately on the world's airlines.

First, he unpacked something that looked like a small, silvery pistol. "No, it's not a firearm," he said in answer to Kevin's raised eyebrows. "It's a Stryker high-speed surgical drill." He pulled its trigger, and at 4,000 rpm, it emitted only a soft high-frequency sound similar to a muffled dentist's drill. "Batteries are fully charged, and they can keep it going for at least a half hour. It even has a vacuum on it to suck up debris."

Kevin said nothing. He simply shook his head in continuing dismay.

Next, Jon opened a small plastic case that held a drill bit with a diamond-edged cutting head less than an inch in diameter. "This one loves to eat mortar," he said.

Finally he hauled out a thin metal wand to which were affixed two tiny strobe lights and two miniature digital cameras, with battery power supply inside the wand and all controls in the handle at its top. "Are you getting the picture, Kev?"

He cupped his chin in hand and nodded slowly.

"I got the idea from the Italian archaeologists who explore the Etruscan tombs in Tuscany. There are so many up there that they excavate only those with interesting contents. And how can they tell which those might be? They bore a hole at the top of their circular ceilings and take flash photos by lowering something like this inside. Only our model here is smaller and much more sophisticated. We might even be able to produce three-dimensional images by using the two cameras."

"Not to burst your bubble, Jon, but I doubt that your gadget will penetrate solid marble very quickly, unless you want to spend an hour or two drilling away."

"I won't penetrate the marble. I plan to use one of the holes already made in the lid but mortared over. This drill should cut it almost like butter. I already promised you that

I'd destroy nothing at all in the process. It's going to be quick, painless surgery."

"I only hope you're right. In fact, I only *pray* that you're right. And please—because of my special relationship with the Holy Father—I never helped you at all in this escapade, right? And if you're caught, I don't even know you." Sullivan stopped and they both chuckled. Since Kevin had originally introduced his friend to the pope, both knew how ridiculous that proposal was. "Okay, then," he went on, "if you *are* caught, get me on your cell phone. I'll have been 'in the neighborhood' and will 'rush over to help my friend' and maybe try to get his tail out of jail if it comes to that."

"Fair enough, Kevin. I couldn't ask for more."

✠ ✠ ✠

Shortly before noon the next day, they were driving back to the basilica of St. Paul. "You look just great in that Italian repairman's getup, Jon," Sullivan said. "Didn't I see you and Mario on Nintendo?"

Jon merely smiled, trying to steel himself for the peril ahead.

"But why in the world you would want to choose the *busiest* time of the day for your escapade is quite beyond me."

"Noon isn't the busiest—tourists will be leaving for restaurants—and I couldn't bring it off if the place were nearly empty."

"Why not? That's when I would have done it."

"Wrong. Same number of guards then, but fewer things to distract them . . . greater chance of detection. Tourists are my protection."

At the basilica, Sullivan parked his Fiat near a service door in the rear and extended his hand to Jon. "God go with you, you crazy fool! I'll be waiting out here, praying for a miracle but with my cell phone handy."

"See you here in fifteen to twenty minutes, Kev."

Jon hoisted his gear, walked up to the service door, and passed through it without challenge. At a very deliberate pace so that he would not attract attention and yet arrive at the crypt exactly at 11:59 a.m., Jon walked through the ranks of pilgrims in line to see the crypt and approached the railing surrounding it. It was 11:58—a minute too early—but no real problem. He slowly opened his toolbox and looked around for guards. Thank goodness noon was also the time for the changing of those guards.

A great boom seemed to explode inside the sanctuary. Although it was merely the Janiculum cannon doing its thing as it did at noon each day, the tourists were sufficiently startled for Jon to make his move. He hauled out his dark green tarpaulin and started spreading it over the glass ceiling of the crypt. *"Mi scuzi! Per favore, mi scuzi!"* Jon said in his best Italian accent, while nudging several pilgrims aside in the process. At the center of the tarp now covering the glass, he placed a large sign in both Italian and English:

CHIUSO PER QUINDICI MINUTI
CLOSED FOR FIFTEEN MINUTES

Then he went to the small doorway near the side of the high altar and tried the door. It refused to open. Was it locked? With prayer and a stronger tug, it opened at last. He crawled through and emerged inside the crypt. Quickly he opened his tool kit, hauled out the drill, and set it to work on his target, which was the most centrally located mortar-filled hole in the lid.

The drill purred away without making the quick progress Jon had counted on. He put more pressure on the drill. This reduced the rpm but the drill seemed to start making some penetration. Still, no breakthrough. *The mortar they used centuries ago was pretty good after all,* he mused. The drilling seemed to go on for endless minutes.

This was all taking too long, he realized. He pushed harder and harder, yet the material refused to yield. His concerns had become worry, and worry was now bordering on panic. He'd have to abandon his wild scheme, cut his losses, and head out ASAP. Yes, common sense dictated that he do just that. After one final push, it would be the end.

Suddenly the drill broke through. It would instantly have crashed into the lid of the sarcophagus had not Jon's gloved left hand been waiting to cushion the blow. Trembling with joyful relief, Jon pulled the drill out and replaced it with his photo wand. It just fit into the orifice. He lowered it exactly one foot down, then turned on the strobes and started tripping the camera shutters. He twirled the wand forty-five degrees and did the same, then the next forty-five degrees, and so on until he had made a complete circle.

Next he lowered the wand nine inches further and repeated the process. He thought briefly of trying a third round but canceled the concept in the name of prudence. He quickly removed the photo wand and retrieved all his gear. As a final touch, he plugged the hole in the lid with color-matched hardening clay.

Then he crawled back out of the crypt. He emerged through the door at the end of the passageway and could finally stand up again. Then his heart almost failed. One of the basilica guards was standing there, looking at him with a great frown.

"Buon giorno!" Jon said amiably, retrieving his wits. He closed the little door, ignored the guard, and walked over to the railing around the crypt, where he removed the sign and the tarp. Then he strolled casually but methodically back to the service door, wondering whether the guard was following him. But he dared not look backward. That would have been too obvious a tip-off.

When he reached the service door, Jon was sure brawny hands were about to seize him by the very scruff of his neck. But no. Thank the good Lord, his bluff had been successful.

He climbed into Kevin's Fiat and they drove off. Jon looked at his watch. Only nineteen minutes had elapsed since they'd arrived. To Jon it had seemed more like nineteen hours.

"Do you mean to say the guard just stood there, *looking* at you?" Kevin asked while driving through the Ostian Gate on their way back to the Janiculum. "I find that a little hard to believe."

"I don't blame you. I was lucky. But it's all in appearances, Kev, *appearances*. To that guard, I was just one of the many handymen tending the place. He probably sees dozens like me every day."

"But how did you ever have the . . . the guts to pull off something like this? When you put on those duds, you must have known something as serendipitous as this could happen."

"I got the idea from something that happened years ago when

I was a freshman at Harvard. One afternoon, some students—dressed like street construction workers—brought a huge air compressor onto the corner where Mass Avenue runs into Harvard Square. They fired up the compressor, and then—with three jackhammers roaring at the same time—they started blasting away at Massachusetts Avenue, tearing up the pavement and stacking huge pieces of asphalt onto the curb. The police quickly came, of course, but what did they do? They carefully directed traffic *around* the construction area so the 'city workers' could get their job done!"

Kevin was laughing so hard, he had to pull over to the curb. Finally he asked, "What did they ever do to those pranksters?"

"Not a darn thing. After a half hour of this, they simply left the scene—air compressor, jackhammers, and all, which they had 'borrowed' from a university construction site."

"They never caught them?"

"Never."

Kevin shook his head, incredulous.

"See," Jon said, "like I said, it's all in the appearances, Kev."

"Maybe it was more like you were Daniel, and the Lord himself closed the mouths of the lions."

"Yeah, maybe so."

✠ ✠ ✠

That evening, they prepared to upload Jon's precious photographs. As he attached each camera to USB cables connected to his laptop, Jon was cautious—trying to keep his own hopes in check more than to convince his friend. "You realize, Kevin, that there are plenty of things that can go wrong here. For one, we could have technical failure with one or both cameras—not the strobes, since I saw the flashing—but if the remote shutter controls failed, we'd have nothing. That's unlikely, but not impossible. Or the camera lenses might have missed their target because I angled them wrong—although I tried hard to get the geometry straight. Or even with all the technical stuff working perfectly, there might well be nothing inside, no target."

Kevin shook his head. "Why so negative? I'm sure there must be something inside the tomb."

"Well, I suppose there probably *are* bones inside, but they might not be St. Paul's."

"But how would you ever know that?"

"Simple. If the skull were attached to the neck bones, then it couldn't be St. Paul because we know he was beheaded."

"Oh . . . of course." With an impish grin, Kevin asked, "Is that all?"

"Well, there is one more possibility," Jon admitted. "There's a remote chance that we have the photos of . . . the real McCoy. Sorry, that's a dumb phrase for something as extraordinary and sacred as this, but you know what I mean."

"Right."

Jon's hand was actually trembling as he turned on his laptop. Why did the booting up take so long? Finally his screen came alive with all its icons. He double-clicked on his favorite photo-imaging program, clicked the Import button for camera #1 at the one-foot level, and waited for the images to appear. They arrived, one by one, with excruciating slowness, yet all were—well, not blank, but showing only the gray marble interior of the sarcophagus. After the eight 45-degree-angle photographs had made a complete circuit, Jon slapped his hand on the table and muttered, "Nothing! Just the same drab interior walls of the tomb. Either there's nothing inside or my lens angles were wrong."

"Well, try camera two, for goodness' sake!" Kevin advised.

"Camera two? Oh yes, of course."

Jon shook off his disappointment and returned to his laptop. The uploads from the second camera started appearing on the screen, but with the same disappointing results: nothing but shots of the interior wall. Jon clapped both hands over his eyes in dejection.

"Jon, *look*!" Kevin yelled. Photo number four from the second camera was coming onto the screen. It showed the top of something that was difficult to make out, but it was most definitely *not* part of the walls.

"Yessss!" Jon exploded. "The hole was near the eastern edge of the sarcophagus, and I aimed the wand there first. Now we're getting the views across to the other side. And just look at seven o'clock!"

"Wow!" Kevin enthused, looking over Jon's shoulder. "Nine o'clock is even better!" Both angles showed bones at the base of each view.

Then there were indrawn breaths: Eleven o'clock showed the top half of a human skull.

Both were silent for some time, savoring the moment. Finally Jon said, "The next series, which was taken nine inches lower, should be even better."

Indeed, this became the series that Jon knew could make history. Both cameras clearly showed the image of a skeletal figure, ranging in height—they estimated—between five-foot-five and five-foot-eight. A shock of what looked to be salt-and-pepper-shaded hair—much on the sides, little on top—was still attached to the skull. And unless this was wishful viewing, there *seemed* to be a break in the neck vertebrae five and six beneath the skull.

"What do you think, Jon? Do we have a gap there or not?"

"It's tough to tell at this point. We've got to avoid letting any bias color our results. In any case, we won't be able to determine that until we enlarge the photos. Then again, if the people who buried this person pushed the head back into position, we may never know, short of a real autopsy."

Suddenly Kevin said, "No, Jon. You're wrong. This . . . this *is* St. Paul." He knelt down, crossed himself, and took several trembling breaths, clearly overcome.

"Easy, man. How can you be so sure?"

He wiped his eyes. "Look at those pieces of purple fabric still attached to one of the ribs!"

"What?"

"And remember how Second Acts closes? 'On his breast we placed a small cross of wood, the emblem of what has become the center of everything he preached and taught.'" Kevin stood and pointed at the latest image on Jon's laptop. "Look closely. Look at that rib cage . . ."

Jon squinted. There it lay, on the sternum: the image of an ancient cross made of darker material that contrasted with the gray of the ribs.

CHAPTER 22

JON SLUMPED DOWN ON KEVIN'S SOFA, moving his head in a slow arc from side to side as the full ramifications ran together in his mind. Then he looked up. "Well, there's our material evidence. And the evidence is actually a keystone, bracing up both sides of our mutual interests: Second Acts *and* the remains of St. Paul. How incredibly, wondrously, fabulous! *Both authentic!*"

Kevin agreed—enthusiastically. "And of course, you can guess my next question."

"I can. 'When may I tell the Holy Father?'"

"You've got it."

"Well, if you tell him now, he *might* not take too kindly to what we've—I'm sorry—what *I've* done."

"I doubt that. He'll be overjoyed that both Second Acts and St. Paul are authentic."

"Maybe, but that cardinal with the five names will be furious."

"True. Done without his sacred permission."

"So why don't we do this? Let's have St. Paul's remains 'discovered' several weeks after we announce the codex to the world. Benedict could persuade Cardinal Many Names to have archaeologists examine the interior of the sarcophagus. We know what they'll find, and it will be a delightful corroboration to silence all the naysayers—"

"Of which there'll be a whole chorus, I'm sure." Sullivan nodded, then added, "Yeah, I think that would be the best way to handle it. And I trust you'll keep me abreast of how the scholarship is moving on Mark and Second Acts."

✠ ✠ ✠

After Jon landed at Logan and hurried into Shannon's waiting arms, he jabbered almost incessantly on the drive back to Weston about his adventure at the Basilica of St. Paul Outside the Walls, though without mentioning his culminating discovery. Never one to mince words, Shannon let him know exactly what she thought of his escapade. It was beyond risky, she said, and more in the nature of foolhardy, rash, juvenile, and even reckless. Jon winced at each of those adjectives but kept his peace until they were home. Then, on the kitchen table, he booted up his laptop and paraded the views of no less than the skeleton of St. Paul. Now Shannon was mute, the back of her right hand covering a mouth that had sprung open in awesome surprise.

While the photographs had exonerated him so far as his wife was concerned, Jon realized that much of her comment was absolutely on-target, and—but for good fortune—things might have turned out very differently, with a massive negative impact on his own good name and reputation. It was a near thing.

The next morning, Jon turned the crypt photographs over to techie friends at MIT for enhancement. He did *not*, of course, disclose the provenance of the pictures or the probable identity of the skeletal remains in them. When they were returned—enlarged and printed in color—his friends had a little fun at Jon's expense with comments like "Aha, so you're professor by day, ghoul by night!" "Dr. Frankenstein, I presume?" and "When do you unveil your new pet monster?"

More significantly, Jon took the prints to a colleague Dr. Theophil Samuel, dean of radiology at Harvard Medical School, who resembled an aging Sigmund Freud. "First off, Ted," Jon asked, "do we have a man or woman here?"

Samuel looked quickly through the photographs, sometimes squinting. "Male. Unquestionably, a male. Not a big person, but male nevertheless."

"How do you know? What do you look for to determine that?"

"Relative bone size. Narrow pelvis—couldn't deliver a baby."

"Okay. Now, perhaps you can't tell from the photographs, but do you have any guess as to his age at death?"

"Hmmm. Oh, I think I can . . . come reasonably close. See those extraphytic accretions at the edge of the bones? They develop over age. So I'd say . . . hmm . . . someone in his sixties—maybe a shade younger. If I had the remains, I could also check the teeth for wear from grinding and therefore age."

"That's quite impressive. All right, please also check out these enlargements of the neck area."

Dr. Samuel studied the new photographs, then hauled out a large magnifying glass to zoom in further. "Strange," he said, "there's definite disarticulation, a definite gap between vertebrae five and six in the cervical plexus. Hmmm, and also a . . . a very consistent, flat abrasion of some kind along the top edges of vertebra five."

"Any idea of what could have caused that?" Jon asked.

"Some very poor neck surgery, perhaps," he trifled. "Where did you get these photos—from Yale Medical School?"

Both chuckled; then Samuel commented, "Well, if someone were, say, beheaded, he'd look very much like this . . . *if* his relatives wanted to make the departed look more natural by trying to piece the bones together again. This isn't King Louis XVI of France, is it—he of guillotine fame?"

"No. Earlier." Jon immediately regretted saying that since he should have pleaded ignorance in the interests of nondisclosure.

"Well, then, Charles I of England? Or even, say, John the Baptist?"

"No," Jon said, chuckling. Then he shaded the truth just a bit. "We really don't know for sure."

"Well, I'd go so far as to say that this poor fellow was probably beheaded by a sword rather than an ax."

"How *in the world* can you tell that?"

"An ax would cause wedge-shaped damage on the vertebrae. But look at the gap between these vertebrae: it's perfectly parallel. A sword had to be used. This fellow was dispatched by one swift cut of the sword. At least his torment was brief."

"And you can tell that because there are no other slash marks on the neighboring vertebrae?"

"Exactly."

Twenty centuries after the fact, Jon felt relief that Paul's pain had been brief. Still, he cringed a bit at what Paul had to suffer, and while on the nasty subject, he thought of other victims. "Reminds me of 'Crazy Boots' Caligula, the sadistic Roman emperor who ordered a victim killed 'with a blow and a half so that he could *feel* he's dying.'"

"Pleasant fellow indeed! Still, you do seem to have a good hunch as to the identity of these bones. And if so, why aren't you telling me? Remember, you started hinting with that word *earlier*."

"You don't miss a thing, do you, Dr. Ted?"

"Aw, c'mon, Jon. How about a little hint?"

"Can you keep a confidence?"

"Of course."

"The bones are probably part of . . . a skeleton in Rome."

Dr. Theophil Samuel thought for a moment, then shook his head. "I'll need more than that," he said. Clearly the eminent radiologist was hardly an expert in the early church.

"Best I can do, Ted. When it's time for the news to break, you'll be the first to know. I promise. But thanks for your help. It was . . . more strategic than you may realize."

"Anytime."

Again, every last clue only further identifies the remains, Jon thought on the way back to his office.

✠ ✠ ✠

Now there was strong material evidence indeed, despite the theft of the codex, evidence of an extraordinary nature. "Isn't this all we really need, Jon?" Shannon asked when she saw him clenching his fist at mention of the missing codex. "We have every word, for goodness' sake. We can publish exact facsimile copies of the codex—even in the exact colors to match the ink of the lettering and the tan of the vellum on which it's written. All the scholars working on the codex are content with black-and-white facsimiles, which are actually clearer than the codex itself. Fact is, we don't even *need* the codex anymore."

"Lots of truth there," Jon admitted. "But we're treading sacred ground here. It's almost like tampering with God's Word and the faith of believers to suggest, in effect, 'Hey, your Bible has been fine up to now, but we have several necessary improvements.' Without the genuine article, I'm afraid that copies will simply not convince them."

"Maybe, maybe not. Anything more from the CIA on their search for the codex?"

"Only this: Dillingham learned that three of the men who were on duty at the airport security line the morning Bartholomew and his party took off are members of Islam Forever, a far-right religious party in Turkey. Whether or not that's significant, no one knows at this point, but I think it could be *very* important. The switch had to have been made at the Istanbul airport."

"But why go to all that trouble making a crude replacement? Why didn't they simply take the codex and run?"

"Can you imagine the huge fuss the patriarch would have made when the attaché case came out of the scanner much lighter than before? Of course, that could have happened anyway had he opened the codex after it exited the scanner. But they played their chances, and it gave them enough lead time to make off with the codex. Or maybe pass it on to others."

Earlier, Dillingham had asked Jon for help on a watermark the CIA labs had discovered on the foolscap paper. Instead of a literal cap with bells attached to its flaps in the headgear of a medieval court jester—the origin of *foolscap* after all—the consistent watermark looked like a crescent and star over an earth surface with the Star of David and a cross embedded in dust. Such a logo was obvious, and both Jon and Osman al-Ghazali quickly translated it: Islam victorious over Judaism and Christianity.

Could it help identify the perpetrators? "Unfortunately it's not a big clue," Dillingham told Jon. "The paper is manufactured in Egypt, but it's used throughout the Middle East."

"But this had to be an inside job, Mort," Jon said, giving the privileged appellation a test run. "Else how could the perpetrators know when the patriarch was coming through the security line and, above all, the exact dimensions of the codex for their copy?"

"That's clear," he agreed. "For some time now, our operatives in Istanbul have been using the Orthodox Patriarchate as their second home, checking out every last person on the staff there."

"They have? I hope they aren't disrupting the business of the patriarchate now that Bartholomew has returned."

"Quite the opposite. Bartholomew is just as eager as you to locate the codex. He's cooperating in every way possible."

Jon thought of another tack. "Has anyone received a . . . any kind of a ransom note for the codex? We haven't. Has Bartholomew?"

"No, not that I've heard."

"Well, where do things stand as of now? What are your plans?"

"We're doing a stronger background check on the three religious party members at the airport security line. Our Turkish counterparts are a big help—all secularists, thank goodness."

"Good move. And . . . *thanks* for all your continuing help, Mort."

"Not at all, Jon. I'm still trying to make up for that tongue-lashing I gave you some weeks ago."

"Aw, don't worry about that," he said.

+ + +

Jon received regular updates, assuring him that the Constantine Codex and Canon committees of the Institute of Christian Origins were working with a near-maniacal drive to complete the opening scholarship on both documents. Slogans like "Urgency, Security, Action" had proven quite unnecessary in urging them on, so very extraordinary was the excitement associated with the Constantine Codex.

Computer studies of the material proved most helpful. The Gospel of Mark was programmed for grammar, syntax, vocabulary, and favorite phraseology, as was the book of Acts. The newly discovered texts were then subjected to the same programming with stunningly similar results. The *immediately* adverb, so typical of Mark, appeared also in the new ending, which had no mention whatsoever of those clearly embarrassing references to snake-handling and drinking poison that showed up in later attempted conclusions to the Gospel and had always been regarded as spurious by the best scholarship. Jon and Shannon found it particularly pathetic that several cults in Kentucky and Tennessee made this central in their worship.

Similarly, just as computer studies had shown the book of Acts to have been written by the same hand as Luke's Gospel, so the same hand was demonstrated in First and Second Acts. Above all, not a single verse in any of the newly discovered material conflicted in any way with the existing biblical text.

Should the newly discovered texts become part of the Bible? The Canon committee had been asked to explore that question, but it was quite divided on the issue. Jon and Shannon concluded that it was still too early to venture much of a working plan for that group.

Perhaps the greatest of all wonders in the entire enterprise was that confidentiality seemed to be holding. In Rome, no one had noticed the plugged one-inch circular hole in the lid of the St. Paul sarcophagus, according to a communication from Kevin Sullivan, although Benedict XVI was constantly inquiring about Jon and the codex.

In Cambridge, the only slight breach in security seemed to be the day that Zachary Alexander, an Associated Press stringer in Boston, came to Jon's office to inquire about "some important document" he was supposed to have discovered somewhere in Turkey after the debate at Hagia Sophia and then delivered to the Ecumenical Patriarchate in Istanbul. Even as his heart nearly froze in midbeat, Jon affected a forced smile and asked the man where in the world he had heard such a thing.

"My cousin Brett has the AP desk in Istanbul," Alexander

said, "and he wanted an interview with the patriarch because of all the in-and-out traffic there after you left."

"And did the patriarch grant it?"

"No, he didn't. It was Brett's guess that some old manuscript—or whatever—was involved."

While a "white lie" of denial might have been justified at this point, Jon tried redirection instead. "It was my wife Shannon who found an old document at Pella, which really isn't all that important. But she'd prefer no publicity on it until she's done the usual translation and commentary."

"Hmm . . . figures, I guess."

"Tell you what. Let's make a deal—you stay mum on this for now, and you'll be the first media person I call when it's time to go public. Deal?"

"Deal."

It was a close shave, but no cigar. Obviously—despite the stolen codex—the good Lord *was* watching over their enterprise. If only the missing codex weren't such an unforeseen and totally loathsome complication!

CHAPTER 23

JON WOULD NEVER FORGET THE DAY, the hour, or the event. No known expressions in the English language could cover it. Nor, he thought, could those of any other language spoken by the civilized. "Bolt from the blue" came close, but that was still pathetically inadequate to describe what actually happened.

He was sitting at his office desk at Harvard, reviewing the latest findings from the ICO committees, when Marylou Kaiser announced, "The FedEx man just delivered something for you, Dr. Weber, and I signed for it. Want me to bring it in?"

"Sure—if it isn't big and heavy."

"Well," she admitted, "it *could* be both."

Jon immediately got up and went to the receiving table in her office. The large box measured something like eighteen inches square and over a foot in height. It was well wrapped with brown tape and was indeed surprisingly heavy. Quickly Jon looked for the name of the sender and read:

Al-Azhar Mosque and University
Office of the Grand Sheikh
Madinat Nasi
Cairo, the Arab Republic of Egypt

"Well, what in the world?" Jon wondered. "Abbas al-Rashid and I haven't been in contact since the debate, other than the usual exchanges of thanks. What do you think's inside?"

"Probably a big, ornate copy of the Qur'an," she opined. "He wanted to convert you to Islam, didn't he?"

"You know, you could be right, Marylou. And that would be *very* sticky. I'd love to maintain the man's friendship, but I doubt I'll be making *that* particular pilgrimage!"

"Well, that's a relief! Muslims don't treat their women very well, and that would include secretaries."

Jon cut through strip after strip of tape, then opened the lid of the box. All he saw was packing popcorn. Marylou hurried over with a wastebasket to prevent her office floor from being littered with Styrofoam pellets. Finally Jon saw the dark tannish cover of what appeared to be some large tome, lifted it free of the packing, and set it on the table.

It was then that breath and heartbeat nearly failed him. It was a codex.

It was *the* codex.

He slumped down onto a chair, held his forehead, and mumbled, "How? . . . Why? . . . It's simply not possible . . ."

His eyes were locked in wonderment on the codex. Nothing else existed for him at that moment.

"Are you okay, Dr. Jon?" Marylou asked.

"This is . . . beyond . . . all . . . belief." Slowly he came back to life. "It shouldn't have been sent FedEx. It shouldn't have been *sent* at all, and yet here it is."

Marylou seized the moment, opened the codex, and withdrew a letter that was inserted just under the cover. "Shall I read it to you?" she asked.

Jon was too dazed to reply, so she took it upon herself to read him the following:

Dear Professor Weber:

I greet you in the name of the God we both serve!

I am sure that the document I have enclosed has much meaning for you and the faith you so ably represent. It was only by great fortune that I was able to obtain it. I knew nothing of your connection to this document until it arrived at al-Azhar University.

It was sent from Istanbul by a radical group of jihadists in Turkey. They wrote that they had managed to take the document from the Ecumenical Patriarch at the airport in Istanbul. But they could not translate it or risk having it translated by any local Greek Orthodox Christians, so they sent it to a Greek scholar in our Department of Classical Languages here at al-Azhar for translation. That would help them know how much to ask for ransom, they wrote.

They trusted this scholar—nameless, for his own security—because he was a secret member of the Muslim

Brotherhood, and so a fellow jihadist—or so they imagined. In fact, he is a Muslim moderate—our own agent in their radical ranks, since we have also learned to play their game by way of defense. You should not worry about his future safety or that of his family. His role here was becoming more and more difficult, and this was his last service for us before leaving Egypt to teach elsewhere under a new identity.

At first, I had planned to return the document to the Ecumenical Patriarch, but those who stole the document also mentioned your strong interest in this work, and I thought it safer to send it directly to you in America. Later, you may return it to the patriarch with proper security.

I am glad to have this opportunity of being of some service to you, since I place great value on our continuing friendship. You would be more than welcome to give a presentation at al-Azhar University at any time you see fit, and I hope that our paths will indeed cross in the future.

Yours, with admiration,
Abbas al-Rashid
Grand Sheikh

Jon shook his head. "What extraordinary *nobility*. Abbas has a higher standard of ethics than I've seen in many Christians. What a man! What a truly *great* man!"

Swimming in waves of elation, Jon picked up the phone and called Shannon. Her *"What!"* was so loud it nearly damaged his eardrum.

His next call was to Morton Dillingham. The least a good citizen could do was to save the CIA—and the federal government—any further expenses in a search that was no longer necessary. Not everything was solved, to be sure, especially the question of how the jihadist perpetrators at Istanbul learned about the codex and were able to get its dimensions right for their fake copy of the codex, but those problems could be solved later on. For now, the codex was *here* . . . present . . . real . . . and in the U.S.!

Jon's last call was to the Ecumenical Patriarch in Istanbul, who wept for joy at the news. Before leaving his office, Jon also dictated the most cordial, most enthusiastic letter of appreciation to Abbas al-Rashid he had ever written to anyone, anywhere, at any time.

✢ ✢ ✢

Jon determined to make short work of the authenticity tests on the codex itself. Putting on white gloves, he cut a small hanging flap of aged tan leather from the cover of the codex and inserted it into a lead-lined pouch. Then he opened the codex and turned through ten pages of Matthew's Gospel until, on page eleven, he found a dog-ear at the upper right corner that was threatening to separate from the rest of the vellum. Carefully, he cut it free. This he also inserted into a separate pouch, then sent both via UPS Express to his friend Duncan Fraser at the radiocarbon labs of the University of Arizona in Tucson.

Fraser had helped him with crucial C-14 tests before, most recently on the leaves Shannon had brought back from Pella, so when Jon phoned to alert him to the express shipment, he seemed unsurprised.

"Since it's you again, Jon," Fraser commented genially, "I'll bet your samples came from, say, Lincoln's Gettysburg Address."

"No, Duncan. Earlier."

"Okay, how about the Magna Carta?"

"No, earlier still. But no more clues, Duncan. That wouldn't be scientific, now, would it? You and TAMS will have to tell me the date, but do treat those samples as if they were a letter from God himself."

"Got it."

✠ ✠ ✠

Under normal circumstances, Jon would have sent the codex itself to the Smithsonian Institution in Washington, D.C., where another friend, Sandy McHugh, would have given it a variety of forensic tests. But Jon decided that the reverse had to happen. The scientists would have to come to Cambridge instead, so very priceless was the codex. He was simply unwilling to risk its safety again.

In fact, a parade of scientists came not only from Washington, but from other points on the compass for an extraordinary, secret conclave. Members of the ICO filed one by one to examine the precious document, as well as Daniel Wallace and his delegation from the Center for the Study of New Testament Manuscripts. Wallace quipped that he felt like Simeon: ready to depart this life since the ultimate manuscript discovery had been made and he had seen it.

Perhaps the most colorful, yet crucial of the many imported experts was Lancaster Whimpole, curator of manuscripts for the British Library in London. Here was the man who was largely responsible not only for that library's immense collection of papyri, but who also served as curator for the until-now greatest of all New Testament manuscripts, the *Codex Sinaiticus*. Whimpole was a tall, tweedy Oxonian sort who looked like James I of England, though even more slender, his teeth yellowed from years of contact with a meerschaum pipe. Whimpole did not suffer fools gladly and could detect fraud with one eye at a distance of fifty paces. Jon knew the man would have to be skeptical regarding the codex since nothing could dare rival "his" *Sinaiticus*.

Watching Whimpole examine the codex was an event in itself. He bent over the document like a Sherlock Holmes—with magnifying glass but without the silly cap. His gloved hands felt the texture of the cover and swept across the pages of vellum. From time to time he would stop, squint, use the magnifying glass, and then move on. He pulled out an orthography chart of Greek writing styles from the first to the fifth century AD and compared the uncial lettering for each era. He then superimposed another chart of the uncials in the *Sinaiticus* and nodded briefly—the first sign of any sort that his poker face or bodily mien had betrayed.

It seemed to Jon that he spent an eternity going through almost every page of the codex, again without registering any sort of response. Jon looked helplessly at Shannon, who stood beside him, just as eager for the verdict as he.

Whimpole failed to notice the Markan ending, but his eyes widened when he came to Second Acts. And they seemed to remain wider for the rest of his perusal. When he had finally finished, he stepped back, looked up, pieced his fingers together, and then said to Jon, "I hope you'll provide more detail on how you discovered this. You gave some information in your phone call."

"I will indeed. But what's your impression of the codex thus far, Dr. Whimpole?"

"Well, I would call it an *extremely* clever fraud . . ."

Jon froze.

". . . were I given to what you colonials call 'practical jokes.' But this codex is authentic. Absolutely authentic. Beyond all debate. The orthography—those beautiful uncials—are fully consistent with the *Sinaiticus* and other manuscripts from the fourth century. I . . . I must congratulate you, Professor Weber, on the manuscript find of the century—no, of the millennium. And—quite naturally—I'm also fiercely jealous of your success!"

A round of laughter was enough to transform the stiff and stodgy Brit into a fellow human being.

✛ ✛ ✛

Two weeks later, all the material test results arrived at Jon's Harvard office. It began with a phone call from Arizona, Duncan Fraser genially announcing, "I guess you want a pair of dates, Jon, right?"

"That would be very helpful, Duncan."

"How about 1650, plus or minus fifty years—both samples?"

Jon's heart plummeted. "AD 1650? You mean . . . you mean the vellum's less than four centuries old?"

Fraser laughed. "I knew I'd catch you on that one! No, Jon, 1650 BP, and I don't mean British Petroleum."

"So, 1,650 years before the present?"

"Yes. Of course."

Jon quickly calculated, then broke out laughing. "Perfect! Right on target! Early to mid-fourth century AD. You and your TAMS toy do great work, Duncan!"

"Only to keep you amused, Jon. What did you discover this time, the memoirs of Constantine?"

Jon was startled for a moment by the name but then said, "No, a shade more important than that. Tell you what, because you've been so kind, I'll phone you about it just before we make the general announcement."

"TAMS and I will be honored."

Sandy McHugh phoned from Washington with similar results. Every test of the adhesive swipes he had taken from the leather cover and vellum pages showed a progression of pollen running up to the present day, yet also strains that went back to the fourth century.

All tests, then, were conclusive: the codex was absolutely authentic. As Jon told Shannon, "Obviously, we didn't need the tests in the first place, since no one today could have forged 140 pages of perfect, fourth-century Greek."

"Why did we go to all that bother, then?"

"The public, Shannon. The skeptical public, not to mention an army of critics."

That evening, Jon put in two calls, the first to the Ecumenical Patriarch in Istanbul, the other to Kevin Sullivan in Rome. Both were for the purpose of establishing a date for the announcement to the world. His All Holiness Bartholomew II would have the honor of making the initial announcement. Pope Benedict XVI would be invited to attend and participate in the presentation or be represented by Monsignor Sullivan. The location should have been the Ecumenical Patriarchate in Istanbul, but for obvious security reasons, it would instead be the Greek Orthodox Cathedral of the Holy Trinity in New York.

CHAPTER 24

"GLAD I CAUGHT YOU before your flight to Cairo this afternoon, Osman," Jon said as he chatted with his associate. It was a mild spring morning in early May, warm enough for Jon to open the windows of his office. "Like some coffee?"

"Please."

As Jon poured two mugs, he continued. "I understand you're visiting relatives in Cairo?"

Osman nodded. "In the western suburbs. At Giza—near the pyramids."

"Do look in on our publisher while you're there, Osman, and try to iron out any remaining problems in the Arabic edition of our book—if there are any."

"Will do. Soon, maybe, I'll have to do the Arabic translation of Mark 16 and Second Acts from our magnificent codex there." It was lying atop Jon's desk.

"Could well be. By the way, didn't you once tell me you could face death if you ever returned to a Muslim country after converting to Christianity?"

"True for Islamic theocracies like Iran but not for secular states like Egypt. And you'll recall that we all got back safely from Turkey."

"True enough."

"Of course, if they knew about me, Muslim fanatics in any country would find me fair game."

"Better watch your back, then. I understand that Osman Mahmoud al-Ghazali's fame is rising in the world of Islam!" Jon was smiling, but then he grew serious. "Hate to bring this up again, but a couple weeks ago, you'll recall, we talked about the remaining problem in the disappearance of the codex?"

Osman nodded. "How could the perpetrators in Istanbul have known its dimensions, when the patriarch would fly here, et cetera, right?"

"Exactly. We all agreed that it had to be an inside job by someone in the patriarchate over there. But then I recalled that when we told you and Dick Ferris about the codex at the Istanbul Hilton, it was *you* who asked me about its size."

"Right. And your point is . . . ?"

"Well, I told you about the size of its pages, but then you also asked me how thick it was."

"So? Both Dick and I wanted very badly to see the actual codex. And that was as close as we could come at the time."

"Fair enough. And it's just possible that my awful vector of suspicion may be pointed in the wrong direction."

"At me, Jon? *Me?* After all we've been through together?"

"Hate to say it, but yes, Osman, even though it absolutely tears me apart to admit it."

"Well, you can spare yourself that kind of personal agony because I'd never ever go back to the other side. Conversion is conversion. A Judas Iscariot I am not!"

Jon clenched his jaw muscles and rolled his knuckles on the desk. "I'd like to believe that. I really would." He paused, avoided eye contact with Osman, and stared out the window. Then he turned in his chair and faced al-Ghazali directly. "Yesterday evening, Mort Dillingham called me from Washington. He hated to admit it, he said, but yes, the CIA asked the FBI to check all phone records on all of us during the weeks preceding the theft of the codex and the weeks afterward. After we hung up, Dillingham faxed me this record. It's a long list, but please note the items I've underlined in red."

He handed Osman the faxed pages. "To the left is your home phone number in Watertown, dated a week before Bartholomew's flight to the U.S., and to the right . . . do you see that number in Istanbul?"

"Where?"

Jon pointed.

"Oh . . . there."

"It belongs to one Tawfik Barakat, who is a member of the Islam Forever religious party, *and one of three men on duty at Istanbul's airport security* the day the patriarch flew off."

Al-Ghazali reddened a bit. "But . . . how can that be? Obviously there has to be some . . . some ridiculous mistake here. Besides, how could the perpetrators know *when* the patriarch would fly off?"

"Osman, Osman, we had all that information here in Cambridge, and you certainly had access to it."

A long silence followed, tense and embarrassing to both of them. Finally Osman cleared his throat. "All right, Jon. Very well. I have a long, *long* story to tell you, and I think you'll like the ending. But first, might I have a bit more coffee?"

Jon walked over to the hot plate and turned his back to prepare a fresh pot. Carafe in hand, he returned and refilled both mugs. Then he said, "Please continue, Osman. I'm listening . . . listening quite carefully, in fact."

Al-Ghazali began with the story of his descent from the great eleventh-century Muslim mystic, Abu-Hamid al-Ghazali, who despised women and hated science in his concern for rigorist orthodoxy. He went on to the story of his childhood in Cairo, while Jon, his patience wearing thin, let his coffee cool. Details of Osman's schooling followed, until Jon said, "To the point, man, to the point. This is all interesting, but you have a plane to catch, don't you?"

"All right, Jon, I'll give you the short version."

Jon took a long sip of coffee, noting a slightly off flavor. "Almost tastes like Irish coffee. That's what I get for not giving the carafe a thorough washing. Is yours okay, Osman?"

"Just a little strong."

Then he continued with the story of his conversion to Christianity and how his eyes were finally opened to the greater historical reliability of the Bible versus the Qur'an. Despite Jon's advice to move on with his explanation, Osman seemed to continue dawdling. Jon let him speak on, grasping his mug a little unsteadily as he took another long sip. Soon he looked at Osman with some concern because the man was becoming clouded in some sort of haze. But his office was also suffused in a growing fog, and the whole room seemed to lurch to one side. He quickly set the mug down, lest he drop it, and put both hands on the desk to steady himself. But the desk seemed to be tipping and sliding sideways. Was he having a stroke?

✢ ✢ ✢

Osman watched the changes coming over Jon with quiet satisfaction. The man was starting to shiver and hyperventilate as Osman continued. "But truth to tell, Jon, for all the evidence you tried to marshal on behalf of Christianity, I found that, in the end, I could never give up Islam. *Never!* I was convinced that I could best help our cause by intruding into your circle."

Jon tried to reach for his phone, but Osman swiftly pulled it out of his reach. "You won't need that," he said. "Of course, I *intentionally* made that error in the Arabic translation of your book, hoping a fatwa would quickly settle things. But when that failed and you discovered the codex instead, I had to—wait, here, let me help you."

Al-Ghazali stood and shoved Jon and his chair deep inside the space under the middle of his desk. "You won't be able to speak, Jon, so why even try? And don't even *think* of standing up because you'd fall on your face."

Jon tried nevertheless. He squirmed feebly in attempting to use his feet to shove the rolling chair away from the desk while his hands reached up to assist by grabbing the desk's edge. But his grasp faded, and his arms dropped limply on both sides of his chair.

"Probably you'll recover, Jon," Osman said, pulling a small, empty vial from his pocket. "It's an improved version of the old Mickey Finn, but it acts quicker. With any luck, you should get over it in a day or so. Tell you what: we've had some good times together, so I'll even help you recover." He scribbled *chloral hydrate* on a slip of paper and stuffed it into Jon's shirt pocket. "Be glad I didn't *really* poison you, chum," he added. "Call it a parting gift."

Just then he heard the long, grinding sound of a huge garbage truck outside the back windows of Jon's office. "And, oh yes, the codex." Al-Ghazali picked up the tome, went to the back window of Jon's office, broke out the screen, and heaved the codex directly into the compacting maw of the garbage truck. "There! Your precious codex is exactly where it belongs, thanks to Waste Management. Live a good life, Jon!"

Al-Ghazali hurried out of the office, relieved that Marylou Kaiser had apparently gone to lunch. He would be over the Atlantic before Jon could even control his tongue. It would also be a one-way trip for Osman since he had planned to flee the U.S. for the past several weeks, suspecting that the discovery of his true role in Jon's circle was only a matter of time.

Several hours later, he was aboard EgyptAir Flight 986 to Cairo. He gazed out the window, a low smile forming on his lips. Suddenly, though, they formed a pout instead. *What utter* fools *those Turks were,* he mused, *trying to get a* ransom *for the codex when I had told them simply to destroy it.* Well, he had corrected their wretched mistake. Allah would be more than merciful.

+ + +

Marylou Kaiser came back from lunch, walked into Jon's office, and screamed. Jon was sitting at his desk, motionless, glassy-eyed, and unresponsive. In a frenzy, she dialed 911. When the paramedics arrived, they quickly suspected a stroke of some kind—not poisoning: this was Harvard, after all. One of them, however, saw Jon's half-empty coffee mug and tasted it. Then he spat it out and grumbled, "Irish coffee. Evidently these Harvard sages start drinking early and often."

They strapped Jon onto a stretcher and carried him downstairs and out into an ambulance that had invaded the sacred turf of the Yard. Although nearly comatose, he started mumbling things like "Kowbage," "Gowbage," "Tuck," and finally "Truck." But no one understood him. Sirens wailing, the ambulance sped eastward on Massachusetts Avenue, crossed the Charles River bridge, and delivered him to ER at Mass General Hospital.

Marylou had, of course, accompanied Jon in the ambulance, and Shannon soon arrived from Weston, pale and shaken. The only one with some context for Jon's situation, Marylou finally started interpreting his mumbles. "Police," she translated from "powice," "garbage" from "cowbage," and "poison" from "paw-zun." None of it made sense, except for *poison* and *police*, and the latter were summoned immediately.

The ER at Mass General was crowded with patients on the road either to death or to recovery assisted by vast arrays of high-tech equipment. In one of the curtained cubicles surrounding its central core, Jon was starting to fight with his restraints. One of the supervisory nurses saw it and quickly injected a sedative.

Marylou had the presence of mind to object. "No," she said, "I wish you hadn't done that. He's trying to regain control. What he needs, I think, is the *opposite* of a sedative."

"No, madam," the nurse sniffed. "We know what we're doing."

✠ ✠ ✠

Still unnerved from Jon's ordeal—and now a bit peeved by the nurse's attitude—Shannon happened to notice the slip of paper in Jon's shirt pocket. Something prompted her to take it out and read it. "Anyone know what *chloral hydrate* means?" she asked.

"You bet!" said an intern on duty, who sprang into action, asking, "You're his wife, I understand? Was he taking any sleep medications?"

"No. Jon sleeps like a baby," Shannon replied.

"I hate to ask this, but . . . did he seem depressed recently? Did he have any suicidal inclinations?"

Shannon shook her head emphatically. "He'd be the very last person on earth to try anything like that."

The intern was joined by Jason Hopkins, MD, the chief internist at Massachusetts General Hospital. Apparently, word had traveled quickly regarding a certain Harvard celebrity in the ER. For once, Shannon was grateful for her husband's celebrity status.

Hopkins read the slip proffered by the intern and checked Jon's vital signs while dictating to an attending nurse: "Blood pressure low: 80 over 50. Pulse rapid: 120 beats per . . . Breathing shallow, apparent hypothermia. . . . Pupils pinpointed. Patient comatose. . . ."

And indeed, Jon had lapsed back into deep sleep.

Shannon and Marylou exchanged a glance. At Shannon's nod, Marylou informed the doctor about the sedative the nurse had administered.

"What?" he bellowed. "How come it's not on the record? Which nurse? That one?"

Marylou nodded.

"We'll discuss this later, ma'am!" he said, glaring at the nurse. "Now get me five hundred milligrams of caffeine sodium benzoate for injection—*immediately*."

All the excitement was doing little for Shannon's nerves. "What's the situation, Doctor?" she asked, blinking back tears.

He removed his stethoscope and asked, "Was he taking medications of any kind, especially barbiturates?"

"Nothing. Other than an occasional vitamin."

"Well, all the symptoms are quite consistent with chloral hydrate overdosage—or even poisoning. The slip in his pocket seems accurate in that respect. Strange that it should even have been there."

"But what are his chances?"

Dr. Hopkins seemed to ignore her as he took Jon's blood pressure again. "Nurse!" he barked. "It's only 66 over—what? Can't even tell. We could be losing him." He called out, "Gastric lavage! Possible Code Blue! And where's that caffeine? Oh . . . thank you, nurse." He now injected the caffeine into Jon's arm.

Then he turned to Shannon. "Sorry, Mrs. Weber, first things first. I just ordered a stomach pump that will replace the contents of your husband's stomach with sterile water. That's to clear out any remaining toxins."

"But he will . . . he will pull through, won't he?" She heard her voice break with apprehension.

"It all depends on how much toxin he ingested. I understand that one of the paramedics thinks it was in his coffee. Does he use cups or mugs?"

"Mugs," Marylou interjected.

Hopkins frowned as he made the obvious comment, "They hold more."

A tube was inserted into Jon's mouth and down his esophagus. The dual procedure began: infusion and evacuation, much as a dentist treats the mouths of his patients. Jon stirred a bit during the process, which all interpreted as a positive sign.

When the procedure was completed, Dr. Hopkins said, "Now it all depends on his blood pressure, Mrs. Weber." Again they cuffed Jon's left arm and pumped.

The pressure released in a welcome hiss. "Good," Hopkins said. "We're at 92 over 64. Better than the last. If he keeps this up, he should soon be out of the woods."

Shannon slumped down onto the couch where Marylou was already seated.

The older woman put a comforting arm around her, and Shannon finally surrendered to her tears.

+ + +

Jon slowly felt himself coming to. He'd been only vaguely aware of being whisked to the hospital, but there was no doubt now that's exactly where he was. He shook his head and tried hard to focus on those around him. "Shannon, sweetheart," he said thickly. "I'll be okay, I think."

She threw her arms about him.

Eventually Jon's mind was clear enough to relate the full story to all present, including a detail from the Boston police who had stood in the background until the medical procedures were completed. The Hub's finest sprang into action at once. They radioed colleagues at Logan to arrest Osman al-Ghazali but learned that he was long gone. They had only slightly better luck with Waste Management, Inc., of Somerville, which supposedly handled refuse from Cambridge. The dispatcher there wanted to get the details from Jon, particularly the time and place of the garbage pickup, so the police officer handed the phone to Jon, and he was able to respond with reasonable clarity.

"And exactly *what* is it that you're looking for?" the man asked.

"A valuable codex . . . that's an ancient book of manuscript pages sewn together."

"Oh. Sorry. That'd be impossible to retrieve, Professor, because Harvard tries to show the world how to recycle—green's their favorite color, not crimson—but you know that. So your book is probably being recycled, even as we speak."

A stab of despair hit Jon as he handed the phone back to the officer. Both his hands turned into fists, and if Osman al-Ghazali had been within range, he personally would have throttled the traitor for manuscript murder. "It's destroyed," he told the women. "This precious, precious treasure is now being *recycled*, if you can believe it! Into what? Maybe toilet paper . . ."

Obviously in despair, Shannon and Marylou appeared to search for appropriate words but found none.

The phone rang. It was the dispatcher again, and he wanted to talk to Jon.

"I had it wrong, Professor," he said. "Turns out that the recycling plant is shut down for repairs, so as of a couple days ago, they're trucking all waste to the North Andover landfill so that it doesn't pile up."

"That's wonderful news!" Jon said.

"Well, I'm not sure why. . . . I really hate to tell you this, but our chances of actually *finding* that thing in the landfill are next to impossible. A needle in a haystack would be easier."

"Please, please," Jon said, "I really beg of you. You *must* try to save one of the most important documents in the history of Western civilization."

"We'll do our best, Professor, but I'm afraid . . . Well, we'll really try."

They wanted to keep Jon at Mass General that night, but he would have none of it. His wits had now returned and fury was burning through his brain, yet he was still rational enough to let Shannon take the wheel on the drive back to Weston.

+ + +

Early the next morning, Waste Management phoned again. "It was truck number 68, Professor Weber, that picked up the waste from Harvard Yard about noon yesterday. Driver was Jim Peabody—a good reliable fellow from Bar Harbor, Maine. That's pronounced 'Bah Habah' up there!"

Ordinarily, Jon would have told him to skip such peripheral details, but now he savored every syllable.

"Anyway, Jim dumped his waste at the landfill in North Andover—oh, it's about twenty miles from Harvard Square—and I'll tell you what we've done. We've cordoned off the area in the landfill where our trucks discharged yesterday, and we're dumping elsewhere while we *try* to find that big book you told us about."

"Thank you. Thank you ever so much," Jon said.

"Again, though, I hate to tell you, it's going to be a downright miracle if we find it. And even if we do, three thousand pounds of pressure probably crushed that Kotex thing . . ."

"That's 'codex,'" Jon advised.

"Fine. Codex. But it was probably crushed into pulp."

Jon winced. The statement was true enough. "Just try, please, *try*. I'll be driving out to the landfill to help you look."

"Well, I don't think . . . Hold it, on the other hand, it'd be helpful to know exactly what we're looking for."

"I'll be there at eleven, with photographs of the codex."

✢ ✢ ✢

For the next two hours, he and Shannon called the secretaries of all departments with offices at or near Harvard Yard with a question that must have seemed quite ridiculous: "What sort of waste did your department discard yesterday?" Of course, there was a quick follow-up to explain the context of that inane query. Clearly grasping at straws, Jon was trying to see if some marker might not be found within all the tons of waste.

But there seemed to be nothing at all unusual. Most of the waste mentioned consisted of cardboard mailers for books sent to professors by publishers in hopes of adoption, interdepartmental communications, intradepartmental memos, book catalogs, advertisements, and the like—nothing with real value as a marker.

One slight glimmer of hope came from the economics department. The secretary there reported that they had discarded about three years' worth of unclaimed examination blue books the previous day. But could they serve as a marker? Doubtful.

By late morning, Jon, Shannon, and Marylou had raced up Highway 193 to the North Andover landfill, where they were obliged to put on yellow hard hats. Jon passed out photographs of the codex to the dozen or so in the search party that Waste Management was kind enough to supply, all armed with picks to try to pry apart the great, caked slabs of waste. With enormous good fortune, the huge bulldozer that further compacted the slabs of waste by traveling back and forth over them had not yet accomplished that task, or the search would have been fruitless even to attempt. The dozer and all Waste Management trucks were discharging at least a hundred yards away from the zone management had marked off. Jim Peabody, the driver of truck number 68, had shown them approximately where he had dumped his load—to the best of his recall—and was now one of the search party.

But it seemed to be a futile effort. Slab after slab was picked apart, only to disgorge everything from orange peels to coffee grounds to flattened tufts of used Kleenex. By midafternoon, despair started setting in. Jon, returning to Plan B, wondered if the world would have to be satisfied with mere copies of the codex. After all, they did have copies of its every word, so that was at least something.

Yet another part of his mind was telling him, *It is humanly possible to examine every last piece of garbage in this sector. Yes, it could take weeks. Yes, it would be enormously expensive. But it* can *be done.*

He was ready to draw up a formal request that exactly this

be done when he noticed a thin vein of light blue in one of the untouched slabs. Well, the Department of Economics *was* near his office, so why not let that vein be the blue-book marker he was seeking. Gently he picked into that slab, and it generously fell apart for him. They were blue books indeed. Student names were written on them, of course, and the department listed on each cover was "Econ."

Another vein of cardboard framed them off, then a vein of Styrofoam packing. Jon pried the packing material apart and found . . . the codex. Mercifully, it had been wedged between sheets of protective Styrofoam. In worshipful awe, Jon meticulously disengaged it from its whitish shroud and opened it with tender care. Only a few pages had been detached from their sewn binding by the compacting pressure, but they were still there, nestled underneath the ancient leather cover now embedded with flakes of Styrofoam. The thin board inside had been cracked, but with no apparent damage to the pages of vellum. Only the coverless last page of Revelation had been torn and damaged, though not beyond hope of restoration.

Jon knelt down on the heap of garbage in the North Andover landfill and gave thanks to God.

CHAPTER 25

AS MIRACULOUS AS IT WAS TO FIND THE CODEX in the landfill, Jon thought an even greater wonder was the fact that—with a considerable number now in the know—there had been no real leaks to the media about their astonishing manuscript discovery. Now, however, it was time—high time—to tell the world.

The Ecumenical Patriarch and his party flew in from Istanbul for another visit to New York, where he would have the privilege of making the initial public announcement. His venue would be the Holy Trinity Greek Orthodox Cathedral in Manhattan. Several weeks earlier, Jon had sent out invitations to the most significant religious bodies and media outlets across the world "to attend a press conference in New York at which a significant biblical manuscript discovery will be announced." He intentionally underplayed the language in his letter for purposes of security, although by now he was developing something of a track record for issuing bland invitations that led to extraordinary announcements.

Kevin Sullivan arrived from Rome with seven cardinals in tow, including Augustin Buchbinder, the Vatican secretary of state. Kevin confided to Jon that Pope Benedict XVI would have loved to come himself, but in Christian concern, he did not want to risk upstaging the Ecumenical Patriarch. Nevertheless, he could not contain his joy that the codex had been found again and implored divine blessing on its reception.

Many of the major religious bodies in America and beyond were allowed four representatives each—including Jews and Muslims—but no political leaders were invited, intentionally so. Seats along one side of the cathedral were reserved for the newspaper and magazine media, as well as the radio and television networks. When Anderson Cooper of CNN arrived, he looked at the forest of TV cameras and commented, "Well, they're all here—even Kol Israel and Al Jazeera—though I haven't come across Radio Nepal, yet."

Before arriving at the cathedral, Jon had put in a busy early morning, making good on his you'll-be-the-first-to-know promises by putting in calls to all the curious crucial experts who had aided them. All now readily understood the reason for his previous silence.

At 10:06 a.m. on announcement day, the dean of Holy Trinity Greek Orthodox Cathedral stood before a thicket of microphones and said, "We welcome you all in the name of the Lord, distinguished ladies and gentlemen. It is my great honor to introduce to you His All Holiness Bartholomew

II, Archbishop Patriarch of Constantinople, New Rome and Ecumenical Patriarch."

Bartholomew stood to enthusiastic applause that he tried to terminate by holding up his arms. At last he succeeded. His clear baritone resonated across the cathedral as he gave the Trinitarian invocation in Greek: "*Eis to onoma tou Patros, kai tou Huios, kai tou Hagiou Pneumatos.* Amen! But since some of you may not know Greek, I shall continue in English."

Ripples of laughter erupted. The audience was now his.

"For centuries, the Ecumenical Patriarchate in Constantinople—many of you may know the city as Istanbul—possessed a literary treasure of immense significance for Christians everywhere. It is a magnificent New Testament manuscript codex, written in Greek uncial lettering that dates from the early fourth century—that is, the AD 300s—and is thus a document even earlier than the great *Codex Sinaiticus* in the British Library, which, up to now, has been the most important of the earliest versions of the Bible. But more. This newly discovered codex is also one of the fifty copies of the Holy Scriptures that the Emperor Constantine commissioned Eusebius, the church historian, to prepare for distribution across Constantinople and elsewhere. Scholars have long searched for one of these codices, but without success. Now, I am privileged to announce, the lost has been found."

Vast waves of applause splashed across the sanctuary and even some unliturgical whistling and cheering.

Bartholomew continued. "This precious document we have officially named the *Codex Constantinianus*, but you may simply call it the Constantine Codex. It lies before you on the pedestal to my left, and it is open to the Resurrection account in the last chapter of the Gospel according to St. Mark, chapter 16. After this conference, you may view it briefly in an inspection line, but kindly do not try to touch it in any way. Guards will assist you in this request.

"The codex was discovered by Professor Jonathan and Mrs. Shannon Weber of Harvard University and the Institute of Christian Origins. I am deeply embarrassed to report that the codex was not recovered from our library or archives, but from a room at our patriarchate devoted to manuscript repair and storage. The entire Christian world is in your debt, Professor and Mrs. Weber. Dr. Weber will now provide some extraordinary additional information regarding the codex."

As Jon walked to the microphone, nothing less than a standing ovation greeted him, and a raucous one at that, complete with cheers and whistling—in a cathedral, no less. He'd wanted Shannon to have this honor—after all, she had really discovered the codex—but she had demurred. "You're much better at public speaking than I," she'd said, needlessly buttering him up.

When silence finally fell, Jon looked to the patriarch and began. "Thank you, Your All Holiness. Without your magnificent cooperation, none of this would be possible. I must now tell you, distinguished ladies and gentlemen, of two additional discoveries *in* the text of the Constantine Codex that some will greet with shock, others with disbelief, and still others with exuberant joy. I would remind the press that all this material will be available in press releases in the narthex after our conference. These have been translated into the ten most widely used languages in the world, identified by an appropriate sign over each stack.

"The first discovery lies before you. If you file by the codex, you will notice that there is *more* text regarding the resurrection of Jesus at the close of Mark 16 than the traditional last verse you find in all your Bibles. And here, please, understand that the text we do find after chapter 16, verse 8, in your Bibles was added later. The Constantine Codex, however, preserves *the original ending that Mark actually wrote.* It not only accords perfectly with the other Resurrection accounts in the Gospels, but also helps explain their variations."

Stunned shock seemed to vacuum all life out of the cathedral, until a veritable explosion of response replaced that void. Shouting, laughing, and cascades of applause reechoed across the cavernous expanse of the cathedral from the sector where the churchmen were sitting. They knew well enough that the broken ending of Mark's Gospel was one of the greatest problems in New Testament scholarship. Non-Christians, in fact, used it as one of their prime arguments against the Resurrection. But at last, Jon was happy to announce, the problem was solved.

When quiet returned, Jon reported the other "surprise" in the discovery of Second Acts. The vast assembly sat in stunned silence as he sketched its contents: Paul's trial before Nero, his trip to Spain and subsequent journeys, and finally his martyrdom at Rome. This time the mood of the audience was one of profound awe rather than the raucous elation over Mark's Gospel. Clearly they were equally thrilled, but totally unprepared for the profound implications of a missing book of the Bible being found. But then a din of discussion seemed to well up from each pew, as church leaders and scholars started putting the pieces together and understanding, for the first time, why Luke ended the book of Acts as abruptly as he did in chapter 28.

It was time for Jon to finish his prepared statement. "Translations of the new material in Mark 16 and Second Acts will also be available in the narthex after our conference. These may be freely copied and used anywhere—with only one exception: they may *not* be appended to any new editions of the New Testament or the Holy Bible by any publisher. The Institute of Christian Origins holds the international copyrights for all the new material and will prosecute any publisher anywhere trying to add Mark 16 and Second Acts to any projected new version of the Bible or the New Testament.

"I'm now open for your questions. In each case, please wait until a page brings you a microphone and first identify yourselves as you start speaking."

Representatives of the press and the media were seated in the front of the sanctuary on the opposite side of the aisle from the religious leaders. Jon recognized a man in the fifth row.

"David van Biema, *Time*. I'm intrigued by your last statement, Professor Weber. Why that restriction? Why couldn't the new material be published in future Bibles? Is there some question about its authenticity?"

"No, David, not at all. In fact, there's a separate handout in the narthex showing all our test results to date, and they're all positive. The reason we can't permit the inclusion of this material in future Bibles *at this time* is because that would require opening the canon of Holy Scripture, and we simply cannot arrogate to ourselves so solemn a responsibility. Only an ecumenical council of the entire church could make such a decision."

"Do you think that could happen? Will happen?"

Yes, Jon wanted to say, but he held his tongue and simply replied, "Again, the church will have to decide." He looked toward another reporter. "Yes?"

"Mark Galli, *Christianity Today*. But wouldn't that be very difficult, Professor Weber? Most Christians assume that the canon of Scripture is *closed.* I can almost hear fundamentalists using Deuteronomy 4:2: 'You shall not add to the word which I command you, nor take from it; that you may keep the commandments of the Lord your God.'"

"Indeed, but that passage, as you know, refers to Mosaic law rather than the whole canon of Scripture itself. But you're right, Mark: opening the Canon could prove terribly difficult and provoke the darkest suspicions, however unjustified, among some of the faithful. . . . Yes?"

"Hang Wha Sing, *Taipei Telegraph*. What means *Canon,* and how books get into 'Canon'?"

"Yes, sorry. I should have defined that earlier. *Canon* comes from the Greek word *kanown,* which means 'rule' or 'standard.' It's the authoritative list of books that belong either in the Old or New Testament. The early church included in the Canon only those books that were written by eyewitnesses or those who had immediate contact with eyewitnesses, *and* that were widely used in worship, *and* that were consistent with the other teachings of Christianity. The new material in the Constantine Codex more than satisfies all three criteria. . . . Yes?"

"But the Canon is still *closed!*" the tall figure nearly shouted. "Oh—Jimmy Lee Curtis, *Southern Baptist Messenger.*"

"*Is* it really closed, Mr. Curtis? One of our great Greek textual scholars, the now-sainted Professor Bruce Metzger of Princeton, has an interesting passage in his book *The Canon of the New Testament* that speaks to this very point." Jon had the book at his lectern and read aloud:

> "One may also speculate what the Church should do if a hitherto unknown document were to turn up that, on unimpeachable external and internal grounds, could be proven to have been written, let us say, by the apostle Paul. . . . Though from a theoretical point of view the way is open for the possible addition of another book or epistle to the New Testament canon, it is problematic that any would, let us say, meet the standards, either ancient or modern, of accreditation."[1]

Jon closed the book and commented, "That was almost prophetic on the part of Professor Metzger. But now you'll understand why the matter of canonicity must be left up to an ecumenical church council. . . . Yes?"

"Cedric Marshall, London *Times*. What about the other alternative? If a book could be *added* to the New Testament canon, might one or another also be *subtracted* from the Canon?"

A bit of commotion greeted that query. Jon smiled. "I will admit that several members of our Institute of Christian Origins suggested that the book of Revelation might be surrendered in favor of Second Acts—to keep the number of biblical books at sixty-six. They were not serious, of course, but merely

[1] **Bruce M. Metzger, *The Canon of the New Testament.* Oxford: Clarendon Press, 1997, pp. 272–273**

concerned about how often Revelation is misinterpreted today. But no, I'm confident that no church council would ever try to *subtract* any book from our present Canon. Yes?"

"Willis Torrington, *Sydney Times*. Don't you think there will be a huge outcry from conservative Christians across the world that you are tampering with their Holy Book, that you are *changing* God's Word, so to speak?"

"There may indeed be such an outcry, Mr. Torrington. But such Christians should know that we'd be the very last to try to shake anyone's faith. Instead, our ICO scholars are firmly convinced that not one syllable of the new material conflicts with anything in the Bible but instead *correlates perfectly* with everything else in it. In fact, it nicely *supplements* the New Testament. If you'll pardon a personal reference, I think my wife, Shannon, put it rather well: 'Two missing pieces in the mosaic of Scripture have finally been located and are now in place.' . . . Yes?"

"Diego Bustamente, *O Dia*, Rio de Janeiro. Do you think *other* books of the Bible will be discovered in the future, Dr. Weber?"

Jon thought for a moment, then smiled and replied, "I truly doubt that. The canon of the Hebrew Bible—that's the Old Testament, according to Christians—is complete, and not even the new manuscript discoveries among the Dead Sea Scrolls have changed that. To be sure, the Ecumenical Patriarch and his scholars have been going through *all* literary materials at the patriarchate in Istanbul, but now nothing seems to be missing from the New Testament canon—except for one lost epistle of St. Paul to the Corinthians. . . . Yes?"

"Luigi Cherubini, *Osservatore Romano*. In your Second Acts document, *Professore*, when the burial of St. Paul is described, does Luke tell us *where* this took place?"

"Yes, he does in fact, as you will note when you read the text. It happened on the Ostian Way, near the city walls of Rome."

"Really? Perhaps where our Basilica of St. Paul Outside the Walls stands today?"

Jon made eye contact with the ruddy face in row three that belonged to Kevin Sullivan as he smiled and said, "That could well be the case, Mr. Cherubini. . . .Yes?"

"Brian Williams, NBC Television. What will happen to the codex after this conference, Professor Weber? Where might scholars consult it in the future?"

"For the next month, the codex will be on display at Widener Library at Harvard University, Mr. Williams, under maximum security of course. Probably, though, most scholars will use enhanced facsimiles of the codex, as have our ICO committees in Cambridge. This is the same group that prepared the translations and brief commentaries available after the conference. The codex remains the property of the Ecumenical Patriarch, of course, and he will decide its ultimate disposition. . . . Yes?"

"Trevor Hardwicke, the BBC, London. Do you think there *will* be an ecumenical council of the church to discuss reopening the Canon?"

"Only the future will tell."

"But don't you have personal feelings on the matter?"

"I do indeed, Mr. Hardwicke. And I think they're . . . rather obvious by now. . . . Yes?"

"Gamal Hashemi, Al Jazeera. On another matter, Professor

Weber, do you and Grand Sheikh Abbas al-Rashid plan to have another debate?"

Jon was startled by the query, out of context as it was. Then he replied, "Nothing is scheduled at this time, but I'd like to take this opportunity to commend Dr. Abbas al-Rashid as one of the most extraordinary personalities I have ever encountered, a man of great nobility and wisdom and clearly an example of Islam at its finest. We both look forward to a continuing and rewarding friendship." Jon knew that further details on how Abbas had saved the codex might endanger his position in the Muslim world.

He now looked at his watch. "I see that it's approaching noon, patient ladies and gentlemen, so it's time to close. The e-mail address for our ICO in Cambridge is listed in the handouts, and we have a staff ready to answer your further questions.

"Finally, I must announce that, ultimately, only *one* person discovered the Constantine Codex, not two. And that person is my beloved wife. Please stand up, Shannon."

Taken by surprise and with her face flushing a pretty pink, she rose to a standing ovation, then shook her head in embarrassment as it continued.

What a woman, Jon thought. *She could easily have taken the microphone today instead of me. And probably done a better job in the process!*

CHAPTER 26

NOT SINCE THE DISCOVERY OF THE DEAD SEA SCROLLS in 1947 was there such a media mania. Any editor who had not sent reporters to Manhattan on that memorable day now seemed left in the dust once the immense implications of the find became clear on the wire services.

Back at Harvard, Jon's life was no longer his own. If half a dozen network interview requests failed to arrive before noon each day, it must have been because Marylou was turning them down, per Jon's orders. Larry King, willing to come out of retirement for such a big story, pleaded at least once a week to have Jon on his show. Jay Leno offered him the sole guest spot on *The Tonight Show*—something he had never done before—while David Letterman tried, via Shannon, to have them both on his CBS *Late Show*. *60 Minutes*, *48 Hours*, and even Oprah Winfrey fared no better. Jon was not affecting any contrived humility. He simply wanted to avoid showbiz at this point and let the newly discovered texts speak for themselves. *They* were of greatest importance, not the people involved in handling them.

Publishers were even worse, both domestic and foreign. All of them, it seemed, wanted to bring out fresh editions of the *Holy Bible* with the new material included. Jon and the ICO steadfastly refused any thought of permitting this and even filed an international injunction against a publisher who attempted to do so.

The next most frequent query from publishers was this: would the ICO permit the Markan ending and Second Acts to be printed as a separate publication? As Jon had stated at the press conference in Manhattan, the answer was yes. For such a separate format, the ICO had indeed placed the material into the public domain, but it was *not* to be boxed with the Bible, not to have a cover resembling the Bible, or have the words *Bible*, *Scripture*, or the *New Testament* in any combination on the separate cover.

Gauging how the Constantine Codex was being received in world Christendom became a favorite hobby for Richard Ferris. Almost every day he would drop in on Jon with his latest gleanings. "The mainline Protestants are solidly for accepting our addenda," he said, "and so are Rome and Constantinople. And you got that wonderfully cordial letter from Benedict XVI, so you know all about Rome, Jon."

"Yes, but what about the evangelicals? Or the fundamentalists?"

"A few of the evangelicals are raising questions, but most

are extremely happy about the codex. In fact, some evangelical scholars had even predicted manuscript finds such as this."

"And the fundies?"

Dick smiled. "Well, predictably, there we have some problems. A few of their television apostles have denounced you and tried to discredit the codex. They've been thundering away about how you were doing the devil's work, but—funny thing—they didn't raise much of a response from their adoring fans. They didn't go wild, as they usually do, when their spokesman targets something or someone."

"Maybe because they're more intelligent than their idols," Jon remarked. "Many of them read, you know, and our news magazines have reprinted large sections of Second Acts—and all of Mark's ending—so they can see for themselves how beautifully it fits with the biblical record."

"True enough. But now for the pièce de résistance, Jon. I've saved the best for last." Ferris had a huge grin on his face. "Here's how the AP covered a comment by someone you know. Name happens to be Melvin Morris Merton."

Jon groaned. "Here we go again. So *that's* why the AP called me for a statement yesterday. And what did our manic minister have to say this time?"

"Read and enjoy." He thrust page two of the morning *New York Times* onto Jon's desk. He picked it up and read:

> San Antonio, TX (AP)—The Rev. Melvin Morris Merton denounced the Constantine Codex this past Sunday in a sermon during his current Texas crusade. He called the document a fraud, and Professor Jonathan

and Shannon Weber, the discoverers, "aiders and abettors of fraud, perhaps even the hoaxers themselves."

"The so-called Second Acts isn't even an original concept," Merton said. "In 1801, a man named C. S. Sonnini translated and published in London an original Greek manuscript that has the concluding material of Acts in the form of a chapter 29. Scholars have long been looking for such a document, so it seems that Dr. Weber has conveniently 'provided' another one. Christians should take this one no more seriously than other frauds perpetrated upon the church. I have no doubt that Sonnini's 'Acts 29' is far more 'authentic' than what Professor Weber claims to have found.

"This is just another sign that Christ will return very soon," Merton said. "One of the most important markers that the end is near will be when the Antichrist—or people doing the work of the Antichrist like Professor Weber—try to deceive the public."

Neither Professor Jonathan Weber nor his wife Shannon could be reached for comment at this time, although sources assume they are still in the Greater Boston area.

"What a pile of garbage!" Jon said as he finished the piece. "Can't anyone put a muzzle on that braying donkey? Why in the world would the AP and the *Times* take that man seriously?"

"Probably because you didn't return the AP's call."

"Good point, Dick. I'm on it."

Jon opened his laptop and hammered out a statement.

In an Associated Press dispatch yesterday from San Antonio, the Rev. Melvin Morris Merton tried to impugn the authenticity of the Constantine Codex by claiming that a manuscript translation by C. S. Sonnini from the nineteenth century, titled "Acts 29," had greater validity. No scholar in the world has taken the Sonnini document seriously, since it has St. Paul visiting Britain, where he meets druids who claim descent from Hebrews who were in Egyptian bondage. Supposedly Paul then traveled to Gaul, Belgium, and finally Switzerland, where he prayed at Mount Pilatus that God would send a sign proving that Pontius Pilate committed suicide there. "Acts 29" goes on to claim that a great earthquake followed, waters of a lake in the mountain turned into the form of Jesus on the cross, and a voice from heaven absolved Pilate of guilt over his role on Good Friday.

If Reverend Merton prefers to believe this clumsy forgery rather than the Constantine Codex, he is welcome to it. His latest attack on my wife Shannon and me in connection with the codex does not merely border on libel but is fully libelous in fact. Considering the source, however, I will not exert a moment's effort in filing a suit. Reverend Merton's sad record speaks for itself, and I extend my sympathy to all his followers.

"What say, Richard? Approve?"

Ferris read the screen on Jon's laptop, chuckled, and gave him a thumbs-up.

"Then it's enough for that flake. What I really wanted to do was quote an old Chinese proverb as a bit of advice for Merton: 'It is better to let people think you are a fool than to open your mouth and remove all doubt.'"

✠ ✠ ✠

While Merton's negative responses were frivolous, others were not. Most criticism came from responsible conservative Christian theologians who were not disputing the authenticity of the codex, but who worried lest the new material be included in the Canon. Opening the Canon would set a dreadful precedent, they argued, and could lead to "hopelessly subjective tampering with God's Word," as one of them wrote. "Our present Bible has served us well for the past two thousand years, so there's no need to change it now."

Jon, Shannon, and the ICO made no attempt to respond to such informed concern, since the issue was entirely out of their hands and was instead something that time and the global church would have to decide. They did, however, notice a powerful swelling support for calling an ecumenical church council to discuss the issue.

The swell became a near tidal wave two months later when Monsignor Kevin Sullivan served as Vatican spokesman at a much-heralded press conference in Rome. He began by reporting that archaeologists had returned to the basilica of St. Paul to resume work on what was believed to be the tomb of the great apostle. His next statements would produce world headlines.

> "A thin probe was inserted through a small hole in the lid of the marble sarcophagus through which

pilgrims used to drop petitions. Because the hole had since been mortared over, drilling was necessary. In the words of Vatican archaeologist Giuseppe Montini, 'We drilled a hole only where there had been a hole.' Strobe photography through small cameras attached to the probe revealed much of the interior, which showed skeletal remains partially covered with purple linen that was laminated with gold trim, some of which the probe was also able to retrieve. Small bone fragments were also recovered, which were then subject to radiocarbon testing. The tests revealed an age of about eighteen hundred to nineteen hundred years, thus a provenance from the first or second century.

"This is powerful evidence not only that the mortal remains of the apostle Paul are inside, but it also confirms, and is confirmed by, the recently discovered manuscript titled Second Acts within the Constantinian Codex. The last lines in that document tell of the execution of the apostle Paul, his burial in a purple cloak near the Ostian Way, and even the detail regarding a wooden cross placed on his chest. Such a cross was indeed discovered atop the sternum of skeletal remains in the sarcophagus.

"Furthermore, the skull and highest neck vertebrae in these remains are separated from the rest of the spinal column, testifying to death by decapitation, exactly as church tradition and, most recently, the Constantinian Codex have indicated.

"Accordingly, church tradition and archaeology have now confirmed both the identity of the skeletal remains and the authenticity of this newly discovered text. This is indeed a marvelous day in the history of Christianity!"

✠ ✠ ✠

Over the next months, a prodigious number of scholarly papers dealing with the Constantine Codex were read at special theological conferences across the world. Just as the discovery of the Dead Sea Scrolls spawned entire libraries of monographs, dissertations, articles, books, commentaries, and indices, so the codex soon became the central focus of academic attention.

Jon and Shannon had to curb overzealous colleagues in the ICO who were pleading with them to become publicly proactive in the gathering momentum to have the new codex material admitted into the Canon. They steadfastly refused because it would detract from the objectivity of their discovery were they to declare, in effect, "We discovered this material, and now we want it in the Bible."

Accordingly, news several months later greeted them as a shock, albeit a happy one. The Vatican in Rome and the Ecumenical Patriarchate in Istanbul made the announcement simultaneously at noon on September 15 (1 p.m. in Istanbul). His Holiness Pope Benedict XVI and His All Holiness Patriarch Bartholomew II invited world Christendom to an ecumenical council to be held in the city of Jerusalem beginning on March 15, six months hence. The conclave would be known officially as the Ecumenical Council of Jerusalem. The purpose of the council was to discuss matters involving the canon of the New Testament, although other items of general concern to Christianity would also be part of the agenda.

Jon was on the phone to Kevin Sullivan the moment he finished reading the announcement, which had flashed across his computer screen, courtesy of Reuters.

"Thanks for letting me know about this in advance, Kevin," Jon said in what passed for a tone of annoyance, whether feigned or genuine.

"Sorry, Jon. I was going to call you this evening, since I thought the announcement wouldn't come until tomorrow. Benedict sometimes does things without the benefit of my advice."

Jon chuckled. "Not a problem! So it's *really* going to happen, is it? But why Jerusalem and not Rome?"

"Well, we had the last one—Vatican III—so it was time for the East—Constantinople. But Muslim Istanbul is hardly the best place on earth for a great Christian gathering, is it? Jerusalem's in the East, and Israelis are a shade more hospitable to Christians."

"Figures. But now to the big question, Kev: format?"

"You'll be glad to know that we're following the suggestion you made the last time I was in the U.S., just before I had to fly back to Rome."

"You mean the 'Logan Plan'?"

"The same. Remember, I wanted to call it the 'Weber Plan,' but in your great humility, you deflected the name to that of the airport instead?"

"That's right, Kev; I'm famous for my humility!"

Both chuckled at the oxymoron.

"Well, we're going to use that plan," Kevin continued. "All participating church bodies will be assured that any decisions made by the Ecumenical Council of Jerusalem will be advisory only, not binding. If individual church bodies wish to endorse them officially or not is up to them."

"Fabulous. It's really the best way to go. We agreed that the new council will not have the overpowering authority of the great ecumenical councils of the past, or the smaller delegations across the world could get paranoid."

"Exactly. And yet decisions by the council will have major importance for all of Christendom since most of the world's Christian church bodies will be represented."

"True enough. Well, it looks like you'll be busy again with the invitation list, no?"

"You've got *that* right, but using the list for Vatican III as a template should be helpful."

Jon thought for a moment. "Wait, it should really be easier, right? Last time the heads of state and many others came to Vatican III. This time it'll be only churchmen and scholars, right?"

"Right. And of course, you'll be there, Jon, won't you? And Shannon?"

"We haven't been invited . . ."

"You are now, you blazing buffoon! Oh, and a personal message from His Holiness: in the name of the See of Rome and all over whom he has supervision, Benedict extends profound thanks to you and Shannon."

"And our greetings, no, blessings to him!"

"By the way, it's looking good for opening the Canon, so far as Catholics are concerned. I haven't heard much negative flak, even from our rigorists."

"Wow! That's a happy surprise. And the Eastern Church seems favorably disposed too."

"So! Do you really think our Bible will expand just a bit?"

"That, my friend, is for the Ecumenical Council of Jerusalem to decide."

CHAPTER 27

JON AND SHANNON FLEW TO ISRAEL a week before the Jerusalem Council was set to begin. One reason for their early arrival was to take a nostalgic excursion. Their "sacred romance," as they called it, had unfolded in the Holy Land. Here they had first met one another—she, the daughter of the famed British archaeologist Austin Balfour Jennings, and he, the Harvard prof on sabbatical who stumbled onto something at their dig that merely set the entire world on edge.

They rented a car at Ben Gurion International Airport and drove north along the Mediterranean coastlands to the Megiddo Pass, thence, over the hills of Nazareth to their favorite haunt in Israel, the seaside city of Tiberias. It was along the western shore of the Sea of Galilee at Tiberias that the two had finally unveiled their feelings for one another. Several months earlier, they had fallen in love, but neither dared reveal that wondrous secret to the other. Jon was more timid about it than Shannon, who asked him for their first hug one evening after dinner when they were taking a moonlight swim in that immortal lake. The explosive joy suffusing Jon when they kissed rapturously after that first hug he later called "one of the greatest moments in my life."

Again they rented a sailboat and plied the very waters that Jesus had so masterfully controlled in calming waves or making them buoyant enough to serve as his personal sidewalk. Again they roared over the memory of a boatload of pilgrims ogling them as they were making out while becalmed in the middle of the Sea. Again they scampered across the waterfalls at the head of the Jordan up at Caesarea Philippi. What a blessing was Galilee at the time of Jesus—what a blessing now to Jonathan and Shannon Weber.

✠ ✠ ✠

The Ecumenical Council of Jerusalem became a world event almost from the start. Its festive opening took place inside the holiest shrine of Christendom: the Church of the Holy Sepulchre in the Old City of Jerusalem. This was the very Golgotha where Jesus was crucified but then resurrected from the nearby tomb situated under the great rotunda at the western end of the sanctuary.

"All this may be sacred," Shannon remarked to Jon, "but what I'd love to see here instead would be the open hillock of Golgotha and a tomb with a rolling stone as a door."

"You don't go for all the candles and lanterns and icons and incense, I take it?"

"The endless crowds and the hubbub don't help either. But I've finally learned to control my disappointment."

"What's your formula?"

"I just shut my eyes and realize that in terms of longitude and latitude on earth, *this* is where it all happened."

"Otherwise it could get to you," he agreed. "And it's hard to believe that a Muslim is the warden here with the keys, to keep peace between Roman Catholics and Eastern Orthodox. Some centuries ago, they actually shed blood over the boundaries of their separate enclaves inside the church."

"Let's hope that's history now."

They hurried over to the central nave of the church for the opening service of the ecumenical council, from which the army of pilgrims had temporarily been excluded in view of the equal host of churchmen filing inside. What impressed Jon and Shannon the most, however, was not the magnificent sacred music and solemn liturgy that followed, but the moment when the Ecumenical Patriarch and the Bishop of Rome embraced publicly and sincerely. This was not a simple Bartholomew-meet-Benedict formality, they knew, but a very powerful and moving symbol of reconciliation after centuries of hostility. The three thousand church leaders present shouted *hosanna*s and applauded wildly.

As a further exercise in ecumenicity, several of the council worships would also be held in the beautiful white interior of Redeemer Lutheran Church in the Old City—the church nearest Golgotha—as well as at St. George's Episcopal Cathedral at the northeastern edge of Jerusalem.

"I asked Kevin how he ever brought that off," Jon commented to Shannon.

"What do you mean?"

"I mean, Orthodox and Roman Catholics worshiping in a *Protestant* church—when they're quite sure they're not part of the true church?"

"What did Kevin say?"

"That both Benedict and Bartholomew agreed on the arrangement because it would be 'an irenic gesture to the separated brethren.' But he had a little more trouble convincing the other Protestants that Anglican and Lutheran sanctuaries, as those of the two largest Protestant denominations, would have to represent all Protestants. Still, they finally agreed."

"It's a new era, Jon."

✠ ✠ ✠

Jon and Shannon spent most of their time in the Holy City attending sessions of the Ecumenical Council. These were held at the National Convention Center in West Jerusalem, wired as it was for simultaneous language translations and the latest in media technology, including electronic voting.

In the interests of balance and fairness, the council was chaired on alternate days by the Ecumenical Patriarch and the Pope. Voting delegates, all of whom were the highest officers of their respective church bodies, were allotted in terms of percentage of world Christian church membership size, which yielded the following results for the 2,800 delegates:

1,390 Roman Catholics
352 Eastern Orthodox
236 Anglican

232 Lutheran
590 other Protestants

To prevent Roman Catholicism from controlling the conclave, however, it was agreed that for the great issues at the council, passage of a measure would have to be approved by no less than three-quarters of the delegates, a true super-majority. This was also designed to showcase Christian unity, if possible.

"Our paragon example here," Jon told Shannon, "was the Council of Nicaea in 325, where they decided the greatest issue by a vote of 312 to 2."

"Not exactly a cliff-hanger."

"Right. No hanging chads."

Shannon grew serious and asked, "Jon, tell me true: how do you rate our chances? We hear a lot of threats and saber rattling from the far right, also in the Catholic and Orthodox camps . . ."

"True. They also have their rigorists who've been condemning the council in advance for admitting Protestants. 'They're not part of Christ's true church on earth,' they scream."

Shannon started chuckling. "But that claim doesn't get very far, since that's the very same thing Catholics say about Orthodox and vice versa."

"Exactly. I'm more concerned that all the fundamentalists—Protestant, Catholic, or Orthodox—are uniting on the slogan *Don't break God's Word by tearing the Bible open!* They seem to be raising a rage with it in the media. It's catchy, but simplistic and wrongheaded."

"And yet you and Kevin always seem so upbeat about the possibilities of success."

"I know. That could be a big mistake, though I do have one reason for hope: the ultras—right or left wing—rarely get elected to leadership posts in their church bodies, and it's the leaders who are delegates here."

"Speaking of which, here they come."

It was quite a sight indeed. Filing into the convention hall were two popes/patriarchs—actually, three, since Coptic Pope Shenouda III was there—a variety of cardinals, archbishops, bishops, metropolitans, archimandrites, abbots, moderators, presbyters, presidents, and other colorful names of Christian magistrates. If their offices had different titles, so did their apparel, which ranged from pure white for the Bishop of Rome and pure black for the Ecumenical Patriarch to every variety of color and style in between, with the African delegates taking the prize for showing every tint in the rainbow. Some of the churchmen were hirsute, others bald by nature or intention. Some were bearded, others clean-shaven.

"I haven't seen such variety since the UN in New York," Shannon observed.

"Too bad we're only observers here, Shannon. Otherwise we could have joined the parade."

"You're kidding, right?"

He merely grinned.

✠ ✠ ✠

The Council of Jerusalem did not take on the issue of the Canon until later. First there were some animated preliminaries, since the rare opportunity to solve problems affecting all of Christendom could not be missed. It took an entire week of debate before Roman Catholic and Lutheran bishops admitted that they misnumbered the Ten Commandments and finally abandoned St. Augustine's mistake in parking the true second commandment against idolatry under the first.

"Remember, Shannon, he was afraid that the 'You shall make no image or likeness' commandment would ruin art among Christians as it had among Jews," Jon commented, "when idolatry was the only issue in play here."

"I *do* know my church history, Jon," she replied, affecting a pout that quickly changed to a grin. "So now Augustine has only nine commandments instead of ten. What does he do? He takes the *least* offensive commandment—coveting—and cuts into two for nine and ten."

Jon breathed a sigh of relief. "From now on, the whole Christian world can agree that 'Don't kill' is number six, and 'No adultery' is number seven."

Then another great concession was made—this time from Eastern Orthodoxy. While the Council of Nicaea had agreed that Easter should be celebrated on a *day*—Sunday—rather than on a *date*—as in the case of Christmas, Eastern and Western Christendom still rarely celebrated the Festival of the Resurrection together. Why? The Eastern church still used the old Julian calendar, whereas the West adopted the Gregorian ever since 1582. The council agreed on the latter but changed the name to the "Common Calendar," since Gregory was a Western pope.

"Hard to believe," Shannon said, "but when to celebrate Easter almost split the early church. Now there's even talk of making the first Sunday in April the universal time to celebrate the Resurrection."

Jon nodded. "It's a really excellent idea, but I think it's going to be tabled for a future council to decide. They're hanging on to the rules for when Jews celebrate the Passover."

And finally the Council of Jerusalem turned to matters canonical. No longer would Jon and Shannon be passive observers.

✢ ✢ ✢

The debates were long and, at times, impassioned, but they largely stayed on track. Both Shannon and Jon were asked to testify in detail as to their discovery of the Constantine Codex.

Before Shannon stepped up to the dais, she asked him, "Is this really happening, Jon? My addressing the council?"

"History is being made at this very moment, my darling. A woman has never before addressed a church council, and it's high time."

"I'm . . . just a bit nervous."

"Don't be, sweetheart. Break a leg! Just be yourself and tell it like it was."

Shannon did just that. Jon was never more proud of her, as she once again recounted the chain of events that began with the dig at Pella. She was poised, confident, and convincing. Knowing that there were a few misogynists at the council, Jon mused, *I'll bet they're shocked that a* woman *could even bring this off.*

When it came to his turn, Jon continued the improbable story of the Constantine Codex but never made any recommendations as to its canonicity. He even applauded the Vatican for "discovering" the remains of St. Paul without tying this into the codex. His objectivity was obvious, although everyone could read between the lines.

His testimony was followed by that of Christianity's most authoritative Greek manuscript scholars. When their opinions were added to the scientific evidence, the debate over the authenticity of the codex concluded rather quickly.

As Jon and Shannon left the convention hall that afternoon, Katie Couric of CBS News buttonholed them and asked, "It looks rather good for opening the Canon, doesn't it, Professor Weber?"

Jon shook his head. "Authenticity of the codex is one thing, but including the new material in the Canon is quite another."

"Do you mean that the council, after all this evidence, might *still* vote against including the last of Mark and Second Acts in the Canon?"

"That's exactly what they might do."

+ + +

The date was July 10. The time was 3 p.m. Every argument on both sides of the issue had been aired. A few church magnates, known to be garrulous, tried to extend debate so that their set speeches would also be included in the official record of the council. That prompted Shannon's whisper to Jon, "Everything's been said, but not everyone has said it."

Jon chuckled, leaned over, and kissed her cheek. "Oh, oh," he murmured, "I wonder if *that's* ever been done before at an ecumenical council?"

She grinned and tickled his ribs. "Or that either."

Now, by a vast majority vote, the council voted to end further discussion. All knew what would come next. A hush of silence filled the vast hall. The atmosphere was electric with expectation. Jon and Shannon clutched hands.

His All Holiness Bartholomew II now stood and led the entire council in a solemn prayer, invoking God the Holy Spirit to guide their vote. Then he announced solemnly, "My colleagues in Christ, if it is your sacred conviction that the newly discovered ending to the Gospel of Mark should be regarded as valid by the church and added to the canonical Gospel of Mark after chapter 16, verse 8, then please vote Yes on your keypads. If not, vote No. Please vote . . . *now*!"

On a giant computer screen hanging over the dais, the data came on slowly. The first image on the screen gave the statistic: "Of 2,797 votes cast, 2,790 are valid."

"Why's that?" Shannon asked Jon, in a whisper. "What about the other seven?"

"Seven delegates probably pressed both yes and no. Or they tried to change their vote."

"Oh."

Endless moments seemed to pass. The screen remained dark. All Jon and Shannon's efforts over the past months—the whole extraordinary odyssey—was now compressed into electronics that would fire pixels on a screen declaring their success or failure. Jon's grip on Shannon's hand tightened even more.

Suddenly the screen came alive. To the left was a tall green column, showing 2,694 votes in favor. On the right side was a very low graph in red, showing only 96 negative votes. Jon and Shannon embraced each other in tears. The convention center erupted in deafening applause and cheering.

When Bartholomew finally reestablished order, he said, "The Holy Spirit has indeed spoken through you, my beloved colleagues. I prayed that this would be your decision! I now turn the gavel over to my most esteemed brother in Christ, the Bishop of Rome."

Jon wiped his eyes and whispered, "The next vote is still in doubt, darling. The Mark ending doesn't really open the Canon. Second Acts will."

She nodded. "They could call Mark's a textual variant. Well, half a loaf is better than none."

Benedict XVI stood and also solemnly invoked the Holy Spirit to guide their decision. Then he announced, "My colleagues in Christ, if it is your sacred conviction that the newly discovered Third Treatise to Theophilus, popularly known as Second Acts, should be regarded as valid and added to the canon of the New Testament following the canonical book of Acts, please vote Yes on your keypad. If not, vote No. Please vote . . . *now*."

Again Jon and Shannon were taut with tension. For some reason, the phrase *"You win some; you lose some"* flitted across his mind, causing his heart to pound.

Again the huge screen came to life and reported, "Of 2,794 votes cast, 2,794 are valid."

"Looks like they all got it right this time," Jon whispered.

"But there are three fewer votes. Wonder what happened . . ."

"Three delegates probably had to go to the john," he responded.

"Happens," she chuckled, grateful for a wisp of humor to relieve their anxiety.

Again it seemed an eternity, waiting for the screen to return to life. Shannon had closed her eyes. Jon assumed she was probably in prayer to a God who could intervene even in electronics if it came to that. Their clasped hands showed knuckles in white.

The screen flashed on. Two graph columns again materialized. To the left stood a tall green column that registered 2,665 votes in favor, and to the right its stubby red neighbor with only 129 votes.

Jon grabbed Shannon in a crushing hug. Thunderous applause and boisterous cheering followed. Benedict indulged it all for several minutes before banging his gavel, fruitlessly. Again, it was a super-super-majority.

A new page had been turned in the history of Christianity. Its Holy Bible now had sixty-seven books rather than sixty-six.

Now the entire Ecumenical Council rose and joined in singing the Common Doxology in dozens of different languages, though with the same melody:

Praise God from Whom all blessings flow,
Praise Him, all creatures here below;
Praise Him above, ye heavenly host,
Praise Father, Son, and Holy Ghost!

Although Jon and Shannon had sung the familiar verse hundreds of times, it never carried more meaning for them than at the present moment. Tears filled their eyes and everyone else's as well. The profound unity in diversity among Christians at the council, they hoped, would serve as a model for the future.

Benedict now called on Jon to address the council. He had asked the pope for a brief opportunity to do so *if* the votes so warranted it. He walked up to the dais. "Thank you, Your Holiness," he began. "I would respectfully ask all of you, distinguished church leaders, to remind your followers of something extremely important; namely, that this council has *not* approved 'a new Bible,' as it were, and has *not* replaced the traditional Scriptures. The 'old family Bible' is as relevant as ever with its sixty-six books. The sixty-seven-book version simply enhances the text of that great traditional document which has served the church so well for almost two thousand years. My wife and I now commend the enhanced edition and its reception in the church to the providence of God."

As he left the dais, shouts of "Amen" and even "Hallelujah" ricocheted throughout the vast reaches of the hall. No one present would ever forget that memorable day, which became a milestone in church history.

Jon and Shannon were treated to endless rounds of congratulations by the church's great, which they vigorously tried to deflect. In fact, they were the last to leave the convention hall. Jon looked into Shannon's sapphire eyes, still a bit misty, and said, "Thanks, my darling, for—how did you put it?—for finding the two missing pieces in that sacred mosaic called the Holy Bible and setting them safely into place."

EPILOGUE

ALTHOUGH THE DECISIONS OF THE JERUSALEM COUNCIL were not binding on individual church bodies, 96 percent of world Christianity did adopt them in fact. Holdouts were the extremely conservative sects, rigorist splinter groups, and the Appalachian churches that practiced snake-handling as a centerpiece of their worship. The assurance that not one syllable of the newly discovered material contradicted any part of Scripture fell on deaf ears. As one of their elders put it, "If the King James Bible was good enough for St. Paul, it's good enough for us."

Publication of the sixty-seven-book Bible became the greatest statistical phenomenon since Gutenberg invented movable type printing. When Jon and the ICO had first permitted the fresh addenda to be published separately as part of the public domain, publishers privately deemed them "crazy," in view of the incredibly valuable property they were giving away. Now they called them "crazy like a fox," since publishing any new Bible with the addenda would have certain strings attached, spelled "royalties." The newly discovered Greek texts in the codex and any translations thereof were fully protected if they became part of any new edition of the New Testament or the Bible.

Jon explained that the reason for the copyright was far more than royalties. A restriction clause in all publishing contracts gave the ICO the right to approve any translation. A "dirty little secret" in Bible publishing had been the intrusion of denominational interests in slight shadings in translating some verses of Holy Writ.

To be sure, new Bible editions had been flooding the market of late. A whole cavalcade of specialty Bibles were crowding the bookstores, such as women's Bibles, men's Bibles, Scriptures for the young, for the aged, and every niche market imaginable. Jon once cracked to Shannon, "Next there will be *A Bible for Left-handed Mothers-to-be in the Second Trimester of Their Pregnancy.*" But all these were only adaptations of the traditional text. The new sixty-seven-book Bible rewrote the sales records in Bible publishing.

The ICO had authorized the Boston law firm of Allen, Stover, Gemrich, Haenicke, and Hume to handle the crush of publishers lining up at their doors. Known for their expertise in international rights and permissions, they monitored worldwide sales of the new edition so well that a record 93 percent of global sales were legitimate. There were exceptions, of course. Customs officials in Long Beach, California, had to seize a whole boatload of the new Bibles because they were pirated editions printed in China with a fake Zondervan imprint.

Although Jon and Shannon disliked the name "The New Bible" because it could suggest that the traditional version was now supplanted, this was the name bestowed on it by the vast public. And because global sales of the New Bible quickly reached truly biblical proportions, the phrase "an embarrassment of riches" had fresh meaning for Jon and the ICO. Their royalties were not large; they were simply prodigious.

Meetings of the ICO were now devoted to the happy task of deciding how to share the wealth. The repository was the Institute of Christian Origins Foundation, and interviews with Warren Buffett and officers of the Bill and Melinda Gates Foundation were helpful. While theirs were secular in nature, the ICO Foundation would serve primarily Christian and biblical interests. Accordingly, the primary beneficiaries were:

- The Institute of Christian Origins, Cambridge, Massachusetts

  Charity began at home. A large endowment fund was established to underwrite an expanded research program for the ICO in all its endeavors, present and future.

- The Ecumenical Patriarchate of Constantinople

  The enclave in Istanbul was landlocked and needed to expand. Now it could buy up surrounding properties in overcrowded Istanbul and enjoy something that actually resembled a campus. This was but a debt repaid.

- The Center for the Study of New Testament Manuscripts

  Its program of photographing and/or purchasing biblical manuscripts across the world could now be fully funded and, in fact, prioritized because of the race against time to secure the texts before inevitable deterioration.

- Endowment for Interfaith Dialogue

  In greater efforts toward Christian unity, far more interchange between Eastern and Western Christendom was necessary, as well as between Protestants and the rest of Christendom.

Soon other beneficiaries included an Endowment for Christian-Jewish Dialogue and an Endowment for Christian-Muslim Dialogue. The list eventually ran to seven pages.

✠ ✠ ✠

Abbas al-Rashid and Jon remained in close touch. Abbas's commencement address at al-Azhar University, "Freedom for Truth," was widely published in tract form throughout the Islamic world, provoking the ire of the orthodox but kindling a powerful response among moderate Muslims everywhere. Some were calling Abbas the long-awaited Muslim Martin Luther for championing the cause of reform in Islam. Too long the moderate Muslim majority had failed to speak out. Whether their long silence had been prompted by fear of the jihadists or general passivity, they now became far more vocal through such moderate organizations as the American Islamic Forum for Democracy, headed by Dr. Zuhdi Jasser. An American version of Abbas al-Rashid, Jasser and his colleagues vigorously opposed extremism in Islam in all its forms.

A European counterpart surfaced to oppose the fiery rhetoric of the radical mullahs who were trying to hijack Islam. In March 2010, Tahir ul-Qadri, a Pakistani sheikh in London, had issued a public declaration declaring that terrorists were the very *enemies* of Islam and that suicide bombers were destined not for heaven but for hell. Abbas included his statement in tracts that were published in the hundreds of thousands and dropped over Taliban strongholds in Afghanistan and al-Qaeda camps in Pakistan and elsewhere. Some of the tracts were released from helium balloons floating over their targets, and they had a surprising impact. Double agents told of heated discussions now taking place in jihadist camps, recruits no longer satisfied with their instructors' calls for violence.

The tracts quoted the Qur'an as prohibiting attacks against the innocent (Sura 5:32) and against suicide in both the Qur'an (Sura 4:29) and the hadith (Bukhari 23:446). They concluded with the warning:

Remember, you are being deluded by false teachers
into committing
murder against the innocent and against your own selves.
This violates the very heart of Islam.

Thinking for themselves, many Muslim youth started abandoning terrorist cells. As an overlooked communication device, the lowly tract was accomplishing big results.

✠ ✠ ✠

Having escaped American justice, Osman al-Ghazali had pleaded with his wife and daughter to join him in Cairo. But they were genuine converts to Christianity and were perfectly horrified to learn of his role as Judas Iscariot. Osman promised that they could remain Christian and attend the Coptic Cathedral in Cairo, where Christian Pope Shenouda III was in charge.

They countered with what they thought a far better plan: Osman must, instead, return to the States, sincerely repent of his crime, and suffer whatever civil or criminal consequences were necessary. In view of the horror stories regarding American women moving to the Middle East only to learn that the husbands they had trusted were now misogynist tyrants operating under sharia law, their response was inevitable.

When Osman refused their terms, Fatima al-Ghazali was granted a civil divorce by the Massachusetts courts on the basis of desertion. She later wrote a bestselling exposé, titled *Women Victims of Islam*. Needless to say, it was banned in Baghdad and throughout the Middle East.

Some months after Osman arrived in Egypt, he had business in Istanbul and used the occasion to visit the radical cadre that had engineered the theft of the Constantine Codex. He called the cell members "greedy, stupid swine" for trying to get a ransom for the codex instead of destroying it, as he had specified. He even suggested that they rename their group "Idiots for Islam" for having blown his master plan out of the water. It seems they didn't like to be called such nasty names, so they pounded Osman bloody. He emerged with a broken nose that never healed properly, and he spent his days in a low-paying job as translator at Cairo University Library, a lonely man bitter at the world, bitter even at Allah.

✠ ✠ ✠

For Jon, Shannon, and the ICO, as the months rolled on, the royalties rolled in. The charity list lengthened. A generous sector of their largesse, however, would always be devoted to the purposes for which the ICO was founded: to expand knowledge of the biblical world in general, the origins of Christianity in particular. Spending their massive sums turned out to be a true chore for the ICO, but a welcome one. In time, however, at Jon and Shannon's urging, the ICO surrendered its copyright of the new material in the Constantine Codex and threw it open to the world for scholarship and publication. The codex itself was finally committed to the Library of Congress for the ultimate in security, with ownership retained by the Ecumenical Patriarch.

✠ ✠ ✠

At last, Jon and Shannon could spend more time at Cape Cod. In previous exploits, they had defended Christianity against diabolical fraud as well as a false Christ. Now they had even enhanced the credibility of its Holy Book—all in all, a rather respectable record. They could only wonder what intriguing adventures might await them in the future.

REALITY NOTE

The first draft of this novel was completed six months before the Vatican announcement on June 28, 2009, that a probe *had* in fact been drilled through the lid of the sarcophagus at St. Paul Outside the Walls in Rome and that some purple linen and bone fragments were retrieved that dated back to the first or second century AD. The plot in this novel, then, turned out to be prophetic in imagining how the interior of the sarcophagus might be revealed. As of this date, however, the Vatican has not undertaken any further examination of the interior of the sarcophagus, especially to determine if there is a skull, attached or detached.

That Constantine the Great authorized Eusebius of Caesarea to have fifty elaborate copies of the Bible prepared for use in the early church is absolutely historical. Strangely, not one of these has been found to date, although some scholars think that the *Sinaiticus* might be one. Whether such a discovery would have included the two documents featured in this novel is not known. But it is indeed possible that either or even both might surface someday or that a biblical manuscript might be discovered that would merit inclusion in the Canon.

Such inclusion would certainly require action by an ecumenical church council. Unfortunately, however, the way any such universal council might be constituted, as set forth in this novel, is quite remote at present. The two largest components of Christendom—Roman Catholicism and Eastern Orthodoxy—have not yet achieved a degree of mutual trust even to hold a joint conclave. Perhaps in decades (or centuries) to come it might indeed be possible, with Protestants participating as well.

Accordingly, the Vatican III ecumenical council referred to in this book is also fictional and first appeared in my prior novel, *More Than a Skeleton*. A council with such a name, however, might indeed take place in the future.

As for the two new biblical documents "discovered" in this novel, one should not conclude that our present Scriptures are in any way incomplete or insufficient without such addenda. They are merely what many biblical scholars would put at the top of their wish list were such a manuscript discovery to take place in fact.

Finally, the question of whether ancient texts—biblical or secular—may be copyrighted successfully is rather open, especially if the texts require some critical reconstruction. In America, the prevailing view is that such texts are in the public domain and do not have copyright protection; whereas in Europe and elsewhere, this is not necessarily the case. Several years ago, for example, the German Bible Society invoked copyright protection on the Nestle edition of the Greek New Testament, claiming that Zondervan's New International Version translation relied too heavily (though justifiably) on the Nestle text. Yet it has not brought suit against the Grand Rapids publisher to date.

Thank you for reading these pages.

ABOUT THE AUTHOR

Dr. Paul L. Maier is the Russell H. Seibert Professor of Ancient History at Western Michigan University and a much-published author of both scholarly and popular works. His novels include two historical documentaries—*Pontius Pilate* and *The Flames of Rome*—as well as *A Skeleton in God's Closet*, a theological thriller that became a #1 national bestseller in religious fiction when it first released. A sequel, *More Than a Skeleton*, followed in 2003.

His nonfiction works include *In the Fullness of Time*, a book that correlates sacred with secular evidence from the ancient world impinging on Jesus and early Christianity; *Josephus: The Essential Works*, a new translation/commentary on writings of the first-century Jewish historian; and *Eusebius: The Church History*, a similar book on the first Christian historian. More than five million of Maier's books are now in print in twenty languages, as well as over 250 scholarly articles and reviews in professional journals.

Dr. Maier lectures widely, appears frequently on national radio, television, and newspaper interviews, and has received numerous awards. He has also penned seven children's books and hosted six video seminars dealing with Jesus, St. Paul, the early church, and current Christianity.

Visit his website at www.paulmaier.com.